LAKE MANAWA SUMMERS, BOOK 3

The Ride of Her Life

A NOVEL

LORNA SEILSTAD

Revell

a division of Baker Publishing Group
Grand Rapids, Michigan

Published by Revell
a division of Baker Publishing Group
P.O. Box 6287, Grand Rapids, MI 49516-6287
www.revellbooks.com

Printed in the United States of America

Library of Congress Cataloging-in-Publication Data
Seilstad, Lorna.
        The ride of her life : a novel / Lorna Seilstad.
              p.   cm. — (Lake Manawa summers ; bk. 3)
        ISBN 978-0-8007-3447-3 (pbk.)
        1. Widows—Fiction. 2. Manawa, Lake (Iowa)—Fiction. I. Title.
     PS3619.E425R53 2012
     813'.6—dc23   2011045606

Scripture is taken from the King James Version of the Bible.

This book is a work of fiction. Names, characters, places, and incidents are the product of the author's imagination or are used fictitiously. Any resemblance to actual events, locales, or persons, living or dead, is coincidental.

The internet addresses, email addresses, and phone numbers in this book are accurate at the time of publication. They are provided as a resource. Baker Publishing Group does not endorse them or vouch for their content or permanence.

Published in association with Wendy Lawton of Books & Such Literary Agency.

12   13   14   15   16   17   18   7   6   5   4   3   2   1

To my husband, the risk taker.
Thank you for taking me on the ride of my life,
and for being a man of God.

That your faith should not stand in the wisdom of men, but in the power of God.

1 Corinthians 2:5

1

May 1906, Lake Manawa, Iowa

"Look, Mama!"

What had Levi dragged in now? Lilly rolled her eyes as she eased a large slice of peach pie onto one of the diner's plates. She wiped her finger on her starched apron before she turned toward her son.

Swinging his arm in a wide arc, he thrust a monstrous, writhing snake toward her nose.

With a shriek, she leapt backward.

"Isn't she pretty?" Levi ran his finger over the snake's scaly head. "You wanna pet her?"

Inching backward until her shoulders lodged against the cold metal pie safe, Lilly fought the fear seizing her voice. The counter between her and that monster dangling from her six-year-old's chubby fist hardly seemed an adequate barrier. "N-no, I do not want to pet that thing."

"Shhh. You'll hurt her feelings." He lifted the snake's head to his cheek. "She won't hurt you, Mama. See? She's just a gardener snake."

"Get it away from your face! And, Levi, it's a garter snake, not a gardener."

"What's the difference?"

She swallowed hard, vaguely aware of the roller coaster workers seated in the corner chuckling. She lowered her voice.

"A gardener works in a garden, and a garter—well, uh . . . holds up a lady's . . ."

"A lady's what?"

"Stockings," she whispered, but more chuckles ensued from the men in the corner. She pointed at the front door. "Why don't you take your friend outside? I think she wants to go home."

"Silly Mama. Snakes are like you and me. She ain't got no home."

"She doesn't have a home."

"That's what I said."

The snake twisted beneath Levi's grasp, and Lilly scooted even further away. "Please, put your friend back where you found her."

"Out front? Under the diner's front stoop?"

Lilly's heart squeezed. *Lord, haven't I been dealing with enough snakes lately? You had to put one where I have to walk every day?*

A wooden chair grated against the floorboards, and seconds later one of the workers, the one the others called "Boss," laid a hand on Levi's shoulder. Lilly winced. Great. He must think her a simpering female. But when she lifted her gaze to his face, even his cobalt eyes seemed to smile.

"Hey, buddy, your snake's a beauty. Must be a whole foot long. Why don't we find a new home for your 'gardener' snake?" He grinned at Lilly, and his eyes twinkled. "Ma'am, do you mind if we *men* take care of this little creature?"

She did mind, because she should be the one helping her son. She was the parent. But given the fear nailing her feet to the floor, she didn't expect that escorting Levi and the snake to a new home would happen anytime soon. Besides, the man seemed nice enough. She nodded, and Blue Eyes took her son's hand and led him through the door of Thorton's Lunch Counter.

She picked up her dishrag and wiped down the counter. What was she going to do with that boy? Six years old, afraid of nothing, and way too much like his father.

God rest his soul.

"Hey, where's my pie?" one of the workers called, smoothing a hand over his rounded belly.

Like you need more pie. Lilly snagged the plate and skirted around the end of the counter. "Here you are, sir. Can I get you fine fellows anything else?"

The door banged open, and Lilly spun, expecting the triumphant return of her son. Instead, her breath caught.

"Lilly." Claude Hart's silver hair peeked from beneath a stylish bowler, and he leaned heavily on the ivory greyhound topping his cane.

Beside him, her former mother-in-law, Evangeline, stood ramrod straight with her lips turned downward in a nearly permanent frown. "May we speak to you—in private?"

Lilly sighed. Would she ever be free of these people? *Dear Lord, gentle my spirit, 'cause just seeing them makes me feel like a big ol' grizzly.*

She glanced around the almost-empty diner, wishing this was a month later. Once Lake Manawa Park officially opened, there wouldn't be an empty table in the place, and she'd have a better excuse not to speak to her meddling in-laws.

"I think this corner is about as private as we're going to get." With a flick of her wrist, she indicated the empty table.

Claude strode over, pulled out a chair, and held it for his wife. Evangeline scowled at the chipped paint on the chair. Pinching her lace-trimmed handkerchief between her thumb and forefinger, she dusted the sunny yellow seat and finally lowered herself in place. Claude sat down opposite her.

Lilly remained standing. She needed to use every inch of her small stature to her advantage. Claude and Evangeline Hart were used to getting whatever they wanted, but it wasn't happening this time. Not when the object they sought was her son.

"What can I get you?" Tilting her head toward the chalkboard on the wall, she mustered a smile. "I pulled the peach pie out of the oven less than an hour ago."

"You know we don't want the food here." Evangeline said the word *here* as if the snake had crawled back in and was lying coiled beneath her chair.

"Please have a seat, Lilly." Claude laid his hand on the back of the chair beside him.

"I think I'll stand."

"You are the most stubborn person I've ever known. I don't know what my Benjamin saw in you." Evangeline touched her handkerchief to her eye as if the thought of her dearly departed son brought tears to her eyes.

Lilly's heart softened, although she suspected Evangeline was using her grief to get her way this time. Still, no matter how difficult Evangeline was, Lilly couldn't discount that the woman hurt over the loss of her son. Lilly understood.

"If you two came to get me to reconsider moving back

into your house, you might as well not waste your breath. Levi and I are doing fine."

Claude scowled. "You're working in a Midway diner, serving food to common workers. You call that fine? What would Benjamin think if he could see you now?"

Lilly's heart splintered at the mention of his name. Why did it sound different coming from someone else's lips? He'd always be her Ben.

She swallowed the hard lump in her throat. "He'd be proud I'm rearing our son the way we planned."

"In a tent? On the lake?" Evangeline's voice quaked. "My son didn't plan that."

Lilly heard the bell on the door jingle but didn't turn. If it was Levi, he wouldn't come running over. Her in-laws frowned on public displays of affection, so he would avoid his grandparents.

Claude's gaze met Lilly's. "You had a home with us."

"I had a room." Lilly glared back. "You made sure I understood it was your house. Then you insisted I send my son away."

Evangeline tugged at her cape. "We simply want him to have the best."

"What's best about sending a little boy halfway across the country to a boarding school?"

"Surely you, of all people"—Evangeline wrinkled her nose—"should understand what our grandson is going to need to compensate for—"

"For what? For being my son? The son of a lowly household servant?" Lilly's voice rose.

"This is ridiculous." Claude stood. "The boy belongs with us. Levi, come here. You're going home with your grandmother and me."

Lilly whirled to find Levi standing beside Blue Eyes. She

stepped beside him and grabbed her son's hand. "He is not going anywhere."

Claude took a step forward.

"You heard the lady." The words fell like a stone in a pond and rippled across the room. Blue Eyes crossed his arms over his broad chest. "The boy is staying here."

Gripping his cane, Claude pointed the ivory greyhound toward Lilly. "This isn't over. I didn't want to take legal measures, but I will. No grandson of mine is going to shiver in the cold in a tent. He belongs with us."

Guilt tugged at Lilly's heart. The temperatures had dipped last night. Had Levi been cold? No. They'd piled on blankets, and besides, living with her former in-laws was another kind of cold—a cold touching the soul, much harder to stave off.

"No sir." She squared her shoulders. "Levi is my son. He belongs with me."

Claude turned to Evangeline. "Come, darling, we'll return when Lilly is ready to be sensible."

Fighting the urge to retort, Lilly clamped her mouth shut. They were still Ben's parents and, as such, deserved every morsel of respect she could bestow on them. She nudged Levi forward. "Say goodbye to your grandparents."

"Please don't take me away, Grandpa." Levi hid behind Lilly's skirt.

"See what you've done?" Evangeline glowered at Lilly. "You've made him fearful of his own grandparents."

"You did that all by yourself."

Evangeline's mouth dropped, but she snapped it shut. "Please be reasonable. He's all we have left of our Benjamin, and it's our duty to do what's best for him. We have the means, and you'll certainly never be able to give him all he deserves."

"Even you must admit Levi deserves a home." Claude let the words hang.

Lilly squeezed Levi's shoulder. "I agree, and as his mother, I'll do whatever it takes to get him one."

⚬⚭⚬

Silverware scraped against the china plates, echoing through the otherwise silent diner. Not one word had been uttered since the Harts' departure. When Lilly turned toward the roller coaster workers at the corner table, they averted their eyes.

Humiliation and anger burned in Lilly's chest. How could she honor Ben's memory by treating his parents with respect when they wanted to steal her son?

Blue Eyes cleared his throat beside her. "Hi. I'm Nick Perrin."

She stared at the large hand extended in her direction, then lifted her gaze to his face. Concern filled the cobalt-blue pools, and she bristled.

"And I suppose you expect a thank-you." She jammed her fists onto her hips. "I'll have you know I didn't need your little 'you heard the lady.' I was doing fine all by myself."

"Hey, I was only trying to help." Nick started toward his table and then turned back. "You know, if I were you, I'd take all the friends I could get. Those two seem determined to take your boy from you."

"But he's my son. Mine." The tremor in her voice betrayed how unnerved she was. "I'll take care of him, Mr. Perrin, and I don't need help from you or anyone else."

"Fine."

"Fine."

Levi tugged on the seam of Nick's tan work pants. "Mr. Nick, can you be my friend even if my mama doesn't like you?"

2

"Mrs. Hart, may I speak to you?"

Lilly whirled at the sound of her employer's formal tone. "Be right there, Mr. Thorton."

She hastily piled the remaining dishes from the roller coaster crew's table. Balancing the dishes on her left arm, she zigzagged around the other empty tables and then deposited the dishes in a tub of soapy water. She wiped her hands on her apron, smoothed the sides of her hair, and took a deep breath before nearing Mr. Thorton's tiny office.

Warmth from the oven after this morning's baking had left the area cozy, but the stern look on Mr. Thorton's face sent chills up Lilly's spine. When had he arrived? It was easy enough for him to slip in the back door and hide in his cubbyhole of an office set off to one side of the kitchen. Had he seen her in-laws? Maybe he believed she'd taken liberties while she should be working. Her pulse quickened. She could not lose this job.

"Good afternoon, sir." She smiled, attempting a cheerful appearance.

Mr. Thorton nodded toward her. "Good afternoon, Mrs. Hart. I have a matter to discuss with you. Please have a seat."

She sat down on the stool in the corner, the only place to sit besides Mr. Thorton's desk chair. Her heart thundered against her ribs. "Is there a problem?"

"I'm afraid so." He rubbed his wiry, peppered beard. "You know I value your work. You've been the best employee I've had in a long time. Since Mrs. Thorton's passing, I'd not found anyone who could cook and run this place as well as she until I found you." His lips gave way to a hint of a smile.

She swallowed. "Thank you, sir."

"But . . ." He paused. "I heard the way you were talking to Mr. Perrin, the roller coaster boss. He's an important man. Not only is he in charge of the project, he also designed the whole shebang. Mrs. Hart, you've got to be nice to that man."

"But he—"

Mr. Thorton held up his hand. "I don't care if he tracks in a sty's worth of mud on your newly mopped floors. He and his workers are the only reason this lunch counter is open this early in the season. If he decides to arrange food at a different location for his workers, then we'll close down until the regular park season begins. That would mean no work for you. Do you understand?"

Lilly's mouth went dry. Her stupid pride had made her spout off to the man for his act of kindness. What if Nick Perrin took his men and left? She licked her lips. "I understand, sir, and I apologize."

"Don't be apologizing to me. It's him you need to apologize to." Mr. Thorton sat down in his chair. "And I expect you to do just that the next time he's in. Do I make myself clear?"

Lilly eased off the stool. "Perfectly."

"Good." Mr. Thorton picked up his pen. "Now, did I smell peach pie?"

"Yes, sir. I'll get you a piece." Lilly hurried from the office area, all too ready to have this confrontation behind her. As far as dressing-downs went, this one probably wasn't significant. But apologize to Mr. Perrin? That was not only unfair, it was unnecessary. She doubted the roller coaster builder had given their little disagreement a second thought.

Nick jammed the shovel into the recently thawed earth much harder than need be. He'd only been trying to help when he'd spoken in the lunch counter on the lady's behalf. Wouldn't any gentleman do the same?

He heaved a load of dirt mixed with grass onto the ground and again plunged his shovel into the hole. The scent of damp soil rose to his nose.

"Boss, whaddya think yer doin'?" Sean McGready, his Irish heritage apparent in every word, walked over and hooked his thumbs in his suspenders. "Boyo, let the men do their jobs and ya do yers."

"We've got to dig a hundred footings. I don't think the men will mind if I do one." Nick deposited a clump of dirt onto the pile.

Sean placed a beefy fist on the handle of Nick's shovel. "Aye, but I do. Yer usin' me shovel and I'll be wantin' it back. Can't let the boys go thinkin' I'm a lazy dosser."

Nick held fast. In a tug-of-war with most of the workers, Nick would easily win. He'd been building roller coasters so long his muscles were solid. But against a bear like Sean, he wouldn't stand a chance even though Sean had a good ten years on Nick's thirty. Finally, Nick huffed and pushed the shovel toward Sean.

"There now. Go be a good engineer and study those drawings some more."

"I like to be a hands-on builder. You of all people know that."

Sean scooped a huge load of dirt from the hole. "I do. And ya have a lot to prove on this job."

"So I won't have you stopping me every time I lift a hammer."

"Knew that too."

"So?"

Sean leaned on the shovel handle and met Nick's gaze. "So, why don't ya be saying what's got ya knotted tighter than a ball of yer mother's yarn? The lass inside?" He paused, and a smile slowly spread across his face. "Ah, it's the lad, isn't it?"

Nick swiped his sweaty brow with his forearm. "What were his grandparents thinking? Don't they realize that poor kid is going to have nightmares over what he heard today?" A familiar tightness wrapped around Nick's chest. Nightmares. He could still recall the ones from his childhood in vivid detail.

Sean raised a thick, reddish eyebrow. "Seems to me his mother said she could take care of the lad just fine."

"She certainly thinks so anyway." Nick gave a halfhearted chuckle. "But the boy wants to be friends, so I might stop by from time to time and keep an eye on him for myself."

"No denyin' it, Nick Perrin. Yer a rare character."

Nick squeezed the older man's shoulder. "And so are you, my friend. So are you. I'll catch you before supper."

As Nick crossed the grassy area, he checked on the progress of the other workers. Already this week, they'd drilled holes and built sturdy wood forms for each point of the concrete foundation. It would take until the end of the week to finish this preliminary work for the coaster.

Nick stopped and pushed against one of the thick Douglas fir posts already set in hardened concrete. It didn't budge. Perfect. This roller coaster had to be the best in the West—and the safest. The last thing Nick wanted was his name attached to an accident.

Taking a deep breath, Nick leaned against the beam and looked out over the choppy waters of Lake Manawa. He'd seen bigger lakes while traveling with Fred Ingersoll's company, but he hadn't seen many other places that rivaled the splendor of this resort. From his vantage point on the lake's southeast shore, he could see two large pavilions, one on each side of the water, and a host of other buildings. Off to his right, the resort's Midway lay quiet, waiting for the park to officially open in another month. And along the shore's edge, a few rowboats lay upturned like turtles on the shore.

"Perrin!"

He turned and spotted Avery Nash approaching. Nick's long legs covered the distance between him and the manager of Lake Manawa's development in seconds. "Good afternoon, sir. To what do I owe the privilege?"

"I've got investors worried you won't get this monster done in time for the park's opening." Nash, a wisp of a man who stood a good foot shorter than Nick, tried to sound authoritative.

"And as I told you before, we won't be done by the opening, but we will be ready for business soon after."

Mr. Nash hooked his thumbs in his vest pockets. "They were hoping you could speed things up."

"I'll keep on schedule, sir, but safety has to be a priority. We can't rush or lives might be at stake, which wouldn't do well for your business or mine."

"Are you sure you can handle this job, Mr. Perrin? I know you're new at this."

"Sir, this may be the first roller coaster I've personally designed, but it's the fifth one I've built. And my designs were approved by Fred Ingersoll himself."

"So you said." Nash sighed. "I'll take the news to the investors, but I expect you to do everything in your power to hurry the construction."

Nick met the man's beady eyes. "If I can speed things up safely, I will, but I don't take unnecessary chances with my coasters or my workers."

3

Tears whitewashed Levi's dirty cheeks. Lilly turned from the dishes she'd been washing and squatted in front of her son. "What's got your face all scrunched up like a roly poly?"

"I lost him."

"Who?"

"Mr. Wiggles."

Lilly snagged a damp rag from the sink and dabbed at his face. "Your snake?"

"No, Mama. My snake's a gardener snake. Her name is Flower."

"So Mr. Wiggles is a worm?" Lilly stood and dipped her hands back in the sudsy water.

"No, silly Mama, he's a spider." He held up his hands, making a big circle with his thumbs and forefingers. "And he's not in his tin anymore."

Lilly glanced at the coffee tin lying upturned by the front door and shivered. *Lord, have mercy.* "Did you lose him before or after you came inside, Levi?"

"If I left him outside, he mighta got away." Levi wiped his nose on his sleeve. "And he was happy because he had friends."

"Friends?" Lilly bit her lip. Did she even want to know?

"Four daddy longlegs."

She spotted one of Mr. Wiggles's "friends" crawling across the floor and raised her foot to step on him.

"No, Mama! No!" Levi dove for the spindle-legged creature and scooped him up. "There, I saved you from the wicked witch."

"Levi!" She stomped her foot. "I am not a wicked witch. Now, take that thing outside."

"But what about his family?"

"You can come back in and find them as well."

"You promise not to squish 'em while I'm outside?"

"I promise."

Levi scampered outside, and Lilly glanced around the room for any signs of the daddy longlegs—or Mr. Wiggles. Seeing nothing, she hurried back to the kitchen to stir the stew simmering on the stove. The men would be in for supper soon, but with Mr. Thorton already gone for the day, at least she wouldn't have to apologize to Mr. Perrin.

Lilly opened the oven door, and a gust of hot air blasted her face. She grabbed the hem of her apron and used it to pull the pan of golden cornbread from the oven. The sweet aroma set her stomach growling, but she cut only one square to set aside for Levi's supper. If there was enough left after the men ate, she'd enjoy a piece as well. If not, well, it wouldn't be the first time she'd gone without.

"Lilly? You in there?" Marguerite Andrews called from the dining room. "Lilly?"

Lilly met her at the counter. "And it's a good thing it's

only me, the way you're shouting like a banshee. What if Mr. Thorton was here?"

"Oh, he wouldn't care. He loves you." She pulled off her lacy gloves and set them down on the counter. "I've got a surprise for you."

"Is it hairy with eight legs?"

"What are you talking about?"

"Never mind. What's the surprise?"

Marguerite rounded the counter and took hold of Lilly's arm. "Close your eyes."

"Marguerite, I don't have time for this nonsense." Lilly stood firm. Why did her best friend always see life as a game?

"Don't be so stubborn. Do as I ask and let me lead you to the door."

"Why can't I close my eyes after I get there?"

"Oh, all right." Marguerite nudged her closer in the desired direction.

Once Lilly complied, the bell above the door jingled, and a cool breeze kissed her oven-warmed cheeks. She heard Levi along with Marguerite's two children, Tate and Faith, fighting over some toy outside the diner. But it didn't cover the sound of someone stepping onto the lunch counter's stoop.

"Okay." Marguerite laid her hands on Lilly's shoulders. "You can open your eyes now."

Lilly peeled her hands away and squealed, throwing her arms around Emily Stockton. "When did you get in?"

"This morning. I came to the lake as soon as I could get away from my aunts and my grandmother."

Glancing at Marguerite, Lilly frowned. "And you knew she was coming all along?"

"Truthfully, no. I saw her on my way over here."

Lilly captured her friend's hands in her own and drew her

24

inside the diner. "I heard your aunt Ethel was doing poorly. Is that why you've come home?"

"Partly." Emily jostled the bundle in her arms. "And Carter didn't think baby Kate and I should be traipsing around the country in a railcar all summer—even if it is a Pullman Palace car."

"He's right." Lilly pulled the blanket away and smiled at the cherub-faced infant. "Now, let me get you some lemonade, and then Aunt Lilly wants to hold this little angel."

"After Aunt Marguerite." Marguerite slipped the baby from Emily's arms and smiled.

Lilly wagged a finger at her friend. "Marguerite Andrews, you'd better be ready to give me that baby the instant I get back."

"Don't worry, I'll share her. Eventually."

After Lilly returned with a pitcher of lemonade and three glasses, Marguerite passed Kate to her. "Is she three months old already?"

"Turned it yesterday." Emily yawned. "Sorry. She doesn't sleep through the night very well."

"I remember poor Benjamin having to take Levi out on the porch swing nearly every night. Oh, how Ben's mother hated that. She said it wasn't proper for a father to be caring for his baby." The picture of tiny Levi propped on his daddy's broad shoulder made tears cloud her eyes. She blinked and forced a smile. "The colic will stop soon enough. Besides, living with your grandmother and aunts, you'll be lucky if you even get a chance to take care of her yourself."

"I'm not staying there. I'm staying here at Lake Manawa in my family's cottage." Emily sipped from her glass. "This brings me to a question I want to ask you, Lilly."

"Oh?"

Emily set her glass down. "Marguerite told me about where

you and Levi are living, and I'd like for you to come and stay with me at the cabin. I'd love the company and could use your expertise about babies."

Lilly handed baby Kate back to her mother. "Thank you all the same, Emily, but I'll have to decline."

"Why? There are two bedrooms, so you'd have your own room, and Carter will be on the road managing the Bloomer Girls team for at least two months. Wouldn't it be nice for Levi to have a bed and a warm place to sleep?"

Standing, Lilly smoothed her apron. "Levi and I have a place, and I can assure you I keep him snug as a bug."

❧

"I told you she'd say no." Marguerite shot a glare at Lilly before turning to Emily. "I offered to let her stay with us too, but she's as stubborn as an ink stain, and she thinks she has to manage all on her own."

Lilly fisted her apron. "You don't understand."

"I understand perfectly." Marguerite poked the table with her finger. Lilly might have changed quite a bit in the last ten years, especially since Ben's death, but in the area of mulish independence, she hadn't budged.

Emily glanced toward the kitchen. "Uh—"

"You don't need to go standing up for her, Emily. Lilly's got some foolish idea about not letting anyone—including her best friends—help her."

Emily stiffened in her chair. "Do you smell something burning?"

"The stew!" Lilly raced into the kitchen and yanked the pot off the burner. She lifted the lid and dipped her spoon into the contents. She pushed some to the side. The stew in the bottom of the pot lay blackened.

"Is it ruined?" Emily asked.

"I believe I can salvage it." She scowled at Marguerite. "If no one distracts me again." She lifted a chunk of carrot, blew on it, and slipped it between her lips. "It's charred, but nothing a few raw potatoes and a bit of sugar won't take care of, thank the Lord."

She dumped the stew from the charred pot into a second clean pot and surveyed how much of the main course clung to the bottom like paste. "Oh well, my supper will be a little crisp tonight."

"Is it okay?" Marguerite bit her lip. The last thing she wanted was to get Lilly in some kind of trouble.

Using a paring knife, Lilly cut the peel off a potato in a long string. "It'll be fine."

"What can we do to help?"

"Nothing."

"That answer is not acceptable." Marguerite remained planted in Lilly's path. Why did Lilly still insist on keeping her at arm's length when they'd been through so much together?

Hands planted on her hips, Marguerite studied her petite friend. Lilly's chestnut-colored hair was pinned up in a fashionable Gibson girl style, and the ruffles of her white shirtwaist peeked over the top of her apron. If this were a home, she'd look like any other wife tending to the needs of her family.

It wasn't fair. She should be enjoying a love-filled life with Ben, not fending for herself as a cook. A very stubborn cook. Since she'd married Ben, many of Lilly's rough edges had been smoothed. It wasn't that Ben had ever said a word. Lilly had simply wanted to be the best wife she could be and had been determined to become the kind of lady others expected at his side. She'd learned the proper way to speak, sit, and entertain. She'd attacked the task with the same determination that kept her from accepting help now.

"Why don't you go check on Levi when you see to your own young 'uns?" Lilly pointed with her knife toward the door.

"All right. Then I'm coming back to finish our talk."

Lilly dropped the potato chunks into the stew. "And you called me stubborn?"

"I learned it all from you."

"The only thing you've learned was how to get into trouble, and you did that all on your own."

"We each have our talents." Marguerite gave Lilly a flippant smile and turned, her skirt swishing against the door frame as she left.

After cleaning up quickly for dinner, Nick hurried to the lunch counter so he could spend a little time with Levi before the other men arrived. The bell above the diner's door jangled as he entered.

Mrs. Hart—Lilly—emerged from the kitchen, wiping her hands on a towel. "Mr. Perrin, about yesterday. I feel an apology is in order."

He stepped back. Did she honestly expect him to say he was sorry for standing up for her? Taking a deep breath, he swallowed the bitter pill of pride. "All right. I apologize."

"No, not from you. From me." She looked down at the towel in her hands. "I spoke rashly, and I now realize you were simply trying be kind." She glanced toward the kitchen. "I'm afraid dinner won't be ready for another forty-five minutes."

"I know, but I thought maybe Levi would like to go bug hunting before supper."

She paused, and he guessed she was considering whether

she trusted him. At last, her lips curved in a smile. Why hadn't he noticed her smile earlier? Pure sunshine.

Too bad she had so little to smile about. Perhaps he could fix that.

"Did you hear me, Mr. Perrin? I said Levi is out back with Mrs. Andrews's children." She motioned toward a table with two other women. The blonde woman nodded. So that was Mrs. Andrews. He tipped his hat in her direction. "Is it all right with both of you, then, if I take the children to collect bugs?"

"If you want to do that, you go right ahead." Mrs. Andrews, a pretty woman near the same age as Lilly, laughed.

"Mrs. Hart?" He didn't want to consider how she'd react if he didn't have her permission to take her son somewhere. The little pistol of a woman couldn't be an inch over five feet tall, but he had no doubt her quick tongue made up for any size she lacked. "Ma'am?"

She rolled her eyes. "Far be it from me to keep a man from his bugs."

❧

Lilly carried a stack of plates to the workmen's tables and began setting them in place.

Marguerite sauntered over with a handful of forks. "And who exactly was that handsome gentleman?"

Emily's jaw dropped. "Marguerite! You're a married woman."

"I'm not looking for me. I'm looking for Lilly."

"Which is a shame, 'cause I'm not looking either." Lilly snatched the forks from Marguerite and laid one to the left of each plate.

Emily shifted the baby into her left arm and brought Lilly

29

a stack of red-checkered napkins. "It's been three years. Ben wouldn't want you to be alone forever."

"You need a man." Marguerite folded the napkins and slipped them under the forks.

"The only man I need is less than four feet tall and is six years old." Lilly straightened. "Don't you two have families to get home to?"

"My grandmother was having the cottage aired and my things moved in this afternoon," Emily said. "I'll head over there in a while. I was hoping to order some dinner here."

"I'll save you some stew."

"And I can't leave until that man comes back with my children," Marguerite said.

"His name is Nick Perrin."

"How do you know him, and how does he know Levi likes bugs?" Emily asked.

"He's the engineer in charge of building the new roller coaster, and Levi's taken a liking to him."

"And what about you?"

As if Marguerite's brain were made of glass, Lilly could see her friend was already making plans, conspiring against her. "I have a lunch counter to run. If you two will excuse me, I'm gonna go stir the stew before I burn it to a crisp."

❦

"Lassie, I believe that was the best stew I've ever tasted."

Lilly picked up the plate in front of the man the others called Sean McGready. His Irish brogue gave away his heritage, and she couldn't help but smile at the twinkle in the man's green eyes. "I think you were simply unusually hungry, Mr. McGready."

"Boss works me hard, he does." Sean grinned at Nick

30

Perrin. "A real slave driver. Maybe ya could sweeten him up with some of that apple cobbler I smell."

"Or maybe she could have a piece with us." One of the younger men reached out to her. "We'd sure enjoy your company." Nick cleared his throat, and the man dropped his hand quickly. "Sorry, ma'am. I was trying to be friendly."

She collected the remaining empty plates, all nearly licked clean, and nodded to Nick. "I'll be right back with cobbler—for all of you."

With the dirty plates piled high in her arms, Lilly headed for the kitchen.

Emily hurried from her table to join her. "Want some help?"

"I can handle it."

"I know you can." Emily touched her arm. "But I want to help."

What was she going to do with all these well-wishers? Why couldn't they understand that relying on other people was not her way? She never had, and she certainly didn't dare start now. This afternoon, Emily and Marguerite had spent an hour trying to persuade her to take Emily up on her offer of staying at the cabin. If she didn't let Emily do something now, they'd pester her all evening as well.

She sighed. "All right, why don't you grab those plates and let's dish up some cobbler?"

After placing a large serving of cobbler on each of the red-rimmed plates, Lilly reached for the coffeepot. My, but these men could drink coffee.

No sooner had she refilled Mr. McGready's cup than he'd downed its contents. She laughed and began to fill it again.

The diner's door opened. Lilly turned her head and spotted her in-laws enter with the sheriff.

"Whoa there, lassie." Mr. McGready held up his hand. "I'm thirsty, but not that thirsty."

She jerked the spout of the coffeepot upward and stared at the overflowing cup. She grabbed a napkin and blotted the spill. "I'm so sorry."

"No worries, lass."

If only that were true. Why had her in-laws brought the sheriff?

The sheriff removed his hat. "Can we speak to you, Mrs. Hart?"

Her heart pounded like a kettledrum. She caught Mr. Perrin watching her and noticed he sat up straighter. Did he intend to intervene again? She certainly hoped not. It would only make matters worse.

She moved closer to the table where her two friends remained. Besides needing their moral support, it would save time later explaining what had transpired. "Certainly, Sheriff. Can I get you anything?"

"No, ma'am," he said. "Would you care to sit down?"

She glanced at her father-in-law's hard face and took a seat, pressing a shaky hand to her stomach. She forced her words to take on the formal tone she'd learned the Harts expected from her as their son's wife. "I don't have a feeling this is a social call, sir. Why don't you tell me why you're here?"

"Mrs. Hart, your husband's parents—"

"My deceased husband."

"Yes, ma'am." The sheriff shifted his feet. "They are concerned about your son's well-being."

"I can assure you my son is perfectly fine, Sheriff. I would never do anything to harm him in any way."

"Yes, ma'am, but your in-laws are worried about where

the two of you are living. They said you left their home and have been living in a tent here at the lake."

"Yes, sir, we have."

"While I know a lot of folks camp in tents here all summer, it's still awfully cold at night this time of year, don't you think? They've offered to let the boy come stay with them."

Emily stood and moved next to Lilly. "Excuse me for interrupting, but that was only temporary until I arrived back here at the lake. She's now staying at our family's cabin." Lilly sucked in a gulp of air, and Emily grabbed hold of her hand and squeezed it hard. "Sheriff, you're familiar with the Graham cottage here on the lake, aren't you?"

"Of course I am. Your grandma Kate's been spending summers out here for years."

Emily looped her arm in Lilly's. "Then you know there's plenty of room for Lilly, her son, my baby, and myself."

"That's not true! I don't believe her." Evangeline huffed. "She's making it up."

"Ma'am?"

Lilly took a deep breath to calm her knotting stomach. She didn't want to accept Emily's charity, but what choice did she have now? She met the sheriff's gaze. "Yes, I'll be moving in there tomorrow."

Evangeline mashed her lips together. "This is ridiculous. We have a perfectly wonderful home where Levi can have the best of everything, and yet she insists on keeping the boy with her at this mosquito-infested lake."

"Ma'am, if the boy isn't being mistreated—"

Evangeline propped her hands on her hips. "And how do you know he isn't being mistreated?"

"My wife is right. Perhaps she's starving him." Claude locked eyes with Lilly.

Anger burned in her chest. How dare they imply she wouldn't feed her son!

"May I see the boy, Mrs. Hart?" An unspoken apology seemed to fill the old sheriff's deep voice.

"I'll get him," Marguerite offered. She returned a few minutes later with a mud-splattered Levi and her own dirt-dappled children. "I'm afraid they've been playing outside—collecting bugs."

"They look like they've been wallowing in a pigsty." Evangeline pressed a handkerchief to her scrunched-up nose. "And they smell as bad."

Lilly laid a hand on her son's shoulder. "Levi, greet your grandparents and the sheriff."

Levi wiped his dirt-caked hand across his shirt and held it out. "Hello, Grandmother." He paused and his eyes grew wide. "Sheriff, is that a real gun?"

"Yes, son, it is." The sheriff shook Levi's offered hand, which his grandparents had ignored, then turned to Claude. "Clearly the boy is being well cared for."

"But look at him!" Evangeline motioned toward Levi with a gloved hand, the handkerchief dangling from her fingertips. "Where are his shoes?"

"I took 'em off." Levi puffed out his chest. "Mama wouldn't want me to get 'em dirty."

The sheriff let out a loud chuckle. "He's 100 percent boy, but there's no crime in that. Had me three of my own." He patted Levi's sandy-haired head. "You had supper yet?"

"Mama feeds me after she feeds the men."

The sheriff glanced at the workmen seated around the corner tables. "Since I can see they're finished, I'm guessing you'd like us to leave so you can eat. Am I right, son?"

"That'd be mighty nice." Levi rubbed his ribs. "I might

faint dead away if I don't get some food soon. 'Sides, when I'm finished, Mr. Nick said I get to go see how the rollie coaster is comin' along—if it's okay with Mama."

"Then we'd best be hurrying." The sheriff turned to Lilly's in-laws, and the timbre of his voice dropped. "As for you two, I don't appreciate being called in on a family dispute even if you have all the money in the country. I've seen this kind of thing before, but I'm telling you, this boy belongs in the care of his mother. As long as the boy's needs are being met and she's not harming him, I suggest you let her live in peace with him at the Grahams' cottage. They've been through enough already."

The sheriff placed his hat back on his head and touched the brim in the ladies' direction before opening the door. He held it for Claude and Evangeline but didn't seem to notice the look of warning Claude flashed Lilly—a look of cold determination that made Lilly's blood freeze in her veins.

A look that said this was far from being over.

4

Daffodils winked at Lilly from the front yards along High Street. Despite the morning's cool temperatures, Lilly felt warmed by the sun as she walked to the Westings' home. Her glass-beaded purse, a gift from Ben on their first Christmas, jingled in her left hand, a few coins lighter since her streetcar ride to the city. Levi's sticky fingers remained clasped in her other hand.

Lilly straightened the jaunty hat on her head and reinserted a hat pin into her Gibson girl chignon. The wide, rose-colored satin ribbons hanging down the back tickled her neck in the breeze. "Now, remember, Levi, Grammy works for the Westings. This isn't her home, so you have to be extra good and not touch any of Mrs. Westing's pretty things."

"Why does Grammy live at Tate and Faith's grammy's house now?" Levi licked the sugar stick Nick had given him this morning. "I liked it better when she lived with us."

"So did I, but the Westings have managed to spring back from a difficult time a few years ago, and Grammy wanted

36

to work there." Lilly released his hand. "Why don't you run up the block and get rid of some of your energy? Let's see how fast you are."

Pumping his little arms as hard as he could, Levi flew up the sidewalk and stopped at the walk leading to the Westings' front doorstep. "Race you to the knocker, Mama."

Lilly caught his collar. "Not so fast, speedy. We'll go around to the back."

"Huh? But I like to use their shiny knocker."

"Not anymore." Lilly sighed. She'd loved the first time she walked into the front door of the Westing home on Ben's arm, but those days were over. Her heart pinched. Although she'd worn one of her fancier frocks, a rose chiffon day dress with a gathered bolero trimmed in lace, the outward trappings didn't mean a thing to those who knew the truth. Ben was gone, and so was any equality she'd once had with this affluent family.

Lilly followed the brick sidewalk and led her son around the side of the two-story Victorian home. She glanced at the trellis Marguerite had once snuck down to get out of her piano practice, and chuckled. How Mrs. Westing had shouted when she discovered a hole in her daughter's new sunny-yellow dress.

"You used to live here, right, Mama?"

"I did. Grammy was the Westings' housekeeper."

"And you was Grammy's baby and you growed up with Aunt Margreet like a sister."

"Mostly. Someone had to keep Aunt Marguerite out of trouble." She paused near the clothesline in the backyard and touched the calico drawstring bag holding the pins—her first sewing project under her mother's watchful eye. Guilt clutched her heart. Her mother was too old to be lugging baskets of wet clothes around. Worse, it was Lilly's fault her mama had to.

The back porch door opened wide, and Mama waddled out wearing an apron over her dark work dress. Sweat beaded on her forehead despite the cool spring morning. She dabbed at her cheeks with the towel in her hand. "Who's that big boy with you, Lilly? He couldn't possibly be my little Levi."

"Grammy, it is too me." Levi ran to Mama.

She bent low and hugged him to her ample bosom. "I sure missed your sticky sugar kisses. How much have you grown? A foot? Lilly, what are you feeding this boy to make him grow so big in only one week?"

Beaming, Levi held his striped stick out before him. "I'm eatin' candy."

"And what kind of stick candy do you have?"

"Cimamum." He licked his lips. "Want some?"

Mama held back a chuckle. "Thank you kindly, but I'll pass on your *cimamum* candy this time. Lilly, pull up those chairs while I go fetch the mess of apples I need to peel. Then we can sit and talk while I work."

"Bring two paring knives and I'll help."

"You'll do none of that. This is your first morning off in a week except for the Lord's Day, and you should be relaxing." The screen door banged shut as Mama went inside.

Lilly arranged two wicker chairs side by side, then moved to what had been Marguerite's play table and called Levi over.

"I have a surprise for you, Levi." She opened her handbag, pulled out a folded sheet of paper, and smoothed it on the table. Creases still remained, but it would be usable. She withdrew a box of Crayola crayons from her handbag. The box had cost her five cents out of her first week's pay.

"What is it?"

She eased open the lid to reveal the eight crayons inside before handing him the box. "You draw pictures with them on the paper."

"Like paints?" His lips bowed in a broad smile so much like his daddy's.

"Sort of. Only these are like colored pencils. You can draw pretty flowers and blue skies. Be careful with them. You don't want to break one."

By the time Mama returned with a bowl of apples to peel, Levi was deep in artistic thought, the candy stick propped between his lips. She set her bowl on the table between the wicker chairs and walked over to Levi.

"Well, aren't those the dandiest things?" Mama examined the box of crayons. "My, my, a person could paint the world with all those pretty colors. Think of all the possibilities."

"I'm hoping it will keep him out of trouble when I'm working during lunch. He loves to create things." Lilly snagged the paring knife before Mama sat down and stripped the apple peel in one long string.

"Lilly, I told you that's my job." Her mother held out her hand until Lilly laid the knife in her palm, then dropped into the wicker chair and pulled her shawl more tightly about her shoulders.

"But I don't mind, and it's my fault you even have to work here again."

"Listen to me. You did the right thing in leaving that house. I know. I was there."

"And if you were still there, you wouldn't have to be back making pies for Camille Westing."

"Mrs. Westing's not the same woman she was when you were a child. Ask Marguerite. And she's happy as a lark I'm back cookin'."

"And cleaning and polishing and doing laundry."

"Heavens no. Wilhelmina does all that." She cut the core from the apple. "She even does the dishes after I cook. Mrs. Westing won't let me do a thing. That whole financial scare changed her. She's a new person now. And so is Mr. Westing. Hasn't gambled a bit since that time. Praise the Lord for blessing him with a whole new business and for letting them keep the house in the meantime."

Lilly glanced toward the clothespin bag on the line. "Mama—"

"I help Wilhelmina some when no one's watching—if I have time and if I'm feeling up to it." Mama chuckled, and her salt-and-pepper-colored bun bobbed. She cocked her head at Lilly. "I recognize that look in your eyes, and you need to stop. I don't want you to go feelin' guilty. I got a good place here. You know how warm my room is, and the Westings even bought me a new feather tick for my bed. Softest thing you ever laid on."

"You deserve a real home, Mama. When I married Ben, I thought I could make a home for all of us."

"Lilly May, God wanted me here."

"How do you know?"

"Because I prayed about it." Mama chose another apple. The slightly swollen knuckles of her hands didn't keep her from making quick work of chopping the fruit. "I wanted to witness to Mrs. Westing, and I've been praying for years for the right time. Her heart is open now. I think she may come to know the Lord." She dropped the naked apple in the bowl. "Besides, this world is not my home. Oh, I know you've wanted us to have a house since you were ten years old, but I learned to be content without one a long time ago."

"When I was ten, Marguerite got a beautiful dollhouse for

40

Christmas." Lilly closed her eyes, and the gingerbread-clad toy structure came into view. "I wanted a big, white, grand house too, with pretty carpets and velvet draperies."

"And a nursery for the baby." Mama touched her hand. "You had those fine things at the Harts', but it still wasn't a home."

"It wasn't *my* home. Ben's mother made that perfectly clear. But I promise you, Mama, I'll earn enough money to make a home for you and Levi. After the season at Lake Manawa is over, I'll get a job at Woodward's Candy Factory, and I'll work hard. I don't want my son growing up feeling like he has no place to call his own."

"Like you did?"

"Mama, you did your best. What else could you do after Daddy died before we could head West? The Westings were good to us most of the time. And you made sure I always felt loved."

"But you were always afraid Mrs. Westing would get in a snit and send us away."

Lilly dropped her head. "Not us, Mama. Me."

Levi waved his paper in the air. "Done. Wanna see, Grammy?"

"Sure do." Mama leaned over the picture and touched the boy in it. "This must be you. Look how handsome you are with your brown hair and blue eyes. But who is this?"

"That's Mr. Nick. He has blue eyes like mine, but his hair is black like coal."

Lilly smiled. "You drew him very well."

"And why is Mr. Nick holding a spider?"

"'Cause he's my friend, and we hunt bugs. Mama don't like him, but I do. And Mr. Thorton told her she has to be nice to him. That was before the sheriff came and we had to move in with Emily and crying baby Katie."

"You don't say?" Mama turned to Lilly. "Well, I guess you can go in the house and get yourself a paring knife after all. It looks like you're gonna be here awhile fillin' me in on your life at the lake, so you might as well make yourself useful."

⁂

Staring at the massive Hart mansion, Lilly took a deep breath. How her mother had convinced her to visit her former in-laws, she'd never know. Actually, she did understand her mother's point. They were Ben's parents, and if she loved him, then it was her duty to make sure they had a chance to have a relationship with their grandson—even if it made Lilly uncomfortable.

And it certainly did. Her stomach churned like the lake on a stormy day. Would they take her visit as the peace offering she hoped it would be?

She knelt in front of Levi and straightened his jacket. "Remember, use your best manners when you see your grandparents."

"They don't like me."

"Yes they do, honey, but they aren't used to being around little boys."

Levi cocked his head. "But wasn't Daddy a little boy once?"

"Yes, but he had a nanny who took care of him most of the time." She stood and lifted the latch on the heavy iron gate. It creaked as she opened it far enough for the two of them to pass through. The ominous clang as it shut behind them made her shiver. Taking Levi's hand, she started up the walk.

"But why didn't Grandmother take care of Daddy?"

"She didn't think it should be done like that." Lilly squeezed his hand.

"Did I have a nanny when I lived here?"

42

"When you were little, you had a nurse your grandmother hired, but your daddy and I let her go. Your daddy and I never wanted you to be away from us. We wanted to take care of you all by ourselves."

"Didn't Daddy like his nanny?"

"Daddy loved his nanny a great deal. He said her name was Rosy. He used to call her Rosy Posey." Lilly gave the brass knocker on the front door two solid whacks. "Now, remember your manners."

The door opened, and Jerome, the Harts' butler, motioned them inside. He took Lilly's cape and draped it over his arm. "I'll let the Harts know you are here, ma'am, and may I personally say you and Master Hart are greatly missed here."

"Thank you, Jerome." She smiled down at Levi. *Lord, please help me say and do the right thing today for his sake.*

Lilly took a deep breath and glanced around. Nothing had changed since she'd left. A garish painting of a fox hunt still hung in the foyer over the entry table. Beneath it lay the tiny silver tray for Jerome to collect calling cards from visitors. Of course, as family, she didn't need to produce one.

Levi fidgeted beside her. Maybe she shouldn't have brought him after all. The Harts had never doted on him the way most grandparents would, and while she understood that it wasn't their way to show affection, he didn't.

"Can I slide down the banister like I used to do when Grandmother and Grandfather weren't home?" Levi hopped over the base of the staircase. "'Member, Mama? You used to hold on to me until I slid all the way down."

"And then we'd go in the kitchen and Mrs. Kauffman would make us hot chocolate and give us cookies." She smiled. At least he held some fond memories of living here.

"Can we go see her now?"

43

"No, honey. Today we're here to visit your grandparents. Remember, use your very best manners."

Jerome reentered and asked them to follow him. Lilly could have said she didn't need to be shown the way, but she found comfort in the butler's company. As she expected, he led them to the sunroom at the back of the mansion where her mother-in-law loved to sit in the mornings. She spotted Evangeline first, sitting on a cushioned rattan love seat. Around her, green plants, airy ferns, and ivy-filled baskets drank in the sun's rays in front of the large windows.

Claude Hart rose from his chair beside her and nodded. "Lilly, have you come to tell me you are reconsidering our offer?"

"No, sir. I came because I wanted you to have the opportunity to see your grandson." She swallowed hard, the words feeling stiff on her tongue. "I'm praying this will be a pleasant exchange for all of us. Ben would have wanted that."

"Ben would have wanted a lot of things." Evangeline sipped tea from her china cup.

Claude motioned to an empty chair. "Won't you have a seat?"

"Thank you." She sat down, and Levi stood beside her with his hand clutching her skirt. "Go tell your grandmother good morning." After she pried his fingers loose, he walked across the room and stood before her.

"My, you've grown. Give your grandmother a kiss." She pointed to her cheek and waited.

Levi bestowed the wet kiss with a loud smack, and Lilly stifled a giggle. If Lilly knew Evangeline, she was dying to wipe the slobber from her cheek. To her credit, the woman simply patted the love seat beside her.

"So, Levi, tell Grandmother what adventures you've been having at the lake. Do you have any friends?"

"I have lots and lots of friends. There are crickets and toads and spiders, and Mr. Nick helped me with Flower, my pet snake."

Evangeline's mouth formed a perfect O, then she scowled at Lilly. "You let him play with snakes?"

"It's only a harmless garter snake."

"Well, I would never—"

Lilly smiled. "I know, but he's my son."

"I ain't got a cage yet, but Mr. Nick said maybe he'll help me build one."

Evangeline tsked. "You don't have a cage, and who is Mr. Nick?"

Folding her hands in her lap, Lilly tried to relax. "Nick Perrin is the man who's building the roller coaster. I cook for him and his men, and he's been kind to Levi."

"Levi's grammar is atrocious, Lilly. You really must let us send him to—"

Lilly held up her hand. "We will leave this instant if you insist on discussing a boarding school."

"We only want what's best for him." Claude's deep voice, so perfect for the courtroom, jarred her. "He could have the best of everything—just like our Ben. Think about how Ben turned out. Don't you want that for your son?"

"Ben hated being sent off to boarding school. He and I discussed it, and it was never our plan to send Levi away. If Ben were alive, he'd tell you himself. Besides, Levi would be devastated without me."

"You can't let a child's emotions make these decisions." Evangeline pinched Levi's cheek. "No matter how sweet he is now, he will grow up to become a man, and what kind of man is determined by the opportunities presented to him."

"What kind of man Levi becomes will be determined by

45

me and by God. And already I can see God has blessed Levi with a generous and caring spirit like his father." Lilly smiled at her son. "Levi, you haven't greeted your grandfather."

After scampering off the love seat, Levi walked slowly to the white-bearded man. Claude extended his hand. Levi took it and pumped it vigorously. "Hello, Grandfather. Lovely day, isn't it?"

Lilly had to bite her lip to keep from laughing.

"Excuse me." Jerome appeared at the door bearing a box. "I thought young master Levi might enjoy playing with some of his father's blocks."

Claude nodded. "Splendid idea."

While Jerome set the box down near the window, Levi hurried to claim it. In seconds he'd begun to construct a tower.

"Lilly, about the other day." Claude cleared his throat.

"Please, I know you don't agree with me, but I have to do what I think Ben would want me to do to raise our son. I understand Levi is all you have left of Ben—but he's all I have left too." She dabbed the tear blurring her vision. "I have to raise Levi the way Ben and I planned."

Claude leveled his gaze at her. "And would Ben want you working all hours of the day while your son played with snakes and strangers? Would he want you living off the charity of friends when your family is willing to provide for you?"

"Ben would want me to be happy." The words came out soft and wistful.

"But he'd want you here, and never living off the charity of the Grahams." Evangeline picked up her teacup. "Levi, what do you have in that cosmetics jar?"

"Levi, stop!" Lilly jumped to her feet, but she was too late. Levi gave a final twist to the metal lid on a small jar and dumped the contents into his newly created structure.

5

The ants immediately scattered to the corners and climbed the blocks.

Levi tried to corral the ants with his hands. "Stop, you naughty ants. This is your new house."

"Ants?" Evangeline squealed, jumped up, and backed against the bookcase as if the ants would eat her alive. "Claude, do something! Get them out of my house."

Lilly dropped to her knees beside Levi and grabbed the empty jar. "Let's put the ants back in your can. I don't think they'll like living at your grandparents' house."

Levi frowned at his grandmother and picked up an ant-covered block. "Neither do I."

Finally, Lilly and Levi collected the majority of the ants, and Lilly told her son it was time to say goodbye. Evangeline kissed the top of his head and asked him not to bring any more creatures with him to his grandmother's.

Claude followed her to the door. "Lilly, it's clear Levi has far too much freedom—playing with ants, toads, snakes, and who knows what else." At over six feet, Claude loomed over her. "Ben would not have allowed you to be so permissive, and since he is not here, we must act in his stead. How will Levi ever take on the Hart fortune if he isn't taught refinement? Given your upbringing, I don't think you understand all Levi may be called on to do. And you are certainly ill-equipped to teach him."

Lilly opened the door and told Levi to go to the bottom of the stairs and wait for her. "Levi will be fine. He's a little boy, and he's only acting accordingly. There's plenty of time for him to learn to be as stuffy as you. However, I do appreciate your concern, and I know you love him in your own way. But I beg you to understand—he's my son, and I will raise him the way I see fit."

Claude pinned her with his penetrating gaze. "We do understand what you want, but that is clearly not what is best for him. Therefore, we will press forward in our efforts to gain custody of Levi because it's in the child's best interest—unless, of course, you relent in allowing us to send him to the boarding school."

"Would that be in Levi's best interest or yours?" She scalded her father-in-law with a final glare and marched down the stairs. With her heart thundering in her chest, she grabbed Levi's hand and hurried toward the gate. Why had she ever thought she could reach the two of them?

Now things were worse than ever.

❧

If Lilly and Levi didn't hurry, the roller coaster crew would have no hot coffee for lunch. The ham sandwiches they'd handle fine, but not having coffee would make them gripe for sure. As soon as the streetcar arrived at Lake Manawa,

Lilly hurried her son off, and the two of them made their way toward the Midway.

"Look, Mama." Levi pointed to the fence housing the Manawa zoo. Although there were no elephants or tigers, the zoo had enough species that the children loved it. "Can we go see the alligator?"

"Not today, sweetheart. We don't have time." She pulled him along.

"But, Mama, you never have time."

"I know, but right now, we really have to hurry."

"Please—"

"Levi, hush now. You don't want to miss seeing Mr. Nick, do you?" She shouldn't use the man as a reward, but sometimes a mother had to do whatever it took.

"Can I show him my picture?"

"Yes, and you can even show him your new crayons."

As soon as they reached the lunch counter, Lilly snagged her apron from the hook. She'd hoped there would be time to return to the cabin to change out of her good dress, but she didn't dare. After stoking the fire, she put the coffeepot over the cookstove's firebox and helped Levi set the silverware in their places on the table. When he'd finished, she dismissed him to go check on Mr. Wiggles and Flower with a warning to stay within sight of the lunch counter.

Since the men didn't have breakfast on Wednesdays at the lunch counter, she knew they'd be extra hungry. She cut thick slices of ham and laid it on the crusty bread. Soon she had the serving tray filled, along with two bowls each of preserved peaches and coleslaw.

After mixing the freshly ground coffee with two eggs and some water in a bowl like her mother always did, she poured the egg/coffee mixture into the boiling water in the enameled coffeepot. She took a deep breath. In two to three minutes it would be done. She'd made it.

She gasped. Dessert! How had she forgotten? Of course the men had come to expect something sweet with their meals. She glanced around the room. No leftover cookies or cakes. No pies or pastries. These men ate everything.

Her gaze fell to the milk can that had been delivered in her absence, and she got an idea. She could cook some pudding. She wouldn't be able to chill it in the icebox, but they could enjoy it warm all the same.

Before she forgot the coffee, she removed the pot from the heat and poured a cup of cold water in it to settle the grounds. She set it on the back corner to keep it warm.

The back door to the kitchen opened. Lilly didn't look up from measuring milk into a pot. "Levi, go wash before lunch."

A man cleared his throat.

She turned. "Mr. Thorton, I'm sorry. I didn't know it was you." She smiled at the young woman beside him. Her strawberry-blonde hair seemed to have a mind of its own, and her bright pink dress didn't match the peach-colored hat on her head in the least. A smattering of freckles across her nose and cheeks brought a whimsical quality to the girl Lilly guessed to be in her late teens. Lilly nodded and swished the spoon around the bowl. "Hello."

"Mrs. Hart, this is my niece Eugenia. My sister's daughter. She's going to be your new assistant. Eugenia, Mrs. Hart."

Lilly dropped her long-handled spoon in the milk, then fished it back out with another spoon. "An assistant?"

"I know this lunch counter is going to be too much for you to handle alone once the season starts, and as I told you, I plan to add two to three more workers by then."

50

"That's mighty thoughtful of you, Mr. Thorton, but it's still early May, and I'm doing fine by myself."

"Yes, you certainly are, but Eugenia's mother and I were talking, and we both thought she might need some extra instruction."

Lilly glanced at the girl, who stood staring wide-eyed around the kitchen. "Let me guess, she doesn't cook a lick."

Mr. Thorton seemed to take an interest in his pocket watch. "If anyone can teach her, I'm sure you can."

"But, Mr. Thorton—"

"I have to meet an old friend. You two can work out the details of Eugenia's duties." He kissed his niece's cheek. "Eugenia, you listen to Mrs. Hart and do exactly what she says."

"I will, Uncle Clyde." She wiggled her fingers at him as he departed.

Lilly took a deep breath and looked at Eugenia's hopeful face. She smiled again. It would be nice to have some company. "Have you ever worked in a kitchen, Eugenia?"

The girl shook her head. "I'm not sure I've even been in one, ma'am, except when I snuck cookies, but I've been reading up on cooking. I've learned a lot."

Reading had its place in the world. Folks could learn a lot from books, but Lilly doubted cooking was one of them. "The men will be in soon, but I want to get this pudding done. Since you've been reading, have you learned how to separate eggs?"

A smile blossomed across Eugenia's face. "Of course. I can do that."

"Good. We'll need twelve eggs separated. The eggs are over there." Lilly pointed to the Hoosier cabinet with a crate on top of the porcelain counter. Then, humming to herself, she returned to stirring her scalding milk. Yes, this could work out fine.

51

"I'm done, Miss Lilly," Eugenia said.

"Already?" Lilly poured the sugar into the pan and turned. On the surface of the cabinet, Eugenia had certainly separated eggs—five brown ones on the right, seven white ones on the left.

Lilly shook her head. Now she didn't have one child to raise, she had two.

The bell jingled above the door, announcing the arrival of the roller coaster crew. Did she dare use Eugenia to serve? Maybe she could do something simple. "Eugenia, why don't you pour coffee for the men while I bring out their food? The pot is on the stove."

The girl bounced away, the silly peach flowers on her hat bobbing as she walked. Lilly grabbed the tray of sandwiches, removed the towel from the top, and carried it through the doorway. The men grinned when she approached.

"I'm as hungry as a horse, Mrs. Hart." The worker she'd learned was Percy Leonard wrapped his fingers around a thick sandwich. He was the youngest but also had the biggest appetite. Tall and thin, Percy made her wonder where the young man put all the food he consumed. "Those doughnuts you left us were delicious, but they didn't stick to my ribs long enough."

"We're lucky she did that." Nick Perrin took his own sandwich from the tray. "My agreement was there'd be no breakfast on Wednesdays. Mrs. Hart deserves a morning off."

"But we can't make it without breakfast," the worker with the broadest girth whined.

"Frank, I don't think you need to worry about fainting dead away."

Eugenia approached with the coffeepot in hand. Thank the Lord she had the good sense to use a towel over the handle to protect her hand.

She reached for Sean McGready's coffee cup and smiled. "Maybe I can make you all breakfast on Wednesdays."

Lilly offered the tray of sandwiches to Mr. McGready. He selected one and set it on his plate. "I don't think you're ready for that yet, Eugenia," Lilly said.

The girl jerked when Lilly spoke and spilled coffee on Mr. McGready's sandwich. Eugenia grabbed for it, and the top slice of bread fell onto the floor. She quickly scooped it up and started to replace it on the sandwich.

"Stop!" Lilly ordered as she picked up Mr. McGready's plate. "Let me go get you some fresh bread on this. Then I'll be back to fill your cups. Eugenia, come with me."

"Does this mean I can't make the men breakfast?" Eugenia's lower lip protruded.

Lilly rolled her eyes and shook her head in disbelief. This was going to be a long, long summer.

Sweet, rich, and creamy, the pudding slid over Nick's tongue. Mrs. Hart could cook better than any woman he'd ever met. They were blessed to have her cooking for them, but he worried they were overworking her. At least it seemed she had some help now.

He grinned. Would that girl be considered a help? From the little he'd seen, he wondered.

He pushed back from the table. "Well, fellows, guess it's time to get back to work."

The others grumbled but followed suit. A tug on his tan work pants made him look down. "Hello, Levi. Where have you been hiding?"

"I was eating my lunch in the kitchen."

"With your mama?"

He shook his head. "She gave hers to the new girl."

Nick glanced over the lunch counter into the kitchen and caught a glimpse of Mrs. Hart sitting on a stool, nursing a cup of coffee. The new girl, Eugenia, had a sandwich in hand. Concern made his gut twinge. Had he seen Levi's mother eat anything in the last week?

"Mr. Nick, can I still go see the stuff you're building?"

"If your mother says yes, I'll be glad to take you. Why don't you go ask her while I wait?"

Levi rushed into the kitchen, and Nick remained even though the other workmen filed out. They knew what to do without him. He laughed when Levi dragged his mother around to the front of the lunch counter.

She'd removed her apron, revealing a pleated rose-colored dress with lace placed in the most attractive places. Not the usual costume of a lady doing kitchen work. Must be one from her days in the rich in-laws' house. He bristled. How could they turn their backs on the widow of their son? And why hadn't her husband provided for her?

"Tell her you said I could go, Mr. Nick."

Nick laughed and tapped Levi's nose. "I said if your mother said yes, you could go."

"Do you, Mama? Do you?"

"Levi, Mr. Perrin is a busy man." She pushed a chestnut curl away from her temple.

"I do have some time to spare this afternoon, and it would be my pleasure to show Mr. Levi the progress we're making on the roller coaster. That is, if you can spare his assistance here."

"Please, Mama?"

"Levi, you could pester a magpie to death." Mrs. Hart rolled her eyes. "If Mr. Perrin is sure it isn't too much of a bother. Just be back by supper time."

"Will do." Nick tipped his hat and placed a hand on Levi's shoulder. "Good day, Mrs. Hart."

"Thank you, Mr. Perrin."

She smiled. Pure sunshine, once again, and it warmed him more than he expected.

6

Why hadn't Nick Perrin returned with her son?

Lilly quickly gathered the last of the workmen's dinner plates and carried them to the kitchen, dropping them so hard into the washbasin the suds splashed onto her apron.

"Would you like me to wash those while you go fetch your boy?" Eugenia brought in the coffee cups.

Lilly started to decline but reconsidered. Washing dishes had nothing to do with cooking, so surely Eugenia could master the task. After untying her apron strings, Lilly slung the piece of clothing on a peg by the kitchen door. "Thank you. If you'll wash them and let them air-dry, I'll put them away in their places when I get back."

"You don't need to do that. I'll put them away too. Don't worry about a thing."

But no one could take care of the worries growing inside Lilly. What if Levi was lost or injured? Her stomach rolled and churned more than Lake Manawa on a windy day, but Sean McGready had said Nick told him to let her know they'd be along shortly. Why had Mr. Perrin not returned with Levi for supper?

She quickened her step on the dirt path leading to the roller coaster site. When she found Nick Perrin, she was going to educate him on the definition of *shortly*.

Taking a deep breath, she inhaled all the scents of spring but didn't have time to savor it. The late afternoon sun would soon sink behind the bluffs. The tall foundation posts came into view like a forest of matchsticks as she approached. My, they'd gotten a lot built in the last week, and it looked like the coaster would be as long as ten or eleven streetcars lined up end to end.

Moving along the length of what would soon be a roller coaster, she searched the area for Levi, but not even one of the work crew was in sight. She shouldn't be surprised. Their day was over. Hers, however, was not.

"Levi!" she called.

From around the side of a stack of lumber, his head poked out. "Here, Mama." Like a turtle, he pulled his head back in.

She hurried to the pile and marched around it. "Where on earth . . ."

When she rounded the stack, she stopped. Levi sat perched on top of a large, homemade worktable holding a much-too-heavy hammer in his right hand. Mr. Perrin bent over her kneeling son, his hand covering the boy's.

"Remember." Mr. Perrin held a nail in place. "First you have to set the nail with a little tap. Then you can drive it in." He demonstrated the motion and pulled his hand away. The nail remained standing upright.

With his tongue stuck between his lips, Levi tapped the nail. "I wanna try it by myself."

"Okay, but don't hit your thumb." Mr. Perrin stepped back

and placed his hands on his hips, making his already broad shoulders widen further.

Lilly couldn't take her eyes off the two of them. Intent on his project, Levi focused on the nail and Nick Perrin focused on her son. Levi drove the nail, albeit crookedly, through the wood.

Levi swung his legs over the side of the table and grinned at her. "We're building a snake cage."

Chicken wire had been tacked to four sides of a frame. She guessed Levi was working on the lid.

Nick tousled Levi's hair. "And you've done a fine job. It'll need a hinge and a latch, but I can pick those up in town when I go for supplies."

"Did you *boys* even notice the others had all departed for supper?" Lilly's words came out with more bite than she intended.

"I apologize, ma'am. I guess we got a bit carried away with our project."

"Mama, we're working men." Levi hooked his thumbs in the suspenders of his knee pants. "We can't quit till the job is done."

"Well, working men need to eat too." She ran her hand along the cage, and her irritation evaporated. Even though Nick Perrin should have kept his word and brought Levi back, how could she be angry with someone who'd been so kind to her son? "I was worried, is all."

"Of course you were." Mr. Perrin took the hammer and set it in his wooden toolbox. "Again, I apologize. I should have been more mindful, but as long as you're here, why don't you let Levi and I show you around?"

She took a step backward. "I really should be getting back to the dishes."

"But, Mama, it'll only take a minute."

She released a long breath. Her nerves were spent, and she had no desire to face Eugenia too soon. "All right, my little pestering magpie. Perhaps I can spare a few minutes."

"Excellent." Mr. Perrin lifted Levi off the table. "Levi, why don't you lead the way?"

Lilly followed her son, who led her around the structure as if he'd built it all himself.

"These here posts will hold the track." Levi laid his hand on the rough wood. "The cars will race on it faster than a horse can run on the streets."

"Really?"

"Up to thirty miles per hour." Mr. Perrin walked several yards away. "This is where the depot will stand. There will be a forty-foot climb at the beginning, which will give the cars the momentum they need to make it around the rest of the track. There will be a few more rises in the middle to keep things interesting."

"How long will it be?"

"A little under two thousand feet."

"It's going to be shaped like a number eight." Levi drew the number in the air with his index finger. "Right, Mr. Nick?"

"That's right. And the whole thing will be painted white."

"And it'll have bright flags waving off the top of the . . . the coup."

Mr. Perrin chuckled. "Cupola."

Lilly tilted her head. "Cupola?"

"Ours will be a little pointed structure built on top of the highest point of the coaster. It will make it look even taller."

"Very impressive, Mr. Perrin."

"Please, call me Nick. Mr. Perrin was my father, and it makes me feel like I'm a hundred years old."

"And is your father a hundred years old?"

Nick opened his mouth to speak, and nothing came out.

Poor Mr. Perrin didn't know how sassy she could be. Except for Marguerite's husband, Trip, and Emily's husband, Carter, she'd not called another man by his given name since her husband passed. And if she called him Nick, would he expect to address her by Lilly?

He found his voice. "Even the boys call me Nick. I'd consider it a personal favor if you'd do the same."

"Mama." Levi rubbed his belly in a big circle. "All this work has made me powerful hungry."

Lilly and Nick shared a look and a smile. Where had he heard that? "Well, perhaps I could find something back in the kitchen for you and Mr. Per—uh, Nick."

Nick nodded, and they started down the path together. Levi bounded ahead with Lilly and Nick following. Nick again apologized for not bringing her son back on time and said she needn't worry about feeding him.

"Nonsense," Lilly said. "If I have to make something for Levi, I might as well fix two plates."

"Three." Nick stopped on the path.

"Excuse me?"

"Levi and I want you to eat with us too. Don't we, Levi? I'm sure with all the fuss, you didn't eat. Surely Mr. Thorton includes meals with your salary."

"I'm allowed three meals a day."

"And Levi said you gave the new girl your lunch, so I know you have to be powerful hungry, as your son would say." He grinned, bringing a twinkle to his cobalt eyes. "So?"

"You're as bad as Levi in the pestering department."

"And?" He lifted his eyebrows.

"And I'll join you both this once."

60

7

"Pork chops have never tasted so good, Mrs. Hart."

Lilly attempted to hide her smile by dabbing her lips with her napkin. She lowered it to her lap. "They aren't difficult to make."

"But they taste better with company." Nick tickled Levi's stomach. "What do you say we help your mama do up these dishes?"

"No, that's not necessary. I can do them." Lilly stood and collected the empty plates.

"Of course you can, but you shouldn't have to." He hurried to his feet and gathered the glasses. "Actually, why don't you rest and let us men handle cleanup? After all, it's our fault you had to cook an extra supper."

"Nick, I can't let you wash dishes."

"Don't you have other work to tend to before morning?"

"Yes, but—"

Nick tucked the glasses in the crook of his arm and gathered the silverware in his fist. "Then you see to that while we boys do these up. I used to help my mother with dishes all the time."

"Where?"

Nick grinned. "In the kitchen."

Lilly gave him a mock scowl and placed her load of dishes in the washbasin. "Where did you live?"

"Near Pittsburgh." Nick removed his coat, rolled up his shirtsleeves, and tied a towel around his waist.

"Pennsylvania?"

"Is there a Pittsburgh, Iowa?"

She smiled. "No, I don't think so."

After pouring a kettle of hot water into the washbasin, Lilly added a small amount of Gold Dust Washing Powder, making a mental note to put another box of soap on her grocery list. How much had Eugenia used tonight?

She pumped a little cold water into the hot and swished the water until suds formed. "Are you the youngest child?"

"No, I'm near the top." Nick nudged her aside. "Let me show you how it's done."

"You're going to show me how to wash dishes?" She stepped to her right and he grinned at her. After rolling up his sleeves, he sunk his arms in the suds up to the elbows and set to work on the glasses first. Maybe he did know what he was doing.

"How many of you were there?" She measured the flour for tomorrow morning's biscuits into her favorite stoneware mixing bowl.

"Ten altogether. Two older brothers and seven younger brothers and sisters. A whole peck of Perrins." He laughed, low and warm. "Hey, where's my half-pint helper?"

"I'll check." Lilly went into the dining room and found Levi's head resting on his crossed arms. His steady breathing told her he was sound asleep. Poor guy. He'd had quite a day. A visit with Grammy, new crayons, dumping ants on his grandparents' floor, building a snake cage—all the excitement must have taken its toll.

She returned to the kitchen and picked up a towel. "I'm afraid you've lost your assistant to dreamland. I guess you'll have to settle for me."

For several minutes, they worked in silence. Not once did Lilly have to return a dish back to the water because Nick had missed something. She prayed Eugenia had done as well with the dishes she'd washed and put away.

"What about you, Mrs. Hart? Only child?"

"How did you know?"

"Guessed."

"Did my bossiness give me away?" Only half teasing, Lilly slipped the dried plate onto the stack.

"No, your independence." Nick wiped his hands on a towel and leaned against the sink. "With ten of us, independence was an unusual trait—except in my youngest brother. He was determined to do things his way."

"Where is he now?"

"Gone." Nick's voice caught, and he swallowed before going on. "He died when he was Levi's age."

"I'm sorry." So that was why Nick had taken such an interest in Levi. He must have reminded Nick of his brother.

"If you're ready to go, I'll carry Levi back to your cottage." Nick wiped his hands on a tea towel and walked into the other room.

"You needn't trouble yourself. I can wake him."

"Mrs. Hart, I realize you probably can out-stubborn me any day, but I can assure you, I will not let any lady and her son walk unescorted home in the dark—especially you." He passed her cape to her from its hook on the wall.

She sucked in her breath, her stomach churning. This was wrong. All wrong. But it felt so right. How had she allowed Nick Perrin to spend the evening with her and Levi? And worse, she'd enjoyed it. How could she do that to Ben's memory?

Goose bumps prickled her flesh. She wrapped her cape about her shoulders while Nick hefted Levi onto his shoulder with ease. Levi's head lulled against Nick's broad shoulder. A memory of Ben, doing much the same after Levi fell asleep in the parlor, flitted through her mind. Only three, Levi had been much smaller, but she'd never forget the way Ben had brushed the hair from Levi's head and planted a kiss on his forehead.

Ben had left on his business trip the next morning, and Levi never saw his daddy again.

<hr />

When had such a pleasant evening gone south? Nick shook his head, and Levi nestled further into his neck. Mrs. Hart had not spoken a word since they'd locked up the lunch counter. She walked beside him, her bearing stiff, her mouth clamped shut.

He shifted Levi in his arms. He hadn't expected a forty-five-pound boy to grow so heavy in a half-mile walk. He kept his two charges on the graveled service road surrounding the lake, as it was much easier to navigate at night. Plus, as chilly as it was tonight, the grass would soon be frost covered. Mrs. Hart may not like how it happened, but he was glad she'd been forced into a position to take her friend's offer. Staying in a warm cabin was better than some chilly tent.

The path wound around the lake's southeast tip before reaching the rows of neat cottages. In the distance, the lake lapped the shores.

Levi's breath tickled Nick's cheek. The boy was a great deal like Nick's brother Toby. Toby would have liked the lake and would have loved the roller coaster. What had his mother said boys were made of? Snips and snails and puppy dog tails? Well, that sure described both Toby and Levi.

Nick patted Levi's back when he stirred. "Which one is your place?"

"None of them."

Her voice sounded far away. What had she been thinking? "Mrs. Hart, in which cabin are you staying?"

"The fourth one." She reached for Levi. "I can take him from here."

He turned to the side to prevent her from removing Levi from his arms. "I've got him. Lead the way."

She huffed but continued down the path. In a few more yards, they reached the Graham cottage. Only a couple of small lights flickered inside, but the wails of an infant filled the air.

Levi lifted his head and rubbed his eyes. "Baby Kate, shhh. You cry too much."

His head dropped back onto Nick's shoulder, and Nick laughed. "He's not fond of the baby, I take it."

"Emily's Katie has colic." Mrs. Hart opened the screen door and held out her arms for Levi.

"I can carry him in if you like." After all, if Lilly's friend was there, no rules of propriety would be breeched.

"No, really, I'll carry him inside."

Nick eased the six-year-old into his mother's arms. "Good night, Mrs. Hart, and thank you for a pleasant evening. Perhaps next time you'll allow me to treat you and Levi to an evening in town."

She didn't lift her eyes to meet his gaze. "There can't be

a next time, Mr. Perrin. I'm sorry." Without a glance back, she slipped through the door of the cottage.

Nick stared at the door for a few seconds before stepping off the stoop and onto the path back to the service road. What had he said? He'd only suggested another family outing.

Realization hit him. Mrs. Hart and Levi were not *his* family.

Levi looked so sweet when he slept. Lilly brushed the sandy hair off his forehead and glanced around the small room she shared with him in the Graham family cottage. Emily had left a lamp burning there for her, and its light bathed the little room in a warm glow. It was still early enough that she should probably go spend some time with Emily or spell her with Kate.

"I'm not sleepy." Levi, slurring his *s*'s, tried to open his eyes.

Lilly pulled the covers around his shoulders and laughed to herself. "I can see that."

"Got to finish my snake cage 'morrow."

"We'll see."

"Mama?" He opened his eyes a slit.

"What, sweetheart?"

"You like Mr. Nick now?"

She kissed his forehead. "Go to sleep, my sweet boy. I love you."

"Mama, you like him lots now. Don't you?" His voice trailed off as sleep claimed him again.

She fingered a little curl forming around his ear. "Yes, Son," she whispered. "I do like Mr. Nick, but I shouldn't." Tears filled her eyes. "I can't, and I won't."

Frost crystals glittered on the cobweb hanging from the eaves of Thorton's Lunch Counter. The sunrise pinked the sky as Lilly unlocked the back door and entered. Thank goodness Emily offered to keep Levi and let him sleep in this morning.

If she hurried, perhaps she could get the biscuits in the oven for breakfast and the ham and beans started for lunch before she had to fry the eggs and bacon for the men. Soon she'd have Eugenia trained to help her. She chuckled. At least, she hoped she could teach the girl, although it might take a miracle.

She sent up a prayer asking for one, knowing that probably would not be God's plan since He had a tendency to teach her patience in concrete ways.

After mixing the biscuits, Lilly rolled them out on a floured board and cut them in circles with an upside-down glass. She slipped a biscuit-filled pan into the oven as the back door opened. She gasped and banged the oven door shut.

"Sorry, Miss Lilly. I didn't mean to startle you."

"Eugenia, what are you doing here so early? I thought I told you to come in around nine."

With a smile, Eugenia removed her enormous orange bonnet and slipped an apron over her head. "I couldn't let you do breakfast all by your lonesome."

"I don't mind." Lilly poured dry beans into a pot of water and set it on the back of the stove to soak before hefting the cast-iron skillet into its place in the front.

"Oh, but I do. I want to help. What can I do?"

Lilly complimented the young woman on her desire to help, but not ready to trust Eugenia with food, Lilly glanced around the kitchen for a task to assign. "I know. Why don't you set the tables for the men? We need ten place settings."

Eugenia nodded and scooped a stack of plates into her arms. "Will they need bone dishes too?"

"Excuse me?"

"Well, full place settings have bone dishes. Soup bowls too, now that I think of it."

Lilly stopped placing slices of bacon in the pan. "Eugenia, have you ever needed a bone dish or a soup bowl for breakfast?"

"No, ma'am, I guess not." She hung her head.

"Plates, cups, napkins, and silverware will be fine. You figured out where all those were last night." Lilly went back to her work, chuckling to herself. *Lord, if You sent Eugenia to teach me patience, please help me learn this lesson fast.*

No sooner had Lilly pulled the last crispy slice of bacon from the skillet than she heard the heavy footfalls of the men entering. She grabbed a dry towel and wrapped it around the handle of the coffeepot before passing through the kitchen door into the dining room. "Morning, gentlemen. Breakfast will be out in a minute."

"I can pour the coffee, Miss Lilly," Eugenia offered.

Nick flashed Lilly a knowing smile, but Lilly pretended not to notice it. After hesitating for a second, she passed the girl the coffeepot. "I'll be out with your bacon and eggs shortly."

"That's good, lassie," she heard Sean McGready tell Eugenia as Lilly turned to leave. Maybe the girl would work out after all.

"Blech!"

Lilly whirled and saw Mr. McGready spew his coffee across the table.

8

"Are ya trying to poison me, lass?"

Rushing over, Lilly grabbed the pot from Eugenia. "Is there a problem?"

"Taste it." Mr. McGready thrust his cup in her direction.

"If you don't mind, I'll . . ." She picked up another cup and began to fill it. Easing the cup to her lips, she took a sip. A rancid taste filled her mouth.

"Go ahead and spit it out, lass." Mr. McGready handed her a napkin. "Ain't fit for a soul to drink."

She forced the liquid down. "That won't be necessary."

"So, what's wrong with it?" Nick asked. "The girl mix it up wrong?"

"I made it myself." Lilly stared into the cup. What was the film on top of the brew? What had she tasted?

The answer hit her so hard she nearly dropped the cup in her hands.

Soap.

She turned toward Eugenia. "When you washed the dishes, did you rinse them well?"

"You didn't say to rinse them. You said wash and dry them."

Chuckling broke out among the men, and soon the room was filled with full-bellied laughter.

Tears pricked Eugenia's eyes, and Lilly took her arm and guided her into the kitchen. Poor girl. Lilly chastised herself for not speaking to her in private. After giving Eugenia a hug and apologizing for not giving clearer directions, Lilly returned with fresh cups and gathered the soapy ones. "I'm so sorry about all of this."

"'Tweren't yer fault." Mr. McGready tugged on his beard. "Besides, this is the best laugh I've ever had before me mornin' biscuit."

His humor was infectious, and she found embarrassment ebbing and a smile forming on her lips. She handed him a cup brimming with coffee. "Want me to taste this first?"

He chuckled. "I'll take me chances." After a tentative sip, he grinned. "Good as it gets."

She quickly poured coffee for them all. When she reached the kitchen, she found Eugenia sobbing in the corner. What had her mother been thinking, never teaching her a thing about kitchen work? If she was from a wealthy home, perhaps they had household servants, but if so, why was she working now?

"Eugenia, it'll be fine. You'll catch on." She patted the girl's arm, then began to crack eggs into the skillet. "Why don't you come over here and I'll show you how to crack eggs?"

A few minutes and some shells later, she had a platter full of fried eggs ready to serve. "Here, you take the bacon out and I'll serve the eggs."

"Are you sure, Miss Lilly? What if the men tease me?"

"I'm sure they will." She passed her the Blue Willow platter, its oriental scene obscured by bacon. "And you can laugh right along with them. We all make mistakes."

She caught Nick's gaze on her as she approached the table.

Lilly's chest constricted. And some mistakes were worse than serving soapy coffee.

∽≫≪∼

"Mr. Perrin, may I have a word with you?"

Nick halted on the sidewalk at the sound of Avery Nash's voice. He moaned. Why did the man in charge of the Lake Manawa management company annoy him so? He watched as the small man with the big attitude hurried toward him.

"You fellows go on," Nick said to his men. "I'll be along shortly." When Nash reached him, he offered his hand. "Good morning, Mr. Nash, what can I do for you?"

Mr. Nash looked at the offered hand and crossed his arms over his chest. "You don't look like you're far enough along on your roller contraption."

"Roller coaster?"

"You know what I meant." Nash grunted. "I don't know if I mentioned it, but I wasn't in favor of the monstrosity. However, the investors felt like it would be advantageous to the resort, so naturally, I gave in to their wishes."

"Naturally."

"And I'd hate to have to tell them what you said about it not being ready by opening day. Surely even you can see the importance of meeting the deadline."

"Mr. Nash, I do understand, but it may not be feasible for safety reasons."

"Fred Ingersoll himself assured us you could handle this job, and I will not hesitate to inform him if you do not meet the deadline."

Nick stiffened and his jaw tensed. Was Nash threatening him? While he believed Mr. Ingersoll had faith in his abilities, he didn't want to jeopardize his reputation with his employer, especially since this was the first coaster he had designed without oversight.

After inhaling a steadying breath, Nick met Nash's gaze. "I can assure you my workers and I are doing everything possible to ensure the coaster is ready for the guests on May 27, but as I told you before, much depends on factors beyond our control—such as the weather."

Nash thrust a finger toward Nick's chest. "Just see that it opens."

Nick sighed as Nash walked away. If the irritating little man didn't wield so much power, he would have insisted he leave him, the roller coaster project, and its crew alone. But Nick knew in the amusement-ride business, reputation was everything. And if he wanted to start his own company soon, his name had better be golden in the world of trolley park investors.

⚬◈⚬

With Levi in tow, Lilly slipped away from the diner to meet her friends at Marguerite's home. Trip had promised to take the children on a boat ride. With supper already under way, she could spare a few hours this afternoon for enjoyment. Besides, it would take Eugenia most of that time to de-flour the kitchen from this morning's baking lesson.

Running ahead on the boardwalk surrounding Lake Manawa's north shore, Levi scooped up a stone and attempted to hurl it into the lake. It fell short and landed with a plop in the shallows.

They passed the Grand Pavilion and waved to the men

putting a fresh coat of white paint on the large building. Further down, she saw a gardener clearing a planter of dried leaves. In another month, the whole park would be teeming with patrons. Most likely, even more people would visit than last year because of the roller coaster.

Guilt tugged on her heart at the thought of the coaster. She'd had another reason to leave this afternoon. Every day about this time, Nick came by, offering to take Levi to finish his snake cage. Even on Sunday, when she'd crossed paths with Nick following church services, he'd asked if Levi could spend some time with him, but Lilly had made a lame excuse to keep her son with her. She hated seeing the two deep lines that had formed between Nick's brows when he frowned.

"Lilly!" Emily waved from a park bench in front of the Rowing Club and stood with Katie in her arms. "I saw you two coming and thought I'd wait and walk the rest of the way with you." She turned to Levi. "So, are you excited about your uncle Trip taking you on a boat ride?"

He kicked a stone with the toe of his shoe. "I'd rather be working with Mr. Nick."

"Levi, you silly boy, you're gonna love sailing." Lilly ruffled his hair.

His lower lip protruded. "But I wanted to finish my snake cage."

"Remember, I told you Mr. Nick is a busy man."

"But he asked me to go, Mama. You aren't never gonna let me go, are you?"

"Levi, we'll talk about this later." She squeezed his shoulder. "Now, run ahead and let Aunt Emily and me talk."

He shuffled off with a frown on his face, but spotting several geese, he seemed to forget about being upset and began honking at them to get their attention.

"What was that all about? It sounds like Levi's grown quite attached to Nick Perrin."

"Levi is attached to the snake cage, not the man. Mr. Perrin is only helping him construct it. You know how Levi is with anything having to do with slimy, slithering creatures."

Emily lowered Katie into the wicker baby carriage and tucked the soft wool blanket around her. "I heard you two talking last week when he brought you home. I didn't say anything then, but I've been dying to ask what that means."

"It doesn't mean a thing," Lilly said more forcefully than she intended.

"Okay, don't get upset." The wheels of the baby carriage clacked on the boardwalk, and its fringed, cardinal-red parasol swung back and forth with the beat. "So, how did Nick Perrin come to be carrying your son home?"

"It's a long story."

Emily grinned. "In that case, hold on to the story until we get to Marguerite's, because I know she'll want to hear it too."

"You're so thoughtful." Lilly gave her a fake smile.

"I'm only thinking of you. I'd hate for you to have to tell the same story twice." Emily giggled.

Lilly tipped her chin in the air. "Maybe I won't tell either of you."

"You will."

"How do you know?"

"If you don't, you'll imply there's something going on that we should know about, and even if there isn't, you wouldn't want us to think that, so you'll have to explain."

Lilly sighed. So much for her relaxing time away.

When they reached the front of the boat shop, Marguerite met them. As soon as Trip Andrews and a couple of his crew had corralled the children, they took off for the sailboat. The ladies then departed for the yard behind the Yacht Club to enjoy a bit of croquet.

After taking one look at the croquet mallet Marguerite offered her, Emily held up her hand. "I think Kate and I will sit this out. Remember the last time I played croquet?"

Lilly grinned. Even though Emily had overcome a great deal of her clumsiness, last summer had proven the tendency was still there. During a match between Emily and her husband, Carter, Emily had tripped over a wicket and sent her mallet through one of the Yacht Club's windows. Good-natured Carter had kissed his wife and said he'd replace the window by nightfall.

"How about we play Poison? You can sit out the first game, but whoever wins gets to hold Katie while you play in the second." Lilly fished a nickel from her pocket for the coin toss.

"If I have to." Emily sank onto the park bench and propped Kate on her shoulder.

From the wooden box containing the equipment, Lilly selected a red-striped ball, and Marguerite, a blue one. Lilly passed Emily the coin. Marguerite won the toss and placed her ball midway between the stake and the first wicket. She gave it a soft strike with the mallet, and the ball landed inches short of the wicket.

"Well, Lilly, I'm ready." Emily patted Katie's back, a telling smile on her face.

"Ready for what?" Marguerite looked up from her disappointing shot and scowled. "Did I miss something?"

"No, you didn't miss a thing except Emily's overactive imagination." Lilly nudged Marguerite to the side and set her own ball on the ground. Her swing sent the ball through the first wicket. "I believe the first point goes to me."

"Well done!" Emily adjusted the blanket around Katie.

"And now you can tell us why Levi suddenly prefers Nick Perrin's company over sailing and how that same gentleman came to escort you home the other night."

"At night? You have been keeping secrets." Marguerite's ball tapped Lilly's after going through the wicket. She held up two fingers, indicating the points she received for the shot.

"Don't be ridiculous." Lilly sighed. "If you two magpies promise not to make this more than it is, I'll tell you what happened."

As she and Marguerite took turns throughout the course, she explained how Nick had taken an interest in Levi. Doing her best to downplay any significance, she told them matter-of-factly how he and Levi had become so engrossed in the snake-cage construction that they'd missed dinner. "Since I had to heat a plate for Levi, I figured I might as well make one for Mr. Perrin as well. After all, he'd been kind to Levi."

"So how did he come to carry Levi back to the cottage?" Emily asked, her green eyes alight with a twinkle.

Lilly crouched to get a good look at the post at the end of the course. If she hit it, her ball would be poison, and hitting Marguerite's ball would mean eliminating her friend from the competition. "Levi fell asleep while Nick and I were washing the dishes."

"Nick?" Marguerite tented her eyebrows.

"He washed dishes?" Emily giggled. "My, my, my."

"You two are as bad as Emily's meddling aunts. The whole thing meant nothing." Lilly whacked her ball hard, and it sailed beyond the striped post at the end of the course. "See, you made me miss my shot."

"Oh." Marguerite grinned. "I think you've still got a shot, but you simply refuse to admit it."

9

Spring was measured in flowers. It might not be manly, but Nick knew it was the truth. First the crocuses and hyacinths bloomed, then the daffodils, a flower to which he was particularly partial because his mother had loved them. Now the bright blooms of tulips lifted their faces to the sky, and soon the air would be filled with the scent of lilacs. He smiled at the thought as he made his way to Thorton's Lunch Counter.

Nick glanced at one of the Lake Manawa gardeners carefully sprinkling seeds from a packet into one of the Midway's large, round flower planters. If Iowa didn't get a late snow as he'd been told sometimes happens, those seeds should be in bloom by June. By then, folks would be enjoying both his roller coaster and a planter filled with marigolds.

Sean had once pointed out that the Lord used a lot of references to sowing and reaping when he taught. Nick found it was Jesus as a carpenter's son, however, that he thought of most often. The sweet smell of sawdust, the grain of wood, and the feel of a hammer would not have been foreign to the Lord. Jesus would have known what it felt like to make something with your own hands, to see it take shape, and to see it finished. He would understand the joy of doing one's best, and Nick felt a kinship to that. But most of all, Jesus would have known what it was like to take a rough piece of wood, smooth its edges, and make it into something usable.

Just as the Lord had done with him.

His musings came to a halt when he spotted Mr. Thorton heading to the lunch counter. Nick flagged him down. God had worked this out perfectly. The last thing he wanted was for Lilly to see him talking to her employer.

The heavyset man met him on the Midway paving. "What can I do for you, Mr. Perrin? Everything okay with your meals?"

"Absolutely, sir. This arrangement has been stellar. Mrs. Hart is an excellent cook, and as I told you, good food makes for good workers."

Mr. Thorton patted his round belly. "We men do like our food."

Nick chuckled and reached for his wallet tucked in his jacket pocket. "But I'd like to pay you extra to see to it Mrs. Hart and her son are both given meals."

"You don't need to pay me. Their meals are included." A deep scowl marred Mr. Thorton's usually jovial face. "You don't think I'd do otherwise, do you?"

"I didn't mean to imply you wouldn't take care of them. Mrs. Hart said three meals a day are included in her salary."

"That's right, and I expect her to eat them."

"What about her son?"

"Well, of course, I thought she'd feed him. I said she could keep him there with her, and she isn't going to let him starve."

Nick shook his head. "No, she'd starve herself before she'd keep her son from eating."

"Are you saying . . . ?"

"I don't know anything for sure, but I've noticed her not eating on a few occasions, and Levi shared a couple of other things that had me thinking. I believe she's a proud woman and an honest one. If you told her three meals, she'd take no more. At least my own mother wouldn't, and I think Mrs. Hart may be a lot like her." Nick opened his wallet. "So I want to pay you for Levi's meals. You shouldn't have to bear the burden."

"That's generous of you, but not necessary. She's the best cook I've ever had. I'll treat her right." Mr. Thorton rubbed his hand over his beard. "Tell you what. I'll make it clear to her today that both her and her son's meals are included in her salary."

"But you won't mention I spoke to you?"

"It'll be our secret." Mr. Thorton held out his hand.

Nick shook it. "Thank you, Mr. Thorton. My men would be mighty upset if she fainted dead away from malnutrition."

A chuckle rumbled from Mr. Thorton. "And what about you, Mr. Perrin?"

"Naturally, so would I." *Even if she is treating me like yesterday's wash water.*

❧

"Levi!" Lilly stood on the stoop of the lunch counter, shielding her eyes from the afternoon sun. After she'd washed up the dishes from the noon meal, Levi had helped her mix some cookies. She'd promised him one when they came out of the oven. "Levi! I've got your cookie."

She waited, but he didn't appear. Scanning the area, she spotted the cast-iron hook and ladder wagon toy he'd been playing with lying overturned near the crate where he kept

Flower. Stepping closer, she eased the board off Flower's crate and peeked inside to see if the snake still remained. The only thing visible was one of the diner's checkered napkins. Would Levi have covered Flower up? He had been worried about how cold the snake was at night.

Not wanting to check but afraid not to, Lilly leaned forward and took hold of the corner of the napkin. She lifted it an inch, but no hiss greeted her. She eased the cloth back. Relief washed over her. No Flower.

As quickly as the relief came, it vanished, replaced by growing fear. Where had Levi taken the snake? He'd never wandered beyond hearing distance before, but he had this time.

She glanced around at the Midway surrounding them. A long row of ghostly booths sat under wide-arched entrances. Still absent of wares and hawkers since the season had yet to begin, they almost begged to be explored. Perhaps he'd gone to do that.

The roller skating rink, shooting gallery, and bowling alley were open on the weekends, but not today. Even the carousel horses had yet to begin their endless circle of trotting. Levi might find any of these places a fascinating adventure.

Why hadn't she checked on him earlier?

She opened the lunch counter's screen door. "Eugenia, I can't find Levi. I need to go look for him."

Eugenia hurried out. "I know he was out here ten minutes ago when I came out to hang up the wet dish towels in back."

"Then he can't have gone far." Lilly called for him again. No answer. A lump the size of a dumpling formed in her throat, panic making it grow more each minute. "Why don't you check in the Midway, and I'll check that grove of trees he's so fond of?"

The girl nodded, and Lilly hurried off. She wound her

way through the grove of cottonwoods and oaks, calling his name over and over. She crossed the top of a fallen log and snagged her dress. Yanking it free, she paused to stick her finger through the tear in the calico print. One more thing to mend.

"Levi!" Scanning the woods, she tried to think like him. Where had Levi said he found the snake? Maybe he'd returned Flower home so she could visit her family.

Home.

Flower's new home.

The snake cage.

Nick.

She hiked up her skirt and ran. Her ankle twisted on a root, but she didn't fall or let the pain stop her. Finally she reached the path leading to the roller coaster. She pressed her hand to the stitch in her side, trying to fight off the fear threatening to consume her. *Please, Lord, let him be safe. Let Nick have him.*

But if Levi were there, why hadn't Nick brought him back?

∞∞∞

Even from a distance, Nick recognized Levi Hart's sure-footed skip. The boy looked happy as a lark as he made his way down the long, narrow path between the diner and the roller coaster site. Did he have a snake in his hand?

Laughter rumbled in Nick's chest. Only Levi would carry a snake around like a pull toy. The boy paused to watch a duck waddle across the path toward the lake. Then he tried to emulate the duck's waddle for several yards.

Nick's chest warmed at the sight. He'd missed the little character and couldn't wait to show him the shiny hinges he'd picked up for Flower's cage.

When Levi spotted him, he broke into a run, the snake's body swinging like a piece of rope from the boy's fist. Thankfully, Levi held the snake just below its head.

"Hey, Levi." Nick squatted down to eye level with the six-year-old. He adjusted the collar on Levi's brown tweed jacket. "Does your mama know you're here?"

"Yep."

"You sure?"

He nodded. "Got to get Flower in her new house. Mama says having a house is 'portant."

"I suppose it is to some folks."

"What about you, Mr. Nick?"

"Not so much." He stood and took Levi's hand. "But I'm sure Flower is going to love her new home. I put the hinges on the door, but I saved putting the latch on for us to do together." Nick led Levi behind the woodpile to the small work area and showed him the cage, now covered in a fresh coat of red paint with the name "Flower" lettered in yellow. Nick had even added a single bud, albeit slightly imperfect. He was certainly no Michelangelo.

Levi squealed. "It's so pretty!"

Nick lifted the cage from the table and lowered it to the ground. "Why don't you give Flower a tour of her new home?"

After lifting the hinged lid, Levi dropped the snake in with a thud. It slithered around with an angry hiss.

Levi frowned. "I don't think she likes it."

"Buddy, I think she might be a little upset from her trip here."

"It's the duck's fault."

"Really?" Nick picked the cage up, snake and all, and repositioned it on the table. "Why is that?"

"Honking. Snakes don't speak honk. They don't like those

loud, honking ducks. They talk hiss. Like this." Levi pressed his nose against the chicken wire. "Hissssssss. Hiss. Hisssss."

Nick pulled the boy back. "Hey, buddy, let's not give Flower a chance to bite your nose. Your mama would feed me to the snakes if you come home with fang marks on your face."

"Mr. Nick, Flower couldn't eat you. You're too big." He patted the cage. "Flower likes worms and lizards."

"And I bet she'd love a nice plump mouse. Any of those at the lunch counter?"

Levi grinned. "I wish there was, but Mama would scream for days if she saw one."

Nick laughed. "Ready to put the latch on?" He lifted Levi onto the table and showed him how the padlock would work.

"And I get my own key?" Levi's soft blue eyes lit up.

Nick slipped a length of leather through the end of a key, tied it in a knot, and dropped the loop over Levi's head. "You keep the key right around your neck so you don't lose it. Now, let's get to work."

For the next ten minutes, Nick let Levi help him put the latch on. Once he'd attached the two pieces, he demonstrated how to lower the hasp and then snap the padlock in place. "Let's see you open it, buddy."

Levi slid the key from around his neck. The tip of his tongue stuck out from between his lips as he concentrated on poking the key into the hole of the padlock. He twisted the key, but the lock didn't give.

"Turn it a little more. Use your muscles."

Forehead scrunched, Levi clenched the key and turned it. Finally the lock clicked open. "I did it!"

"You sure did." Nick snapped the padlock closed. "Now, try again."

"Aw, Mr. Nick. Why?"

"'Cause Flower might get hungry if you can't open her cage every time you need to feed her."

"Or hug her." Levi stuck the key into the lock again. "She gets lonely sometimes. Like Mama."

At the mention of Lilly, Nick's chest warmed. He started to ask Levi about his father but clamped his lips closed. Now wasn't the time. Not yet.

Shouting in the distance drew his attention. He cocked his head to the side and listened for the sound again.

"Levi!" The sound was faint but closer. The voice belonged to Lilly. She shouted again, sounding winded and distraught. Why was she running?

Nick's heart rammed against his ribs. He grabbed the six-year-old's shoulders. "Levi, tell me the truth. Did your mama give you permission to come see me?"

Levi hung his head. "No, sir."

Poor Lilly. She had to be beside herself with worry.

Nick released Levi and jogged to Lilly on the path. "He's here, Mrs. Hart."

Visible relief cascaded over her face, and she wobbled. He took hold of her arm. "He's fine. He's not hurt."

She tossed his hand away. "How could you? Why didn't you bring him back to the diner? You knew he didn't belong here!"

Taking a step back, Nick held up his hands. "Whoa, ma'am. He told me he had permission to come see me. I only found out—"

"But I would never let him walk here alone." Tears trailed down her cheeks, and she swiped them away with the back of her hand.

Nick swallowed. Of course she wouldn't, only he hadn't considered that. "I'm sorry. I thought—"

"You didn't think. That's why I can't let him be with you. You don't think about the consequences."

Nick's mind whirled in confusion. Why did he feel like the conversation had suddenly made a sharp turn and he'd been left without a map? What consequences was she talking about?

Chest still heaving, Lilly glared at him, her amber eyes filled with fire. "Show me where he is so I can take him home."

"Of course. He's at the worktable." Nick turned, motioning for her to precede him.

With her back ramrod stiff, Lilly stomped down the path. She rounded the woodpile and jammed her fists onto her hips. "Where is he? You said he was here."

"He was." Nick leaned over to look under the table. The cage was gone. Levi couldn't go far lugging it, but he had probably hid out of fear. He searched around the pile. "Levi, this isn't funny. Come on out. Your mama won't be mad."

Lilly shot a fierce look at him.

At least she won't be mad at you because she's too busy being furious with me.

10

"Let go of me!"

Lilly whirled at the sound of the familiar small voice, and her heart beat double time.

"Easy, laddie. Yer mum is lookin' fer ya. I heard her calling yer name." With his beefy hand clamped around Levi's shirt collar, Sean McGready gently pushed the boy forward. "Caught him sneaking under the trestles, lugging that cage."

"Thanks, Sean." Nick lifted the cage from Levi's arms and set it on the table.

"Goodbye, laddie." Sean took off his bowler hat and ran a hand over his bald head. "Hope we can still be friends." He nodded toward Lilly. "Ma'am, sorry for manhandlin' your boy."

She'd already dropped to her knees in front of Levi and pulled him to her, showering kisses on his head and face. "Thank you for bringing him to me."

Levi twisted and wriggled free enough to step back in her

arms. He wiped his cheek with his sleeve. "Mama, Mr. Nick is gonna think I'm a baby."

With a smile, she kissed the same cheek again and loosened her hold. Still, she didn't release him entirely. She couldn't. She needed to touch him in order to believe he was truly all right.

"Levi, you frightened me out of my wits." She glanced at Nick, wanting him to see the pain he'd caused. "Why did you sneak off?"

"And, Levi, why did you lie to me about having permission to come here?" Nick asked. "You told me your mother said you could be here. Twice."

Levi's lower lip quivered, and tears filled his eyes. He crumpled into sobs.

Wrapping her arms around him, Lilly stroked him until his sobs softened. "Levi, we want to understand why you did what you did."

He hiccuped. "I wanted to finish Flower's home, Mama, but you kept saying no when Mr. Nick asked."

Recalling all the times Nick had offered to take Levi, Lilly felt her stomach knot. She couldn't let her son get attached to Nick, but how could she explain that to a six-year-old? Nick would leave at the end of the summer, and they'd be devastated.

They? She shook her head. She meant *he.* All this excitement had her as addle-brained as Eugenia.

Nick laid his hand on Levi's head. "No matter what, you need to obey your mama. She's a good lady, and she deserves your respect even if you don't like what she tells you."

"But—"

"No buts, Levi. Listen to her, you hear?"

The authority in Nick's voice declared the matter closed, but Lilly wasn't done yet. At least not with Mr. Perrin. Besides, he had no right to scold her son.

She stood. "Mr. Perrin, I find your part—"

"Wait, Mrs. Hart."

"—in all of this—"

"Lilly."

She stared at him, the sound of her Christian name on his lips echoing in her ears. How dare he?

His gaze dropped to Levi, and he raised his dark eyebrows. "Can we speak privately about this?"

Perhaps he was right. Levi didn't need to hear the things she planned on saying. She touched her son's shoulder. "Mr. Perrin and I need to talk alone. You stay right here, and I mean it."

"I'll obey."

"Good boy." Nick winked at him. "We'll be back in a minute."

Lilly led the way to a grove of trees, blood pumping so loudly in her ears she could scarcely hear the rustling of the branches above. Thoughts shot at her like bullets. The nerve of Nick Perrin correcting her son when he was the one who had let this whole fiasco unfold. And who did he think he was, using her Christian name without her permission? Even if he was the boss of this project, it didn't mean he could do whatever he pleased. Even if Mr. Thorton caught wind of it, she was going to give Nick Perrin a tongue-lashing he'd not soon forget.

She took a deep breath. She was being too harsh, but how else could she keep Nick away from her son—before they became too attached? Emotions churning like the waters of Lake Manawa on a windy day, she whirled toward him.

"You accused me of not thinking of the consequences?" Nick's blue eyes, dark and livid, pierced her.

Shocked, Lilly took a step back.

"Have you even considered that if you'd let him come with

me, this wouldn't have happened?" He grabbed a stick from the ground and broke it in half. "Levi's a boy, and he needs a man around. Lord knows he can't count on his grandfather, and I was trying to be a friend, but you—" He cut his words off and hurled half the stick into the lake. His shoulders heaved with his rapid breathing, his jaw locked in anger.

"But I what?"

He spun toward her. "You deliberately kept him away from me. And why? Am I some kind of monster? Did I not wash your dishes well enough?"

She blinked. Nick a monster? Hardly. The expression on his honest face and his words tickled her. She fought the tug at the corner of her lips. "As a matter of fact, your dish washing could use some work."

A smile began to form on his face as well, and he shook his head. "You could drive a good man to drink."

Her eyes widened.

"Not literally." He sighed and shook his head. "Mrs. Hart, I'm out of line. I'm sorry. Levi's your son. I'm sure you only want what's best for him. I won't bother either of you again." He turned to go.

Her breath caught. "Wait."

"What?" He stopped and faced her.

"I need to apologize to you. I'm sorry I accused you." Lilly forced the words out. Apologizing wasn't her favorite thing to do, not that she had to do it often. "You are certainly not a monster, and you've only been kind to Levi."

"And about my dish washing?" He gave a lopsided grin.

"You just need more practice."

"Is that a fact?" He grew quiet and stuffed his hands in his pockets. "If I'm no monster, why are you keeping Levi away from me?"

When she finally spoke, Lilly's voice sounded soft even to her own ears. "He'll become attached to you more and more, and then you'll leave at the end of the summer."

"You can't protect him from everything."

Lilly's heart constricted. If only she could. "But he's already lost so much."

As if he were trying to see into her thoughts, Nick studied her for a long moment. He pulled his hands from his pockets and crossed them over his broad chest. "You know, he'll only keep sneaking off to visit. He's fascinated with the roller coaster."

"And you." Lilly swallowed. "So what do we do?"

"Nothing today. He needs to stew a little about the consequences of his choices, but tomorrow, why don't you explain to him that I'll bring him over here every night after supper and show him how much we've gotten done during the day? Then you can finish at the diner and pick him up on the way to your cottage. Would that work?"

"Emily's cottage." Lilly glanced in the direction of her current residence, unsure why she felt the need to correct him. "And yes, that might keep him from sneaking off, but it won't keep him from getting hurt at the end of the summer."

"True, but I can promise you this—I'll be the best friend I can be to him for the time we have together."

Lilly's eyes misted. She blinked. Had she really almost kept Levi from this kind man? "I know you'll take good care of him."

He met her gaze and held it. Too intense for her liking. "As if he were my own."

Lilly turned and started back to Levi, her heart inexplicably full and sad at the same time. Nick fell in step beside her.

They walked in silence for a few moments before she spoke.

"Now, Mr. Perrin, about you calling me by my Christian name."

Nick chuckled. "I like the way it feels on my tongue. Lilly. Sweet, like peppermint with a little bite to it."

"But it's hardly proper."

"Funny, you don't strike me as a woman terribly stuck on what's proper. Do you really not want me to call you Lilly?"

Cheeky man. He was certainly hard to say no to. Oh well, maybe he could call her Lilly on occasion. What would it hurt to hear her name from a man once in a while?

She offered him a little smile. "Let's just say too many sweets aren't good for a person."

11

Lilly told Levi he'd have to stay inside the diner with her for the rest of the afternoon as punishment for wandering off. She handed him a bucket and a brush and told him to begin scrubbing the floor.

"But what about Flower?"

"Mr. Nick said he'd bring her over at supper time." She pointed to a corner of the dining room. "You may start there."

Once Levi began, she escaped into the kitchen.

"I'm so glad he's okay." Eugenia looked up from the work-table, flour dotting her cheeks. "When I didn't find him in the Midway, I went ahead and made the pies for supper tonight."

"Thank you, Eugenia. That's so thoughtful." Lilly glanced at the Hoosier cabinet where two pies, the crusts a perfect gold, sat cooling. Maybe the cooking lessons had paid off. Of course, she'd taste them herself before she let another human being near them. She smiled. "They look delicious."

"And I did them like you've been teaching me." Eugenia

beamed. "I was trying to start the noodles, but I don't think I have that down yet."

Lilly chuckled at the noodles hanging like worms on Eugenia's apron. One had even made its way into her frizzy hair. "It looks like you're being eaten by Levi's worms."

"These noodles have a mind of their own."

Lilly draped a fresh apron around her neck. "Let me take a look. I've been known to tame a noodle or two."

Half an hour later, Lilly had helped Eugenia roll the noodles out and cut them into long, thin strips. Together they'd hung the noodles on a rope to dry. The chicken was already simmering, so Lilly asked Eugenia to join her in the dining room so they could polish the silverware.

Drenched in mop water, Levi scampered to his feet when she walked into the room. "All done, Mama. Isn't it pretty?"

If mop water and a scrub brush could make art, Levi was a Rembrandt in the making. Lines crisscrossed the room in a fascinating pattern. Now, torn between having him do the job correctly or praising his artistic creation, Lilly studied her son's face. Was he simply trying to get out of his work? No, there didn't seem to be an ounce of sneakiness in his sweet blue eyes.

She smiled. "It's beautiful, Levi. Why don't you take the mop bucket outside and dump the water?"

Eugenia stepped forward. "But, Miss Lilly . . ."

Lilly could imagine what Eugenia was thinking. Since Levi certainly hadn't done the job perfectly, one of them would have to mop later. With a flick of her wrist, Lilly motioned for Levi to go on, and then she settled in a chair and picked up a tarnished spoon. "Children's eyes, Eugenia."

The girl sat down beside her. "Excuse me?"

"You can always tell whether a child is lying to you if you

look in their eyes." She dipped her cloth into the tin of J. A. Wright's silver polish and rubbed the spoon. "Levi wasn't trying to get out of work. He truly believed he'd created something beautiful. It would be wrong of me to crush his spirit."

"Wish my mother had felt that way." Eugenia set the pile of knives in front of her.

Lilly cocked her head. The girl had said little about her upbringing. But since she was Mr. Thorton's niece, did Lilly really want to know?

"Please don't get me wrong. My mother is a wonderful lady." Eugenia stuck her piece of gray flannel in the silver cream and removed a much-too-large dollop. "She likes things done right, and I have a lot of talent for wrong."

If it wasn't so sad, Lilly might have laughed. "Didn't she teach you how to do things?"

"She tried a few times when I was little, but afterward she said it was easier to do them herself."

The back door slammed shut, and Lilly and Eugenia both startled.

"It's me, girls," Mr. Thorton called from the kitchen.

Lilly selected another spoon. "So you didn't have servants?"

"Heavens no." Eugenia held up the polished knife and studied her reflection on the blade. "Is that why you thought I was inept in the kitchen?"

"Not inept. Inexperienced." Lilly held up her spoon. "Do you think Levi would know how to shine this if I didn't teach him how to do it? That's another reason I didn't get upset with his cleaning job. I've never really taught him how to do it right. I sort of expected him to simply figure it out on his own. It isn't fair to expect folks to know something they've not been taught."

Eugenia smiled. "You're a sweet lady, Miss Lilly. Thank you for teaching me."

"Ugh! Phew! Lilly!" Mr. Thorton's voice filled the diner, followed by hacking and coughing.

Lilly and Eugenia raced into the kitchen. Mr. Thorton frantically filled a water glass from the pump at the sink. He downed one, two, three glasses before whirling toward Lilly. He held one hand to his throat, and with his other, he jabbed a finger toward a piece of pie. "Who made this?"

Eugenia dropped her gaze to the floor. Her shoulders slumped forward.

Lilly met his gaze. "Is there something wrong with it?"

"Something wrong! It's plain wicked." He filled a glass again and emptied it.

She glanced at Eugenia. The poor girl was as pale as flour on a cutting board. What could she have possibly done to the pie? Surely Mr. Thorton was overreacting.

"It can't be that bad." Lilly pushed the hair from her forehead with the back of her hand.

He picked up the slice and shoved it at her. "It's worse. Taste it."

Lilly forked off a small bite and put it in her mouth. Her eyes instantly filled with tears. Oh my, this was bad. Very, very bad. She'd never tasted anything so salty.

She caught a horrified look on Eugenia's face. In that second, she knew she had to swallow it. If she didn't, Eugenia's spirit, like Levi's, would be crushed.

Without the aid of a cup of coffee with which to wash it down, Lilly forced herself to gulp the bite. Her voice choked when she spoke. "It may have a little too much salt."

"May? Since when do you make a pie like that?" Mr. Thorton's face grew as red as strawberry jam.

Lilly flashed her eyes toward Eugenia. Thankfully he followed her gaze. Could she get him to see that his niece was on the verge of tears?

"That was our practice pie, Mr. Thorton. Practice makes perfect, and you know, you shouldn't be sneaking around in a woman's kitchen." She set the remainder of the pie slice on the Hoosier cabinet. "Women have been known to bake all kinds of things into pies to teach men to keep their hands out of the sweets. Right, Eugenia?"

The girl nodded slowly. "Yes, one lady baked blackbirds in her pie. When the pie was opened, the birds began to sing."

Mr. Thorton stared at his niece. "You do realize that's a nursery rhyme, right?"

Eugenia laughed nervously. "Of course I do, Uncle Clyde."

"Anyway, the point is, you'd do best to ask which pies we intend to serve folks and which we intend to try out first ourselves." Lilly dropped the dried noodles into the pot. Inside her, laughter bubbled. "'Cause you never know what we might be fixin'."

Or who might be the one fixing it.

There was no solving this problem. Nick stared at the roller coaster plans in front of him, his chest heavy with the news he'd received. Although his crew had made good time, he couldn't build the roller coaster without the necessary supplies. The end-of-May deadline of Lake Manawa's opening season loomed in his thoughts. His name was on the line with this project. Excuses meant nothing when it came down to getting a job done.

"Did the railroad say why there was a delay?" he asked lanky Milt Hawkins, one of the four men he'd sent to pick up pieces of the Douglas fir they'd ordered for the coaster's support structure. What lumber they had on hand was quickly going into the few trestles they'd begun.

Milt shrugged. "Only that it wasn't on the shipping invoice."

"I'll have to go into town tomorrow and send a telegram." He rolled the plans and reinserted them into the metal tube. They had a long way to go, and the amount of lumber needed was staggering. If they had a supplier they couldn't count on, they were in trouble. But one glitch wasn't worth losing sleep over. "We have enough to keep us busy for a few days, so hopefully it'll come in soon."

"Heard some talk in town about rain coming. Reckon that's normal in the spring."

Nick nodded. "Unfortunately, that's true. We'll have to do what we can with the time God gives us. Thanks, Milt."

As soon as the worker left, Nick pulled out his pocket watch and flipped it open. The tiny compass watch fob, a gift from his former fiancée, brushed his wrist. He should take the silly thing off. He had no desire to remember Ruby Rawlins.

He studied the hands on the watch. The freight office would be closed by now, so there was nothing he could do to clear things up. At least he wouldn't miss dinner and seeing Levi as he'd promised. And the last thing he wanted to do right now was break a promise he'd made to the boy—or to his mother.

⁓

A few moments to herself was a true luxury. Lilly sat down in one of the lunch counter's chairs and finished her supper. For some reason, Mr. Thorton had readdressed the subject of her meals, or, rather, added Levi's meals to her salary. He'd made his position clear: he expected Lilly and her son to eat at the diner for every meal. Although she told Mr. Thorton that was too much and tried to turn down his offer, he refused. Lilly couldn't deny the relief she now felt knowing she didn't need to come up with more money for food. Every penny she saved meant they were one step closer to purchasing a home of their own.

As Nick had promised, he'd taken Levi with him following supper. Lilly stood on the stoop and watched her son skip away with his hand tucked in Nick's. And now, with Eugenia washing—and rinsing—the dinner dishes, she could feel the tension easing from her muscles for the first time in days.

A dish clattered on the floor of the kitchen. Lilly jolted. "Everything okay, Eugenia?"

"I broke the handle off a cup."

"No souls lost," Lilly called back. It did no good to worry over broken china. Besides, those things were bound to happen in a diner, and more so with Eugenia around.

The front door opened, and Lilly turned to see Marguerite and a tall young man enter. She grinned. She'd recognize those protruding ears and handsome face anywhere, but my, how Marguerite's younger brother had filled out.

She hurried to the door. "Well, look who the cat dragged in."

"I told Mark you'd never forgive me if we didn't drop by." Marguerite looped her hand through her brother's arm.

"That's true." Lilly motioned them to the table. "Mark, sit yourself down and let me get you each a cup of coffee. I want to hear all about what you're gonna do now that you've graduated."

"Miss Lilly, I'll get the coffee." Eugenia waved from the doorway. "I'm more than happy to serve, Mr. . . . ."

Lilly grinned. Eugenia might appear a little muddleheaded

at times, but she had no trouble with her eyes, and she clearly liked what she saw in Marguerite's brother. "Miss Eugenia Baker, this is Mr. Mark Westing. He just graduated from law school. Mr. Mark Westing, Miss Eugenia Baker."

Eugenia blushed and dipped her head. "I'll be right back with your coffee."

Lilly sat down across from Marguerite and Mark. "So, Mark, you graduated two weeks ago. Does it feel good to be finished with school?"

"I still have to pass my bar exams, but meanwhile I've got a few nibbles on some law offices where I could get some experience."

"I wish my Ben were alive. He'd be glad to help you prepare." Lilly paused when Eugenia appeared with two coffee cups and the pot. With more grace than Lilly had seen yet, she filled the cups.

"Thank you." Mark smiled, the impish little boy still visible.

Eugenia beamed. "My pleasure. Can I get you anything else?"

"Do you have any pie left?"

"No!" Lilly blurted out. "Sorry, Mark, no pie today. Eugenia, why don't you bring us out a plate of those cookies we made?"

"I hope they're like the ones your mama made." Mark glanced at Marguerite. "Remember when Mother caught me with my pockets full of Alice's gingersnaps?"

"No ginger snaps today, but I'll see if I can make a batch this week." Lilly glanced at the watch clipped to her shirt-waist. "I need to go pick up Levi."

"From?" Marguerite asked.

"He's at the roller coaster site with Nick Perrin. I promised to fetch him by six."

"Nick, huh?" Marguerite's eyebrows formed twin peaks.

"I can tell my sister is conniving again." Mark frowned playfully at Marguerite. "Sorry about that, Lilly, but would you mind if we walked you over? I've been itching to get a good look at the contraption."

"It's not much more than a forest of posts right now." Lilly stood and grabbed her cape from the hook by the door. "But you're welcome to come along."

Mark held the door for Lilly and Marguerite to precede him out.

"Wait! Your cookies." Eugenia rushed from the kitchen. She halted in front of Mark. The cookies on the plate, however, kept going. They flew off the plate and onto Mark's patterned vest before falling to the floor and crumbling to pieces.

"Oh, Mr. Westing, I'm so sorry." A blush turned Eugenia's cheeks crimson. She dropped to the floor and started grabbing chunks of the fallen cookies as though they'd disappear if she couldn't pick them up fast enough.

Mark brushed the crumbs from his clothes, then helped her stand. "It's fine. I've certainly had my pockets full of crumbs before."

Eugenia's eyes glazed as she stared at her hand clasped in his.

Lilly exchanged a knowing look with Marguerite and moaned inwardly. Mark might have no interest in Eugenia, but Eugenia already had the two of them walking down the aisle.

"So, Lilly." Marguerite pulled her through the door. "Nick has Levi. Tell me how that came to be."

Surely this was going to be the longest summer in history.

12

"Run, Levi! Keep going!" Nick cupped his hand to his mouth.

Levi ran, his pudgy arms pumping, a kite string fisted in his hand. Nick held aloft the diamond-shaped kite they'd fashioned. When Levi had gone far enough for the string to grow taut, Nick released the kite, praying it would take flight.

"Pull, Levi! Pull!"

Levi stopped and did as he was told while Nick hurried to stand behind the boy, ready to lend a hand. Levi tugged on the string. The wind lifted the kite in the air.

"Higher!" Levi jumped up and down.

"Let out more string."

Levi followed Nick's instruction, but the kite continued to dive.

Nick reached over Levi's head and tugged on the string several times. The kite resumed its place against the clouds.

"When it starts to come down, pull the string several times like this." Nick demonstrated the pumping motion.

Nick caught Lilly's approach out of the corner of his eye.

He recognized the woman with her as Mrs. Andrews from the diner the other day, but the man with them didn't look familiar. He smiled and waved to them. "Hey, buddy, looks like we have an audience."

"Mama! Look at the kite we made!" Levi pointed toward the sky. "It's flying."

Lilly beamed. "It certainly is. Well done, Levi."

"Do I have to stop now?" His bottom lip jutted out.

"No, you keep going. I want to introduce Mr. Perrin to Aunt Marguerite's brother." After introductions had been made, Nick offered to show Marguerite and Mark what progress had been made on the coaster's construction.

"It's falling!" Levi frantically pumped the string. Still, the kite continued its nosedive.

Nick spun and grabbed the string. He pumped it hard. The string snapped, and the kite dove into an oak tree near the lake.

Tears sprang to Levi's eyes. "My kite."

"Sorry, buddy, kites are fickle. Sometimes they seem like they could keep flying high forever, and other times they come down on you without warning."

"Kind of like a woman," Mark said under his breath.

Marguerite shot him a glare, but Nick couldn't keep the corners of his lips from curling. He glanced at Lilly, who seemed to have missed the exchange because she was focused on wiping her son's tears.

Nick ruffled Levi's hair. "Why don't you let me give these folks a quick tour, then we'll see if I can shake the kite out of the tree? Mrs. Hart, care to join us?"

She nodded. "Levi, you stay close while we look around, okay?"

He sniffed. "Yes, Mama."

With a sweep of his hand, Nick motioned the group toward one end of the structure. "The coaster will be over a quarter mile in length, one of the longest in the West. We're naming it the Velvet Roller Coaster, and she'll be the jewel of Lake Manawa." Nick walked to the center of the structure. "The car shed will sit here, and the depot over there."

"I can't wait to ride on it." Marguerite scanned the structure, seeming to envision the finished product. "I've read that it's almost like flying."

Nick nodded. "Mark, ever ridden a coaster?"

He leaned against one of the posts. "Not yet, but I'll be one of the first in line."

"And how about you, Mrs. Hart? Can we count on your patronage? Can I give you the ride of your life?" Nick cocked an eyebrow in her direction.

Lilly clasped her hands in front of her. "As a matter of fact, I like my feet on the ground, right where God intended them to be."

"Why doesn't that surprise me?" Nick teased. "Mind if I try to change your mind?"

"Good luck doing so." Marguerite gave Lilly a cheeky grin. "So, Mr. Perrin, how many people can ride at a time?"

"Two cars on each run. They can hold up to eight people, but on some days it's best to run only one car of four." Nick scratched his eyebrow. "Brakemen aren't needed on these coasters. The scenic railways have them, but my roller coaster is designed for the cars to be going fast enough for a thrill, yet slow enough to stay on the track."

"What happens if they aren't slow enough?" Lilly asked.

Mark chuckled. "I don't think Mr. Perrin would let that happen."

"But what if it does?" Lilly fixed her eyes on Nick.

He stiffened. Why did she want to hear this now? He held her gaze. "The cars could leave the track."

"Meaning they'd fly through the air, possibly killing those in the cars, correct?" She squared her shoulders. "And that's exactly why my son and I will not be riding your Velvet Roller Coaster."

We'll see about that, Mrs. Hart. I can be as stubborn as you.

Nick turned and shielded his eyes with his hand. "Speaking of your son, where has Levi gotten off to?" He searched the area, and his gaze landed on the tree where the kite had lodged. At the base of the trunk lay Levi's discarded jacket.

He flashed a glance at Lilly, but she'd already hiked her skirts and was racing the short distance to the tree. What did she think she was going to do to get the boy down?

Coming to a halt beside her, Nick scanned the tree for Levi. He spotted him near the top, lying on his stomach, clutching a thin tree branch. In a branch only yards away was the wedged kite. Impressive. He'd almost reached it.

"Levi, come on down. We'll get the kite later," Nick called. If the boy had gotten up there, he could certainly get down.

He didn't move.

"Sweetheart, we need you to come on down." Lilly's voice belied her concern.

"I can't, Mama. I'm stuck."

Nick's chest tightened at the sob in the boy's voice. "He's too scared to move."

"Hang on, sweetheart. I'll be right up." Lilly removed her spring cape and handed it to Marguerite.

Nick clasped her arm. "Where do you think you're going?"

"To get my son."

"You stay here. I'll get him."

"Those tree branches couldn't possibly bear your weight. Look at the one Levi's on now. See, it's bowing like a rainbow."

He glanced upward. "But what do you know about climbing a tree?"

"A whole lot more than you obviously think I do."

She shoved past him, and Nick stared wide-eyed after her. What did Lilly think she was doing? Ladies didn't climb trees—even to get their precocious six-year-olds down from them. Then again, Lilly Hart wasn't like any lady he'd ever met.

"She can do it." Marguerite pressed a hand to his arm.

"She's always been athletic," Mark added. "She could out-swim Marguerite any day. Besides, she's right. Those branches wouldn't hold you or me."

As if she'd been climbing trees all her life, Lilly swung onto the first branch. When she pushed off the lower one with her right foot, it cracked. Her foot slipped.

Nick lunged toward the tree.

⁂

Lilly caught the second branch and pulled herself up with great effort. She risked a glance below to see the lower branch now dangling against the trunk. She released the breath she'd been holding. Another way down would be in order upon her return, but she'd address that concern when the time came. Right now she needed to get to her son.

"Sweetheart, are you doing okay?"

"Mama?" He turned his head to see her, and his hold slipped. He clutched the branch again. "Hurry. I'm scared."

"I know, sweetheart." Lilly moved faster from one branch to another. "Just hold on. I'm coming." She reached for a thick branch, and her shoe slid on the bark. She sucked in a breath. *Slow down. Falling would do Levi no good.*

"Careful, Lilly." Nick's words were laced with concern.

Levi whimpered above her, and guilt pricked her heart. How had Levi climbed to the top of a tree in such a short period of time? She should have been keeping a closer eye on him instead of inspecting Nick's Velvet Roller Coaster. No mother should become so distracted she lost sight of her child.

"Listen to me now, Levi. I'm below you, but I can't climb on the limb where you are. You're gonna have to climb down from that branch."

"I can't move, Mama. It'll break. It's creaking." His chubby fists clinched the branch until his knuckles turned white.

"No, it won't break. Take it real slow." She leaned forward as if her effort would help him move.

"What's going on?" Nick barked the question, and Lilly glanced below to see him pacing back and forth.

"I think she's gone as far as she can," Marguerite said. "Levi needs to swing his legs down so she can get to him."

Lilly risked another glance downward.

Nick cupped his hands to his mouth. "Levi, you need to do what your mama asks you to. Remember, she's a smart lady."

"My tummy hurts." Levi hiccuped.

Despite her prodding, Levi refused to budge. Lilly let out a long sigh. What was she going to do?

"Hey, Levi." Nick's voice filled with a sense of adventure. "Remember when you told me about that book that had all kinds of animals in it? Porcupines and squirrels and—"

"Chipmunks."

"That's right," Nick said.

Lilly moved closer and stumbled on a knot in the branch. She fought for leverage and slid hard against the tree's massive trunk. She winced at the jab of pain but ignored the trickle of red on her white cotton shirtwaist. Scratches would wait. Her son would not.

With more care, she eased herself onto the branch below her son and glanced at the ground. They had to be almost twenty feet off the ground.

Nick's voice rose upward again. "Levi, do you think you can pretend to be a chipmunk and move from branch to branch?"

"I guess." The bravado in his voice was clearly forced.

"You can do it, Chipmunk."

"Okay, Levi." Lilly braced her foot against the tree trunk and reached for her son.

"Not Levi, Chipmunk." This time a note of true bravery rang clear.

Lilly shook her head. *Chipmunk?* How long would it take to get Levi over that one?

"Scoot back a little at a time until you reach the trunk . . . Chipmunk. Turtle speed. I'm right here."

Wiggling his body like a giant caterpillar, he inched back. The branch swayed as he moved, and each little crack sent a jolt of fear through Lilly.

She continued to coax him until he had lowered one foot within reach of her. She touched his calf. "There you go. Put your foot right here." Guiding his boot in place, she resisted the urge to tell him to hurry. "Now the other one."

He slipped the other foot over the branch and slowly eased it to the branch below.

"That's it." Lilly held his waist as he moved beside her.

"Good job, Levi!" Marguerite's words brought a smile to his face, and Lilly hugged him to her side. She glanced below and spotted Nick, a smile playing across his beard-shadowed face.

"Okay, Chipmunk," he called. "You got up there, you can get down. Right?"

Levi took a trembly breath, his shoulders shaking beneath her arm. "What if I fall?"

"I'll catch you." Nick spoke with such sincerity even Lilly found herself believing the man's words.

"And what if Mama falls?"

Despite all the branches, Nick held her gaze. "I'll catch her too."

13

Lilly could not believe Nick Perrin would have to catch her after all. Without the tree branch at the bottom, she would have to let Nick lift her down or risk a sprained ankle. Why had the branch broken when she'd made her ascent?

The thought of his hands on her waist made her cheeks flame hot as a soup pot. Maybe a sprained ankle wouldn't be so bad.

"Your turn, Mrs. Hart." Nick held up his arms. "Just like Chipmunk."

"You jump, Mama." Levi demonstrated the effort from beside Marguerite. "It's fun. Don't worry. Mr. Nick will catch you. You'll be Chipmunk Mama."

Ten minutes ago her son was scared witless, and now he couldn't wait until she launched herself into the arms of Nick Perrin.

"I think I could shimmy down the trunk."

"Don't be silly." Nick moved his extended arms. "Take a leap of faith. It's not far, and I'll catch you. I promise."

Heart dancing in her chest, Lilly studied Nick's sapphire eyes—such a contrast to his almost coal-colored hair. And while his grin teased her, his eyes made promises that scared her almost as much as discovering Levi in the top branches of a tree.

If she leapt, would he truly catch her?

Pride alone wouldn't allow her to remain perched on a branch like a wild turkey, six feet from the ground, but this was asking too much. She tried to imagine how Levi felt earlier, but she was clinging to her branch for a different reason entirely. *Lord, I'm too scared to do this.*

She shook her head. This was only getting down from a tree, not making a lifetime commitment. Taking a deep breath, Lilly counted to three aloud and pushed herself from the branch.

Falling through the air lasted only a split second.

Nick Perrin caught her, just as he'd promised. His hands spanned her waist, and she clasped his well-toned arms as he lowered her to the ground.

He kept one hand firmly on her elbow and glanced at the bloodied tear in her shirtwaist. "You okay?"

"It's only a scratch."

Marguerite draped an arm around her shoulders. "Now that everyone is safely on the ground again, Mark and I had better get going. Trip will be wondering why we've been gone so long."

"Glad you and your son are all right." Mark tipped his hat to Lilly. "And thank you for the tour, Mr. Perrin. I enjoyed hearing about the coaster."

"Come back anytime."

"I may do that." He motioned Marguerite toward the path.

"And, Lilly." Marguerite turned one last time, her eyes twinkling. "We need to have a long talk tomorrow."

⌘

"Tomorrow's your morning off." Nick kept his tone deliberately casual as he walked beside Lilly. Even though she and Levi were fine, he intended to see them both safely home.

They made their way down the path to the cottages with Levi skipping ahead of them. The trees began to cast long shadows on the lawn as the sun dipped behind the bluffs.

"So, will you be heading to town?"

Lilly kept her eyes on the path. "I like to visit my mother on Wednesdays. She works for Marguerite's parents as their cook."

"So culinary talents run in your family?"

Her lips curled in a smile. "Taught me everything I know."

Levi stopped and poked a stick under a rock off to the side of the path. He pried the rock loose and it rolled over. Sitting on his haunches, he stared at the creepy crawlies beneath it as they scrambled in protest at the disturbance.

Nick placed a hand on Lilly's arm to slow her. Levi was so intent on his bug studies, Nick hated to interrupt. Inhaling a lungful of the tangy air coming off the lake, he turned to Lilly. "I have some errands to run in town tomorrow as well. Would you and Levi care to join me for breakfast?"

Lilly raised her eyebrows. "Eugenia is serving *your* breakfast at the lunch counter."

"Eugenia is cooking? Are you trying to kill my men?" He chuckled.

"She's improving." Lilly gave him a sidelong glance, then giggled. "Besides, it's hard to ruin oatmeal."

He raised a skeptical eyebrow. "As I said, would you two like to join me for breakfast—in the city?"

"Nick . . ." She dropped her gaze to the ground and pulled her shawl tight about her shoulders.

"It's breakfast, Lilly." He stuffed his hands in his pockets to keep from lifting her chin. "Nothing more. Three friends eating scrambled eggs *you* didn't have to cook."

She glanced toward Levi. "I'd better get him home."

The wait for her answer dragged on as they walked in silence. He didn't want to push her, but surely breakfast wouldn't be threatening to the ironclad barrier she'd erected around her heart.

"Well?" he asked when they reached Emily's cottage.

"See what I got, Mama?" Levi held up a toad and delivered a kiss to the creature's mouth.

Lilly reached for her son. "Levi! What are you doing?"

"It's not a princess, Mama. It's only an old toad."

"What am I gonna do with you?" She shook her head, and a smile blossomed on her face. It slid away when she looked at Nick. "What if Levi gets the wrong idea?"

"The wrong idea about what? Toads or scrambled eggs?" He flashed her a roguish grin and crossed his arms over his chest. He wasn't giving up so easily. "I can set him straight on the toads, and if you prefer, I can tell him hard-boiled eggs are best—even if they're a little tough to get out of their shells."

"Are you calling me an egghead?" The breeze whipped the soft curls falling free from her bun. One appeared to tickle her cheek, and she pushed it away. She smiled, but a sigh escaped. "I guess we do have to eat, and we might as well do it with you. Where do you want us to meet you?"

"I'll pick you both up at seven thirty."

Before she could protest, he lifted Levi, toad and all, into his arms. "See you in the morning, Chipmunk. We're having breakfast in town."

"Chipmunk Mama too?"

"Absolutely."

112

❧

Adjusting the lace collar on her green-checked day dress, Lilly worried her bottom lip between her teeth. Did the dress send the wrong message? She didn't want to wear one of her nicest dresses, but this one was still a far cry from her white shirtwaist and serviceable dark skirts she normally wore at the diner.

"Here's your hat." Emily handed her the matching straw hat with the large peacock plume and trailing satin ribbons. "You look lovely. You can stop fussing."

"I'm not fussing. I simply want to appear presentable." Lilly pinned her hat in place and splayed her hand over the belt cinched around her waist, attempting to quell the flutters in her stomach. At least the silver buckle wasn't tarnished.

A smile widened across Emily's face. "In that case, you are quite presentable, and so is Levi trussed up in his sailor suit—except for the dirt on his chin."

"Dirt? Where?"

Emily giggled. "I'm teasing you. He looks adorable."

"Why do I feel so strange doing this? It's only breakfast between friends." She pinned her watch to her bodice.

"Because you and I both know the way Nick Perrin looks at you does not say 'friend.'" Emily patted her arm. "But that is not a bad thing."

A knock sounded on the door, and Levi scrambled to answer it.

Lilly gripped the back of a chair. "This is a mistake."

"No." Emily draped Lilly's spring cape around her friend. "The only mistake would be not to go."

Levi swung the door open. "Morning, Mr. Nick."

"My, don't you look dapper." He looked to find Lilly

113

in the doorway. "And doesn't your mama look pretty as a daisy."

"Not daisy. Daffodil." Levi hopped down the steps. "That's her favorite flower, but her dress is green, so I guess she's pretty as a toad."

Nick chuckled. "Only you would think toads are pretty."

"Toads are beautiful." Levi spun in a circle. "Let's go. I'm hungry. I want a stack of pancakes this high." He held his hands a foot apart.

"Well, Lilly, shall we go feed this starving boy?"

She nodded, and they started down the path toward the service road. Lilly stopped at the sight of a waiting carriage. "You brought a rig."

"Sure. I told you I had errands. I rented this one when I arrived and keep it at one of the farms nearby."

"I thought we'd be riding the streetcar."

He shrugged and plopped Levi in the seat. "Same difference. We'll get there either way."

Except this way, she'd have to sit beside him alone all the way to town. What if someone saw them?

"Mrs. Hart?" He held out his hand to assist her.

She took it and sucked in a breath at the roughness of his hand as he helped her in. Of course his hands would be calloused with all of the manual work he did, but she hadn't expected it.

Levi bounced on the leather seat and growled. "I'm hungry as a bear, Mr. Nick."

Nick climbed into the carriage and picked up the reins. "One breakfast for three hungry bears, coming right up."

14

With Levi wedged properly between Nick and her, Lilly relaxed into the carriage's leather seat. The service road wound
around the lake, and she enjoyed seeing the part of the resort
that had yet to spring to life for the summer season. For several
years she'd summered here with the Westings and then with
Benjamin. Only since his death had she not spent the hottest
months of the year here at Lake Manawa.

"Can you tell me about this part of the lake?" Nick pointed
to the structures lining the south shore.

"The beach is called Manhattan Beach. I think the original
developers wanted it to have an upscale eastern feel. The small
building by the electric fountain is Louie's French Restaurant.
The big pavilion jutting out into the water like a peninsula
is the Kursaal. It has a wonderful dance floor upstairs, and
the whole building lights up at night. It's quite something."

"It sounds like you've been there before."

"It's where I met Benjamin."

"If you don't mind telling me, I'd like to hear how you met him."

"It's a long story."

"We've got a ways to go."

"Tell him, Mama. Tell him how Daddy didn't care you were poor."

"Levi." She placed a restraining hand on his leg and looked at Nick. "I wasn't poor, not in the destitute sense, but I wasn't in his social class either. His parents didn't approve."

"I gathered that from the other day. So, how'd you meet?"

"Before Marguerite and Trip married, her family had fallen on some hard times. They've recovered since then, but at the time, they could keep only my mother on their household staff. I moved in with Marguerite and Trip temporarily soon after they wed."

"You two are obviously close."

"Yes, almost like sisters. We grew up together in the Westing household. Except she was their daughter and I was her maid." Lilly paused and let the sunshine warm her cheeks. She closed her eyes, letting the scenes play in her mind. "Since Marguerite had always enjoyed parties and balls, she had quite a collection of frocks. That summer she nagged me until I borrowed one and went to a ball with her. I met Benjamin Hart that night. He had no idea I didn't own the clothes on my back."

"Mama was so pretty he couldn't help but love her."

Nick grinned at Levi. "I bet."

Lilly's cheeks heated. "Ben asked to court me, but I turned him down. I knew with his parents' standing in the community, there was no way they'd accept me."

"He persisted?"

"Let's just say if you think I'm stubborn . . ." She let the words trail off. "By the next year, we married, and we moved in with his parents. Two years later, God blessed us with the arrival of Levi." She hugged her son, surprised at how easily she'd spoken of Ben in front of Nick.

"But his parents never approved." He shook his head in disbelief. "You'd think a good Christian family . . ."

"Ben's parents might attend services on Christmas and Easter to keep up appearances, but I'd hardly say they walk with the Lord on a daily basis."

"But they named their son Benjamin. It's a biblical name. And you two followed suit with Levi."

Lilly giggled. "Benjamin Hart was named after Ben Franklin. His parents wanted him to become a great man like his namesake. His middle name, Davis, was his mother's maiden name. But we did choose Levi because it's biblical. It means *joined*. Ben wanted to remind his parents that we'd been joined together by God."

"And they shouldn't try to separate you two." He nodded. "Smart man."

She brushed a curl from her forehead. "Now it's your turn. How did you become a roller coaster designer? Is there a school for that?"

Nick chuckled. "Not that I know of." He explained that he'd met Sean McGready soon after graduating from high school. "Sean brought me to Mr. Ingersoll and told him he'd never regret hiring me. Talk about pressure. I never wanted to let Sean down, so I worked twice as hard as anyone in the company."

"But you must have shown a bent for the work."

"I've always been good at putting things together and solving problems." He turned the horse to the right at the far end of the lake and paused for a pair of geese to waddle across the road. "After a while, Mr. Ingersoll gave me the chance to start trying some of my own ideas."

"And you've been designing roller coasters ever since?"

"Not exactly."

"Pardon?"

"This is the first one I've designed solely on my own. I've been in charge of Ingersoll's plans on a half dozen coasters. But this is the first one I can call my own, and it's only the beginning."

"Beginning of what?"

"My own company, eventually. Perrin's Park Amusements." His eyes lit up as he spoke.

"Does Mr. Ingersoll realize he's training his competitor?"

"Probably, but I still have a great deal to learn before I can venture out on my own. Besides, he has Luna Parks going up all over the country right now, so I'm not the only one he's been training."

"This company you want to build means a lot to you?"

"I've been poor, Lilly. No-food-for-days poor. I won't ever let that happen again to myself or those I care about." He looked at her, held her gaze for a moment, and then snapped the reins. The horse switched to a steady, clopping gallop.

For several minutes, Levi chattered about the trees and birds, and Lilly risked a glance at Nick as he drove. Wearing a pair of tan trousers, a striped jacket, and a fashionable straw hat, he looked as if he could have been any one of Ben's wealthy friends. He was certainly as intelligent and driven as those men had been. But his calloused and rough hands told another story. As much as she loved Ben, she doubted he'd ever touched a piece of wood or known a night of hunger. Nick knew both intimately.

A warmth grew inside her, and she fought to push it away.

She shouldn't be comparing him to Ben. She'd given her heart to Ben, and it still belonged to him. He'd given her five wonderful years and a son she loved more than she'd ever dreamed.

But why was she thinking about this now? Could Emily be right about the way Nick looked at her?

No, he'd said they were friends. Maybe she was simply lonely. A friendship with Nick wouldn't hurt. He'd leave at the end of the summer, but meanwhile, she'd have a few mornings of companionship to lighten her days—as long as Levi didn't get hurt in the process.

"Mama, look!" Levi pointed to the familiar mansion on one of the city's bluffs. "We used to live there."

"That's the Hart estate?" Nick let out a low whistle. "Was the gate to keep you in or keep others out?"

She smiled. "Probably both."

"Want to stop and say hi?"

"I'd rather eat Eugenia's cooking."

Nick laughed, and the sound of it made her relax.

Friends.

She liked that.

For the rest of the journey, Nick asked Lilly to tell him about the city. She explained how Council Bluffs had gotten its name from the time when the Otoe Indian tribe had a council on the bluffs with explorers Meriwether Lewis and William Clark. She pointed out where Ben had practiced law with his father, her favorite stores in which to shop, and Bayliss Park in the center of the city. Lilly pointed to her right. "And Fairmont Park is in those hills."

"It has lots of deerses in it." Levi wiggled. "And there's a boy with a leaky boot."

"A leaky boot?"

"It's a fountain sculpture in the park with a little boy

holding his boot in the air." Lilly straightened the bow on her son's sailor collar. "Levi loves how the water comes out of the bottom of the boot."

"We'll have to make a day of it and go there." Nick cast a glance at Lilly.

She'd not contradict him, but as nice as the morning was, she couldn't let these forays occur at regular intervals.

Nick made a left turn down the street toward the Kiel Hotel and pulled the carriage to a stop. "Breakfast is served."

"Here?" Lilly stared at him as he hopped down.

He plucked Levi from the seat and then came around the carriage to assist her. "You don't like it? Sorry, it's the only place I've eaten besides your diner."

"No, it's a fine place. Too fine." She spoke the last words softly, intending them for only her own ears. She placed her hands on his shoulders.

He held her waist and swung her to the ground, holding her a bit longer than necessary. "Nothing is too fine for my friends."

Friends. Yes. That's all this was. Breakfast with friends. She could not—would not—let the feelings stirring inside her fan into flame.

Levi needed a man like Nick in his life. She did not.

"Ready for those pancakes, Chipmunk?" Nick took Levi's hand and gave Lilly one of his lilting grins. "And we'll order a nice hard-boiled egg for your mama."

15

After breakfast, Lilly's stomach was satisfied, but her mind remained starving for answers. Following the meal with Nick, she'd gone to see her mother, but it had done little to help make sense of the nagging turmoil in her heart.

Now that she and Levi had returned to the diner, she needed to push her ponderings aside. She glanced around the kitchen and spotted only one pan on the stove. After tying her apron, she lifted the spoon from the oatmeal and watched the congealed blob plop back in the pot. She glanced at Levi, and they shared a giggle. If the men had left this much oatmeal after breakfast, they were sure to be famished when they arrived for lunch.

"Levi, you want something to eat before I feed the workers?"

He scowled at her from the stool where he perched. "You wouldn't make me eat that, would you?"

She laughed. "No, I was thinking of an apple."

"I'm still full to the brim with pancakes." He scampered off the stool. "Can I help you?"

"Sure, why don't you fetch me some potatoes from the bin and put them on the counter for tonight's dinner?"

While Lilly sliced roast beef for sandwiches, Levi gathered the potatoes in his shirttails and carried them to his mother. He set them on the counter, and one rolled off. After chasing it down, he plopped it back in place. "Where's Miss Eugenia?"

"She should be here any minute." Lilly removed two bowls of strawberry Jell-O filled with preserved pears from the icebox. The men loved this wiggly treat almost as much as Levi did. Maybe she should have Eugenia make the next batch. Even she should be able to boil water. Then again, maybe not. Bless her heart, that poor girl's engine was not connected to the rest of the train.

"You like Mr. Nick now, Mama?"

"Of course I like Mr. Nick. He's a kind man." Her stomach fluttered, betraying the rush of feelings the mention of Nick's name caused in her. But she knew any decisions she made concerning Nick couldn't be based on feelings. One look at her son reminded her there was simply too much at stake.

"I'm glad you like him." He dropped the last potato from his load into the sink. "'Cause I do too. He makes you smile."

"I smile all the time."

"More when you're with Mr. Nick."

She tickled his belly. "Now look who's smiling."

The back door opened, and Lilly turned. Eugenia walked in the kitchen, worry etching her face.

"Eugenia, what's wrong?"

"They hated the oatmeal. It was lumpy."

"They'll live."

"But *he* was here."

Lilly stopped measuring coffee grounds. "Who?"

"Mr. Westing, the man you introduced me to yesterday."

"Mark?" How odd. Why would Mark stop by again? "Did he want anything?"

"He asked where you'd gone and where Mr. Perrin was. I told him you had the morning off and I had no idea about Mr. Perrin, but that's not the problem." Eugenia twisted her handkerchief into a knot.

"Let me guess. You fed him breakfast."

"Lumps and all." Tears filled Eugenia's pale green eyes.

"Oh, Eugenia, you're sweet on him, aren't you?" Lilly covered the girl's hands with her own. "He'll be back. You'll have another chance to impress him."

"Do you really think I can, Miss Lilly?"

Good grief. How did Lilly answer without lying? Sure, a man would be fortunate to have someone as loving as Eugenia, but would Mark see beyond her nervous tendencies?

"Eugenia, you're a sweet, kind, giving young lady, and I'm certain you're full of many surprises."

Nick wanted to hit something, but the frail freight clerk with the long face would hardly do.

"What do you mean my building materials were shipped to Columbus, Ohio? Do you think I can build a roller coaster without wood?"

"Apparently someone misread Council Bluffs and directed it to Columbus. Iowa and Ohio are similar." The clerk fiddled with his pencil.

"Similar? How?"

"They both have four letters and three vowels—not that it really makes any difference, Mr. Perrin."

Nick took off his hat and plopped it on the clerk's counter. "This is the second time this has happened."

"I can assure you I've tracked down your order, and it will be here the day after tomorrow."

"Two days!"

The nervous clerk snapped the pencil in two. "I apologize for the inconvenience. I'll have the supplies delivered to you at no extra charge, sir."

Nick sighed. Taking his frustration out on this poor man was no way for a Christian to act. "I'm the one who should apologize. I'm sorry for my outburst. So you'll send them out as soon as they arrive?"

"The very hour."

"Thank you, Mr. . . . ." Nick held out his hand.

The clerk shook it. "Snodgrass. P. J. Snodgrass."

"I appreciate your tracking the order down. And your first ride on the roller coaster is on me, Mr. Snodgrass."

"That won't be necessary."

"I insist."

"Really, it's not necessary." Mr. Snodgrass whipped out his handkerchief and wiped his beaded brow. "You won't catch me near your contraption."

"But you're a railroad man."

"I ship freight on them, but I don't ride them. Not a bit safe."

"Well, if you change your mind, Mr. Snodgrass, let me know." He tipped his hat. "And thanks for sending the supplies out."

Nick exited the depot and shielded his face from the noonday sun. Not only would he miss lunch at the diner, but he'd also miss seeing Lilly again.

Climbing into his rented rig, Nick turned his thoughts

toward the roller coaster. If those supplies didn't come on Friday there would be nothing for his men to do. How would they ever make the opening-season deadline of May 27?

And what would Lilly think of him if he failed? It would be hard to convince her how serious he was about building his own company if he couldn't meet his first obligation.

He turned down the street leading out of the city and snapped the reins. How had that stubborn woman taken his thoughts captive? He'd been to different places all over the country, and not since Ruby had anyone turned his insides to jelly like Lilly. When he was with her, he felt like he was on one of his roller coasters—a thrill one minute and a death-defying plunge the next. And he was only along for the ride.

What made her worth the stomach-lurching trip? Her smile of pure sunshine? The way her amber eyes told what she was thinking even when she tried so hard to remain tough? That stubborn streak that had made her strong enough to handle difficult circumstances?

Perhaps all of those.

Still, she wasn't ready. After the way she talked about her deceased husband, he wondered if she would ever be.

He gave the horse the freedom to run along the last stretch toward the lake. As with the horse, maybe he should simply let Lilly feel in control. Perhaps then her shell would crack, and she'd let him in.

But how long would it take? Because he didn't want to crack her shell if he couldn't stay around to pick up the pieces.

⌘

With no time to change, Lilly rushed to the suffrage meeting after serving the workers their supper. Emily had been asked to be the guest speaker, so she hated to miss the meeting. She'd have been even later if Eugenia hadn't offered to do the dishes.

Pausing on the Rowing Club stairs, she gave her black work skirt and plain shirtwaist a once-over. Passable but not terribly fashionable. At least she'd taken time to fix her hair. Little good that would do when the scent of liver and onions clung to her like the spray of a skunk.

Inside, she made her way to the top floor and eased the door open. If she slipped in the back, perhaps no one would notice her attire or her poor taste in perfume. No chairs remained, so Lilly leaned against the rich wood paneling in the back.

Emily stood at the front podium, delivering a message honoring Susan B. Anthony. When had the suffrage fighter died? And how had Lilly missed hearing about it? Had she even seen a newspaper in the last month or so?

A couple of the members turned toward her, scanned her appearance, and sent her clearly disapproving scowls. They whispered between themselves. Lilly could guess what they were saying. She pressed herself further into the corner. For a time, she'd felt like she belonged at these gatherings, but now Ben was gone, and she often found herself again feeling like the girl who never quite fit in at Marguerite's tea parties.

Her eyes misted, and she dabbed at the corners with her handkerchief. Good grief. The onions must still be getting to her.

"Ladies, let us not fail Miss Anthony and the others who fought tirelessly for a woman's right to vote." Emily stepped in front of the podium. "Let us continue their fight and make it our own. Let us not give up until each of us can drop our ballot into the box electing the next president of the United States."

Emily nodded, indicating the end of her speech, and the room erupted in applause. Lilly resisted the urge to sneak out the back. When the women began chatting among themselves, she made her way around the edge of the room toward her friend.

Lilly wrapped Emily in a hug. "Wonderful speech."

"I'm glad you made it."

"Even if I smell like yesterday's lunch?"

"I didn't notice." Emily quirked a grin.

"You're too nice to say so." Lilly inclined her head toward Marguerite, who was approaching. "On the other hand, I bet it will take her less than a minute to make a comment."

Marguerite skirted around two ladies in a heated discussion and clasped Emily's hands. "Well done. Your grandmother would be proud."

"I practiced the speech earlier today by giving it to her and my aunts." Emily glanced at Lilly, who was holding her watch in her hand. "Oh, Lilly, how did your breakfast with Nick go this morning?"

Marguerite's eyebrows shot up, and a smile curled her lips. "Breakfast? But I do hope you didn't wear that perfume, Lilly. I'm afraid it doesn't become you in the least."

Lilly rolled her eyes. "I doubt if eau de onion is becoming to anything other than a slab of liver." She turned to Emily. "See? Less than a minute."

"What takes less than a minute?" Marguerite asked.

"Never mind."

Marguerite looped her arm through Lilly's. "In that case, the three of us need to find a nice quiet place where you can tell us all about your breakfast excursion."

16

"And Mr. Nick got the zoo to open just for us today, Mama, so you gotta come."

Lilly studied Levi's hope-filled blue eyes, then turned toward Nick and frowned. He'd put her in a difficult place, and she hated disappointing Levi again. "As you and Mr. Nick know, I've got to make supper for the workers."

"No you don't." A cocky grin spread across Nick's face. "I gave everyone the afternoon off, and that includes you. Our supplies won't be in until Friday, so I wanted to save the rest of what we had to do for Monday." He snagged her spring cloak from the hook and held it. "So let's get a move on. The rabbits are waiting."

"How long have you two been conniving on this?" she asked as Nick slipped the cloak in place.

"Since yesterday." Levi pressed a finger to his lips. "But it was a secret."

Lilly squatted in front of her son and buttoned his jacket. "Is that why you couldn't get to sleep last night?"

He nodded. "Monkeys marched in my dreams all night."

"Marching monkeys, huh? Were they munching on marbles?" She stood and shared a grin with Nick.

"Silly Mama. Monkeys eat 'nanas." Levi skipped to the door and flung it open.

Nick caught it before it slammed into the wall and motioned for her to exit. "Marbles? Did you really think he'd buy that?"

Lilly shrugged. "Who knows what nonsense you've filled his head with?"

A chuckle erupted from Nick, and Lilly found herself sharing in the laughter. The threesome followed the sidewalk leading to Lake Manawa's "zoo." She hoped Levi wouldn't be too disappointed. This little setup was a far cry from Omaha's Riverview Zoo. Maybe she could figure out a way to take Levi across the river to see that one, which boasted nearly two hundred animals.

Levi grabbed her hand and pulled. "Come on, Mama. Don't be a slowpoke."

Scooping Levi into his arms, Nick tickled him. "I think somebody's awfully excited. Maybe we should wait until another day when he can be more patient."

"No!"

Nick held Levi in one arm and ran his free hand over his stubbled chin as if he were deep in thought. Lilly studied him. How long would he keep his ruse going with Levi? He seemed to have a natural ability with her son to know how to encourage better behavior.

The afternoon shadow on Nick's face only made his chiseled features more defined. His cobalt-blue eyes sparkled with mischief. "I guess we can still go today—if a certain little boy can be quiet and gentle with the animals."

"I can be quiet." Levi pressed his chubby hands to Nick's cheeks and held his face. "And gentle too. See?"

Nick slid him back to the ground. "I'm impressed. Did you see that, Lilly? Levi can be quiet and as gentle as a lamb."

She smiled. "Good, because we wouldn't want to frighten the rabbits."

"Or the alligator." Nick nodded with a solemn tip of his head. "When alligators get agitated, they get hungry, and we sure wouldn't want to have to deal with agitated alligators."

Levi's eyes grew as wide as dinner plates. "No, we sure wouldn't. I'll be real, real, real quiet."

"You know, Levi, I wouldn't want any of us to get separated and run into any wild animals." They'd reached the zoo, and Nick opened the door to the main office for Levi and Lilly to pass through.

After trotting inside, Levi lifted his serious face toward Nick. "That would be bad."

"I think we should all hold hands just in case." Nick held out his open hand to Lilly.

She shot him a fiery glare.

Levi grabbed Nick's other hand. "Mama, you'd better hold Mr. Nick's hand. You don't want to get eaten by agitatored alligators, do you?"

"That's not the beast I'm most worried about," she muttered.

Nick looked at his empty, outstretched hand and raised his brows.

Holding hands with him in public? Didn't he realize what he was asking? It was nearly a declaration.

"For your safety, ma'am," he said like a sheriff from the Wild West.

With a sigh, she placed her hand in Nick's palm. She only hoped she wouldn't regret it.

Nick closed his hand around Lilly's and squeezed it gently. Warmth spread across his chest, and he fought the urge to sweep her into his arms.

Lord, help me to take this slow. I don't want to scare her.

But fear had never stopped him from doing anything before. Tackling demons head-on gave him a rush like nothing else. Not that Lilly was a demon, but for him, love had certainly been one.

The owner, whom Nick had met previously, was a massive man named Jethro Tallman. He looked up from the reception desk on which he was putting a fresh coat of paint. He placed the paintbrush in a can of turpentine and put the lid back on the pail of paint before turning to them. "Been spiffing up the place before opening day. I'm glad you could make it in, Mr. Perrin." He turned to Levi. "And this fine fellow must be the animal lover."

A broad grin spread over Levi's face. "I am! Thank you for letting us come today."

"No problem, young fellow. As I said, I've been fixing things after the long winter. I had a little ice damage to the roof, and Mr. Perrin sent some of his men to help me with the repairs. Least I could do is let you all have a sneak preview." Jethro tugged a red rag from his back pocket and wiped his hands on it. "Ready for the grand tour?"

Levi bounced once and stopped. He looked at Nick and whispered, "Yes."

"We told Levi he had to be gentle and quiet with the animals." Nick placed his hand on the boy's head. "No agitating the alligators."

A hearty laugh shook Jethro's belly. "Sounds like a good

idea, but I don't think we'll be bothering old Smiley. This way, folks."

With a sweep of his hand, he directed them toward the door on the left of the reception counter. Levi went through first, still clinging to Nick's hand like a lifeline. And since Nick wasn't letting go of Lilly's hand, it meant she had to follow him. If Jethro noticed his breach of etiquette in making a lady go last, he didn't say anything. The three of them stopped in front of the first cage and waited for Jethro to introduce the strange bird inside.

"This little lady came all the way from South America."

Levi pressed his hand to the cage. "That's a long way to fly."

Jethro chuckled. "She didn't fly. She was brought on board a ship. She's a parrot."

They stepped down the line to the next cage, where another large bird stared at them with one eye.

"What's this one?" Levi asked.

"It's a stork." Jethro tossed the bird a handful of corn. "Do you know what storks bring?"

Lilly sucked in a breath.

"No, sir."

Jethro glanced at Nick, then dropped his gaze to Nick's and Lilly's clasped hands. "Well, if you're lucky, you may find out sooner than you think."

Lilly's cheeks bloomed the prettiest shade of rose Nick had ever seen. She pulled her hand away and refused to look at him.

One step forward, two steps back. Thank you, Jethro.

They looked at several other birdcages, then Jethro led them to a much larger cage. A monkey swung from the walls of the cage to the tree branch that had been propped inside. He dropped to the ground and picked up a slice of apple.

"He likes it!" Levi squeaked.

"He likes about everything you and I like." Jethro opened the cage door and held out his arms. The monkey raced over and jumped into them like a toddler. "This is Taffy."

"Let me guess, he has a penchant for that candy?" Lilly stayed a respectable distance away.

"That he does." Jethro pulled a piece from his pocket, and Taffy snatched it from his fingers.

They crossed to the other side of the room, where reptiles were housed. Nick glanced at Lilly, who was clearly not enthralled. Her gaze roamed the room. He saw her focus on the last cage, where an enormous snake lay coiled. The cage sat next to the potbellied stove piping heat into the room. A large pan of water warmed on top of the stove. The combination of the stove's heat and the water filled the room with moisture.

Nick wiped his brow. "Who's that big fellow?"

"Ah, I see you've discovered my main squeeze, and he is a she." Jethro ambled to the cage and reached for the cage's latch. "This incredible lady is Delilah. She's a red-tailed boa."

"You're not taking that thing out, are you?" Lilly grabbed Levi's hand.

"Mama, you're supposed to hold Mr. Nick's hand. Not mine."

"I'm fine, Levi. It's you I don't want to be frightened." She squeezed his shoulders to hold him in place.

"I'm not scared. I'm brave." He wiggled free and pressed his nose to the cage. "'Sides, I looooove snakes."

Jethro pushed the boy's head away. "And Delilah may mistake your nose for her dinner if you get too close. But, ma'am, I promise you this pretty lady is well mannered—unlike Taffy over there."

"I think Levi would be disappointed if we didn't let him

pet the snake, Lilly." Nick ruffled Levi's sandy hair. "Wouldn't you, Levi?"

The boy nodded enthusiastically.

Lilly sighed. "Okay. As long as you don't make *me* touch it."

Lifting the latch on the door, Jethro glanced at the three of them and told them to relax. He reached inside, lifted Delilah from above her tail, and then supported her massive body with his other hand. The snake immediately began to coil on his arm. Easing her off, he hefted her tail over his shoulder and held her neck in his hand. The remainder of Delilah's long body wrapped around Jethro's torso.

Nick felt Lilly shiver beside him. He slipped his hand around hers, hiding the union in the folds of her skirt. Lilly squeezed her appreciation.

"How big is she?" Nick asked.

"She's almost nine feet long and weighs forty-five pounds." Jethro stroked the alternating tan circles and red stripes on her back. "She's an old gal. We've been together since my circus days. She must be almost twenty years old. Go ahead and pet her."

Levi bounced on his toes until his mother finally nodded her permission. He reached for the snake, tentatively at first, and finally touched its skin. "You want to pet her, Mr. Nick? See, she's nice. Smooth and cold. Not slimy. You too, Mama. You gotta pet her. You have to."

Nick felt another shiver shake Lilly's body. Poor thing. She'd do anything for her son, but this? He locked his gaze on her. Her amber eyes, wide with fear, begged him to bail her out of this. Did he want to bail her out? Maybe he should, but then again, it might be fun to face this challenge together. He tightened his hold on her hand. "We can do this."

Ever so slowly, he raised her hand in his own. He felt the

resistance, but she finally gave in to his lead and let him place her fingers on the snake's thick hide. He covered her small hand with his much larger one. With his fingers so much longer than Lilly's, he was able to touch the cool, almost silky snake flesh. It contrasted sharply with Lilly's supple, warm hand tucked beneath his own.

Like a dance, he drew her hand along the path of mahogany stripes on the snake's back. Warmth pooled in his chest, and his heart pounded like a kettledrum. Was she learning to trust him? Did she realize he'd die before he'd let this snake—or anything else—harm her or her son?

All too soon, she withdrew her hand from beneath his. "It's . . . a . . . a . . . rather cold."

"Snakes are cold-blooded animals." Jethro eyed Nick and kicked up the side of his mouth. "Unlike us."

Nick cleared his throat. "Do you have any alligators? Levi was hoping to see those too."

"Sure I do. Let me put Delilah away, and we'll head outside." Jethro gently uncoiled the snake's lower body and laid it in the cage. As if Delilah understood what was happening, she withdrew the rest of her body from around Jethro's torso and slithered to a resting place.

Jethro tugged on his collar. "She likes it warm and humid, but it gets to me. Ready to head out where it's cooler?"

He led them out the back door. The open pen area surrounding the barn was divided into several sections—one for sheep, one for a milk cow, and another for pigs. For a moment, Nick thought he spotted a camel chomping hay inside the barn. Jethro passed that fenced area and said they'd come back. He motioned them toward a solid brick fence several yards from the barn.

"Welcome to the home of Smiley." Jethro swept his arm over the enclosure. Nick looked over the solid wall and found an alligator sunning himself on a boulder in the center of the area. Around him, a small pond had been dug for his swimming pleasure.

Jethro reached over the edge and poked the animal with a long pole. Smiley opened his jaws, revealing rows of sharp teeth. He snapped his jaw shut with lightning speed.

"Oh my," Lilly breathed. "And this thing is practically my neighbor. Imagine if he got loose."

Levi clutched at Nick's leg, so Nick picked him up.

"Can he get out?" Levi asked.

Jethro patted the brick wall. "No, that's why I built these. It's not like an alligator can climb with those stubby legs and all. And Smiley's not so bad, but he likes to show me who's really the boss."

Levi relaxed in Nick's arms. "Can we see him eat something?"

"Hmmm." Jethro rubbed his chin and pointed to a shack. "You see that cabbage over there? Go get it for me, and we'll see if Smiley feels like playing."

Nick set Levi on the ground, and the boy raced off. He returned seconds later with the head of a cabbage and passed it to Jethro.

Jethro poked the alligator. "Smiley, want to play?" He held the cabbage for the creature to see.

Opening his cavernous mouth, Smiley made a move forward. Jethro tossed the cabbage toward the alligator's nose. His jaw snapped down on the cabbage, shredding it in an instant.

Levi jumped up and down and applauded. When Smiley wheeled in his direction, Levi hurried behind Nick's legs. "I agitatored the alligator. Don't let him get me."

"He's not going anywhere, but you ought to see him eat watermelon. He smashes those into bits." Jethro tapped Levi's nose. "Now, young man, I've got a surprise for you."

17

What was that noise? Lilly listened again. It wasn't the sound of a cow bawling or a horse neighing, but it had to be an animal. A sick donkey maybe? They hadn't seen a donkey in the little zoo, but that didn't mean there wasn't one in the barn.

What if Mr. Tallman was in trouble? She glanced at Nick, who gave no indication that the strange noise alarmed him.

"What do you think the surprise is, Mama?" Levi's eyes danced.

"I don't know, but Mr. Tallman told us to wait patiently, and that's exactly what we're gonna do." Lilly knelt in front of Levi to adjust his jacket as a cool breeze ruffled the trees. The raspy, belching sound came again, and this time Nick looked at her and smiled. Did he recognize the source of the noise? She started to ask, but he pressed a finger to his lips, silencing her questions.

Lilly stood still as the barn door opened, then turned to see Mr. Tallman leading a camel. Draped over the camel's back was a blanket of bright, rich colors. On top of that was what appeared to be a saddle of sorts, which was covered in additional layers of blankets. As the camel lumbered toward them, thick, gold tassels swung from the corners of the multicolored blanket.

Levi stared at the beast towering above him. "What's his name, and do I get to ride him?"

Mr. Tallman stopped the camel beside a wooden tack box and patted the camel's neck. "This is my old friend Ali Baba. He's another one of my partners from my time with the circus." Mr. Tallman placed his hand on Ali Baba's front flank and gave him the directive to sit.

The camel folded his legs beneath his massive body until he was sitting on the ground. Still, the top of Ali Baba's hump reached over Lilly's head.

Mr. Tallman tapped Levi's cap. "Ready to ride one of the ships of the desert?"

Levi looked around. "I don't see a ship."

"That's what they call camels." Nick picked up Levi and turned to Mr. Tallman. "You want him right here?"

Lilly put her arm out to block the way. "Wait a minute. Are you certain it's safe for my little boy to ride this thing?"

"My Baba's a gentleman. We've been giving camel rides to folks at the lake for almost ten years now. Haven't you seen him? No one's been bitten or maimed in any way. But since you're worried, why don't you and Mr. Perrin ride first?"

Lilly stepped back and hurried to fold her hands in front of her. "No, that won't be necessary."

"I don't know about that." Nick raised his eyebrows in Levi's direction. "What do you think? Should your mama and I go for a ride, then let you have a turn?"

"Yes!" Levi clapped his hands. "Go, Mama. It'll be fun."

Lilly burned Nick with a glare, but he merely chuckled. "Besides, Lilly, I'll feel safer with you next to me."

"You shouldn't, because I'm gonna kill you the first chance I get," she hissed.

Nick grinned and motioned toward the camel. "It'll probably be easier for you to . . . um . . . ride astride."

"I'll manage to ride sidesaddle."

"That's the spirit." Mr. Tallman offered Ali Baba a treat from his coat pocket.

"Where's the stirrup?" Lilly looked on both sides of Ali Baba and lifted the blankets over the saddle.

"There's not one. You direct a camel with your toes, so a stirrup isn't necessary."

Lilly's eyes grew wide. "My toes?"

Mr. Tallman's belly shook when he laughed. "You won't have to do that because I'll be leading him on the rope."

"And I'll make sure you don't slide off." Nick patted the saddle. "Need help getting on?"

"I can manage." Lilly sat down on the tack box, then tucked her legs beneath her. She stood gracefully before attempting to lift herself into place on the saddle, but she couldn't fully get on. She slid off, her fingers running along the animal's wiry hide. She tried three times.

Nick chuckled, hopped on the crate, and nudged her out of the way. He grabbed the horn and pulled himself up. After swinging his leg over the side, he scooted to the back half of the saddle.

"Maybe Levi should accompany you instead of me." Lilly turned to find her son.

Before she knew what Nick was doing, he'd hooked an arm around her waist and drew her upward onto the camel's back. In one smooth motion, he deposited her on the front half of the long saddle.

"Well done, Mr. Perrin." Mr. Tallman stroked Ali Baba's

head. "Now, here's what you two have to do. When Ali Baba stands, he raises his back legs first, so you'll be tilted this way." He demonstrated the steep inclined plane with his hand. "So you need to lean backward at that point. Then, when he raises his front legs, you both lean forward. See that horn in the front of the saddle and the one in the back? Hold on to those so you don't fall off."

After making sure the two riders were ready, Mr. Tallman signaled Ali Baba to stand. The camel raised his long back legs, and because Lilly was seated sidesaddle, instead of leaning straight back, she leaned to her left. Her shoulder came into contact with Nick's solid chest. She sucked in a breath and started to pull away. When she did, she slid forward a bit. Nick snaked his arm around her waist and secured her against him.

He smelled of pine and outdoors, the scent stirring something deep inside her, long forgotten. The warmth in her stomach mixed with the raw fear coursing through her. How had she let herself get in this intimate of a position with a man? She was a married woman.

Was.

A sob stuck in her throat as the single word pulsated in her thoughts.

No. No. No. She loved Ben. He would hate seeing her leaning against another man. She shouldn't be here. She belonged to Ben. At the very least, she should ask Nick to remove his protective arm immediately. And she would—if she could discover any other way to stay on the camel.

Finally, Ali Baba began to rise to his front legs. This time Lilly was ready and leaned forward when she felt the camel move beneath her. As soon as they were almost upright, Nick's hand slipped away. Good. She wouldn't have to ask him to remove it. That's what she wanted, right?

When Ali Baba reached his full height, Lilly sucked in her breath again. She had to be nearly eight feet off the ground. What if Levi fell from this height?

"What do you think of the view?" Nick asked.

Lilly glanced at the trees as they passed. A robin swooped in with more fodder for her nest, and a black squirrel bounded from one tree to another. Lilly peered between the branches and caught a glimpse of the lake where a couple of sailboats dotted the water.

Levi skipped beside Mr. Tallman. "Can you see forever and ever and ever? I ain't never been that high."

"You haven't ever been this high." Lilly gripped the pommel as the beast swayed beneath her.

"'Course not, Mama. It's not my turn yet."

Nick touched Lilly's arm. "What do you think of Ali Baba?"

"I think it would take me a long time to become accustomed to such a beast as my only form of transportation."

"Riding a camel is all about balance." Mr. Tallman led them down the center of his zoo and around the alligator pen. "Sit confidently and stay firmly planted."

Lilly tried to concentrate on doing that, but inch by inch, she felt herself slipping off the side. Maybe riding sidesaddle wasn't such a good choice. "How much farther are we gonna go?"

"Not far. To that fence and back."

Nick cleared his throat. "You okay?"

"Fine." Lilly sat up straighter. *Or as fine as I can be when I've been hoodwinked into riding a camel.*

"I won't let you fall, Lilly." Nick must have leaned close because she felt his breath on her ear. Shivers rippled along her spine. She glanced at Mr. Tallman. If he'd heard Nick, he gave no indication.

The camel continued to sway to his own clumsy rhythm as

he followed Mr. Tallman. Lilly slid a bit more and hugged the pommel. Only a few more yards. She could hold on until then.

"Lilly?" Nick touched her arm. "Are you having trouble staying on?"

"Heavens no. I merely need to reposition myself." Lilly attempted to use the pommel horn to hoist herself back in place. It didn't work well, but it should suffice. "I'm good now."

The last few yards, Levi bounced in front of them, declaring this had to be better than riding a horse. Lilly had her doubts. Maybe the ships of the desert sailed better on sand than on Iowa's rich soil.

Mr. Tallman led the camel back to the area in front of the barn and stopped. "I'm going to have Ali Baba sit down so you two can dismount, but this can be the trickiest of all. Remember, for a minute it might feel like you're falling off. He has to fold his front feet under first, so pretend you're going down a steep mountain."

Lilly glanced at Nick. He kept his gaze fixed on her as the camel began to lower himself. Her stomach jumped when his right front leg dipped. Despite her iron grip, she lurched forward on the fabric of her skirt. Her ankles showed. If this continued, who knew how much Nick would see before the camel came to a stop? But if she fell . . .

The blankets beneath her slid sideways. She lost her hold and gasped.

As if he'd been expecting it, Nick slid his arm around her waist and pulled her toward him. His muscled arm remained firmly around her, burning her skin through her shirtwaist, as the camel lowered first his front and then his hind legs to the earth.

Nick's hand remained in place this time. "Sidesaddle didn't work so well, huh?"

Mr. Tallman chuckled. "Well, it works better when I have my mounting scaffold ready. I apologize for not having it yet this year. Good thing you were there to catch her, Mr. Perrin."

"Hmmm. That's twice now." A self-satisfied grin tugged at Nick's mouth. "What would you have done without me?"

"Well, for starters, I wouldn't have gotten on the creature in the first place." She tipped her chin up, and Ali Baba made his strangled-donkey noise. Lilly quirked an eyebrow. "See, Ali agrees."

"He just wants us off." Nick released her, swung his leg over, and dropped to the ground.

Before he could assist her again, Lilly slid off the side in a most unladylike fashion, and Mr. Tallman grabbed her arm to steady her. Nick scowled.

Levi hugged her legs. "Was it the bestest ride ever, Mama?" He didn't wait for a response but moved on to hugging Nick. "Do you want to go again with me, Mr. Nick?"

Lilly shook the folds of her gored skirt back in place and flashed Nick a smile. "I'd sure appreciate it. It was awfully high."

The corners of Nick's lips bowed. "In that case, sure, Chipmunk. I'll go with you."

"One thing." Levi wagged a finger at Nick. "Don't hug me like you did Mama. That's for girls."

18

Nick marched up the stairs onto the porch of Mrs. Whitson's boardinghouse. A few members of his work crew lounged on wicker chairs, the remainder having gone to town for the evening. One of his men exited the building, and the boarding-house's medicinal scent followed. Why did Mrs. Whitson's house always reek of camphor?

After shucking his coat, Nick tossed it on the back of a worn chair and then dropped into the chair. He shifted and the wicker creaked. "Can nothing go right?"

Sean peeked over the top of his newspaper, and his eye-brows rose. "Trouble with the lass?"

"All I did was ask Lilly if she'd like an escort to church services on Sunday. What was the crime in that?"

Sean folded the newspaper and set it aside. "I take it she didn't enjoy yer day with the beasties?"

"Oh, I think she liked the animals fine. It's me she doesn't seem to want to be around."

"Nick, my boy, the lassie is sweet on you fer sure, but her

heart is torn. Ya need to be patient." Sean lifted the lid to a box and pulled out the wooden piece he'd been whittling. He handed Nick a second piece.

Nick opened his pocketknife and began to peel away the wood on the toy he'd been constructing. "I keep telling myself that, but when I think she may be letting me into her life a bit, she closes me off."

"I hate to break this to ya, boyo, but even yer blue-eyed charm can't open every door."

"Why won't she trust me?"

"Why should she?"

"What do you mean by that?"

"Don't get your rankles up. I'm asking ya if you've truly thought of what yer asking her to do in taking a chance on the likes of ya."

Nick laughed and glanced at his friend, whose eyes were alight from the good-natured ribbing. He fingered the chunk of wood in his hand, enjoying the feel of its solid structure. "Lilly could do worse than me."

"Could she?" Though he kept his voice casual, seriousness swept the twinkle from Sean's face. "She's already lost one husband, and ya don't exactly have a desk job. Ya want to build a business more dangerous than most anything a man could think of, and near as I can figure, ya haven't asked God to help ya in this once." He set his wood toy on the table. It wobbled, so he shaved off another sliver of wood.

Nick used the tip of his knife to cut an intricate pattern on the side of the cube. "I have prayed about it."

"Truly? A real God-doing-the-leadin' prayer, or a wish-list prayer?"

Nick's chest tightened. His knife slipped and pricked the fleshy part of his thumb. He pressed his forefinger to it to quell the flow of blood and sighed. His prayer had been more about asking God to do what Nick wanted, not necessarily to do what was best for Lilly. Had he been prideful and assumed he was the answer to her struggles?

"Nick, my boy, she needs a friend. Love can bloom out of that—if it's the Lord's will. Ya know that. But make sure ya know what yer gettin' into. A part of her heart will always belong to her deceased husband. Always." He held up the wooden piece he was working on. "Do ya want to quit now, boyo?"

Levi was going to love their surprise, but their project was time consuming. Yet Sean wasn't simply talking about what they were constructing. Good old Sean always asked the hard questions, making Nick consider things he didn't want to.

Nick shook his head. "No. I'm not giving up."

Maybe he didn't know what he was doing, but he did know he couldn't abandon Lilly and Levi like Ruby Rawlins had abandoned him. Trust was a fragile thread and easily snapped. He'd be her friend. He'd pray for her. He'd show her she could lean on him.

He'd be there for her until God told him something different.

⚬

Tapping the pencil against the ledger, Lilly studied the figures before her. Thank goodness summer was coming and she could make Levi's trousers into knee pants. If she wanted enough money for a place of her own by fall, she'd need every penny. As it stood, she already had a tidy little sum set aside.

A chill in the air of Emily's cabin made her shiver and reminded her of the gray clouds that seemed to be blowing in this afternoon. While her spirits had lifted with the church services, they'd sunk with the gloomy weather and the dismal figures.

"How are things looking?" Emily draped a shawl over Lilly's shoulders.

"Thanks to your letting us stay here, I think I'll have enough to get a place by the end of the summer if nothing significant happens. It'll be close, but we should be able to buy a house before school starts in the fall. Maybe sooner, if I can find one that needs a little work."

Emily sat down at the parlor's small table. "My grandmother says you're welcome to stay here as long as you want, even after I go back to managing the team with Carter."

Looking up from her work, Lilly studied her friend's face. Dark circles no longer rimmed Emily's eyes. Since her grandmother had sent a cook/nanny over, at least Emily was getting a little more sleep, but she looked sad at the mention of her husband's name. "Have you heard from Carter?"

"Received a letter today." Emily pulled an envelope from her pocket. "He is missing Katie and me terribly and thinks sending me here for the summer was a horrible idea."

"What do you think?"

Emily giggled. "I think if he had to listen to Katie's crying every night, he'd change his tune." She traced the angular lines of the address with her fingers. "But I don't know if I can stay here all summer without him."

"Think he might visit?"

Emily withdrew the letter from the envelope and smoothed it on the table before them. She pointed to a section toward the bottom. "This is the schedule for the Bloomer Girls team. It's packed so solid I don't see any times he could get away. If I thought Katie . . ." She let her words trail off.

"What? If you thought Katie could make the trip? Emily, are you thinking of traveling to see him?"

"That would be hard to do with a baby just a few months old. Not to mention the girls' games are all on the West Coast this year." Tears filled Emily's eyes. "But I miss him so much it hurts."

"I understand." The empty feeling that had become Lilly's constant companion tugged at her.

"You do, don't you?" Emily wiped her eyes. "I'm sorry. Here I am going on about missing Carter when at least I'll see him again."

"My loss doesn't make what you're feeling any less important, Emily. But I do understand loneliness in a new way now."

"Tell me."

"At first it was crushing. I didn't feel like I could breathe. It felt like it might swallow me whole, and I wanted it to. I didn't know if I could go on." Lilly closed the ledger in front of her.

"And now?"

"I still have days like that, but now when loneliness hits, it's more like a cloudburst than a devastating storm. People say things like, 'You should be over him by now.' Does that make sense to you? Like losing Ben was nothing more than a case of influenza."

Emily shook her head and squeezed Lilly's hand. "How do you deal with the loneliness now?"

"Levi." Lilly smiled. "He's my life. That's why I have to save money for a house. That's why I'd work until my fingers fell off. Levi will have what I never did—a place with roots to call his own."

"Excuse me, ladies." Rose, the new cook/nanny, stepped into the doorway with a tall, flowered hot chocolate pot on a tray. "Would you care for some hot chocolate?"

"Bless you, Rose. That would be lovely." Emily motioned for the girl to bring the service to the table. After Rose set the tray in place and departed, Emily reached for the handle of the skinny pot. "On the road, Carter and I like to have this before going to sleep as often as the hotels have it on hand. I can assure you that this is one beverage that can be made in a number of ways. Rose's is delicious."

"I haven't had hot chocolate since I lived in the Harts' house." The steam rose from Lilly's porcelain cup, and she inhaled the sweetness. "It's one of the few things I miss from there."

"Lilly, I know we were talking about Ben, and I don't want to sound disrespectful, but have you given any thought to marrying again someday?"

"Have you been talking to Marguerite?" Lilly took a drink from her cup. "Today Nick asked Levi and me to join him for church services, but it doesn't mean a thing. He's a friend and that's all, and I did not accept his invitation."

A slow smile spread across Emily's face. "I didn't say anything about Nick Perrin."

Lilly set down her cup. "Yes you did. You were talking about me marrying again."

"Exactly, and you're the one who brought his name into the conversation." Emily pushed back from the table and stood. "I find that interesting, don't you?"

"Wait a minute." Lilly took hold of Emily's arm. "We are not done talking about this. Where are you going?"

"To bed. I'd tell you to have sweet dreams, but I think Nick's got that covered."

❧

It was still hard for Marguerite to believe her little brother had grown into such a fine young man. The whole afternoon and evening had been spent laughing, playing games with the children, and catching up, but finally he announced he needed to head back to the city.

Trip gathered Mark's coat from the stand and passed it to him. "Do you have to leave so soon?"

Mark put on his coat. "Afraid so. After all, I'm a working man now."

"You found a position? Where?" Trip slipped his arm around his wife's waist.

Marguerite scowled at her brother. "And why did you keep your news until now?"

"So you couldn't ask me a thousand questions, my dear sister. I'm working for Claude Hart."

"Lilly's former father-in-law?" Marguerite's stomach flip-flopped at the thought of the man who'd been so cruel to her friend. "How could you? Don't you know what he's been trying to do to her? He's practically put her on the streets because she won't kowtow to his plans for Levi."

Jaw tense, Mark met her glare. "He offered your former lady's maid a chance to educate her son at the best schools, and she ran off with his grandson instead of accepting his offer."

Marguerite's blood pumped so hard she could hear her own heartbeat in her ears. "There's more to it than that and you know it!"

"Easy, honey." Trip kissed her temple. "Mark's been away, and he may not realize the whole story."

"Honestly, Marguerite, I didn't mean to upset you. I took the job because Mr. Hart is the best attorney in town. Until I take and pass the bar examination, I'll be little more than a glorified clerk, but after that, he said he has big plans for me." Mark reached for his hat. "I started last week, and I've already learned a great deal."

"Be careful of him," Trip warned. "He didn't amass that fortune by being kind."

Placing his hand on the doorknob, Mark sighed. "I want to learn everything I can from him. That's all."

Trip clapped him on the back. "Congratulations. I'm sure you'll do fine. Right, honey?"

Marguerite hesitated and then kissed Mark on the cheek. "I'm sure it feels like quite an honor to be hired by someone as powerful and influential as Mr. Hart. Come back and see us soon, okay?"

Mark dipped his head. "Of course. You'll be seeing me so often you'll get sick of me."

After he'd gone, Trip closed and locked the door. Marguerite blew out the lamps, and they climbed the stairs to their bedroom. As soon as they were inside, Marguerite began to unbutton the itchy collar of her dress. "I can't believe he took that job."

Trip turned to his wife and lifted her hand to his lips. "He didn't take the job to spite Lilly, you know."

Marguerite sighed. "I know, but Claude Hart is—"

"Is not here." Trip cupped her face with his hand.

The corners of her mouth lifted. "And your point?"

He ran his thumb over her cheek, making a fire spark inside her. After almost eleven years, how did this man send her heart fluttering with a single touch?

"My point is I've waited all day to get you to myself, and tonight I want to be the only man in here." He kissed her forehead. "And here." He placed his hand on her heart.

"What am I gonna do with you?"

He grinned and his dimples deepened. "I have a few ideas."

19

Nick awoke to the steady drumming of rain on the boardinghouse's roof. He rolled onto his back and moaned. He'd planned to get going on the rest of the trestle since their supplies would be arriving today.

Maybe this was a sweet spring shower. A sweet, *short*, spring shower. He pushed up on his elbow and saw a bright flash of lightning, followed by a thunderous boom. He flopped back on the pillow and groaned. Okay, maybe it wasn't a shower.

Avery Nash, the park manager, would be coming to see him now and would demand to know why things were not as far as they ought to be. The lack of supplies or the rain would never serve as an adequate excuse for the man. He wanted the coaster ready on opening day, and he'd settle for nothing else.

A knock on his door startled him. "Mr. Perrin?"

Nick recognized the nasally voice of Mrs. Whitson, the owner of the boardinghouse. He swung his feet to the floor and scrubbed his face with his hands. "I'll be right there, ma'am. Let me throw on a shirt."

She continued talking from the hallway. "I told your men that even if it's raining, they need to find somewhere to go. I will not have them underfoot all day—"

With his suspenders still hanging at his sides, Nick opened the door.

"And I certainly don't intend to cook for them." Her eyes grew wide. "Were you still asleep?"

Nick drew his fingers through his hair and smoothed it down. "Yes, ma'am. I guess without any sun to wake me, I overslept."

"Well, your men are downstairs, hanging around like lost hound dogs, so you'd better come tell them what you want them to do for the rest of the day before I shoo them off."

Clearing his sleep-scratchy throat, Nick slipped his arms into the suspenders and pulled them onto his shoulders. "Mrs. Whitson, I understand you don't want to cook for them, but do you really expect them to stay out of the house all day? It's raining. We won't be able to work outside."

"That's not my problem." Mrs. Whitson gave him a curt nod. "Today's the day I change sheets. You and your men need to be gone by eight. I won't have them ruining my schedule."

She didn't wait for a response but marched away like a general who'd delivered indisputable orders. Nick closed the door behind her and hurried to the washstand to shave. After lathering his thick-bristled brush, he slathered the soap over his face and neck. He pulled his skin taut and drew the razor along the length of his jaw.

"Nick, do you want me to take the fellas on over to the diner?" Sean asked from the other side of the door.

Nick jerked and the razor slipped. He pressed a towel to

the bead of red that formed on his cheek. "Yeah, go on ahead. Take some cards and the checkerboard too. We may be there all day."

Sean opened the door to the room and leaned inside. "Does yer Lilly know that?"

"*My* Lilly?" Nick chuckled. His Lilly wasn't going to appreciate a hoard of men hanging around her diner any more than Mrs. Whitson wanted them in her boardinghouse. Still, he knew she might grouse a bit, but she was too kind to send them away. "No, she doesn't know. Not yet. Do you want to tell her for me?"

"Sorry, boyo, friendship only goes so far, but I'll be wishin' ya well in that endeavor."

"Thanks, Sean. Thanks a bunch."

❧

All day?

Lilly dropped the heavy, cast-iron skillet onto the cookstove with a resounding bang. What was she going to do with a whole crew of men in her diner all day long?

She motioned to Eugenia to put the lard into the pan to fry two chickens for lunch. That along with gravy over biscuits would have to suffice. Already the men had consumed three pots of coffee and had eaten every sweet she had in the place, including the cobbler she'd intended for lunch. And it was only eleven o'clock. Thank goodness the rain seemed to be coming down a little less hard. Maybe the work crew would be out of here soon.

The worst of the morning had not been the raucous laughter or the incessant munching. The worst had been seeing Nick Perrin over and over. He'd been exceptionally gracious and thankful all morning. He'd even tried to pay her extra money for the hassle of having his men there. Lilly firmly refused his offer. It was storming outside. That wasn't his fault. What choice did they have but to hole up somewhere?

Levi scooted a stool across the wood floor, making a screeching sound that prickled her skin with gooseflesh. He climbed on top of the tall stool and stood with his hands on his hips. "I'm gonna help you now, Mama."

"Not from up there, you're not. Sit down right now, young man."

With an exaggerated sigh, Levi slid down onto the stool and swung his feet back and forth. "It's gonna be hard to cook from clear over here."

"You"—she tapped his nose—"are not cooking."

"But I'm big enough." He puffed out his chest. "'Sides, Mr. Nick told me to go help you for a while."

Lilly rolled her eyes. It figured. She sank her hands into the wash water in the sink. "Are you old enough to grab that dish towel and dry these plates for me?"

With a big grin, Levi hopped off the stool and snagged the towel. "Yes, ma'am, and when I'm done, I'm hunting night crawlers."

Lilly held out a plate to him. "Outside? In the rain?"

"You don't have any in here, do you?" His eyebrows scrunched together.

Laughter bubbled in Lilly's throat. "No, but I don't know if I want you outside right now either."

"But, Mama—"

"Let's do these dishes and then we'll see."

With great care, Levi laid the plate on the stool and rubbed it until it glistened. Then, using both hands, he carried it to the Hoosier cabinet's countertop. Back and forth he repeated his process, returning for more plates. Each time, Lilly blessed him with a smile of approval.

"Miss Lilly?" Eugenia held up a raw chicken leg in one hand and a thigh in the other. "Which one goes in first?"

"First you dredge them in that flour mixture. Remember? Then you put the thickest pieces in first because they take the longest to cook. Like we practiced last week." Lilly passed another plate to Levi. "Is the lard hot already?"

Eugenia dropped in the first piece, and grease splattered out. "Seems plenty hot."

"Lay the pieces in. Don't drop them." Lilly handed Levi another plate. "And remember, don't let the lard get too hot and burn the chicken to embers. If it starts smoking, you need to move the pan to a cooler spot on the stove."

Several minutes later, Levi placed another freshly dried plate on the pile and said, "Mama, maybe we could make something extra special tonight?"

After shaking her hands free of the suds, Lilly dried them on her apron. "Something like night-crawler pie?"

"Mama." Levi's nose wrinkled, and the tip of his tongue jutted out from his mouth. "Only fishes and birds eat worms."

"We eat fish and birds, though, so what's the difference?"

Biting his lip, Levi seemed to be giving her comment serious thought. A few seconds later, he shrugged. "Okay. I'll need to find a whole mess of them if you're gonna fill a pie." He whirled toward the back door.

After Lilly glanced out the kitchen window and saw the rain had stopped, she decided he could go on out. "Try not to turn into a mud puddle yourself." She closed the door behind him and remained there for several minutes to watch his search for night crawlers. She shook her head and smiled when he held up his first treasure for her to see.

Eugenia screamed.

Lilly spun. Flames leapt from the skillet and flashed into the air.

⊗

Who had screamed?

On his feet in seconds, Nick bolted around the counter and through the kitchen door. Acrid smoke poured from a fire on top of the cookstove and filled the room.

"No!" Lilly lurched forward, knocking an enameled water pitcher out of Eugenia's hands. The pitcher hit the stove with a tinny clang, and water splashed onto the hot stove top with a hiss, instantly producing a giant puff of steam that rolled toward the ceiling. Lilly jerked back and pushed Eugenia away from the fire.

The fire in the skillet climbed higher. Nick's insides knotted. He grabbed a larger cast-iron pot from a hook, raced to the stove, and set the heavy pan on top of the skillet fire. Smoke rolled out the sides, but the flames no longer licked at the room.

Lilly flipped the damper closed.

Nick wasted no time. He grabbed Lilly's arm, and she trembled beneath his grip. "Are you okay?"

She nodded.

"Are you sure?"

"Yes." She coughed.

Over his shoulder, he caught sight of his men gawking at the events that had transpired. "You boys, get the doors and windows open to air this place out. Eugenia—" He looked around for the addle-brained girl. "Find Levi."

"Levi?" Lilly coughed again. "Where is he?"

"She'll find him. Why don't you go sit down and catch your breath?"

"Absolutely not." The fire on the stove had nothing on the one in her eyes. "Look at this place. And where is Eugenia with my son?"

"He's right here, Miss Lilly." Eugenia pushed him through the back door.

Mud caked Levi's shoes and trousers, and a pail swung from his hand. "Why is it so smoky in here? I could only find five night crawlers. Will that be enough for a pie, Mama?"

❧

"Levi." Lilly pressed her hand to her aching forehead. "Take the worms outside, sweetheart, then come in and wash up."

"Why don't you go out with him and get a little fresh air? I think the sun has even peeked out now." Nick placed his hands on her shoulders and pointed her toward the door.

Lilly glanced around the wreck of a kitchen and leaned into his gentle touch. The ceiling was scorched. The whole place reeked. What was Mr. Thorton going to say now? And how many hours did she have ahead of her to put the place to rights?

"Whoooo-eeee."

Lilly turned to see Mark standing in the doorway to the kitchen, waving his hand in front of his face. She stepped away from Nick and her cheeks warmed.

"What happened here?" Mark stepped inside and examined the blackened streaks on the ceiling.

"There was a grease fire." Nick took her elbow and nudged her toward the door.

Mark looked at her. "Was anyone injured? Is Levi all right?"

"Everyone's fine, and Levi was outside playing when it happened." Lilly opened the door to the Hoosier cabinet and coughed.

Nick placed his hand on the cabinet door, barring her access. "What do you think you're doing?"

"It's past noon now. The men will be starving soon. I need to make them lunch." She glanced at the stove. "Unless you think they'd like some slightly overdone fried chicken."

"Lilly Hart, you'll do no such thing." He took her arm, led her to the back door, and opened it. "You're going outside for some fresh air like I said before. Mark, will you tell Sean to come in here?"

"Sure, if you tell me who Sean is."

"The big, muscled Irishman with red hair and matching beard."

"Will do. Looks like you have everything in hand here." He turned and disappeared into the dining room.

"Nick," she whispered, "isn't having Eugenia in my kitchen enough of a disaster for one day?"

He didn't respond, but gently shoved her out the door.

"Mama!" Levi broke free from Eugenia, who was helping him wash. He ran to her and threw his wet hands around her waist, leaving little handprints on the fabric. "Was it a big fire?"

Lilly smiled. Only a child would find wonder in a kitchen fire. She glanced at Eugenia and saw tears in her eyes. "Not too bad. Nothing a little elbow grease won't clean."

"I'm really sorry, Miss Lilly." Eugenia sat down on the back stoop. "I didn't mean to catch the chicken on fire."

"Accidents happen, Eugenia. No one means to do them. That's why they're accidents."

"What will Uncle Clyde say?"

"We'll do our best to get it all cleaned before he returns tomorrow from his trip." Lilly patted her shoulder. "Now, why don't you stay out here and keep an eye on Levi for me while I get lunch on for the men?"

"Don't you need my help?"

"Right now, you can help me the most by watching our worm catcher before he manages to collect enough night crawlers for a pie."

Inhaling another lungful of the tangy, lake-scented air, Lilly opened the diner's back door. Smoke immediately filled her nostrils.

When she entered the kitchen, she found Nick's friend Sean rummaging through the icebox.

"Excuse me." She looked from Sean to Nick. "What's going on?"

Pulling out of the icebox, Sean glanced at her. "Nick said you'd be needin' a bit o' help with lunch, and seeing as I'm feelin' peckish meself, I thought I'd make up a mess of bangers and mash for the lads."

"Bangers?" Lilly glanced at the icebox. This didn't sound promising. What did she have in there that she could make?

"Sausages," Nick translated as he breezed back into the room. "And mashed potatoes. It's the only thing he can make, but he does a great job at it."

"Now that's not true. I do a fair job with swimmers and bricks too."

Lilly raised her eyebrows.

Nick laughed. "Fish and slab-cut fried potatoes."

"Sorry, I don't have any fish right now."

"Then you do have sausages?" Nick smiled when she nodded. "Good. Are they in the icebox?"

"Nick, I can make lunch."

"No need, lassie." Sean held up his hand. "I can find them. You've had enough excitement for one day. Why don't you rest a bit?"

Nick swept his arm toward the door. "You heard the man. I

already had the men take a few tables outside, but the dining room is airing out nicely."

Lilly sighed. At least Sean's bangers and mash had to be better than Eugenia's oatmeal or charred chicken. And she did need to make a list of what they'd need to do to get the diner back in order. After grabbing a tablet and pencil, she sat down at a table near an open window.

Nick turned a chair around and straddled it. "Better put repainting the ceiling on that list."

"You don't think it'll wash?"

"Paint's curled. Needs to be scraped and repainted."

She rubbed her burning eyes. "Mr. Thorton is really not gonna be happy with me now."

"He's been unhappy?" Nick's eyes narrowed.

"Never mind." Lilly jotted "repaint the ceiling" on her list. "The curtains will need to be taken down, washed, and rehung. Can't get the smoke smell out of fabrics without a good scrubbing."

Nick covered her hand, stilling the pencil. "What's going on with Mr. Thorton?"

"I can handle it."

"Lilly."

She sighed. "Apparently, my former father-in-law suggested to Mr. Thorton that it would be in his best interest to encourage me to let my in-laws take Levi for regular visits."

"Alone?"

"Well, they certainly don't want to see me." She glanced down at where his hand still held her wrist.

He let it slide away. "What are you going to do?"

"I told Mr. Thorton that I would take him over there for visits, but I wouldn't leave him with them. I don't trust them not to say things against me to Levi or even try to keep him from me. They've tried to take him twice now already."

"What did Mr. Thorton say?"

"He wasn't happy." She glanced around the room. The only person who seemed to know they were still there was Mark. She turned to Nick. Concern lay etched in his cobalt-blue eyes. "He said that although I'm a wonderful cook, it's easier to hire a new cook than it is to deal with the kind of fallout a man like Claude Hart can cause. He said I was skating on thin ice, and not to get too comfortable here after all." She surveyed the smoke-fogged dining room. "Now look at this place. I fear I may be more trouble than I'm worth."

Another cough tickled her throat, and she pressed her fist to her lips. Would her lungs be filled with smoke for a week?

Nick went to the counter and poured Lilly a glass of water. After delivering it to the table, he waited to speak until after she took a drink. "It was his niece who caused the fire. You shouldn't take the blame. Maybe I need to remind him of that."

"Please don't say anything." Lilly set the glass on the table and smiled at him. "But I am thankful for the offer."

20

"You have something to report?"

Mark Westing settled in a leather chair across from his new employer, Claude Hart, and smiled at the elderly attorney's question. Once Mark shared what he'd witnessed, he'd become the powerful man's new favorite person. After all, that's why he'd been hired—to find useful information on the Westings' former maid that would make her more cooperative. The venture would help them both. Mr. Hart would get the information he needed, and Mark would secure a position as an associate with Claude Hart and be well on his way to a most lucrative future.

Marguerite would be furious to know what he was doing, but, like Lilly Hart, she'd never grasped the invisible line between servants and the wealthy—the one that should never be crossed. Lilly should have known better than to defy Mr. Hart, and her son would benefit from an excellent education.

"I hope this is important enough for you to come to my

home on a Saturday morning. Could it not have waited until Monday?"

"I'll let you be the judge of that." Mark tugged on his vest. "It's as you feared. Your daughter-in-law is definitely sweet on the roller coaster builder."

Mr. Hart steepled his fingers. "And what about his feelings toward her?"

Needing to rid his nostrils of the diner's stench, Mark took a deep breath. The air in Claude Hart's office smelled of expensive cigars. Mark crossed one ankle over his knee and leaned back in the chair. "Nick Perrin's clearly smitten."

"Fool." Mr. Hart slammed his fist on the desk. "What power does she have over men?"

The harsh words kicked at Mark's conscience. "Sir, I've never known our former maid to be *that* kind of woman."

Mr. Hart's brows drew close. "Tell me what's going on. I'll be the judge."

"I arrived immediately after there'd been a fire in the kitchen. Nick Perrin stepped in and started barking orders like he owned the place." Mark uncrossed his leg and leaned forward.

"That hardly sounds like he's smitten."

"You'd have to see him. It's the way he coddles her and treats her like a queen. And he even got one of his men to cook lunch so she could have a break." Mark coughed. "Sorry. It was smoky in the diner. And all this happened on the heels of their day at the zoo together."

"Zoo?"

"From what my sister told me when I dropped by, Perrin arranged a private showing at Lake Manawa's zoo. Your grandson said Lilly and Nick rode a camel together. I think the only person who doesn't realize this has taken a romantic turn is Lilly herself."

Mr. Hart frowned. "This is unsettling news."

"Sir, if you don't mind me asking, why are you so bothered by this? Your son has been gone long enough for the mourning period to be over. And Lilly has made it clear she has no intention of moving back in with you. I know you still feel responsible for her, but if she marries Nick Perrin, she'll be out of your hair."

Peering over the top of his reading spectacles, Mr. Hart studied Mark. "If Lilly falls in love with this man, she'll move away with him. If that happens, she'll take my grandson with her. I know I may not show it well, but I love my grandson, and he's all I have left of my son. My wife barely survived losing our Ben, and she'd never recover if Levi were ripped from her as well." His hands balled into fists. "I cannot let that happen."

"How could you possibly stop her?"

"How indeed?" Mr. Hart stood and paced behind his desk. "Lilly is a shrewd woman. She'd catch on too easily if I interfere directly. I have to make her see Nick Perrin isn't the man for her."

"And how do you propose we do that?"

"We?" Mr. Hart offered Mark a nod of approval. "I like how you think, Mr. Westing. Keep this up. I've got big plans for you, son." He drew his hand along the length of his well-groomed, white beard. "I believe if you put your mind to it, you'll find all sorts of ways to keep her and Mr. Perrin apart." Mr. Hart jotted a note on a piece of paper and folded it in half. After addressing it, he handed it to Mark. "Now, I need you to deliver this to the man I've listed and wait for a reply."

"What is it?"

With a flick of his wrist, he dismissed Mark. "The less you know, the better."

"Could I interest you in a chicken leg, well done?"

Lilly turned to see Nick holding up a blackened piece of meat with a pair of tongs. When she'd arrived this morning, he was already there. The ceiling had been scraped free of all blackened signs of yesterday's smoke, a fire roared in the oven, and he'd even made a pot of coffee. Try as she might, she couldn't shoo him away. "I told you to leave that."

"And I told you I would do it." Nick put the leg with the other charred remains and picked up the skillet. "I'll dump this out in the grass somewhere. Some raccoon will be delighted."

"I don't think we should be that unkind—even to the raccoons."

"But they ate Eugenia's oatmeal." With a chuckle, Nick nudged the back door open with the toe of his boot. "I'll be right back." By the time he returned a few minutes later, Lilly had a bowl on the counter with flour measured into it.

"What are you doing?" He thumped his hand on the counter in front of her.

"Making pancakes. Slowly. I'm still a little stiff from Eugenia's and my cleaning jag yesterday."

Nick carried a stool to the center of the room. It wobbled a bit when he set it down, and he frowned at the piece of furniture, but when he glanced at her, a crooked smile lit his face. "This is your throne. You can sit here all morning and rule your loyal subjects, but you can't help them."

"In case you haven't noticed, I have only one loyal subject, and she is decidedly late. At this rate, your breakfast will be more like lunch. I know you're behind at the site, so you need to get an early start." Lilly filled a cup of water from the sink and took a long drink. "I'll abdicate the throne if you don't mind."

He cupped her elbow and led her to the stool. "It is true the Lady Eugenia seems to have misplaced her hourglass, but I have my trusty kitchen weapon at hand." He lifted a wooden spoon in the air. "I will mix these pancakes myself."

"Nick, really, it's sweet of you to offer, but I can do this."

"And probably with your eyes closed. But indulge me. It'll be fun." He set the spoon beside the bowl. "What do I add next?"

She sighed. "Baking powder."

"How much?"

"Three good-sized tablespoons."

Nick dipped a spoon into the Calumet baking powder tin and pulled out a heaping tablespoonful. "How's this?"

"Shake a little off. Too much. Try again." She watched him refill the spoon. "That looks pretty good. After you put that in, add a little salt and some sugar."

"A little salt? Would you care to be more specific?"

"Let's go with three teaspoons of salt and three tablespoons of sugar. That ought to do it."

After checking with Lilly to make sure he had the correct spoons in his hands, Nick deposited the two ingredients into the bowl with a flourish and grinned at Lilly.

"Don't go getting cocky yet. Now make a well in the center of the flour mixture."

Nick carved out a perfect half circle. "Okay. Done."

"See that coffee cup on the Hoosier cabinet? Fill that with milk three times and then add a few splashes more."

"Splashes? How much is a splash?" Nick retrieved the jar of milk from the icebox. "I'm beginning to feel sorry for Eugenia."

Lilly dipped her fingers into her glass and flicked the water in Nick's direction.

He jumped back. "What are you doing?"

"Teaching you about splashes." She suppressed a smile when he shot her a mock glare. "Remember, you're the one who wouldn't let me mix it. You know, I'm gonna have to give added effort to teaching Eugenia to cook. If I do lose my job here, she's the one who'll be cooking for your men all the time. But that means they may have to endure a few Eugenia fiascos in the process."

Nick moaned and wiped his flour-covered hands on the back of his dark trousers. He left handprints. Lilly stifled a laugh.

"What's so funny?"

"Nothing." Her cheeks flushed hot. She couldn't exactly tell him where the handprints were located.

He frowned. "Do I need to add anything else?"

"Three eggs and a little of the melted butter in that tin on the stove."

"I don't suppose you know how much 'a little' is."

Lilly shrugged. "Enough to butter a dozen biscuits? Let me show you."

"No." Nick retrieved the tin can and held it in his hand. "I can do this. Tell me how much."

"I tip the can five times." She moved off her stool to supervise the mixing. "Then you need to beat the whole mixture until it's smooth. Not too long or they'll get tough, but long enough so there aren't any lumps of flour."

He looked down at her and chuckled. "You know, you make building a roller coaster seem simple."

"We could trade jobs for a day if you like."

Before he could answer, the back door swung open. Like

168

a whirlwind, Eugenia flew inside with her hat askew and her face flushed. "I'm ever so sorry. I missed the streetcar and had to catch another ride." She plucked a leaf from her hair. "Mr. Billett, the milkman, spotted me and let me ride with him."

Lilly turned her attention to Eugenia and smiled. "Please make every effort to be on time, especially now when we have so much to catch up on."

Tears filled the girl's eyes. "I know, and I am truly, abundantly sorry. Here you are at the crack of dawn, and I'm sleeping the morning away. Maybe I should move in with you so I can get here on time to help you."

"Sounds like a plan to me." Nick quirked a grin that Lilly would have happily slapped off his handsome face. How could he encourage Eugenia, even in jest?

"While it is kind of you to offer, Eugenia, it won't be necessary." She looked at Nick. "Nick, we'll discuss this more later. When we're alone."

Nick grinned again. "Is that a promise?"

Lilly's cheeks flamed. What was she going to do with him?

⌘

The next half hour was a flurry of activity. Eugenia poured the pancakes, and Nick had never seen such an assortment of shapes and sizes. Still, they'd be edible since he'd made them under Lilly's tutelage, and for that he was glad.

Lilly layered slabs of ham in a skillet, made coffee, and set the table all without a hiccup. By the time Eugenia had created a lopsided stack of pancakes, the ham was heated. Nick scooped up Eugenia's creations and carried them to the men's table, and Lilly followed with the plate of ham.

The comments began as soon as Lilly returned to the

kitchen. Lanky Milt displayed his pancake. "What continent do you think this looks like?"

"China." Archie cocked his head to the side. "No, maybe Africa. No, how about Argentina."

"Argentina isn't a continent." Frank Ward grabbed another three pancakes for his plate.

"Look at this one." Always the comedian, Forest held up a clown-shaped flapjack beside his face. "Who do you think is more handsome?"

The comments went on for several minutes between the crew members. Would they survive Eugenia's cooking? What if Lilly planned to have her cook more often now? Maybe they could hint enough that she'd curtail that idea. Thankfully, Lilly and Eugenia were in the kitchen and couldn't hear their jesting.

Finally, he'd had enough. He hit the end of his knife on the table to get their attention. "I don't want to hear another word about Eugenia's cooking. She and Lilly will do their best. In fact"—he speared a piece of ham—"I think they are going to need some extra help today because of yesterday's fire. Percy, I'm going to assign you to help out at mealtime. The kitchen ceiling needs to be painted, and they may need some help scrubbing the pan after that burnt chicken."

Percy gaped at Nick. "Me? Why me?"

"First of all, you're the youngest man here, so they all have more seniority on the job. Second, you're good at following directions and pitching in wherever necessary." Nick took a swig of coffee. "That's exactly the kind of help Mrs. Hart needs."

"But Mrs. Hart is a she."

"Observant lad, aren't ya?" Sean teased.

Percy's cheeks grew cherry red. "But it's women's work to make pancakes."

Nick chuckled. "Well, not all the time. I made the ones you're eating. Eugenia only poured them on the griddle. Besides, you're still working for me, and I'm having you help out here for just one day. That won't be a problem, will it?"

"No, sir." Percy dropped his gaze to his syrup-drenched pancakes and shoved a bite around on his plate.

Forest elbowed him in the side. "And I bet you'll look good in an apron."

The whole crew roared with laughter. Nick glared at them and prayed he hadn't made a mistake concerning assigning the boy to the kitchen.

21

Lilly plopped a cabbage on the counter. "This vegetable is your best friend."

Eugenia lifted her eyebrows. "A cabbage? I might be desperate for companionship, but not that desperate."

Laughing, Lilly snagged a knife from the drawer. "You're gonna make something the men will love, and it's easy."

"Easy for you, maybe impossible for me."

"Once they taste your corned beef and cabbage, you'll be listening to their praises."

"If you say so." Eugenia walked to the pantry shelf and returned with a jar of preserved corn.

Lilly chopped the cabbage in half. "What is that for?"

"Corned beef."

"Oh, Eugenia." Lilly shook her head and stifled a giggle. "You don't need corn for this."

"Then why do they call it 'corned' beef?"

"I have no idea." Lilly shrugged, chuckling. "Why don't you get the two beef briskets out? I've been brining them for over a week now. They're in a crock in the icebox on the bottom shelf."

After locating the crock, Eugenia set it on the counter. "What's floating in this?"

"Different spices I used in the brine." Lilly used her knife to point to the large pot hanging on a hook. "Get that down, then rinse the beef and set it in the pot."

Eugenia complied. "Now what?"

Lilly wiped her hands on her apron. "Now you are really gonna cook. Get the tin that says Allspice and the one that says Bay Leaves."

"You're going to let me put the spices in?"

"It's now or never."

Once they had the corned beef and cabbage on the stove and simmering, Lilly ventured outside to find Levi.

He sat on his haunches, studying something in the grassy area.

"Levi, honey, let's go for a walk."

"Mama, come see this."

Lilly smoothed the front of her dress. "If we hurry, we can see how Mr. Nick is coming along with the supplies they delivered yesterday."

"Oh, all right." Levi sighed and stood. He walked backward, apparently not wanting to take his eyes off his animal friend. Finally, he turned and skipped to her.

Lilly hugged him. "What was in there?"

"A giant black kitty. It was acting silly." Levi held out his hands about a foot and a half apart. "It was this big and had a white stripe too." With his hand, he drew an imaginary stripe from his head to his bottom.

She gasped. A familiar stench made her scrunch her nose.

"Here he comes." Levi pointed toward the bush.

"Levi, get inside now!"

"But—"

She pushed him toward the door as a skunk emerged from the bushes and turned toward her. Before she could raise its ire, she slipped inside the door to the diner behind her son and thanked God for sparing them both.

"Miss Lilly, I thought you were going for a walk." Eugenia set down the plate she was drying.

"There is a skunk outside. I think it's best if we all stay in here for a while. It's rare for a skunk to come out in the daylight."

"But, Mama, he was funny. He walked real silly. All wobbly-like." Levi demonstrated the uneven gait as he crossed the room, then pressed his nose to the front window of the diner. "See?"

Lilly joined her son and witnessed the skunk's strange behavior for herself. She glanced at Eugenia, but the girl gave no indication she understood that this most likely meant the animal was diseased with rabies or distemper. They needed to get someone to come take care of it before anyone was hurt. She didn't want to risk leaving to do that, but what if Nick or one of his men happened upon it and was bitten?

Sinking into a chair, Lilly sighed. This was ridiculous. They were being held hostage by a skunk. What else could she do? If she found Nick, he might be able to take care of the skunk, but what did he know about rabid animals? Besides, he needed every minute to work on the roller coaster if it was going to be done in time for the grand opening.

Lilly stood and placed a hand on the door. Nick wasn't the only man around. What about Mr. Tallman at the zoo? He understood animals, he was within running distance, and he'd know what to do.

Eugenia touched Lilly's arm. "Where are you going?"

"To find Mr. Tallman."

"Miss Lilly, you mustn't go out there. What if you get sprayed?"

Levi whirled around. "I'll go, Mama. I'm the fastest, and Stinky knows me."

"Stinky?" Lilly shook her head. "Please, honey, don't get attached to him. And I need you to stay in here and keep Eugenia company." She patted Eugenia's hand. "I'll run to the zoo, but if I see the skunk, I won't move a muscle. I'll be fine."

"I should go." Eugenia straightened her shoulders. "After yesterday's fire—"

"Yesterday wasn't all your fault. I should've been watching, and I should've told you not to use water on a grease fire."

"Still, let me go get Mr. Tallman. You'll do a better job keeping Levi from going outside. With my luck, I'd sneeze and he'd be out the door." Eugenia glanced at Levi, whose eyes were fixed on his mother. "Right, Levi?"

He gave them an impish grin.

Eugenia had a point, and they didn't have a lot of time to waste. Nick and his men would be arriving within the hour. "Oh, all right. Run like the dickens, but remember what I said to do if you see the skunk?"

"Freeze in place."

"Exactly."

Levi crossed his heart. "And I'll keep an eye on Stinky for you."

"Thanks, Levi." Eugenia fastened her linen cape about her neck.

Easing the door open, Lilly said a prayer as Eugenia slipped outside. From the window, Lilly could see the skunk hadn't noticed their movement. She exhaled slowly, releasing the breath she'd been holding.

So far, so good.

⁂

"Let's go over this one more time." Nick placed a finger on the drawing in front of him. "If you're going to build roller coasters, you need to know the proper names."

"Why?" Percy's voice cracked, betraying his young age. "The other fellas won't let me do anything but haul boards and nails."

Nick glanced at Percy, whose yellow hair stuck from beneath his wide-brimmed hat like a scarecrow. He had a soft place in his heart for the boy. When he'd first found Percy, he was stealing raw potatoes from a store. After learning he had no family, Nick guessed the hunger in the young man's eyes matched the hunger in his belly and had secured a job for him, much like Sean had done for Nick years ago. "You're paying your dues, Percy. They'll let you do more when they feel you've earned it. Now, let's see if you can remember the parts of the trestle bent."

Percy sighed. "A bent has vertical posts. We're setting our vertical posts in concrete."

"Good." Nick pointed to the horizontal boards set at intervals on the bent. "And what are these called?"

"Those are sills, and this one at the top is called the cap. It's the largest and bears the most weight. It's supported by the rest of the trestle bent."

Nick nodded in approval. "I'm impressed, Percy. So what are these diagonal boards?"

"Braces?"

"Yes, but what kind?"

"Does it make a difference?"

"Not if you're always going to be hauling boards." Nick drew his finger along the diagonal line. "It's a sway brace. So after the bents are up, what do you connect them with?"

Percy glanced at the other workers who'd already erected two trestle bents and were crisscrossing boards between them. "Extra sway braces?"

Nick nodded. "They make the trestle more stable. We add additional braces where necessary. You're a fast learner, Percy. Keep up the hard work." He pulled out his pocket watch and checked the time. "Now, you'd better hustle on over to the diner to help Mrs. Hart and Miss Eugenia."

Percy moaned. "Do I have to?"

"None of that. Doing what needs to be done is what makes you a man. They may have some heavy lifting that requires your strength." He clapped a hand on Percy's shoulder. "Tell them we'll be along shortly."

After watching the gangly youth trot off, Nick turned his attention to the rest of his crew. The men had worked hard despite the mud, and the work had gone well this morning. While some men worked on the engine house, others tackled the roller coaster structure itself. By the end of the week, they'd have most of the trestle bents up and braced if they continued at this rate. Then they'd be able to start adding the decking and rails. For the first time in days, he dared hope they might make the deadline.

"Nick, how tall is this next trestle supposed to be?" Milt Hawkins called from the work site.

Picking up his plans, Nick shielded his eyes from the sun and glanced from their location to his paper. "Forty-two feet. That one is still part of the coaster's highest point."

He watched Milt remeasure the section before giving Al

the signal to hoist the top half of the trestle structure into the air using the small, steam-operated building site crane. Like monkeys, Forest and Archie swung into place on the horizontal beams, took hold of the section, and began securing it. His stomach wadded in a ball. They made it look so easy, but Nick knew that wasn't the case. One wrong move, one slip, could mean a fall where a man could be seriously injured. He took safety seriously on his site, but that didn't mean accidents couldn't happen, and he felt guilty for pushing them. Working quickly could make a man careless.

For the second time that day, he said a prayer for the men and for himself. *Father, please don't let my pride make anyone else fall.*

❧

Pacing from window to window in the front of the diner, Lilly kept her eye on the skunk. He continued his inebriated walk not far from the establishment, but there was still no sign of Eugenia.

Lilly went to the back door and cracked it open. Hearing voices, she paused. *Lord, please don't let Eugenia get sprayed by the skunk. That poor girl has enough strikes against her already. And besides, I'd have to be in the kitchen with her stinking up the place for days.*

"Ahhh!" The shout was followed by a familiar stench wafting through the crack in the door.

Lilly closed the door and moaned. *Lord, was it because I forgot to say 'amen'?*

But where was the skunk? She hadn't seen anything.

"Levi, where's the skunk now?" she called into the dining room.

"Stinky went around the side."

The back door swung open, and Eugenia hurried inside with her nose plugged. Mr. Tallman followed, but neither of them reeked of skunk spray.

Lilly frowned. "I heard someone yell, but if you didn't get sprayed, then who did?"

"I heard it too." Mr. Tallman put his hand on the knob. "Smelled it even more. Glad it wasn't you, Mrs. Hart. You ladies stay here. I'll find out who it was and take care of the skunk. If what Miss Eugenia said is true, it's a dangerous animal. Probably distemper."

22

"Mrs. Hart, can you come out here?"

Lilly turned from the icebox in time to see the look of amusement on Mr. Tallman's face. She set a jar of pickles on the counter, called to Eugenia to finish setting the table for lunch, and followed him outdoors.

"Oh, Percy!" Lilly covered her mouth and nose with her hand. Her heart ached for him. She'd grown fond of the boy who was trying so hard to be a man. "You got sprayed?"

Percy looked up from his seat on one of the Midway's park benches. "I was coming to help you ladies in the kitchen. Nick said I had to, and the stinkin' skunk got me."

"Did he spray you directly? Are your eyes burning?"

"No, ma'am. I saw him raise his tail, and I dove behind a bush. Still got a little on me, I guess."

Mr. Tallman laughed. "'Fraid so, son."

"I'll just go wash in the lake, Mrs. Hart." Percy stood. "I'll be back to help you shortly."

Lilly held up her hand. "I'm afraid bathing in the lake will

180

do no good. You need to get out of those smelly clothes right away. Mr. Tallman, if you'll set up the washtub, I'll have Eugenia help me get several jars of tomato juice from inside."

"There's no way I'm going to take a bath out here in front of God and everybody." Percy's eyes, a soft pecan brown, grew as wide as gingersnaps. "Wait a minute. Did you say tomato juice?"

"It cuts the stench, son." Mr. Tallman picked up the shotgun he'd used to take care of the skunk and leaned it against the bench.

"Do I look like I'm ready for the soup pot?"

"Mrs. Hart, I'll take the boy on back to my place so he'll have some privacy. You can have one of the men bring over the tomato juice and a new set of clothes for the boy."

Percy bolted up. "No! You can't tell them. They'll rib me for months about getting sprayed."

Lilly's head began to throb from the stench. "Nick will want to know, and your clothes will have to be burned."

"But I ain't got but one other set of work clothes. If he hadn't made me come here—"

"Now, son, let's get you washed, and we'll worry about all that later." Motioning to the paved walkway with the stock of the gun, Mr. Tallman indicated it was time to leave. He gave Lilly a nod and followed behind the slumping youth.

Lilly hurried inside to find tomato juice before the men arrived. She slid the stool across the wood floor, wincing when it screeched. She climbed onto the stool and once again noticed it wobbled a bit. One leg must be shorter than the other three. She needed to get that repaired.

Carefully, she stood. She reached for the first jar and tucked it in the crook of her arm, then reached for a second. They'd need at least four quarts, perhaps even five or six. Thank goodness Mr. Thorton had an ample supply of preserved goods. Unfortunately, she'd have to make several trips up and down the stool to secure enough jars without dropping any.

"What are you doing up there?"

Lilly startled at the sound of Nick's voice. The stool wobbled. She grabbed for the shelf to steady herself, then glared at him. "You nearly made me fall."

"Which wouldn't have happened if you weren't climbing around like a monkey." He crossed the kitchen, took the jars from her arms, and set them on the counter. Then he returned and held out his hand to assist her down. "I know Levi calls you Chipmunk Mama, but that doesn't mean you need to live up to the name every time I turn around."

She turned back to the shelf. "I still need four more jars of tomato juice."

"What for? Even my men can't use that much at one time."

"You'd be surprised." She tucked another jar in the crook of her arm.

"I'll get them." Instead of waiting for her answer, he grabbed her waist and lifted her to the ground.

"Nick!" Her face flushed hot.

Giving her a devilish smile, he stood on his tiptoes, lifted another three quarts from the shelf, and set the jars with the others. "So, what are you making with all these?"

"A bath."

Nick's eyebrows peaked. "Excuse me?"

With a laugh, Lilly pointed to an empty crate.

Nick snagged it and began filling it with the jars. "A bath? Wait a minute, did someone get sprayed by a skunk? I smelled it when we arrived. And where's Percy? He should have been helping you get these down. Sometimes I'm not so sure about that boy."

Tapping the toe of her shoe, Lilly waited for Nick to put the pieces together. If he did so on his own, she wouldn't be betraying Percy's confidence.

He set the last jar in the crate and turned to her. "*He* got sprayed?" Laughter shook his chest.

"Your reaction is exactly why Percy didn't want you or your men to know."

"Does he honestly think he can hide it? Tomato juice doesn't work that well." Nick sucked his cheeks, apparently trying to stop his grinning, but another chortle escaped. "So where is the poor kid?"

"The skunk was sick. I had Eugenia fetch Mr. Tallman to take care of it, and he took poor Percy back to his place for a bath. He's there waiting for the tomato juice. So if you'd kindly hand me the crate, I'll deliver it."

"You?" Nick hefted the crate in his arms.

"Yes, and you'll need to fetch Percy another set of clothes. Mr. Tallman plans to burn what he was wearing." Lilly tried to tug the crate from Nick. "Percy is concerned about his clothes. He says he has only one other set."

Nick pulled the crate away, and the jars rattled inside. "I'll take care of the clothes, and I'll deliver these. The boy's humiliation is bad enough without a lady seeing him naked."

"I—I—I had no intention of allowing that to happen," Lilly sputtered.

Turning toward the door, Nick grinned. "Maybe you should go get a drink. You look a little flushed."

After the door banged shut behind him, Lilly patted her burning cheeks. For that, she wasn't even going to keep a plate warm for Nick.

She rolled her eyes. Well, maybe she should if he was taking care of Percy.

༄

Every man was hard at work by the time Nick arrived back at the roller coaster site with Percy. He patted his full stomach. Lilly had kept a plate warm for both him and Percy, and to his surprise, Eugenia's corned beef had gone beyond palatable to downright tasty. Maybe Lilly would be able to teach her to cook after all.

"Now, don't let the men get to you, Percy. Sure, they'll give you a hard time, but it will only last until something else comes along for them to joke about."

Percy shot him a glare.

Not since Nick had delivered the tomato juice had the young man said a word to him. Obviously, Percy felt his boss was somehow to blame for this, but how had this become Nick's fault? "You don't smell nearly as bad as before." Nick clapped him on the shoulder. "Besides, it'll wear off in a couple of days."

Side by side, they walked the rest of the way until they met up with the others.

"Whoooo-eeee!" Forest pinched his nose shut. "Percy, you smell like a skunk dipped in ketchup."

"Fellas, leave him be." Nick pointed to the engine house. "Percy, why don't you work with Archie and Frank today?"

"You're going to make them be inside with him?" Forest snickered.

Nick couldn't keep the corners of his mouth from curling upward. "On second thought, maybe you should continue your regular job out here."

"Hauling boards?" Percy's chest heaved, and he shot Nick another heated glare.

"Yes, Percy. That's one part of your job." He met the young

184

man's hard gaze and held it until Percy looked away. What was wrong with the boy? Nick turned to the others. "Let's get back to work, fellas, and see if we can get as much done this afternoon as we did this morning."

After Nick made sure things were well under way, he took off his jacket and rolled up his sleeves. Another set of hands—hardworking hands—would help this project out the most right now, and his name was the one on the line if this coaster failed.

And with things finally looking more encouraging with Lilly, the last thing he wanted was to let her see she couldn't count on him.

⤬

How hard could it be to put a roast in the oven?

As soon as Eugenia had finally completed the task, Lilly made an excuse to get out of the diner for a while. If she stayed, she feared she might end up using a cast-iron skillet as a weapon. So much for the morning's progress.

Why was she being so intolerant? Eugenia was improving, and she should give her credit for doing so. *Lord, help my words to be filled with kindness and grace toward Eugenia. Help me remember to be patient with her just as You are patient with me.*

Lilly found Levi outside playing with a toad. After he'd washed, the two of them headed for Marguerite's. Levi needed some playmates, and she could use her friend's good cheer.

Levi skipped beside her, and Lilly drank in the sunshine. Spring filled the air with a sense of hope. Every bud ached to burst forth, but only the bravest had done so already. A few more warm days like this, and Lake Manawa would begin to sport its floral finery.

She and Levi found Marguerite at the beach near the Grand Plaza, lounging in a deck chair on the boardwalk. She flipped a page in her copy of *The Virginian*, a Wild West story by Owen Wister, while Tate and Faith used a stick to put windows in their sand castle on the beach.

"Lilly." Marguerite motioned to another chair. "What a pleasant surprise."

After removing Levi's shoes and socks, Lilly set him free to join his friends, then sat on the chair beside Marguerite. She drew in a deep breath of fresh, unskunk-scented air and released it slowly.

"What's going on?"

"All Eugenia had to do was brown the roast and peel a bunch of carrots and potatoes, but the process took so long, I'm afraid the roast might not be tender by the time the men arrive for supper tonight. I asked her why she was taking a month of Sundays to peel the potatoes, and do you know what she told me?"

"What?"

"That she didn't want to poke a potato in its eye." Lilly moaned. "Sometimes watching Eugenia learn is downright painful."

Marguerite set her book aside. "Is she that bad in the kitchen?"

"Worse, but she has such a good heart. Yesterday she started a fire. Didn't Mark tell you?"

Marguerite shook her head.

"It's not Eugenia's fault. Her mother never taught her any of this, and she's trying so hard to learn. I keep praying for more patience."

"You?" Marguerite adjusted her wide-brimmed hat with a grin.

"I know. You'd think growing up with you would have taught me all the patience I'd ever need."

Marguerite turned to her. "I'm glad you stopped by. I was thinking of you."

"Why?" Lilly leaned back in the chair and lifted her feet.

"The sand castles." She glanced at the shore where the children continued building their structure and sat on the edge of her chair. "Remember when your mama took us swimming and we made one? You said someday you'd have a home as fancy as the one we made that day."

Lilly squeezed Marguerite's hand in thanks for her ministrations. "I will have that home, but I doubt it will have any turrets."

"Maybe Nick likes turrets." Marguerite leaned back in the deck chair and cracked one eye open toward Lilly.

"Marguerite Andrews, you are incorrigible."

Marguerite sighed. "I prefer to think of it as unsinkable."

Lilly rolled her eyes. "You would. Before you get to thinking your life is all peaches and cream, Mrs. Unsinkable, did I mention who Eugenia has her eye on?"

"Please don't say it's—"

"Your sweet little brother. Only he's not so little anymore."

"And he's never been all that sweet." They both laughed. "I'm so glad to see he's outgrown his impetuous nature."

"Gives me hope." Lilly sighed. "If he could give up his critters and footraces to become a respectable attorney, maybe there's hope for my Levi."

"Your Levi will be as wonderful as his daddy was." Marguerite turned her head toward Lilly. "Speaking of my brother Mark, Trip and I are having a welcome-home picnic in his honor tomorrow. I've already asked Emily, and I want you and Levi to come too."

"I'd love to, but I'm afraid I'll have to decline. I asked Eugenia to attend church services with me and told her we'd grab a bite to eat afterward."

"Bring her along."

Lilly lifted her brows. "Some welcome home for Mark."

"It would serve him right. Payback for all the trouble he was growing up." Marguerite giggled. "I think it'll make the day all the more fun."

"I believe you have an incurable evil streak."

"Really? I hadn't noticed." She laughed again. "So you'll come?"

"What should I bring?"

With a flick of her wrist, Marguerite dismissed the thought. "Nothing. This time you'll have to suffer through my cooking."

"So you want me to bring bicarbonate of soda?"

"And you call me a friend."

"Just speaking the truth in love." Lilly smiled as the words came out of her mouth. Ben used to make jokes about "speaking the truth in love," and even in the midst of intense discussions, it made her smile every time.

Glancing at the beach, Lilly spotted Levi again. The tip of his tongue protruded from his mouth as he concentrated on his sand creation. It didn't look like a castle. Curious, Lilly stood. She took the steps down from the boardwalk, and her shoes sank in the shifting sand of the beach. As she drew closer, a smile tugged at the corners of her mouth. Levi's creation was the clear beginnings of a roller coaster. Her chest warmed. Nick would like seeing this.

Nick.

Only a minute ago she'd been thinking about Ben and how much her son was like him. Guilt rubbed another raw spot on her heart, and she crossed her arms over her chest. Her eyes misted as she looked out over the choppy lake. How had Nick Perrin crept into the lives of her and her son and made them feel like he belonged there?

But he didn't belong there. And she'd actually encouraged the man in the last two days. What was she doing? She wasn't ready to care about anyone.

She glanced at her son's sand coaster. For his sake, she needed to put some distance between the two of them and Nick. She needed to think. If it was God's will, maybe Nick would be too busy to notice her efforts to push him away.

But what would she do if it wasn't God's will?

23

After Saturday's extra-long workday, Nick's muscles ached. The comfort of the feather ticking and the cool spring morning made crawling out of bed harder than usual. Even the cacophony of birdsong hadn't bothered him. Nick stretched. Surely the fact that it was Sunday made sitting upright worth the effort.

It didn't take Nick long to bathe, dress, and shave. He grabbed his striped tie off the chair. If he didn't hurry, he would miss the start of church services—and miss seeing Lilly and Levi. Today was the first Sunday that tent services were being offered at the lake. The bright sun filtering through the dotted curtains on the window promised a day he'd not soon forget.

He grinned as he recalled yesterday's visitors to the coaster site. Before he'd quit working, Marguerite and Emily had come to invite him to a picnic lunch after services. They'd subtly mentioned that Lilly and Levi would be there. Dangling that particular carrot before him made refusal impossible.

He wrapped the tie around his neck and knotted it before adding a stiff linen collar. He drew a comb through his thick hair one more time, then slid his arms into the sleeves of his dark gray sack coat. Grabbing his felt hat from the dresser, he said a prayer asking God to bless the day. *And if You see fit, Lord, let Lilly open her heart to me. I know she's holding back, and I don't want to push her, but would enjoying an afternoon as a little more than friends really do either of us any harm?*

⤜⤛⤜

"Brothers and sisters, Jesus was tired."

Lilly nodded in agreement toward Brother Hamilton as she stroked Levi's sandy hair. Jesus wasn't the only one who was tired. Only minutes into the sermon at the Sunday tent service, Levi had laid his head on her lap and fallen asleep. Last night it had taken him a long time to fall back to sleep after the nightmare, and even now, Brother Hamilton's rousing sermon had not awakened him.

"How tired do you have to be to fall asleep in the bottom of a boat during a storm?" Brother Hamilton held out his large, wrinkled hands to his sides in question. "Jesus was physically exhausted. And when his disciples saw the storm, they panicked. They woke the Lord, saying, 'Jesus, don't you care that we're going to die?' They saw the waves coming over the sides of their boat and felt it rising and plunging and were afraid they were going to drown. Wouldn't you be?"

Emily, who was seated on Lilly's right, touched her arm and motioned to the other side of the tent. When Lilly looked between the outlandish ribbons on Eugenia's hat, she spotted Nick looking in her direction. He nodded and flashed a rakish smile that tilted her heart. She quickly diverted her

191

attention back to Brother Hamilton and waved a silk fan in front of her flushed cheeks. Did she still feel Nick's gaze on her, or was it her imagination?

Brother Hamilton moved to the front of his podium. "The disciples had been with Jesus day after day. They'd seen him heal the sick and give sight to the blind. They'd seen his hands break bread and feed thousands, but in a moment of crisis, their faith evaporated."

Lilly stiffened. When Ben died, her whole world had dissolved in an instant. Had her faith gone with it? No, she believed in God. Her faith had been the one thing in life she could count on. She obeyed the Scriptures. She was a good person. She did as God asked. Nothing had changed, had it?

Brother Hamilton's gaze swept the believers gathered before him. "Our faith takes a backseat to the storms of life. The disciples questioned the Lord when the storm came, and so do we. But the Lord questioned their faith."

A cool breeze snapped the flaps on the tent. Lilly tugged the hem of her yellow bolero jacket more snugly around her waist. Levi stirred on her lap, scratched his nose, and settled again. She laid her hand on his back, trying to ignore the twinge of guilt stirred by the preacher's words.

"Brothers and sisters." The preacher's voice rose. "I don't know what storms each of you faces, but I can tell you one thing is for certain. Jesus doesn't still every storm, but He is in the boat with you."

Unable to stop herself, Lilly glanced again at Nick. This time he seemed to be listening intently to Brother Hamilton's words. A Bible lay open on his leg. He'd told her Sean had led him to the Lord and had even been the one to baptize him, but she'd not spoken of his faith with him since then. Although she'd considered it, she wasn't sure she wanted to.

If she asked him questions of that sort, then he'd have the right to do the same, and since Ben's death, her walk with the Lord hadn't been an easy one.

Brother Hamilton paused for several seconds before continuing. "We're so busy managing our lives for ourselves, we forget that it is God who is in control. His plans for you may include some storms, but He will be with you through them. Have faith. Trust the Lord to still the storms either in the world or in your heart."

The congregation rose for the closing hymn, and Lilly tried to shake Levi's shoulder to awaken him, but he was simply too tuckered out. Remaining in her seat, she softly joined in the singing. An unfamiliar man's baritone voice seemed to fill the tent. Was it Nick's?

"All to Jesus I surrender; Lord, I give myself to Thee," the deep voice rang out.

Glancing back, she saw Nick singing the words from memory. So the voice as smooth as chocolate belonged to him. Of course it did.

As sweet as her Ben was, he couldn't sing, nor had he ever sung any hymn with much feeling. His faith had never grown to where he wholly depended on the Lord. He had never needed to. Everything in his life had come easily.

Nothing in Nick's had.

Swallowing the lump in her throat, she attempted to lift her own soprano to join Nick's strong voice. But the words refused to flow. She simply couldn't say, "All to Thee, my blessed Savior, I surrender all."

After the closing prayer, Lilly coughed to clear her throat. What was wrong with her?

Emily turned to her. "Are you all right? I didn't hear you singing, and you have such a lovely voice, I missed it."

"I had a frog in my throat." She offered a reassuring smile first to Emily and then to Eugenia. "Did you enjoy the services?"

Eugenia nodded, and the bows on her hat bobbed. "Yes, and thank you for inviting me. It feels like a family."

"Speaking of family, we'd better get going to the picnic to welcome Marguerite's brother home." Lilly looked around. "I think she and Trip have already left."

Baby Kate lifted her drowsy head and stared at her mama with round brown eyes.

"Katie will want to eat before the picnic, so I'm going to hurry back to the cabin and feed her." Emily brushed a kiss on the top of the baby's head. "Tell Marguerite I'll be along shortly."

Lilly smoothed Levi's hair. "I will—as soon as I can figure out how to wake my own sleeping little prince."

"I can help with that," Nick said from behind her.

Before she knew what was happening, he scooped Levi up. Levi's eyes flickered open. He looked at Nick, smiled, and tucked his head into the space between Nick's neck and shoulder.

Lilly stood and shook the wrinkles from her skirt. "I'll still need to wake him. We have plans."

"I know." Nick's smile made his blue eyes light. "With me."

"N-no. I have plans with Marguerite and Trip."

He grinned. "Well, isn't that a coincidence. So do I."

Lilly was going to wring Marguerite Andrews's pretty little neck.

⸎

No matter how many times Marguerite told Lilly to sit down and relax, the stubborn woman refused.

Nick had had enough.

With Levi awake, Nick again had the use of both arms, so he approached the picnic table in Lake Manawa's Shady Grove where Lilly attempted to put on the tablecloth against the breeze. He took it from her, snapped it in the air, and let it float down over the table. When it fell into place, he looked at her, only to discover a glare rather than a look of appreciation.

She placed her hand on the table. "I can do this alone."

"I know, but you don't have to." He quirked an eyebrow. "Besides, why do you want to?"

"It's easier that way." She reached for the picnic basket she'd set beside the table.

Even before she touched the handle, Nick picked it up and plopped it on the tablecloth. She reached for the handle to pull it toward her, but Nick held fast, refusing to release the basket. "It may be easier to do it yourself when you're with some people . . ." He glanced at Eugenia, who was batting her lashes at Marguerite's brother. "But with others, you can let them help."

She lifted her face to his, appearing ready to retort, but he locked gazes with her. Her jaw was set firm. Hmmm. A battle of wills. Oh, she was a stubborn one, but he'd let her know she'd met her match. Maybe some people might be put off by her tough, I-don't-need-anyone exterior, but he wasn't. She was not going to chase him away.

Lilly Hart needed to realize he was here to stay.

His gaze dropped to her lips. Her tongue darted out and swept over their ripe fullness. Warmth pooled in his chest and spread until he could barely keep from tasting what she offered.

"Nick!" Levi pulled on his sleeve. "Come play ball with me and my friend."

Lilly blinked and stepped back. Nick cleared his throat and turned toward Levi. "What friend?"

"Him." Levi pointed toward an athletically built man wearing a baseball uniform. A mop of dark, curly hair hung from beneath his baseball cap.

Lilly squealed. "Carter!"

Who was Carter, and why did Lilly's face light like fireworks on the Fourth of July when she saw him?

⸎

The next twenty minutes blurred with hugs and shouts and tears. Lilly stepped back and watched Carter run his finger along his wife's cheek and kiss her tenderly. A deep ache balled in her stomach. She missed intimate moments like that when she knew she was the most important person in the world to someone.

Baby Kate lay nestled in the crook of Carter's arm. Lilly doubted the baby girl would be more than two inches from her daddy's side for days.

She glanced at Nick and smiled. Relief seemed to wash over his face. How odd. What was he thinking?

"That's Carter Stockton—Emily's husband?"

Lilly glanced at the couple. "Yes, of course it is. Who did you think it was?"

"I didn't know." Nick released a long breath. "He's a baseball player?"

"Was. He and Emily own and manage a Bloomer Girls team now. You know, an all-women's team that competes from town to town."

Nick nodded. "But since Emily had the baby—"

"They thought she and Kate would be better off here for the summer, rather than traveling all the time." Lilly glanced at the couple. "Emily's been missing Carter something fierce."

196

Nick opened the picnic basket. "A husband and wife should be together."

How often had she thought the same thing? But after Levi was born, things had changed. When Ben had to leave on business, she could no longer join him. They had a child to consider. "Even if one of them has a job that requires travel?"

"Even then." Nick lifted a covered glass dish of potato salad from the basket and set it on the picnic table. "I understand the choice they made, but I want my family where I can take care of them."

"You can't take care of everything."

He grinned, but a serious note clung to his voice. "I can try."

Lilly's heart skipped. The hidden promise in his words scared the daylights out of her, but it also created a thrill she dared not admit.

She shook her head. She was imagining things where they didn't belong. Seeing Carter and Emily together had simply addled her thinking more than she realized.

Forcing her mind to think quieted her errant heart. Nick could never be there for her. It wasn't possible. His job made him travel around the country. She wanted a house—a home to call her own. And Nick was too much of a dreamer to realize he couldn't have it all.

Working silently, they unloaded the remainder of the basket's contents. When Marguerite directed them to sit, Lilly wasn't surprised to find her friend had seated her beside Nick, but she was caught off guard when Trip asked Nick to say grace.

After he removed his hat, Nick bowed his head. Beneath the table, he took Lilly's hand in his own. "Dear heavenly Father, thank You for bringing Carter home to his family safe and sound. Thank You for each of the new friends I've made here." He squeezed Lilly's hand. "And thank You for being with us in each and every storm. Give us courage to face them. Bless the hands that prepared this meal and the souls that are going to consume it. In Jesus' name."

When the whole group joined in the "amen," Nick released her hand. Those gathered began to pass the picnic fare, and Lilly glanced at Eugenia. She couldn't believe Marguerite had seated the girl across from Mark. That poor man was going to suffer her moony eyes and twittering giggle for the entire afternoon.

Carter regaled them with stories from their travels with the team. Crowds came to watch their team, and Emily always made sure they got an earful about suffrage as well. "And did Emily tell you she's speaking at the next National Suffrage Association meeting in Washington, D.C.?" He beamed at his wife.

Her cheeks bloomed pink. "I haven't said yes yet, Carter, and I'll probably trip walking to the podium."

He kissed her cheek. "If you do, it'll only make your speech more memorable."

Nick nudged Lilly's arm and leaned close to her ear. "Your buns are better."

Choking on a bite of fried chicken, Lilly reached for her lemonade. "Thank you, but don't let Marguerite hear that."

"Hear what?" Marguerite, who sat across the table from them, passed the basket of buns to her right.

Lilly dabbed her lips with a checkered cloth napkin. "Nick was telling me how much he enjoys my cooking."

"In comparison to mine?" Marguerite wagged her fork in Nick's direction. "Shame on you, and here I was on your side."

Lilly's cheeks flamed.

"The food is wonderful, Mrs. Andrews." Nick picked up his piece of fried chicken and offered a weak smile.

"But not as good as Lilly's?" Marguerite laughed. "Oh, don't look so nervous. I know she's a better cook than I am—especially her desserts."

Trip draped an arm around his wife and pulled her close. "Honey, I'll eat your desserts any day of the week."

"Speaking of desserts . . ." Lilly stood. "Why don't I start serving the pie?"

"Let's save it for later." Marguerite eyed Nick. "Unless, of course, Nick wants to help you with dessert."

Lilly rolled her eyes and glanced down at Nick's empty plate. "Well?"

He stood and carefully unfolded his legs from the bench. "Actually, I'd love to." He turned to Marguerite. "May we be excused, madam hostess?"

"Absolutely." Marguerite's lips curled in a knowing smile. "We'll keep an eye on Levi. And, Nick, Trip put everything you and Lilly will need by the dock."

"The dock? The pie isn't on the dock. Everything you need? Nick, what have you planned now?"

Nick cupped Lilly's elbow and winked. "Dessert."

24

"We're going out in that?"

Nick glanced at the rowboat Trip had pulled onto the sand and raised his eyebrows at Lilly's question. "You're not afraid of the water, are you?"

"Me? Heavens no, but—"

"Good." Nick held out his hand to assist her. "In that case, get in."

"I'm not going anywhere until you tell me what's going on. What will people think if they see us alone?"

"They'll think we're courting."

"Which we aren't." She stuck her fists on her hips.

"Who says?"

"Nick!"

"Lilly, I simply wanted to spend a day with you without interruptions—or adorable interrupters." He swept his arm toward the boat. "So, if you'd care to join me."

"And if I don't?"

He crossed his arms over his chest. "I'll kidnap you."

"Honestly, Nick. It's not like you're some kind of pirate."

He scooped her into his arms.

Lilly gasped and wrapped her hands around his neck. "Put me down!"

"Arrgh, prisoners don't make demands." He crossed the sand to the boat and gently deposited her on a seat. In a smooth motion, he shoved the boat into the water and hopped inside. Flashing her his best pirate grin, he added another wink. "Fair maiden, consider yourself kidnapped by Captain Nick."

"All right, Captain Nick, where are you taking me?" A crease in her brow warned him he may have gone too far.

"The other side of the lake." He inserted the oars in the locks and began to row. The boat surged forward with each stroke.

"Why are we going there?"

"Do you always ask your captors so many questions?"

"I wouldn't know. This is my first abduction."

He grinned. "We're going to that wooded area in search of a treasure you'll love."

"Me? What do I want from the trees?"

"Mushrooms. We're going mushroom hunting. Marguerite told me they were your favorite and that the rain the other day and the extra-warm temperatures in the last few days should have made them pop out."

"Truly? That's what we're doing?" A wide smile replaced Lilly's frown. "Marguerite's right. I do love morels."

"Morels?"

"Yes, that's the official name for the mushrooms we eat."

"So you know what we're looking for?"

"Yes, of course I do."

"Good, because I don't know a mushroom from a toad-

201

stool." He studied Lilly sitting across from him. She'd worn her hair down today. He liked the way it looked, framing her face. What color would he say it was in the sunlight? Cinnamon, maybe? And the fancy daffodil-yellow dress brought out the amber flecks in her eyes.

He winced. She probably shouldn't be traipsing through the woods in her Sunday dress. So much for thinking of everything.

She lifted the basket Trip had placed in the boat. "How do you like your mushrooms? Fried? With eggs?"

He grinned. "With you."

Lilly diverted her gaze to the lake. "It's a perfect day to be on the lake." She pulled the edges of her little jacket more tightly around her. "Only a little bit of a chill in the air out here. It's been unusually warm for late May in Iowa. Don't get too used to it. We could have a blizzard yet."

"A blizzard in May?"

"It happens."

Was she telling him the truth? The playful expression on her face was new to him. "So, will you forgive me for kidnapping you?"

"It will depend on how many mushrooms you find." She adjusted a hat pin.

He glanced at the shore. "I guess that gives me an incentive to look hard." After he pulled the rowboat ashore, he helped Lilly out. "Lead the way, great mushroom hunter."

Lilly made a beeline for the woods. Under the canopy of the oaks, cottonwoods, and elms, the air cooled considerably, but she didn't seem bothered. She snagged the first long stick she could find and used it to nudge the foliage aside. "They'll be under brush, around old logs, or any place that's damp."

"What do the mushrooms look like?" Nick lifted a branch out of her way so she could pass beneath.

"They look like a brownish-gray sponge. They can be as small as this." She held her thumb and forefinger a half inch apart. "Or as large as this." She left the span of a foot between her hands.

"Are you serious?"

She laughed. "Well, I've never seen them that large, but I've heard they can grow to be that big—kind of like fish stories. Mushroom hunters are quite competitive."

Nick leaned against a tree and watched Lilly move from place to place, digging beneath a bush or overturning a pile of leaves, apparently energized by the conquest.

He joined her near a tree stump. When she moved to step over a log, she slipped a bit. He caught her waist. "Whoa. Careful."

"Look!" She pointed to a spot beyond the log. This time she sat on the log and swung her legs over in front of her. She hurried to the area and plucked the morel mushroom from the earth. "Our first one."

Nick joined her and examined the sponge-topped mushroom lying on her outstretched hand.

"What do you think?" she asked.

"Not bad for a fungus."

"I promise you'll love them. I'll cook them tonight in butter and you'll see." She dropped her find in the basket. "Don't stand there staring at it. Start looking, Captain." She scampered off, seeming much more like Levi than herself.

He had to hurry to catch her. "I think you like the thrill of the hunt as much as finding the mushrooms."

"The huntin' is the best part." She ducked beneath a branch.

He liked her relaxed, playful tone. "Hey, wait up."

"You're supposed to be hunting mushrooms—not me."

"Who says I can't do both?"

"Nick—"

"I found one!" He bent and snapped the mushroom off above the roots as Lilly had instructed.

"Keep looking in that area," Lilly called from several yards away. "Sometimes if you find one, there are more."

As he hunted, he became engrossed in the task and discovered three more. A twig snapped, and he turned his head but saw nothing. Probably a rabbit or a deer. The woods always made him a little jumpy.

In a matter of minutes, he'd picked another three mushrooms. "Lilly, look at the size of this one!" He held a four-inch mushroom in the air, but she didn't answer. He scanned the area. Where had she rushed off to now? "Lilly?"

"Over he—" Her words cut off. Branches snapped. Lilly gave a muffled scream.

Nick raced toward the sound of her voice. "Lilly?"

"I'm down here."

Peering over the embankment, Nick spotted her in a heap at the bottom. Her hat askew and her dress muddied, she looked at him and smiled with a mushroom in hand. "Look, I found one."

❦

Embarrassment warmed Lilly's cheeks as Nick lifted her to her feet.

"Are you sure you're okay?"

"Yes. I heard a noise. When I turned, I lost my footing." After shaking the dead leaves and sticks from her dress, she adjusted her hat. She sighed. She must look a mess.

He plucked a twig from her hair. "Did I mention how lovely you looked today?"

She laughed. "*Looked*, as in past tense."

"You still look beautiful even with dirt on your cheek. Come here." He withdrew his handkerchief and tipped her chin up with his thumb. With a gentle touch, he wiped the smudge. "I'm sorry about your Sunday dress. I shouldn't have brought you out in it."

Lilly's heart skipped at his nearness. She swallowed. "It'll wash." Tearing her gaze from his face, she looked down and noticed the black piping on her bolero jacket had come loose.

Nick followed her gaze. "Washing won't fix that."

"Mending will. I can work miracles with a needle."

"I think you can probably do miracles with about anything." He cupped her elbow. "Let's take a break for a minute and catch our breath." He led her to a nearby log and drew her down beside him, then released a long sigh. "So much for our fun afternoon. I'm sorry."

"I'm the one who fell, and I'm fine. Do you take responsibility for everything?"

He shrugged. "Natural big-brother response?"

"So, you think of me as your sister?" Her peaked eyebrows issued the dare, and the words were out before she could pull them back. What was she doing?

Nick stood and held out his hand. She slipped her hand into his warm grip and let him pull her to her feet. But instead of releasing her hand, he brought it to his lips and touched the back with the softest kiss. Warmth spread over her body. She should pull away, but she couldn't. It was as if she were held in place by the earth itself.

"Lilly Hart, I certainly don't think of you as my sister." His gaze dropped to her lips.

Her heart hammered and fear shot through her. Was he going to kiss her? She needed to step away. To Nick, a kiss would be a promise of possibilities, and she wasn't ready to give that to him or to herself. She didn't dare.

Looking into her eyes, he paused for a second before lifting her hand again. He pressed another kiss to it and smiled. "It's getting late. We should probably be heading back."

She blinked and nodded, not trusting words to come. After exhaling the breath she'd been holding, she bent to retrieve the basket of mushrooms. She hurried ahead of him, needing some distance to sort out her feelings.

If she didn't want him to kiss her, why did she feel so disappointed?

❧

Fear. Nick saw it in Lilly's eyes. Oh, how he'd wanted to kiss her, but she wasn't ready, and now she'd bolted away like a frightened bunny.

Lord, give me wisdom and patience.

Nick caught up to her but didn't try to walk too close. "Do you want to find some more?"

"This should make a good batch." She didn't look his way. "Nick." She swallowed. "Has there never been anyone special in your life?"

He grinned. She might be scared, but curiosity was winning out, and that had to be a good sign. But did he want to tell her about Ruby? Did he even have a choice? If he ever wanted her to open up to him, he had to go first. Taking a deep breath, he slipped his hand around hers. If he was going to bare his soul, Lilly was going to know his intentions.

"I was engaged before." He paused when he saw her bite her lip. When she didn't say anything, he continued. "Her name was Ruby Rawlins. She broke off the engagement."

"Why?" Lilly halted and faced him. "I apologize. That's none of my business."

"Yes, Lilly, it is." They began walking back toward the boat again. "It was two years ago. Ruby was a stage actress and had hopes of making it into silent films."

"Did she make it on screen?"

He shrugged. "I don't know. I've avoided films for that reason alone. Ruby wanted more than I could give her."

"You must have been devastated."

"I was. I loved her." He drew in a deep breath. "But love isn't always reciprocated."

"And you've never spoken to her again?"

"No." A rustle in the bushes made them stop at the edge of the woods. He glanced around and spotted a doe and a buck emerge from the tree line several yards away. He grinned. Spring had a way of bringing out the romance in everyone.

He looked down into Lilly's face. Doubt clouded her eyes. He swallowed. "I won't lie to you, Lilly. I've thought of her. I've wondered where she is and if she got what she wanted." He cupped her cheek. "But she doesn't hold my heart anymore."

A hint of a smile curled Lilly's lips. "I guess we'd better go."

Reluctant to sever the connection, he let his hand slide from her cheek down the length of her arm.

They walked for another minute before Lilly spoke again. "Was she beautiful?"

Nick shrugged. "You could say that, but I wasn't smart enough to look beyond the outside and into her heart."

They reached the shore, and after helping Lilly seat herself, he pushed the boat off the sand and hopped in. Using an oar, he pushed them out into the water, then faced Lilly. "Your turn."

She raised her eyebrows. "You want me to row? I can, you know."

"I bet you can, but no. I mean it's your turn to answer a question." He dipped the oars into the water, which rippled away in circles. "If you could have anything in the world, what would it be?"

"To keep Levi safe."

"No, I mean something tangible."

The smile that broke across Lilly's face made his heart stutter. "That's easy. I want a house of my own. I've always lived with someone else. First with Marguerite's family, then with Ben's, and even now, with Emily. I want Levi to have a home, a place that says, 'This is where you belong.'"

"You were a part of Marguerite's household since you were a little girl. Didn't it feel like home?"

Lilly sighed. "Maybe a little, but Marguerite's mother was a difficult woman. She made it clear I was not a member of the family. I was help, and nothing was guaranteed."

"But your mother worked for them for years. It wasn't like she could throw you out, right?" He stopped rowing for a minute and studied her face. "Lilly, tell me what you're thinking about."

"Mrs. Westing isn't like Marguerite. She wanted to be someone in society, and she felt treating Mama and me as a lower class was part of that."

The boat bobbed in the water. "Go on."

Her gaze dropped to the bottom of the boat. "One time, when I was about four, she caught me in her dressing room, trying on her powders and perfumes." She laughed a bit. "I must have been a sight, all dusted and smelling like an old lady's boudoir."

"What did she do?"

208

"She beat me with her brush and said if I ever did anything like that again, she'd throw me and Mama out on the streets. She said we were only there because she and Mr. Westing were good people, and I should thank God they'd taken Mama and me in after my daddy died. She said we'd have to live on dog scraps, and if my mama died too, it would all be my fault." Tears laced her long lashes. "I was a little girl. I wanted to smell pretty like she did."

"Did she ever try to make you leave?"

"I heard her threaten to send me away several times, but Mr. Westing always stopped her. The summer before Marguerite married Trip, she was ready to let me go, but then he said Marguerite would need her lady's maid at the lake."

"So you never felt secure?"

"I wouldn't say never." Lilly forced a smile. "It's over now, but I don't want Levi to go through that." She swept a finger under her eye. "Am I gonna have to row after all?"

Nick frowned, took hold of the oars, and began the steady thrust-dip-pull sequence. Anger at what Lilly had gone through burned in his gut. How could anyone treat a child so cruelly?

Lord, how do I take away that pain?

Deep inside, he knew he couldn't. His own childhood demons told him that, but it wouldn't stop him from trying.

25

"I think you could use this information to convince Lilly to see the wisdom in your plans for Levi." Mark Westing laid the report he'd completed after Sunday's picnic on Claude Hart's desk. "Simply suggesting you could use this to prove she isn't morally fit to raise the boy should be enough to make her go along."

For two days he'd considered whether he should share the report's contents with Mr. Hart. At last, his need to impress Mr. Hart trumped his conscience. It was the former maid's own fault. Lilly had gone off alone with Nick Perrin, and now his employer would be pleased with the news he had to offer.

Mr. Hart picked up the report and thumbed through the pages. "Alone, I doubt it would be enough. Spending an afternoon unchaperoned picking mushrooms after attending church services would hardly make her look morally bankrupt."

Standing, Mark paced the floor. "I'm sorry. I thought—"

"You did good work, Mr. Westing, but we'll need more.

Obviously our efforts to dissuade her interest in him have not worked. Eventually I had hoped Lilly would be forced for financial reasons to submit to our wishes for Levi."

"And now it appears Nick Perrin has come to her rescue."

Mr. Hart glanced up from the report and held Mark's gaze. "And as I said before, that is why I hired you. We simply need to make sure Lilly sees it's in her best interest to keep away from that man. I can use this as added leverage to that end."

"Nick Perrin seems pretty determined. Even the delays at the roller coaster site haven't slowed his courting efforts. I'm planning something more significant, but it will take time to get everything in order."

"Keep working on it. I want their courtship to come to an abrupt end." Mr. Hart rubbed his beard. "In fact, perhaps I'll pay my former daughter-in-law a visit and suggest her presence may be drawing Mr. Perrin's attention from his work. If I know her, she'll give him up before she'll let him suffer because of her." Mr. Hart redirected his attention to the report. "You've done a thorough job researching Nick Perrin's past." He flipped a page, grinned, and tapped the center of the paper. "Ah, now this, Mr. Westing, is information we can use."

Mark grinned. "Apparently we think alike, Mr. Hart. I've already started working on that."

⋘⃝⋙

The bell on the front door of Thorton's Lunch Counter jingled. Lilly backed through the swinging door from the kitchen with a fresh order of fluffy scrambled eggs and pancakes in her hands.

"Be right with you," she said, scooping up an extra napkin before turning. She stopped when she spotted Claude Hart, and her pulse thundered. Swallowing hard, she delivered the plate to the customer and walked over to greet her former father-in-law.

"I'm afraid you're a bit early for pie. It's not out of the oven yet. But can I get you pancakes and coffee?" She smiled. *Please, Lord, help me extend this man grace and season my words with kindness.*

"You know perfectly well I have no intention of eating here." He motioned for her to sit down at the empty table in the corner. "We need to have a discussion."

She bit back the acidic replies that threatened to roll off her tongue. *Kindness. Kindness. Kindness.* With a slight nod, she took the seat he offered.

He lowered his large frame into the chair across from her and placed both hands on the top of his cane as if he were there to comment on the lovely weather they'd been having. He dipped his head. "I heard that Nick Perrin has been having some difficulties with his roller coaster construction."

Lilly clutched her apron at the mention of Nick's name. "Why do you care about that?"

"I care about everything—and everyone—who comes in contact with my grandson." His hard mica glint bore into her.

She shivered but forced her voice to remain calm. "Nick can tend to his own affairs."

"If you care about the man, perhaps you should consider what any alliance with you might do to his precious project." He tapped the cane on the floor twice and stood.

"Are you threatening his roller coaster project? Because of me?"

"I'm merely pointing out that Mr. Perrin might be wise to spend more time there and less with you."

"Or?"

"Or he may find it nearly impossible to finish this job. It's the first roller coaster he's designed, isn't it? I'd hate to see him fail." He tipped his hat. "Good day, Lilly."

⁂

"How's the boy and his stubborn mama?"

Nearing Sean's work area, Nick grinned. The Irishman had a way of cutting to the chase. "Levi's fine, and I think I made some headway with Lilly while we were mushroom hunting."

Sean drew his paintbrush across the first of over twenty short boards. After they were painted green, the boards would be secured and used to keep the roller coaster cars from rolling backward if the chain would slip on the first incline.

"You're getting rather attached to those two. Sure that's wise?"

"I can't help it. It's like we're being drawn together by some invisible force."

Sean chuckled. "Sounds like the hand of God is doing some powerful nudging."

"And Lilly digs her heels in at every turn." Nick handed Sean his bucket of paint. "She takes two steps forward and one step back."

"Ya can't blame her. The lady needs time to adjust to the likes of ya." Sean drew the back of his hand over his brow. "Besides, can she trust ya?"

"What do you mean? Of course she can trust me." Nick motioned to the men to bring the rest of the short boards over. "I'd never do anything to hurt her."

"Not intentionally anyway." Sean set the brush in the bucket and crossed his arms over his chest. "So, what do ya want me to tell the boys concerning yet another delayed supply shipment? We needed that lumber to finish the safety rail."

"If need be, we can use the scrap lumber on the machine shed and exchange them with the whole boards there to use on the railing." Nick raked his hand through his hair and pointed to the pile under a tree. Another delay in the arrival of supplies had sent the roller coaster crew scrambling, but if they could keep on, they might make it within a few days of the park's opening season. "We'll replace the siding after the shipment comes in."

Sean scratched his head. "That'll work, boyo, but I'm still worried about the lift chain. She's not arrived, and without her, the whole coaster is a bust for opening day."

Nick flipped through his notepad. "True, but if we have everything in place, we ought to be able to install the lift chain as soon as it arrives."

"It'll take at least two days to hook her up, get the tension set, and check her out, but we could rush that a wee bit, I suppose."

Nick shook his head. "No, we'll open a day or two late rather than let anyone on this coaster before it's been checked and rechecked."

"Whatever ya say. Yer the boss." Sean reached in his pants pocket. "By the way, Lilly sent this note with me when ya didn't stop for lunch. She seemed a mite upset."

Nick tugged his leather glove off with his teeth and unfolded the paper. His blood ran hot through his veins as he read the contents. The Harts had gone too far this time.

"Sean, can you hold things down again for a while? I need to take care of something right away."

"If yer sure ya can spare the time away, boyo."

Nick stuffed the paper in his pocket. "I'll have to make the time. This can't wait."

The screen door banged open as soon as Lilly sat down in the shade in back of the diner. She jerked, nearly toppling the large bowl of apples on her lap. What did Eugenia need now?

But instead of seeing Eugenia, she looked up to find Nick marching toward her, his face filled with fury. Her heart thudded to a stop.

Since the day they'd gone mushroom hunting, things had changed between them. All week they'd spent time together talking, laughing, and sharing. No words concerning an official courtship had been declared, but they were there all the same.

He thrust the note toward her. "When was he here?"

"This morning." She set the bowl on a picnic table. "I won't let you sacrifice all your hard work for me."

"And I won't let that man bully you!" He hit the table with his fist, and the apples jostled in the bowl. He stepped closer. "Tell me what he said."

"Nick, please, calm down. You have to see the wisdom in my decision. He made it clear that as long as I continued to let you spend time with Levi and me, your coaster project would be in jeopardy." She backed away until a tree stopped her. With her back against the oak, she dug her nails into the bark.

Lord, help me do this. I can't let Nick suffer for me. Help him understand I have to still this storm before it destroys him.

"I know you've already had supply shipments delayed over and over. You said yourself that the lift chain you ordered from the ironworks company back east has yet to arrive. I'm certain now Ben's father made that happen. He's a powerful man. I can't let him ruin you."

Nick's chest heaved. After a minute, he met her gaze and held it. "He's not going to blackmail you."

215

"It'll only be for a while." Lilly closed her eyes. She couldn't look in those telling blue eyes or she'd lose her nerve. "Once the roller coaster is running, I'll bring Levi by again."

Nick stepped so close she could feel the warmth of his body. She opened her eyes and blinked.

He put one hand beside her head on the tree. "No." The answer was soft but firm.

"But, Nick—"

"No." He traced her cheek with his thumb. "Lilly, he's not going to use me to get you to do his bidding. I won't let him hurt you ever again. That's my choice."

"And don't I get a choice?"

"Sure you do." A rakish smile curled his lips. "You get to choose whether I kiss you now or later."

Her pulse raced. His masculinity engulfed her, but it was his eyes—so honest, so sincere, so safe—that begged her to accept his offer. But what would Ben think? Would he approve of Nick Perrin? Would he want her to be with another man?

The answer, hidden in her heart, pushed its way to the surface. He'd want her happy.

And Nick did make her happy.

"Now," she whispered.

His eyes darkened, and he slowly dipped his head and brushed her lips with a feathery kiss. Pulling back, he waited for a second as if giving her time to change her mind. He lowered his head again, and her lips parted beneath the pressure of his kiss. Her knees weakened, and he tightened his hold—both the hold around her waist and the one on her heart. Oh yes, even with all this turmoil, Nick Perrin definitely made her happy.

Nick broke the kiss even though it was the last thing he wanted to do.

He trailed his hand down her arm and squeezed her hand. "I still need to go take care of this problem with your former father-in-law."

"I'll get my cape." Her eyes dared him to argue with her.

He nodded, but there was no way she was going with him. This was between Claude Hart and him. The only way to deal with a bully was to stand up to him, and that man needed to understand that anything concerning Lilly was off-limits. And Nick was willing to make his point in whatever way he found necessary.

As soon as Lilly went inside, he slipped away.

Begging forgiveness later would be easier than getting her to agree with him now.

❧

Nick and Sean approached the large brick building housing the law office of Claude Hart. Although Nick had planned to go alone, when Sean learned what was going on, he insisted on joining him.

Nick glanced at his beefy friend whose hot temper had settled more than one dispute in what Sean liked to call the "McGready way." He clapped a hand on Sean's shoulder. "Why don't you wait out here for me? If I need you, I'll call."

"Why don't I come in with ya? I know yer thinkin' to talk this out, but sometimes ya got to back up yer words."

"Sean, he's a lawyer. I don't think he's given to violence, and I certainly don't want to hit the man."

Sean tented an eyebrow.

"Okay, I'd love to punch him, but God wouldn't want me to handle things that way."

"Yer a better man than me, boyo." Sean opened the door for him. "I'll be out here if ya need me."

Nick stepped into the foyer of the office. He looked down when his foot sank into a thick Oriental rug.

"May I help you?" a prim, middle-aged lady asked from behind a desk.

Nick glanced at the nameplate on her desk. "Miss Fallwell, I'm here to see Mr. Hart."

"And you are?"

"Nick Perrin."

She ran her long, slender finger down a ledger. "He doesn't have an appointment scheduled for you, Mr. Perrin."

"If you'll tell him I'm here, I'm pretty sure he'll see me anyway."

Miss Fallwell folded her hands. "He's not in."

"When do you expect him to return?"

"I can make an appointment for the day after tomorrow." The stenographer picked up a pencil. "Say, ten o'clock?"

"No, that won't be necessary." The door opened, and Nick turned to see a familiar person walk in. "Mr. Snodgrass, what a surprise to see you here."

The jumpy freight clerk pushed up his glasses and cleared his throat. "I . . . uh . . . have some legal matters to attend to."

Miss Fallwell opened a drawer and withdrew an envelope. "Here you go, Mr. Snodgrass. Mr. Hart said it's all there and to thank you for a job well done." The stenographer passed the envelope to the clerk, but Mr. Snodgrass's hands shook so badly the envelope fluttered to the floor.

Nick snatched it from the floor. Miss Fallwell and Mr. Snodgrass both dove for it, but he stepped beyond their reach and opened the unsealed letter. After a peek inside, he released

218

a long, low whistle. "What did you do for Mr. Hart that earned you such a lucrative profit?"

"That's none of your business."

"Really?" Nick counted the bills inside. "I wonder if the railroad would feel the same way if I share what I know and your possible connection to missing freight."

Sean filled the doorway. "Problems?"

"No. Mr. Snodgrass, the freight clerk, was about to help us find something we need quite badly."

Mr. Snodgrass swallowed hard. "What do you want?"

Nick stepped close and pressed the envelope against Snodgrass's chest. "I want to know where the lift chain is that I ordered for my roller coaster."

"I really must protest to this treatment of Mr. Snodgrass." Miss Fallwell rose to her feet. "If you don't cease badgering him, I shall be forced to telephone the police."

Sean moved next to Snodgrass and draped an arm around his shoulders. "We're not badgering ya, laddie, are we?"

"No," Snodgrass croaked. He tried to shrug off Sean's arm, but Sean held firm. "Mr. Perrin, your chain is in Atlantic, Iowa."

"And how can I get it here?" Nick crossed his arms over his chest.

"Please, Mr. Perrin, I shouldn't have told you as much as I have. Certain people will be furious with me if they learn I said anything. Besides, all the trains heading this way have full loads."

Anger bore a hole in Nick's gut. "I guess I'll have to pay the clerk in Atlantic, Iowa, a personal visit. You'd better hope he's willing to make an exception."

Sean let his arm drop from Snodgrass's shoulder and turned to the stenographer. "And it'll please me to bits if ya let Mr. Hart know that Mr. Snodgrass is no longer in his employ. Isn't that right, laddie?"

"I think that might be in my best interest." Mr. Snodgrass shoved his glasses up again.

Sean clapped him on the shoulder, nearly sending the frail man sprawling. "Now yer being a smart lad."

"Come on, Sean," Nick said. "We've wasted enough time here."

❧

Nick Perrin's men deserved to eat Eugenia's burnt sponge cake. They could eat her dry pork chops too.

It was Nick's fault for abandoning Lilly. She'd gone in to get her cape only to find smoke wafting from the oven. By the time she'd gotten Eugenia, her charred cake, and Levi settled and returned to meet Nick, he'd taken off. She had to hurry to keep him from doing something foolish enough to land him in jail.

Quickening her steps, she made her way from the streetcar stop down the block to Ben's former law office. Since Ben's death, she'd not been inside. She pulled the heavy door open, and instantly the heady scent of dusty law books and leather pulled her heartstrings taut. She used to keep a baby carriage in the office's back room. How many times had she met Ben there for lunch or run her hand over the mahogany of his desk?

"Lilly?" Nick's eyes widened. "You shouldn't have come."

"And you shouldn't have left me." She turned to the stenographer. "Miss Fallwell, I want to see my father-in-law."

"As I told these men, he's not in."

"Then give him a message from me." She leaned on the desk. "Tell him to leave me and my son alone. I'm not afraid of him." She glanced at Sean, then Nick. "Anymore."

220

She spun and marched from the foyer, letting the door slam behind her. Outside she leaned against the cool brick building, her pulse racing and her body trembling. She took a deep breath. What a lie that had been!

Sean climbed in the rig and rode off, but Nick joined her. "You okay?"

She took another shuddery breath. "I'm fine." She should still be furious with him, but the concern on his face removed all her resolve to remain angry. What was Nick doing to her?

"You were quite something in there." He placed his hand on her arm. "But you're shaking."

"It's not what I said to the clerk. It's being here."

"I figured that it would be hard. That's one of the reasons I left."

"And the other?"

"It's my fight now." Nick glanced at the gold letters on the window of the office. "He's messing with my roller coaster and—"

"And?"

"And the woman I love."

26

Lilly blinked.

"Miss Lilly, I'm really sorry about the cake." Eugenia poured the blackened ring of sponge cake into the trash basket. "I'll try to watch things more closely."

Shaking her head, Lilly removed her hands from the sudsy dishwater and dried them on a towel. What was Eugenia prattling on about? Lilly needed to focus on the moment and not on what Nick had said.

He loved her.

The thought warmed her to her soul but sent a paralyzing bolt of fear through her at the same time. Nick was a man she could respect. He was honest and thoughtful, and although she believed his declaration, he wasn't being practical about the two of them. He wouldn't be around much longer. That was the nature of his job.

She placed the towel back on the hook. She'd already let him into their lives more than she ought. When he left, how was Levi going to take it?

And how would she handle it?

The all-too-familiar pain of loss knifed through her. She couldn't do this again. But the lurch in her heart told her what she already knew.

It was too late.

She loved him too.

But he didn't have to know that.

"I don't know if I'll ever get the hang of this." Eugenia slipped the empty cake plate into the dishpan.

Pushing her thoughts of Nick aside, Lilly turned to Eugenia. "You are improving. Learning to cook and bake takes time and practice, and I'm impressed with how far you've already come. As soon as we get these lunch dishes done, why don't I show you how to make cinnamon rolls?"

❦

Stepping back, Nick surveyed the coaster and grinned. They wouldn't make opening day tomorrow, but the next day she should be running. His men had worked harder in the last two days than any men ought to have to, but they'd done it. Tomorrow, when they were testing the coaster, at least folks would get to see what it was like.

He snaked an arm around Lilly's waist and kissed her cheek.

"Yuck!" Levi said, sticking out his tongue. "Mr. Nick, you're going to get all gooshy kissing a girl."

"I don't think kissing your mama will make me gooshy. Will you make me gooshy, Lilly?"

She rolled her eyes. "Sometimes I don't know who is the grown-up when you two get together."

"Mama, Mr. Nick is more growned up than me, and he's more growned up than you too."

223

"Taller does not make him mature."

Nick grabbed Levi, whirled him in a wide circle, and then set him back on the ground. "Being mature isn't nearly as much fun as playing. Lilly, what do you say? Shall we ride the miniature train? Or maybe the carousel? I saw they were both getting set up for tomorrow."

"Please, Mama?"

"Nick, you said you have work to finish here."

"I can come back later."

"In the dark?"

"Sure."

Lilly stood beneath the first incline of the mammoth roller coaster and stared at the lift chain. "Maybe we'll go in a while, Levi." She turned to Nick. "I know you got all this installed in one day, but tomorrow—"

"Is the park's opening day. I know." Nick wiped his hands on a rag and chuckled. "We were lucky that the freight clerk in Atlantic miraculously found a spot for it on one of the trains headed to Council Bluffs after Sean had a visit with him."

Levi jumped up and down. "When can I ride it?"

"Never!" Lilly snapped.

Nick cocked his head in her direction. He fought the urge to argue with her. Levi was her son, but how overprotective could she be? The boy had been watching the coaster go up since the beginning. Naturally, he wanted to ride it.

He drew in a long breath. "Apparently your mama and I need to discuss that, buddy. Would you go get me my canteen out by the worktable?"

"Sure, Mr. Nick."

Her back ramrod straight, Lilly propped her hands on her hips. "I do not want him on this contraption."

"Well . . ." Nick drew out the word. "Why don't you at

224

least let me show you how this 'contraption' works? Let's go inside the engine shed." He held the door for her, then walked toward one of the cars set on a sawhorse stand. She remained by the door. "Come here. You can't see anything from over there."

Lilly sighed and moved closer. "I won't change my mind."

"This is the chain dog." Nick indicated a horseshoe-shaped piece of steel beneath the car, then he stepped toward Lilly and wrapped his arms around her waist. "It engages the car to the lift chain. It bears the full weight of the car as the chain pulls it up the first lift hill."

She licked her lips. "What if it slips? Mistakes can easily happen."

"Not with me." He held her gaze for a second, then took her hand. "Let's go back out and I'll show you."

They joined Levi at the foot of the first incline. After a long drink from his canteen, Nick pointed to the lift hill. "See those green boards? We use those to keep the cars from rolling back. They allow a car to pass by going up, but if it were to slip and try going down, the boards would stop it."

He wasn't sure which was worse, the doubt in Lilly's eyes about him or about the coaster, but he wished he could make both go away. Unfortunately, relationships didn't have anti-rollback devices.

Pressing his hand to her back, her urged her closer to the lift chain. "Each of these sections is called a lift-chain barrel. That's what the chain dogs under the cars attach to."

"So once the motorized lift chain pulls the car to the top, what keeps the roller coaster going?"

He smiled. "Gravity, excitement, and magic. The trick is to design a track that keeps the ride going fast enough for a thrill, but not so fast you lose control."

She stepped out of his reach. "You need to be careful. Going too fast can get someone hurt."

Why did he feel the conversation had taken an unexpected plunge? How could he make her see she needed to give them a chance?

He glanced at the top of the roller coaster, the red flag on the cupola waving in the wind. "But, Lilly." He gave her a sidelong glance. "Some rides are worth the risk."

⁂

"The miniature train is harmless, Lilly!"

Lilly glared at Nick. He couldn't possibly understand why she didn't want her son on the train any more than the roller coaster. Why didn't he leave it alone? "It's my choice to make. Not yours."

"Then at least tell me why."

Levi's lip jutted out, and tears filled his eyes. "Why, Mama?"

"I said no and I mean it." She took his hand. "Come on. Maybe Mr. Wissler will still be at the merry-go-round. I'm not promising anything, Levi, but if he is, he might let you give it a go." Nick started to follow them, and she turned to him. "You can go back to work now. Levi and I will be fine."

"Lilly, what has gotten into you? One minute you were fine, then the next, well, you were acting like someone put molasses in your flour. Is it me, the roller coaster, or the train?"

"Maybe all three." She whirled and walked away.

He caught her elbow. "Or maybe it's not any of that. Maybe it's you."

"Or me." Levi hung his head, and his voice choked with tears. "I'm sorry, Mama. I know I shouldn't want to ride the train. You told me before."

Nick lifted Levi and dried his tears with his handkerchief.

"Hey, Chipmunk. Don't cry. It's only a train. I think we can ride the merry-go-round, and it's way better. Look! It's all lit up." He glanced down at Lilly. "You coming, or are pretend horses riding in circles too dangerous as well?"

Her stomach ached as if she'd swallowed a loaf of sourdough. She pressed her hand to it. "You go ahead. I've got some thinking to do."

"I imagine you do."

On the carousel, Nick waited while Levi bypassed the long-eared rabbit and the portly pig and headed for a dappled white steed. It had an ornate blue saddle blanket and gold-trimmed saddle. "Good choice, Levi."

Despite Levi's protests, Nick selected the less decorated black horse on the inside. The boy claimed good guys always rode white horses.

"This good guy wants to ride beside his buddy," Nick said. He lifted Levi onto his mount, then swung his leg over his own black stallion. Unfortunately, having long legs meant his feet still touched the floor of the carousel.

When the music commenced, Nick smiled at Levi. "Wave to Mr. Wissler. It's mighty nice of him to let us have an early ride and test this out for him."

Tears now replaced by a wide grin, Levi waved his arm back and forth at the gray-haired man. He gave a loud "giddyap" to his horse, followed by a rousing "yee-haw."

Nick added a "yee-haw" of his own, and Levi giggled. As the carousel turned, Nick caught sight of Lilly on a park bench near the turnstile. She gave them a halfhearted wave each time they passed. On the third time around, she was gone.

Nick's heart felt like it had a kink in its chain. Maybe he shouldn't have whisked Levi away. Perhaps he'd been too harsh. But that woman could be more complex than a set of drawings for a hundred coasters. What would make anyone react that way to a miniature train ride designed for children?

The merry-go-round slowed, and Nick spotted Lilly waiting with Mr. Wissler. The older man took her hand and helped her step on the carousel. She walked between the horses, holding on to the brass poles for balance since the ride had yet to come to a complete stop.

She looked at Nick and tilted her head toward a swan-shaped chariot seat for two mounted behind Levi's horse. "Want to join me?"

Nick nodded and stepped over the back of the black stallion. He squeezed Levi's shoulder. "You hold on tight, Levi. Your mama and I are going to ride behind you."

"In a bird?" Levi scowled.

Chuckling, Nick held out his hand to Lilly. "Apparently he doesn't approve of our choice, but I think this is perfect."

The lively organ music began again, and the carousel picked up speed. Nick glanced at Lilly. Twice she'd opened her mouth to speak, then clamped her lips shut. He draped his arm around her shoulders and pulled her closer.

A long sigh escaped her. "I don't like trains."

"I gathered that."

"Ben was killed in a train accident. He was on his way back from Minneapolis when the train derailed."

A weight settled on Nick's chest. No wonder she'd gotten so upset. He should have guessed it was something like that. "Have you ever told Levi how he died and why you don't like trains?"

Her eyes fixed on the little railroad as they passed. "It's not fair to burden him with my fears."

"He's your son, but the way I see it, you're doing that already by getting so upset about the train ride. He's a smart boy. I'm sure he senses your fear. Have you ridden a train at all since the accident?"

She shook her head. "I don't know if I could, and Levi doesn't understand."

"He's not going to understand anything unless you explain it to him."

Lilly said nothing for a full turn of the carousel. Nick glanced at her. The evening light cast shadows on her weary face. How he wished he could erase the last hour's events.

The merry-go-round began to slow. Lifting her face to his, she said, "I need to ride it."

"If you can't, Lilly, you can't. It's okay. It's understandable. I'll even explain it to Levi for you."

"No, I can do this. I'd do anything for him. Anything."

"I know." Nick nodded and kissed her cheek.

The merry-go-round came to a stop, and Levi turned toward them with a big grin. "My horse had to be more fun than that silly bird."

Someday maybe Nick would get the chance to tell the boy the truth.

Placing her hands on Nick's shoulders, Lilly let him swing her off the carousel and onto the ground. He lifted Levi high into the air before depositing him beside her.

"Let's go ride the train." Lilly took Levi's hand.

"But you said—"

"I changed my mind." She linked her arm in Nick's. "Right, Nick?"

"That's a fact. I only hope Mr. King is still there."

They came around the side of the bowling alley and discovered Mr. Thorton walking toward them.

Halting, Lilly pulled her hand free from Nick's arm. "Mr. Thorton. I didn't expect to see you around this evening."

"Obviously." He glanced down at Lilly's clasped hands. "Aren't you three a happy little family?"

Nick frowned. "Lilly and I were on our way to take Levi on a train ride. Several of the operators are gearing up for tomorrow's opening and told me earlier today to bring him by."

"Mrs. Hart, I thought you'd be busy preparing for the opening day as well."

"I'll be heading back to the diner after Levi's train ride."

"I see. Have you given any more thought to what we spoke about? Your in-laws would like to take the boy for the weekend."

"Sir, they are my *former* in-laws, and as I told you before, if they want to see Levi, they can come here and do so any time they want." Levi tugged on her hand. "Now, if you'll excuse us, Levi is pretty excited about possibly riding the train."

"By all means. Excuse me." Mr. Thorton stepped out of the way. "But be careful, Mrs. Hart. I'd hate for you or your son to get hurt."

Was that some kind of veiled threat?

Nick pressed his hand to the small of her back and directed her around Mr. Thorton. When they were out of earshot, he glanced at Lilly. "More trouble?"

"Ben's father has been passing along some messages through Mr. Thorton."

"I'm surprised he's still pressuring you. Mr. Thorton seemed like a kind man."

"He is, I think. But he's a businessman too. I don't know if you realize how powerful Claude Hart is. Ben used to say his father could ruin a man in twenty-four hours if he wanted to."

"Yet you still are fighting him."

"And now so are you. I don't have a choice, but you do. If he wanted my business, he could have it. But he wants my son."

"Mr. King is there! I see him!" Levi ran on ahead.

Lilly spotted the train and stopped. Her pulse drummed, and she rubbed her sweaty hands on her skirt. "I know it's ridiculous and I'm ashamed, but I don't know if I can do this."

"First of all, there's nothing to be ashamed of. Second, you can do this. Have a little faith. We'll do it together—like we petted the snake."

They caught up with Levi, and Mr. King smiled at them. "Mr. Perrin, I was wondering if you folks would be coming by."

"Sorry, we got delayed on the carousel." Nick reached in his pocket and pulled out some tickets. "These are for the roller coaster. Please come as my guest."

"Tomorrow?" Mr. King tugged on the bill of his black-and-white-striped railroad cap.

"'Fraid not. Still have some safety checks to do, but it'll be running by the end of the week."

"I can't wait." He looked down at Levi. "Are you ready for a ride on my train? Since I'm the engineer, I need a good conductor who can yell, 'All aboard.' Would you do that for me?"

A smile blossomed on Levi's face, and he nodded. "I can yell real loud."

"Good for you." Mr. King pointed to the cars. "Okay, go ahead. Say it as loud as you can."

Levi took a deep breath, leaned back, and cupped his chubby hands to his mouth. "Aaaaaaall aboard!"

"Well done. Maybe you can have my job someday."

"Nope. I'm gonna build roller coasters like Mr. Nick."

The miniature train bumped along with a steady *clack clack*, but Lilly couldn't relax. She clutched her pocketbook in her hands, her knuckles whitening. Nick pried her hand free and held her sweaty palm in his as if he didn't notice. All the while, he and Levi chattered like railroaders about the track, the engine, and the cars, contrasting and comparing them to those on the roller coaster.

"Isn't this fun, Mama?" Levi twisted in his seat to face her and Nick.

Nick squeezed her hand and chuckled.

She elbowed his ribs. "It's certainly an adventure."

Levi whirled the other way and leaned out over the side.

"Get back in and sit right, Levi Hart," she snapped.

He frowned and glanced at Nick.

"She's the boss." Nick patted the back of the boy's seat. "Sit back here and enjoy the rest of the ride." He shot Lilly a devilish grin. "I know I am."

Heat infused her cheeks, and her pulse quickened again, but for a whole new reason. What was she going to do with Nick? Didn't he realize this could never work between them? He kept saying to trust him and trust the Lord, but he didn't know what she did. The only one she could trust was herself. Bad things could happen to anyone. Perhaps God had blessed her with love again only to rip Nick away as well.

27

Nick dropped into a wicker chair outside Emily's cottage. He rubbed his face with his hands. Lilly was pulling away again. He knew it as surely as he understood how fast the cars of his coaster had to go to make it through the whole figure eight. What did he have to do to convince her they had a real chance?

The incessant chirping of crickets annoyed him. He needed to think. No, he needed to pray. *Dear Lord, show me what to do.*

The screen door opened, and she stepped out of the cottage. The sweet scent of her rose cologne greeted him first, making him want to pull her into his arms and kiss the daylights out of her.

"That didn't take long." Nick patted the wicker chair beside him.

"All the excitement must have worn him out." She buttoned her spring cape around her neck. "I can't sit. Remember, I have to do some additional work at the diner. Emily said she'd watch Levi."

"You're going back tonight?"

She shrugged. "I have to. Care to walk me over?" She started down the path that led to the Midway, and he fell in step beside her.

"You'll be there alone." The thought made his neck prickle. That spidery feeling had been niggling at him all night. He glanced around.

"I've been alone before."

"But you've already worked a full day, and I know you're tired. Why don't I stay and help?"

She stopped and faced him. "Absolutely not. The last thing we need is for my former father-in-law to get wind of you and me spending time alone together at night. Can you imagine what he'd do with that information? He'd have Levi taken away by morning."

"I would never let that happen, Lilly." He swallowed hard. "A child belongs with his mother."

He took her elbow, and they began walking again. The lapping of the lake and the whir of cicadas filled the silence between them. He didn't like the idea of her being in the diner by herself, but he liked the idea of causing her more heartache even less.

"Nick, when you said that a child belongs with his mother, it sounded—personal." Her voice was soft and gentle. "Why is that?"

"Maybe I should tell you another time. I don't want you to have to work even later."

"I can spare a few moments, and I'd like to hear now."

Having reached the Midway, he motioned toward a park bench lit by the lights emanating from the shooting gallery.

Even though he was concerned about the lateness of the hour, she was reaching out to him, and he wanted to encourage that more than ever. Perhaps this was the chance he'd been praying for.

They sat down, and he drew in a long breath. "You know I'm from a large family."

She nodded.

"And you know we didn't have a lot of money." He shifted on the bench and watched a frog hop by in the dim light. "Things got real bad one winter. My dad lost his job, and we were living on the money my mother made washing clothes and ironing for other folks."

Lilly touched his arm. "What else?"

He sighed. "When I say bad, I mean worse than anything you can imagine. We were starving. They couldn't afford to feed all ten of us, so they took the four oldest of us to an orphanage."

She gasped. "They sent you away? How could they? How old were you?"

"I was twelve, and Lilly, you've got to understand, my parents were good, hardworking folks, but a storm was upon them." He met her gaze. Her eyes filmed with tears. He drew in a deep breath. "When my parents took us there, I remember my father squeezing my shoulder and telling me I had to be strong for my younger brothers."

"And your mama?"

"She kissed me and cried. She said she'd be back for us as soon as they could come." His voice cracked. "I believed her that day, but soon the other orphans made it clear to me that parents never returned like they promised. I still remember seeing her walk away and turning to blow me a kiss. I held on to that memory and tried to recall it every night. I was afraid

I'd forget what she looked like." He stopped. He couldn't tell her he'd cried himself to sleep every night for months—a twelve-year-old boy, crying like a baby for his mama. "Then one couple came and decided they wanted to adopt me."

"Oh no. What did you do?"

"I pitched such a fit the couple changed their minds." He chuckled. "After they left, the matron beat me."

"And that was your last chance at a home?" she whispered.

He squeezed her hand. "No. After a year, my parents did come back."

"What a horrible thing for a child to go through. Not knowing if they'd return. Not knowing if you'd ever see them again. Nick, I'm so sorry."

"I only told you this so you'd believe me when I say I won't let those people take your son from you. I know how much a boy needs his mother." He stood and pulled her to her feet. "Now, I guess we'd better get you inside. I'll be waiting right here to walk you home."

"You'll be bored silly. I'm perfectly capable of walking back to the cottage."

"It'll give me some time to pray." He cupped her cheek, brushing the creamy softness with the pad of his thumb. "I have some people I'd like to talk to the Lord about."

❧

The iron bed squeaked every time Lilly rolled over. Front, side, back—no position gave her body rest, let alone her thoughts. She could still taste Nick's good-night kiss, his breath fresh from the clove-flavored Necco wafers Levi had shared with him. She could feel the cool touch of his calloused hand against her cheek, and after the story he'd shared with her about his childhood, she'd ached to comfort him in a tangible way.

And he'd waited for her to finish her work.

The thought sent another wave of emotion coursing through her. Better than that, he'd sat in the dark and prayed for her. Had Ben ever brought her name before the Lord? For that matter, when was the last time she'd prayed for Nick or anyone else?

She scrunched the feather pillow beneath her head. What had Nick said about his parents? A storm was upon them?

The wind sent a branch tapping on her cabin window. She jolted. Her heart pounding, she rolled over and sat up. Perhaps a glass of water would help her get back to sleep.

After pulling on her wrap and slippers, she padded down the hall to the parlor. Carter's snores echoed from the room he and Emily shared. She stopped when she found Emily sitting in the parlor, nursing Kate.

"I thought I heard you." Emily smiled and nodded toward the empty chair. "Can't sleep?"

"I was thinking about storms."

"I didn't see a cloud in the sky today, but I can hear the wind picking up. Do you think we're in for a storm?" Emily stroked Kate's face with her thumb.

"No. Nick was telling me about a storm his parents faced. They fell on hard times and sent him and three of his brothers to an orphanage to live."

"How horrible."

"I know. They did come back for them, but Nick didn't know if they would. Can you imagine living with that uncertainty? Nick says they are good people, but—"

"Lilly, we mustn't judge them."

"I know." Lilly understood storms—both the ones in nature and the ones in life. How a person dealt with them said a lot about him or her. Making a decision like that had to be the hardest thing Nick's parents had ever done. She sighed. "I can't help but wonder why his parents hadn't given their storm to the Lord."

"Maybe they had. Maybe taking Nick to the orphanage was the answer God had given them."

"But how can God rip parents and their children apart?"

"Or a wife and a husband?" Emily met Lilly's gaze and held it. "Isn't that what you really want to know?"

"You think I blame God for Ben's death?"

"No, but I think you stopped trusting Him then."

Lilly stiffened. "I trust God. I have my whole life."

"You have in the past, but are you sure you trust Him now?"

A prick of guilt stabbed Lilly's heart. It was a good question, and one that had been in the back of her thoughts. What Emily didn't understand was there were different kinds of trust. Before Ben died, Lilly had believed trust to be simple too. But now—well, she was more cautious. She had to be.

"Emily, you're becoming more like your grandma Kate every day."

"Thank you."

Lilly rolled her eyes and yawned. "I think I should go back to bed. Tomorrow's a big day."

"Sleep well, my friend." Emily shifted Katie to her other side to nurse. "And be sure to say a prayer about those storms."

◈

Crowds circled the fence outside the roller coaster. It seemed that every person in Council Bluffs had taken the streetcar to Lake Manawa as soon as church services concluded.

With powder-blue skies and a bright sun, opening day promised to be perfect. Nick shielded his eyes with his hand and glanced at the myriad of curious onlookers. When this roller coaster was up and running, there'd certainly be no shortage of patrons.

"Forest," Nick called, "help Sean get those sandbags in the cars. I need them to weigh as much as four people."

He turned and spotted all five feet nothing of Mr. Nash marching toward him. "Mr. Perrin, where have you been?"

"At the tent church services."

"But it's opening day."

Nick nodded. "And we need God's blessing for that more than anything."

Mr. Nash flung his hand toward the ride. "Why isn't this coaster running? Look at all those people. I told you it needed to be done today. I even advertised it in the newspaper."

"If guests are disappointed, that's your problem. I told you it wouldn't be ready. Today I have safety checks to do and adjustments to make accordingly." Nick pointed to the sandbags. "First we check her out with sand. If everything goes okay, then I ride at least twenty times. The only person I'm taking any chances with is myself. Unless, of course, you care to join me."

Mr. Nash stepped backward. "No, that won't be necessary. I hope you realize the investors will not be happy. They will be notifying Mr. Ingersoll."

"Neither the investors nor Mr. Ingersoll would be happy if someone got hurt." Nick glanced around, and his gaze fell on Lilly and Levi. His chest swelled. After church, he'd told them the coaster would have its first trip at two o'clock, and now they'd made it to witness the occasion. "Mr. Nash, if you'll excuse me, we're about to make the inaugural run of Lake Manawa's Velvet Roller Coaster." He left Mr. Nash standing there, mouth gaping at the dismissal, and strode over to the fence. "Want to see things close-up, Levi?"

"Yes!" Levi clapped his hands, and Lilly laughed.

"Follow me then." He led Levi and Lilly along the fence until they came to the turnstile. He motioned to Milt Hawkins to let them through. Scooping Levi into his arms, he said, "We're going inside the loading station. Soon as we get every-thing set, I'm going to let you pull the lever and start the whole thing."

Levi clapped again.

"You spoil him." Lilly laughed. "But I suppose everyone needs a little spoiling now and then."

"Does that include you?"

She rolled her eyes. "I'm much too practical for that."

"We'll see." He motioned for her to climb the steps into the loading station. "Patrons will give their tickets to the clerk here and then line up in that section." They swung a half door open and passed through. Nick helped Lilly step down onto the track, cross it, and step back onto the other side where some of his men stood.

Nick set Levi down and turned to Sean. "Let's get a car on these tracks, Mr. McGready."

"I'd be honored." Sean snapped his suspenders.

"What's he doing?" Levi tugged on Nick's hand.

Lilly drew him back. "Levi, Mr. Nick is busy."

"No, he's fine." Nick squatted down beside Levi. They watched as Sean flipped two latches on a six-foot section of track and pushed it beneath the walkway. "We have to have a way to change cars to do maintenance and to store them. That section of track is movable so we can wheel in our cart section."

Next, Sean pushed a second wheeled section of track down the walkway from the car storage area. Two more men as-sisted him in angling it into the open slot.

"The section Mr. McGready is moving now is built on wheels. It slides right into the empty space. See?" Nick pointed to Sean's area.

"But how did the roller coaster car get on it?" Levi stood on tiptoe to see into the car storage area.

"That special track section is the same height as the ones in the car shed. We can easily move cars onto it, wheel it in place, and slide them off. Watch."

Sean and two other workers pushed the section holding one of the two-seated red cars into the vacant slot. The newly arrived cars sported leather seats with yellow curlicue designs on the side panels and a safety bar inside for the rider to hold on to.

Once the car-bearing track was in place, Forest and Lars helped Sean roll the car from the temporary track onto the regular one. Forest held it in place while Sean pulled the wheeled section away. Finally, he tugged the original track section from beneath the walkway and secured the latches on each end.

"Impressive, isn't it?" Nick beamed.

"If it runs," Mr. Nash said from behind them.

"It'll run." Nick stood. "Okay, let's get those sandbags loaded into the car. Percy, be prepared to push the car around to the chain lift when I say so."

Nick waited until the guys put the sandbags in the cars, then checked the placement of the bags. He patted the top one and turned to Levi. "Are you ready to make this work?"

Levi nodded.

"Okay, when I count to three, help me move this lever forward. One, two, three."

Levi's face scrunched with effort as he pushed, but Nick still had to help. The motor began to crank the chain on

241

the lift hill with a steady chinking sound. He watched it for several minutes. So far, so good.

Nick waved to Percy, and the young man wheeled the sandbag-filled car around the loading station's track until it reached the foot of the lift hill. The lift chain grabbed the chain dog beneath the car and began to carry the car up the first forty-two-foot climb.

No one spoke. The crowd seemed to hold its breath.

Nick squeezed Lilly's hand.

Please, God, let this work.

28

The car climbed the first hill, clacking as it passed over each anti-rollback board, ticking off the footage to the summit with clocklike precision. Lilly reminded herself to breathe, but when the car reached the summit, rolled around the first curve, and made its descent, her breath caught. She pressed her hand to her mouth.

The crowd cheered.

Lilly glanced at Nick. He kept his eyes on the car as it rose and dipped and clunked around each corner. By the time it made it back to the loading station, its speed had slowed considerably. Percy applied the brakes, and the car came to a rest.

Nick's crew clapped one another on the back, and several men shook Nick's hand. Leaning to his right, he bent to speak into Lilly's ear in order to be heard above the celebration. "If we weren't in front of a couple hundred people, I'd kiss you senseless."

"And if you did, I'd send you on a roller coaster ride to the moon."

He chuckled. "Percy, let's get some of these sandbags out. Time for me to go for a ride."

Lilly grabbed his arm. Fear jolted through her. "You're going to ride now? But it's only had one test run."

"And now it will have two—only this time I'll be the passenger."

"But—"

He covered her hand. "I'll be fine. Trust me."

Trust you? Lilly stared as Nick climbed into the backseat of the roller coaster car. Her heart pounded like a drum against her rib cage. Trusting Nick wasn't the issue. Trusting a contraption that could catapult him halfway across the Midway before he could blink concerned her.

Percy pushed the car around the track to the base of the lift hill again. Nick waved to her and the crowd, but Lilly couldn't look as the car began to climb. Still, the urge to see forced her to open her eyes. Each time the car passed one of the forest-green anti-rollback boards, she wanted to cheer. The car cleared the first curve, then plunged into the first dive and flew up the other side. Lilly sucked in her breath. The car continued on its path, twisting around the curves of the figure-eight layout and through the undulating dips and rises.

Prior to reaching the next curve, the car came to an abrupt halt. Nick grabbed the safety bar in front of him and braced his arms. If he hadn't, Lilly was certain he'd have been thrown from the car.

Sean moaned.

"Look, Mama!" Levi tugged on her skirt.

With slow, deliberate movements, Nick climbed into the front seat. He tossed one of the sandbags into the back, then stood, holding on to the safety bar for balance.

Lilly turned to Sean. "What's he doing?"

"If there's somethin' wrong with the car, he'll have to push it all the way back. If the car slowed because of the track, he'll have to push it to get it going again. Either way, I bet the lad will be tired when he gets back."

Nick stuck one foot out of the car and pushed off of the high sideboards along the track. The car began to move again. Did Nick do these things every day? What if he slipped and fell? He had to be over twenty feet in the air.

As if he were running beside a sled, Nick continued to urge the car along. It picked up speed after rolling down the last hill but limped its way into the loading shed.

After the car stopped, he stepped onto the boarded walkway. He looked at Forest and Lars. "We'll need to smooth out the track before the number three curve. Can you two get on that right away?" He walked over to Lilly. "See, that wasn't so bad."

"Standing here watching you almost kill yourself? No, that wasn't bad at all." She could scarcely speak over the lump in her throat. She grabbed her son's hand. "Come on, Levi." She strode from the platform. The crowds around the fence had begun to disperse, and except for Marguerite, Trip, Mark, Emily, and Carter, she recognized few remaining faces. "We need to get back before this crowd all decides the show's over and wants to eat."

"Lilly, wait," Nick called.

She stopped on the loading station's last step but didn't turn. Tears burned her eyes. How dare he take those kinds of chances? What if Levi had seen him fall?

Nick touched her arm. "I'm sorry I scared you. I think it looks worse than it is."

"Was it fun, Mr. Nick?" Levi tried to spin around to see the roller coaster again.

"Yes, Levi, it was." Nick tousled his hair. "I know what I'm doing, and I was perfectly safe the whole time."

"You couldn't have been." Her voice came out pinched. "You were nearly thrown out of that thing."

"Lilly, it's my job." He tilted her head to see her face. "Are you crying?"

She pulled free and cleared her throat. "As I said, I have work to do and so do you. I need to be on my way."

"I promise you I was not in any real danger." Nick fell in step beside her. They reached the turnstile, and he caught her hand. "Let's celebrate tonight. I already told the crew I was letting them leave early as a reward for all of their hard work in getting the coaster going, so you don't need to make them dinner. We'll have dinner at Louie's French Restaurant, then go to the new vaudeville show."

"Vaudeville, Nick? I don't know." Besides, she wasn't ready to stop being furious yet.

"I checked. The poster says the show is family friendly." He gave her a lilting smile and tipped his head toward the roller coaster. "Besides, don't you think I deserve a little celebration?"

Levi jumped up and down. "Please, Mama. Let's go cell-break with Mr. Nick."

"Yeah, Lilly, cell-break with me."

The infectious sparkle in his eyes touched her, and her resolve to be angry at him for risking his life ebbed. Maybe she'd overreacted. He'd been doing this for a long time, and he didn't seem to be careless in any other way. Besides, like he said, it was his job.

He locked his hopeful gaze on her. Those cobalt eyes should be considered lethal weapons.

She sighed. "I suppose you do deserve to celebrate. Your

coaster is rather impressive—except for the almost killing yourself part."

"Remember, I told you I wasn't in any danger."

She raised her eyebrows and gave him a cheeky grin. "But you will be if I see you doing anything dangerous like that again."

Customer after customer entered Thorton's Lunch Counter. Lilly wiped a hand across her brow. If crowds continued like this all summer, they'd need more help. As it was, she'd not had a moment to breathe all afternoon.

She opened the oven door, and the sweet scent of cherry pie tickled her taste buds. Before all the pie was gone, she'd save a piece for Nick for the evening. She imagined he'd be too busy to come get one for himself.

Eugenia rushed into the kitchen. "He's here!"

"Who?"

"Mark Westing." Eugenia patted her frizzy hair into place. "What do I do?"

"Take his order. And remember we only have two entrée choices on the menu today. Pulled pork sandwiches and those new hot dogs on rolls."

"Yes, ma'am." Eugenia smoothed her surprisingly clean apron. "Do I look okay?"

Lilly wiped the smudge of mustard from the girl's cheek. "You look lovely."

Gathering her skirt in her hand, Eugenia hurried out. Unable to resist watching the scene unfold, Lilly finished removing the pies and followed Eugenia into the dining room a few seconds later.

"We have papple, cherry, and cheach pie." Eugenia's cheeks

247

filled with color. "I mean apple, cherry, and peach pie. Would you like a slice? Not of each of them, of course, but one of them? Nobody would eat all three, but if you want to, that's fine too."

Lilly snickered and refilled a customer's coffee cup at a table near Mark's. Poor Eugenia. All aflutter simply being in the presence of Marguerite's handsome little brother.

Mark chuckled. "I'd love a piece of cherry pie, Miss Baker. And if Lilly can spare you, would you care to join me?"

"Me?" Eugenia squeaked. "Here? Now?"

"Yes." He laughed again. "Be sure to select a piece of pie for yourself as well. My treat."

Lilly stepped back into the kitchen and pressed her hand to her mouth. Had she heard that correctly? Eugenia was going to be over the moon for a month. If Mark was indeed interested in her, it would explain why he'd been hanging around so much. Lilly shrugged. She'd seen stranger matches, but she wouldn't have predicted this in a hundred years.

Eugenia flew into the room. "He wants me to eat pie with him!"

"Shhh." Lilly held up her finger. "You don't want to give him the impression that you are overeager."

Clasping her hands to her chest, Eugenia cast a dreamy look at the ceiling. "Oh, but I like him so much. Wouldn't he make the most wonderful husband?"

"Husband? Eugenia, it's pie, not a proposal." Lilly took hold of Eugenia's shoulders. "Why don't you focus on the moment? What did he want to eat?"

"Just pie—with me."

"Any particular kind?" Lilly stepped to the Hoosier cabinet where the two hot pies now rested and pulled out a knife.

"I'll have peach."

248

"No, Eugenia, not you. What does Mark want?"

"Red-cherry pie for his red-cherry lips," she said dreamily.

Lilly rolled her eyes and cut a slice from the fresh pie. She slid it onto an ironware plate. "Take this out to him. Then I'll cut you a piece of peach from one of the pies in the pie safe out front. Be careful now. This is still warm."

After taking the pie, Eugenia nearly ran from the room. Lilly eased out the door behind her.

"Here's your cherry pie." Eugenia thrust the plate toward Mark, and the pie slid off, flying onto his crisp, white shirt. He yelped and pulled his shirt away from his chest. The steamy cherry filling oozed down the front, leaving a crimson trail.

"Oh my goodness." Eugenia's hand shot to her mouth. "I'm so sorry. Are you all right?"

Mark removed a chunk of crust from his lap and dropped it on the empty plate. His eyebrows cocked, he smiled at her. "Do you suppose you could find me a towel?"

"Yes, of course. Hold on. I'll get something and clean you right up."

Before Lilly could intercede, Eugenia snagged a towel from the lunch counter and rushed back to Mark. She extended her hand toward his shirt.

"I can take care of it." Mark reached for the towel.

"No, it's the least I can do." Eugenia began to mop the cherry filling with the towel, but it left yellow mustard streaks in its wake. "Oh my." She stopped and stared at the mess.

Lilly hurried over with a fresh, damp cloth. "Here you go, Mark. This ought to take off the worst of the damage. Eugenia, why don't you go in the kitchen and cut Mark another slice of pie?"

"Yes, of course." With tears in her eyes, the girl scurried away.

"It didn't burn you, did it?" Lilly watched him gingerly dab at the stain.

"No, it wasn't that warm. It surprised me more than anything."

"Let me get you some coffee, and if you bring that shirt back later, I'll wash it for you. A little lemon juice will work magic on those cherry stains."

Lilly brought Mark a fresh cup of coffee, and Eugenia arrived with the pie. Using both hands, she set the slice on the table. "I really am sorry."

Mark grinned at her. "Don't worry about it. So, where's your pie?"

"But after—I didn't think you'd—I didn't get a slice." Eugenia balled her apron.

Lilly slipped away and returned with a slice of peach pie. "Here you go, Eugenia. Now sit down and enjoy it." She winked. "And try to keep the pie on the plate."

Still chuckling under her breath, Lilly walked back into the kitchen.

"What's so humorous?" Mr. Thorton glanced up from his desk as she entered.

Lilly startled. "When did you arrive?"

"A couple of minutes ago. I saw you made it to the roller coaster's inaugural run."

Lilly's stomach soured. "I hope you didn't mind. There was no one in the restaurant, and Eugenia was still here."

Mr. Thorton leaned back in his squeaky chair and tucked his arms behind his head. "No, that was fine. I saw that Nick Perrin let Levi pull the switch to start the whole affair. I bet your boy loved that."

"He certainly did. It's all he can talk about." Lilly paused and blinked. Why was Mr. Thorton watching her? Could he be the one relaying information to Claude Hart? Someone had told her former father-in-law about Nick, and Mr. Thorton had already made it clear that he'd spoken with the Harts.

"By the way, where's little Levi at now?"

"He's outside playing." Her nerves tingled, and she glanced toward the back door. She could see Levi playing with a toad. Surely Mr. Thorton had seen him when he arrived as well. "I'd better get back to the dining room and see to our customers."

Mr. Thorton nodded. "Yes, of course, but don't forget to check on your son from time to time. You never know when a boy is going to get a hankering for an adventure."

A cold hand of fear drew a line up Lilly's spine. She only wished she knew why.

29

With her hand tucked in the crook of Nick's elbow, Lilly mounted the steps to enter Lake Manawa's vaudeville theater with Levi in tow. Boisterous conversation echoed from within, and she smiled. A little laughter was exactly what she needed tonight. She'd considered sharing her fears with Nick concerning Mr. Thorton, but now was not the time.

After Nick secured tickets, they entered the theater. Nick led them toward the front, and they slipped into an empty place on the pew-like seating. Within minutes the auditorium filled, and Lilly was glad she hadn't taken the time to change into yet another dress. She'd already tried on two, but she still feared the one she was wearing might be a bit too fussy with its black, lace-edged flounces on the silk skirt.

She smoothed the lapel of the matching tailored jacket and glanced at Nick, who was speaking to Levi beside him. Levi's eyes lit up when Nick told him an animal act would perform.

Her gaze swept the rest of the crowd. Other women wore equally fancy dresses, although most were more fashionable.

While beautiful, her frocks lacked the latest details that would make them in vogue. She doubted Nick would notice, but it was yet another thing that had changed since Ben's death.

She shouldn't complain. Many women had only a few dresses from which to choose. Thanks to Ben, she'd been blessed with three trunks full, and this dress had been one of Ben's favorites.

"You look beautiful." Nick touched her arm. "That color brings out the golden flecks in your eyes. What do you call it? It's not quite green and not quite true gold."

"The color? I call it ocher, but who knows what someone else might say." She smiled.

Nick looked rather handsome himself in his double-breasted suit and knotted tie. But it was the stylish homburg hat with its dent in the center that she liked the most. It was so different from the bowlers most of the men wore, but it must have cost him a week's salary.

She blinked when she realized she'd been staring. "How's Levi doing?"

"Chomping at the bit to see the animals." Nick placed his hand on the boy's bouncing knee. The heavy curtains opened, and lively organ music filled the air. He leaned close and pressed his lips to Lilly's ear. "Ready for a show filled with endless surprises?"

His hot breath on her skin sent chills coursing through her. She was ready as long as the surprises were onstage and not coming from the man next to her. How did he convey so much in a few words?

He winked at her.

She pulled out her fan and waved it in front of her flushed cheeks. What a night this was turning out to be!

The show opened with a barrel-chested man singing a

lively patriotic song. He was followed by two Irishmen, the Brady brothers, billed as novelty bag punchers. The men demonstrated pugilistic techniques on a fast punching ball and ended their act with a mock boxing match. Nick applauded their display with great enthusiasm.

When a woman known as "only Lizette" took the stage with her collection of trained poodles and cockatoos, Levi sat on the edge of his seat. The poodles leapt over one another as if they were children, balancing balls on their noses, jumping through hoops, and even climbing a ladder. The crowd had to hush to hear Lizette's cockatoo, Cookie, speak. Levi giggled when the white bird bobbed its feathered head and said, "Hi, dolly." Lizette persuaded Cookie to kiss her cheek and say, "Love you."

Nick leaned over and brushed a kiss on Lilly's cheek. "I like the way Cookie thinks."

Lilly's cheeks grew warmer under the implied message.

While another performer sang a teary ballad, the curtains closed for the stage hands to set the scenery for the next skit. When the curtains parted, a park scene was revealed. A woman entered wearing a dark veil. She sat down on the bench and closed her parasol.

Seconds later, a mustached actor approached her and spent several minutes trying to persuade the woman to remove her veil, wanting to see her beauty. No matter what he did, she neither spoke nor took off the veil. He even performed acrobatics to impress her and sang a love song in a rich tenor voice. He made one final attempt by telling her a sad tale about how his brother had always gotten the girl. Still, she refused to lift the veil. Finally, he departed, despondent over her lack of response.

Another actor then entered the stage. He sat down by the

woman, draped his arm around her shoulders, and asked how her day had gone.

She giggled. "Well, you just missed your brother."

The man laughed, lifted her veil, and kissed the woman soundly.

Nick sat bolt upright. Every muscle in his body seemed to tense. He stared at the actress until she left the stage.

Lilly touched his arm. "What's wrong?"

"That was Ruby."

❧

The strains of the young Greek violinist's aching solo only heightened the tension in Nick's chest. He tried to swallow the lump in his throat.

Ruby was here.

Now.

At Lake Manawa.

He drew in a long breath and released it through his nose. He glanced at Lilly. Her face was pale, her hands clutched in her lap. He should whisper something reassuring in her ear, but his mind refused to formulate words.

It figured. Ruby had always had a way of making his life chaotic, and without knowing it, she'd done it again.

❧

Applause erupted as the last song concluded and the curtain closed. Lilly glanced at Nick. He'd hardly breathed since Ruby's first act. Was Nick having second thoughts about her now?

"Ice cream!" Levi jumped up from his seat. "You promised we could get some after the show."

Nick tore his eyes from the stage and stood. "You're right,

255

Chipmunk. I certainly did." Offering his hand to Lilly, he drew her upward. "Let's get out of here. The sooner the better."

As she and Nick walked side by side down the Midway toward the ice cream parlor, Lilly ignored the hawkers trying to get Nick to play their penny arcade games and win her a prize. Not once did he give them a second glance. Of course, with all his travels, he was used to this sort of fare, but his silence told her something troubled him.

Not some*thing*. Some*one*. Five feet, seven inches of exotic womanhood named Ruby Rawlins.

The buttery scent of freshly popped popcorn filled the air. She smiled as the lights came on, and the whole Midway illuminated in a magical way.

Nick suddenly stopped. "Hey, Chipmunk, have you played the Japanese rolling-ball game?"

"He doesn't need to do that, Nick. If you want some time alone—"

"No." His voice, firm as iron, made her step back. "I'm sorry. I meant I don't want to be alone. I want to be with the two of you." He placed his hand on Levi's head. "So, ready to play?"

"Posilutely."

Lilly exchanged a glance with Nick, and they both snickered. "Levi, honey, it's *positively* or *absolutely*. You can't have both."

"Why not?"

"It's not a word." Lilly took his hand, and the three of them headed toward the Japanese rolling-ball arcade. The red scalloped awning flapped in the breeze. She stepped inside the area, and the heady scent of incense reached her nostrils.

"Who makes up the words?" Levi asked.

"People."

"I'm a people."

"You're a person."

Nick hoisted Levi onto a step stool the proprietors had created for the children to use. "And right now, you're a person who's going to learn to play the Japanese ball game."

"How's it work?" Levi scrunched his brow.

"Here's a man that's a good fella!" the Oriental woman running the game shouted to the crowds. Her deep voice didn't seem to go with her feminine red kimono. "He'll take a chance." She turned to Nick. "You get a present either way, mister. Yes, sir, that's a fact. A nickel per ball."

Nick handed the owner a quarter, and she passed him five small balls. Nick gave two to Levi. "You see the pins at the end of this board? You roll the ball and knock down all ten pins to win a bigger prize." He swept his hand toward the rows of oriental trinkets and dishes. "If you don't get them all down, you don't win much."

"But that's not fair." With a frown, Levi tilted his head to the side to get a better view of the pins.

"There are a lot of things in life that aren't fair." Nick sighed, then gave Lilly a weak smile. "You want me to show you how to do it first?"

"No, I can do it." Levi clutched his two balls to his chest.

"Okay, go ahead and try, but stay behind this line." Nick pointed to the line painted on a yellow board.

Levi rolled the ball and it curved to the right, only taking three pins with it. He clapped. "I did it."

The proprietor set the pins up. "Why don't you try again? See if you get more."

With the tip of his tongue protruding between his lips, Levi rolled the ball. This time several of the pins tumbled, leaving only three standing.

"Good job." The woman handed Levi a reed whistle.

Levi immediately raised the toy to his lips, blew into it, and released a long, shrill sound.

Lilly grabbed it. "I think I'll hold on to this until we're home."

"We don't have a home, 'member, Mama?"

His words jabbed her, but she covered her feelings with a smile. "Then I'll keep it until we get to Emily's."

Nick held out a ball in his palm. "Your turn, Lilly."

"You go ahead. I don't think I need to show you how good I am." She tried to offer him a teasing grin to lighten the moment.

"I disagree. It's your turn." He glanced at Levi. "And we should always take turns with our friends, right, Levi?"

"That's what Mama always says, and she said Mr. Nick was her friend."

"Is that so?" Nick chuckled.

Lilly gave him a mock glare and took the ball.

"Want some help?" Nick offered with a crooked grin.

"I think I can manage." Lilly rolled the ball and knocked down half the pins. The Oriental woman handed her a flimsy paper fan. Lilly rolled her eyes but thanked the lady.

"And how does my girl get a silk fan?" Nick pointed to the pretty ones displayed in a case.

"Only one way. Knock down all the pins. Twice." She pointed to the pins. "Very difficult."

Nick bent to examine the game. "There has to be a trick to the board's tilt or bend that makes it so hard." He pointed to the center. "See there, Lilly, it's a smidgeon higher."

"But that makes it nearly impossible."

"Nearly impossible is my specialty." He moved the ball in his hand up and down, apparently making calculations in his mind.

Lilly smiled. "This isn't a roller coaster."

"But it's all about curve and velocity." He winked at her and gave the ball a shove. It followed an arc, then hit between the first and second pins. One by one, the pins fell.

"You did it!" Levi jumped up and down on his box and clapped.

"Must do it one more time for fan." The proprietor joined her hands in front of her, revealing the tattered edges of her pagoda sleeves. "Very difficult."

Nick rolled the last ball, and the pins clattered on the board.

Levi whooped.

The proprietor, looking none too pleased, pointed to the fans displayed and said to Lilly, "You pick?"

Nick glanced at Lilly. "May I?"

She nodded. Nick selected an ivory one with a greenish-gold bird surrounded by flowers. He handed it to Lilly and pointed to the bird. "An ocher fan to go with your lovely ocher dress."

"Thank you." She waved it in front of her warm cheeks.

"Nick? Nick Perrin?"

Lilly turned at the sound of the lilting voice of a woman. Her heart skidded to a halt.

Lord, help me handle this gracefully.

30

Nick would know that voice anywhere. Perhaps he could pretend he didn't hear Ruby.

"Nick?"

Slowly he turned. He touched the rim of his hat and dipped his head in greeting. "Ruby."

"It is you. I thought I saw you during the performance with this little fellow, so I've been out here looking for you." She eyed Levi. "And who is this?"

Nick slipped an arm around Lilly's waist and found her back ramrod stiff beneath his hand. Regret pressed on his chest for putting her through this. "Miss Ruby Rawlins, may I introduce Mrs. Lilly Hart and her son, Levi."

Ruby locked her gaze on Lilly. "Mrs. Hart, it's a pleasure to meet you."

"You too, Miss Rawlins. I enjoyed your performance this evening."

"I didn't." Levi crossed his arms over his chest. "I liked the bird better."

"Levi, hush." Lilly placed her hand on his shoulder. "I apologize for his rudeness."

"I'm just being honest, Mama."

"I appreciate honesty." Ruby's lips curled, revealing a perfect smile. She flicked a flaming lock of auburn hair off her shoulder.

Nick scowled. Since when had honesty meant anything to her? It certainly hadn't been important to her when they were together.

Scooping Levi into his arms, Nick hugged the boy tight. "Sorry to cut this short, but I promised Lilly and this little man some ice cream." He nodded toward her. "It's nice to see you again."

She stepped closer, laying her hand on Nick's sleeve. "But, Nick, when do you want to talk? We have a lot of catching up to do. Could we meet somewhere tomorrow?"

Nick studied her—the woman he'd once loved. Dark circles rimmed her eyes, and the world-is-lucky-to-have-me spark she always exuded was no longer present. Her life with the vaudeville traveling show seemed to be a hard one.

It served her right.

A twinge of guilt kicked him in the gut. God wouldn't want him to be bitter. Besides, did Ruby really deserve a life like this? Performing after poodles and a cockatoo?

But she wasn't his concern anymore, and the woman beside him was.

"I'll be around. Maybe we'll run into one another."

He ushered Lilly away, leaving Ruby standing alone on the Midway.

"Could you slow down to a fast trot?" Lilly struggled to catch her breath.

"Sorry." He let his steps fall in line with her pace. "I wanted to get away from her fast."

261

"Really? I never would have guessed."

They reached the ice cream parlor, and Nick held the door for her.

Lilly sat down at one of the small round tables, and Levi scrambled into the heart-shaped chair beside her. The ice cream parlor sported rows of sparkling glasses and jars of colorful fruit toppings and nuts.

Nick settled in the remaining third chair. "What kind of ice cream do you want, Chipmunk?"

"Vanilla with butterscotch."

"Mmmm. Good choice. Maybe I'll have that too." Nick stood. "I'll place our orders."

"What about me?" Lilly asked.

"I know what you want."

"How?"

"Trust me."

"That isn't exactly my forte."

"Really?" He mocked her earlier words. "I never would have guessed."

He returned a few moments later carrying a lacquered wooden tray bearing two butterscotch sundaes, one with nuts and one without, and a chocolate soda.

Lilly beamed when he set the treat in front of her. She sank her long spoon into the creamy scoops of vanilla ice cream in the bottom of the tall glass and stirred the chocolate syrup and soda water surrounding it. Withdrawing a spoonful of ice cream, Lilly slipped it in her mouth. Nick watched her lips close around the confection, and he yearned to taste them once again for himself.

"You can't ignore Ruby." Lilly dipped her spoon in the soda again. "She wants to speak with you, and you aren't difficult to find. In case you hadn't noticed, there's a rather large structure at the entrance to this park that points to you like a beacon."

"How did we get back to the topic of Ruby?" Nick took a bite of his sundae.

"What were you thinking about?" She dabbed Levi's chin with her napkin.

"Kissing you." He gave her a rakish grin and slurped down a large spoonful. "Lilly, I don't want to speak with her or about her or have anything to do with her. She's my past. You're my future."

"Some future," she mumbled under her breath.

Nick looked up. "What are you talking about?"

"The coaster is done. You'll be leaving soon."

"No, I won't. Where'd you get that idea?"

"I heard your men talking."

His spoon clattered against his sundae dish. "Most of them are leaving, but I'm not. I'm staying here for the rest of the summer. I have to make sure the roller coaster is working well, and then I have to train whomever the Lake Manawa manager hires to run it. I thought you knew that."

Tears filled Lilly's eyes, but her lips curled in a warm smile.

"You really thought I was leaving soon."

"Not right away, of course, but in a few weeks, I thought—" She dropped her gaze to the few remaining spoonfuls of her soda.

"I'd leave you?"

She shrugged. "Eventually you'll have to, Nick. You can't stay around here forever."

"Or you could go with me."

"Can we, Mama?" Levi pushed his licked-clean sundae dish to the middle of the table. "Can we go with Mr. Nick?"

Lilly's eyes darted from Nick to her son, then back to Nick. "We should talk about this later."

Nick stood and offered her his hand. "We certainly will."

⤜⧓⤏

Hanging out the dish towels on the clothesline behind the diner, Lilly glanced across the Midway to the Velvet Roller Coaster standing proudly against the sky. In the last three days, it had performed flawlessly, according to the patrons who came into the diner still exhilarated by the ride. And the long lines had kept Nick busy far into each evening.

She'd been busy herself. Still, she'd managed to have her usual morning off and had gone into the city to spend time with her mother. It felt good to tell her mother all about Nick, about his declaration of love, and even about his former fiancée.

Lilly snapped a wet apron in the air before pinning it to the line, thinking about how Nick had dismissed Ruby in the Midway. Later he'd asked Lilly to leave with him. Had Ruby been the driving force behind such a bold statement?

Doubt made her stomach churn. This morning, her mother had said she was having a crisis of faith. "Your faith," her mother had said, quoting 1 Corinthians, "should not be in the wisdom of men but in the power of God. Lilly, you're relying on your own wisdom."

Was she? And how was she supposed to trust God when He'd allowed so much pain and disappointment in her life? Even now, God had let Ruby arrive just when her heart was beginning to open to the possibilities with Nick.

Marguerite stepped out of the diner's back door. "There you are."

"Did you come to help me with laundry?"

"It looks like you have it under control." She snickered and handed Lilly a clothespin from the basket. "I'm on my way over to take Tate and Faith for a ride on Nick's roller coaster. Want to join us? The diner didn't look too busy, and now that Nora is helping you, Eugenia said she could hold things down for a while."

Lilly smiled at the thought of the new employee. Nora had proven to be a quick learner and a hard worker, and having her there had given Lilly a bit more freedom. "I don't know. Levi has been pestering me day and night about taking a ride, but I've seen it and I don't want him on it." Lilly stopped hanging the next towel midair and eyed Marguerite. "Wait a minute. I thought you said you might be in the family way."

Marguerite grinned and pressed a hand to her midsection. "I am, but that shouldn't stop me. If the roller coaster is safe for children and old ladies to ride on, why should it be dangerous for a woman carrying a child?"

A twinge of worry for her friend nudged Lilly. Why did Marguerite always have to push the boundaries? She clipped the towel in place. "Does Trip know you're doing this?"

"I told him I was taking Tate and Faith on the new ride. In fact, he may join us there." Marguerite came around the other side of the towels and passed her another clothespin.

"But did you tell him about the baby?" Lilly leveled her gaze over the clothesline at Marguerite.

"Not yet. If I did, you know as well as I that he'd probably not even let me look at the roller coaster, let alone ride on it." Marguerite tucked the basket of pins under her arm.

Lilly snagged the now-empty laundry basket. "And you have no idea why he might feel that way?"

"It's not my fault every bone in my husband's body is

overprotective. Besides, this is the first roller coaster in the area—the whole state. Can you imagine not riding it?"

"As a matter of fact"—Lilly held the screen door for her—"I have no plans to ride that beast."

"But Nick built it."

Lilly slipped the large basket into the corner, then took the smaller one from her friend and placed it on the shelf. "Nick knows how I feel. I tell him the truth."

"Okay, okay." Marguerite held up her hands. "I'll tell Trip—after I ride the roller coaster one time. You coming?"

"To watch you make your stubborn self sick on that thing?" Lilly untied her apron strings. "I wouldn't miss it."

❦

The rare perfect days in Iowa made living through the cold winters and hot summers worthwhile. Lilly took a deep breath of tangy, lake-scented air and decided this was one of those perfect days. Perfect temperature. Perfect breeze. Perfect friends.

She glanced at Marguerite. Well, two out of three wasn't bad. Marguerite certainly wasn't perfect, but at least she was a dear—if a little foolish—friend. Ahead of them, Tate, Faith, and Levi zigzagged through the Midway patrons on their way to the coaster, barely able to contain their excitement.

"Levi, remember, you are not riding on the coaster," she called. "You're only watching."

He twirled around and walked backward. "I know, Mama."

"He says that now, but as soon as we get there, he'll be begging me once again." Lilly slipped her hands into the pocket of her skirt and fingered a nickel. "Sometimes he's as bad at handling *no* as you are. Maybe I can distract him with some popcorn."

"Or maybe you could let him have a ride." Marguerite gave her a sidelong glance. "Sometimes it's okay to take a chance, Lilly."

"And sometimes you can't. Not when it comes to your children."

Marguerite rolled her eyes. "It's going to be fine. You'll see."

As they approached, Lilly spotted Trip waiting for Marguerite at the ticket counter, his horizontally striped, blue sailing shirt standing out among the suit coats of the other patrons. He tipped his white cap to them. "Hello, sweetheart. Good afternoon, Lilly. Did Marguerite convince you to join us on the ride?"

"No, I'm simply here to watch."

"Look, Mama. It's Aunt Emily." Levi pointed down the walk where Carter and Emily approached, pushing Katie in a baby carriage.

"Did you stop by and invite them too?" Trip snaked his arm around his wife's waist and kissed her temple. "You're a regular social secretary."

Marguerite waved to them. "It wouldn't be a party if they weren't here."

After they'd all exchanged greetings, Trip turned to the ticket counter. Forest, one of Nick's men, served as clerk, but Lilly knew that was only temporary. She guessed he was training the young man beside him.

"How much is it?" Trip asked.

"Five cents a ride or six rides for a quarter." Forest smiled at Lilly. "It won't cost you or your boy a thing, Mrs. Hart. Nick already made that clear. You two always ride free."

Lilly's cheeks warmed. "I won't need a ticket, but thank you anyway. Can I still go in and watch?"

"Sure thing."

Trip laid a quarter on the counter. "Give me six. If we don't use the other two today, I'm sure Marguerite will by the end of the week."

"Don't be so sure about that," Lilly muttered.

"Marguerite, you're going?" Emily's eyebrows shot up.

"Of course I am." Marguerite shot her a look of warning.

"But—"

Marguerite linked arms with her husband. "Oh, good. The line's not long, so we won't have to wait. Emily, you can leave the baby with Lilly so you can ride with Carter."

While Carter purchased their tickets, Emily lifted Kate out of the carriage. At Forest's suggestion, they rolled the carriage behind the ticket counter, and Emily and Lilly walked side by side down the paved walk to the loading station.

"Lilly, who's that talking to Nick?" Emily asked.

Lilly scanned the station, and her breath caught. Auburn locks hung loose down the woman's back to her impossibly thin waist.

Ruby.

Maybe that's why Nick had been so scarce for the last three days. A knot of jealousy formed in her throat. She swallowed it down. No, she had finally made a decision. She had faith in Nick, and she would continue to trust him until he gave her a good reason not to.

❧

Ruby ran her hand along her bodice in a way that made it hard for Nick to miss his former fiancée's assets. He averted his eyes and saw Lilly approaching with her friends. His chest warmed. Had she come to ride after all?

"So, Nick, can we meet to talk following the show tonight?

Say, nine o'clock? I won't have had so much as a morsel of nourishment all evening long." She smoothed her hands along the sides of her narrow waist. "Maybe we could grab a bite to eat."

He called to one of the men to oil the chain lift. "Ruby, I haven't been done here by nine o'clock all week. If I do finish by then, I need to spend some time with Lilly."

"Surely she won't mind a couple of old friends catching up."

"We aren't old friends. We were engaged, but we aren't now. We aren't anything anymore." He glanced at Lilly again, her expression unreadable. "Now, if you'll excuse me."

She caught his sleeve. "You've done well for yourself, Nick, and I'd like to hear more. If you can't meet tonight, how about tomorrow? Lunch? We can even invite her."

"No, I don't think so."

She tipped her head and gave him a come-hither smile. "All right, but I hope you know I'll be back every day until you change your mind. We will talk, Nick Perrin, and I won't take no for an answer."

Ruby sashayed away, the feathers on her elaborate hat waving in the breeze. She passed Lilly on the station's stairs and gave her a syrupy smile. She spoke to her, but Nick couldn't hear the exchange. If Ruby said anything rude to Lilly, he was going to wring her pretty little neck.

He met Lilly at the top of the stairs, and his chest swelled at the sight of her. If they weren't in a public place, he'd have kissed her right then and there. "You don't know how good it is to see you."

"Funny, you appeared to have plenty of company."

While Lilly's words were teasing in nature, he heard a note of hurt in her voice.

"She still wants to get together to catch up. I told her no, but she's never been one to take no for an answer."

Trip glanced at Marguerite. "Kind of like someone else I know. So, Nick, how fast does your coaster go?"

"Nearly fifteen miles an hour." Nick pointed to an empty car. "Who's riding with whom? Levi, you want to ride with your mama or me?"

Lilly's eyes widened. "He's not—I'm not—we're not going. We're here to watch. I'm tending Kate for Emily."

"Oh." He couldn't hide the disappointment in his voice.

"Can I ride with Mr. Nick, Mama?" Levi looked up at her with blue eyes full of hope. "Tate and Faith are going."

She scowled at Nick, then turned to Levi. "Remember what I said about pestering me?"

He hung his head and drew a circle on the platform with the toe of his boot. "Yes, ma'am."

Nick ruffled his hair. "Maybe later, Chipmunk."

"Is this safe for everyone, Nick?" Emily glanced at Marguerite.

"Sure. Children, old folks—they've all ridden on it. No problem. Marguerite and Trip, shouldn't be much different than sailing for you. A little speed and some ups and downs."

Lilly locked her gaze on Marguerite. "Ups and downs. Ought to be a lot of fun."

"It is." Nick grinned. "So far, not one complaint."

When the car at the top of the lift hill began its descent, screams rent the air. Nick chuckled and led the group to the loading platform. After Lilly took baby Katie from Carter, he helped Tate and Faith into the front seat of a waiting car. Trip and Marguerite sat behind them. Emily and Carter offered to take the next car along with two people they didn't know. Percy pushed the Andrews family's car around the bottom of the lift hill. Seconds later, it began to make the forty-two-foot climb.

Once the car was well on its way, Percy brought Emily and Carter's car around. Nick glanced at Lilly and noticed she'd not taken her eyes off Marguerite's car. Was she that afraid for them? Didn't she believe he and his men had done everything possible to make this the safest ride possible?

A minute and a half from the time the car left, it returned. No sooner had Sean applied the brakes than Trip was helping Marguerite from the car. Her face, a sickly shade of green, told Nick the woman had not taken well to the roller coaster ride.

Nick took her other arm. "Are you okay, Marguerite?"

Lilly hurried to his side. Before she could even say anything, Marguerite broke free of the two men's holds and raced down the stairs.

Trip started to go after her, but Lilly grabbed his arm. "No, let me." She thrust Katie into Nick's arms. "Take care of her until I get back. Levi, stay here with Mr. Nick."

31

With her skirt balled in her fist, Lilly ran down the steps. She found Marguerite behind the ticket office, hunched over, wiping her mouth with a handkerchief.

Lilly scrunched her nose at the stench and laid a hand on her friend's shoulder. "Better?"

Marguerite stood and leaned against the shed. "Just say it."

"Say what?"

"'I told you so.'"

"I wasn't gonna say that." She pointed to a park bench with a view of the roller coaster. "Why don't we go sit down? It will let you catch your breath. You want to lean on me?"

"No. If Trip thinks I can't walk, he'll probably carry me all the way home." Marguerite wobbled a bit as she straightened but managed to walk slowly to the bench. She sank onto it and patted her disheveled hair. "How do I look?"

"Like a haint." Lilly's lips curled.

"A haint who feels a little foolish." Marguerite sighed.

"Make that a lot foolish. Wouldn't you think a woman my age would know better?"

"You'd think so." Lilly glanced at the loading station and saw Trip now at the bottom of the steps. "Here comes your husband."

Marguerite pressed her hand to her forehead and moaned.

Trip jogged over to meet them. "Marguerite, are you feeling better? Do you need a doctor?"

"No. This is nothing more than a little seasickness."

Trip quirked an eyebrow. "Lilly, thanks for seeing to her." He sat down beside his wife and took her hand. "I'm surprised the coaster bothered you. We've been on sailboats that hit swells worse than any of those dips, and you handled those fine." He snickered. "Except when you were in the family way, of course."

Marguerite glanced at Lilly, and Lilly raised her eyebrows.

Trip caught the exchange. "Marguerite? Are you . . . ?"

"Maybe." She fiddled with the seam in her gored skirt. She peeked at Trip. "Probably."

A grin spread across Trip's face, then slid away. "You knew this and you still went on the roller coaster?" He stood and paced. "What were you thinking? Didn't you realize how dangerous that could be? You put yourself and our baby at risk."

She rubbed her temple. "I wanted to ride it, and I knew you'd forbid it."

"I certainly would have, but not to keep you from having fun." He shook his head in disbelief. "So you kept our baby a secret from me?"

Lilly crossed her arms in her best I-told-you-so pose.

Trip whirled toward her. "And you knew too? How could you let her do this?"

"Let her?" She fired a glare at Marguerite. "I don't let her do anything. She gets in trouble all by herself. Always has.

Always will. The only difference is now she's your problem, not mine."

"She tried to talk me out of it." Marguerite stood, swayed, and pressed a hand to her stomach.

Trip caught her arm and urged her back to the bench. "Easy." He sat down beside her again and rubbed circles on her shoulder. "We'll talk about all this when you're feeling better. By the way, for the record, I'm thrilled about having another child. Lilly, do you think she needs a doctor?"

"No. There are no pills for stupidity, or I'd have had the doctor give me a bottleful for Ben's folks." Lilly glanced at Marguerite, her head now resting on her husband's shoulder. "Take her home and love her, Trip. Yell at her if you have to, but be glad you have her. You never realize what you have until it's gone."

❧

Slipping a fresh apron over her head, Lilly eyed Eugenia's first batch of cinnamon rolls. Light and fluffy, the rolls had risen beautifully, and the whole kitchen smelled of cinnamon. Eugenia had even watched the rolls so carefully that not one of them had a dark spot on the top.

"Eugenia, these are gorgeous. You are truly becoming quite a baker." Lilly set a blue crockery bowl on the counter. "Did you want to put icing on them?"

"Oh yes. That's the best part."

Lilly tapped the blue bowl. "Do you know what to do, or do you want me to walk you through it?"

"I think I remember everything." Eugenia reached for the butter crock. "Thank you, Miss Lilly. You've been such a good teacher, and I know I haven't been the easiest student."

Laughing, Lilly stirred the ham and beans on the stove.

"Every day you get a little better, but lately you've grown by leaps and bounds. Your mother would be proud of you. I know I am. Perhaps you should save her one of the rolls."

Eugenia poured milk and vanilla extract into the confectioner's sugar and butter. "Truth be told, there's only one person I want to give a roll to."

"Hmmm, I wonder who that could be?" Lilly grinned. "I think Mark will be quite impressed too."

After beating the frosting, Eugenia tasted a bit on the tip of her finger. "Delicious. I still can't believe I know how to do these things."

Lilly handed her a knife. "After you spread the icing on the rolls, you can start on the dishes. If you're lucky, you'll have them done in case Mark stops by again."

⚘

"But, Mama . . ." Levi attempted to skip a rock across the lake, but it sank with a splash only a few yards from the shore. "I'm big 'nough."

Lilly sat down on a bench and pulled out a sock from her mending basket. The pink-tinted sky seemed to be lowering its sleepy eyelids. With the days getting longer, she had more daylight to enjoy after her work at the diner was done, and she'd come to treasure these moments at the close of the day. If Nick could get away today, he planned to meet them. Their time together had seemed sparse since the roller coaster opened and Ruby arrived.

Levi traipsed over and tipped his chubby face up to her. "Please, Mama."

"Levi Hart, we're not discussing this again. I don't want you riding on the roller coaster."

"But Mr. Nick said—"

"I don't care what Mr. Nick said."

Levi giggled.

"You don't care what I say, huh?" Nick slipped in place beside her with two bamboo fishing poles in hand. He kissed Lilly's cheek. "What have I said to get myself in trouble?"

"Nothing. Levi's pestering me again about riding the roller coaster."

Nick untangled one rod and passed it to Levi. "Now, wait for me, Levi. Did you bring the worms?"

"Yes, sir. A whole big, big, big bunch." He spread his arms wide.

"Good job." Nick turned to Lilly after Levi had scampered away. "I could go with him on the coaster, and you wouldn't have to be on it at all."

"Nick, I know you feel it's safe, but I can't in good conscience let him ride it. What if something happened to him?"

Nick nodded, hurt evident in his eyes. "It's still a matter of trust."

She laid a hand on his arm. "Not in trusting you. It's in trusting the equipment, the heights, the whole thing. He's all I have."

"Have you ever considered you might be a tad"—he held his thumb and forefinger a half inch apart—"overprotective?"

"No, I haven't." She quirked a smile, tied off the knot on the sock, and bit the thread. "But he is *my* son. How about I promise to think on it some more?"

"And pray about it?" He snagged the sock from her hand and dropped it in the basket.

"What are you doing?"

"We're going to be by the water, handling dangerous hooks and scary fish. You'd better come along to protect us."

"I'm sure you can handle fishing all by yourselves." She reached for another sock.

"Not so fast." He took her hand and pulled her to her feet. "I don't like worms."

"Are you serious?"

He flashed her a grin. "Of course I am. Slimy things give me the creeps."

"I know that's not true."

He shrugged. "Someone has to put the worms on *your* son's line. Looks like it's going to be you."

She sighed and let him lead her to the water's edge. Confounded man. Did he think she was going to give in on the roller coaster because of a worm? With a son like Levi, she'd dealt with plenty of worms. Crickets, cicadas, frogs, and granddaddy longlegs too. It was only the spiders and snakes that got her. She shivered. She hated spiders and snakes.

Once she had Levi's hook baited, she turned toward Nick. "Need some help?"

Nick shot her a glare as he wrestled with a night crawler. "There. Ready to cast, Levi?"

"Yes, sir." The two of them approached the shore. Nick tossed out his line, then turned to help Levi.

"We've got this." Lilly smiled at him. She was already standing behind her son. "Pull the tip of the pole back like so," she told Levi, covering her son's chubby hand with her own. "Now swing it forward." The line landed a few yards from Nick's. Immediately Levi wanted to reel it back in. She stopped him. "Levi, I know it's hard, but it's time to be patient and wait to see if the fish are gonna bite."

Nick and Lilly sat down on the shore. Heedless of the warning, in less than ten minutes, Levi had reeled in his line and recast no less than six times. The poor worm on the end of his hook flopped like a piece of wet rope.

"You never cease to surprise me." Nick glanced at Lilly.

"So, have you heard if the fish are hitting on night crawlers? Ever try corn, Miss Fisherwoman?"

Her stomach cinched when she looked at him. His face was shadowed with beard growth, and she ached to reach out her hand and run it along the rough surface of his solid jaw. Nick Perrin, undeniably handsome, made her insides jelly.

Jealousy poked her hard. Was this how Ruby felt when she was near him? Were all Ruby's feelings for Nick coming back to her?

She swallowed. "I think folks use a lot of different baits to get what they want."

"Are we still talking about fishing?" Nick took up the slack in his line.

"Yes and no. There are all kinds of fishing. You can fish for answers or fish for information. You can fish like we are right now, or you can look at all the other fish in the sea." She cast a sidelong glance in his direction.

"I'm not looking, Lilly."

Oh my, he knew whom she was talking about. She gave him a fleeting smile. "She's beautiful."

"I'm not interested."

"She sure is interested in you."

"But she won't be reeling me in. Understand?" Nick stood and offered her his hand. His eyes dropped to her lips. Would he kiss her in front of Levi and make her forget Ruby Rawlins even existed?

No sooner was she on her feet than his line pulled taut. He braced his feet and reeled the catch in. A fifteen-inch catfish dangled from the line. He held it up triumphantly.

"You did it!" Levi set down his rod and applauded.

"Beginner's luck," Lilly teased.

"The trick is to make sure the fish want the bait you're

278

offering. If they don't, it's a waste of your time." He met her gaze. "Goes double when you're fishing for a person."

Levi cast his line again. "Silly goose. Nobody fishes for people."

Lilly walked over and laid her hands on his shoulders. "You'd be surprised, Levi. You'd be surprised."

"Besides, Levi, remember, Jesus told His apostles He was going to make them fishers of men." Nick managed to remove the fish from his hook. "Gotta use the right bait there too."

Lilly's insides warmed. Nick Perrin had a good heart.

The rest of the evening passed without another mention of Ruby. Nick caught a couple of additional catfish along with a few unwanted small crappies he threw back, and they headed to the diner to clean their catch. By the time Nick had finished, Levi had fallen asleep at one of the tables, his head resting on his arms.

Lilly soaked the fish in milk in the icebox and then set a piece of pie in front of Nick.

"Where's yours?"

"I'm not hungry."

Nick speared a bite and held it to her lips. "You go first. That way I know you aren't poisoning me."

She laughed and ate the bite. The blueberries burst on her tongue. She moaned as she swallowed the sweet juices. "This is really good."

"Your pies are usually good. Delicious, in fact."

"Mine, yes. Eugenia's, no."

"You were trying to poison me!" Nick laughed and took a bite of his own. "This is great. You've done wonders for her, Lilly."

"She is improving, but I wouldn't say it was me. She's working hard. My mama always said everyone needs someone who believes in them."

"You gave her the chance and made her believe in herself. You make people want to be better." He gripped her hand. "You make me want to be a better person."

She let the warmth spread from her hand to her heart, not daring to speak for fear the moment would evaporate like steam over a pot of soup.

"I love you, Lilly."

His blue eyes searched hers, and her insides quivered like gelatin fresh from a mold. If she told him how she felt, would he stay in the city for good? But if she truly loved him, could she ask him to do that?

Trust Me.

The words pressed on her heart as surely as if the Lord had spoken them aloud to her.

But, Lord, he'll leave me. I'll be alone again. I can't bear to give him my heart and then lose him.

Nick drew circles with his thumb on the tender flesh of her hand, seeming to say she had all the time in the world.

Her heart swelled even more.

Trust Me.

She licked her lips, still tasting of blueberry, and whispered, "I love you too, Nick Perrin."

He didn't finish his pie. He pulled her to her feet, his gaze locked on hers.

She closed her eyes and felt the heat of his breath. His lips covered hers, and the spark flamed until she forgot about fishing and Ruby and roller coasters and anything in the world—except the man she loved holding her in his arms.

Please, Lord, don't let this be a mistake.

32

There had to be some kind of mistake.

As the messenger pedaled his bicycle away from the roller coaster site, Nick read the words of the telegram again. His chest tightened. How could a morning holding so much promise sour so quickly? He and Lilly had enjoyed a wonderful weekend, and now this?

"Problem, boyo?"

Nick looked at Sean and crushed the telegram in his fist. "I have to leave early."

"I can cover for you here this afternoon. Does Lilly need you or something?"

"I don't mean leave early today. I mean I have to leave Lake Manawa and this city earlier than we planned."

"Why don't ya come explain yerself whilst I check the motor and chain?"

Nick followed the burly man to the motor shed beneath the coaster. Sean eyed the lift chain, looking for any potential problems, then turned to Nick. "So, laddie, ya want to tell me what that telegram said?"

After reaching the roller coaster's engine, Nick primed the motor and prepared to start it. "Fenton Evans fell while working on the Kansas City coaster. He broke his leg and some ribs, so he won't be working for the rest of the summer. Mr. Ingersoll says he can cover for him until the end of June, but then he's scheduled to start on a new project down South."

"So Mr. Ingersoll needs ya to be takin' over for him on the Kansas City project come July?"

"I have to be there after the Fourth." Nick oiled one of the gears on the motor. "I thought I'd have the rest of the summer here. That's what I told Lilly. How am I going to tell her I have to leave so soon?" He fired the motor, and the chain began to turn.

Sean adjusted the tension on it. "Ya thinkin' the lassie will be a bit miffed at ya?"

"Miffed? Try furious." Nick wiped his hands on a rag. "And scared. I don't want to rush her, Sean. We need more time."

"Guess the good Lord thought ya didn't need it." Sean clapped his hand on Nick's shoulder. "Ya still have a month, laddie. If God created the whole world in seven days, I think He can move a mountain of stubborn like yer lassie in a month. The question is, are ya ready to make a commitment like that?"

Nick's chest tightened. Was he ready? Up until this point, everything had been about convincing Lilly to take a chance on him. But now? Was he prepared to become both a husband and a father? And would he ever measure up to Ben Hart in Lilly's eyes?

After leaving Sean to finish a few things in the engine shed, Nick rounded the corner of the loading station and stopped short. This day kept getting worse. He took a deep breath, forcing a calm he didn't feel. Ruby was not taking no for an answer.

Nick rolled his eyes. *Like that's a surprise. Ruby Rawlins expecting to get her way.*

He met her at the foot of the loading station's stairs. "Morning. We're not open yet."

She flicked her gloved hand in the air. "Silly, I know that. But since you wouldn't join me in the evening, I thought we could talk this morning. Surely Mrs. Hart wouldn't be jealous of that?"

"Lilly's not jealous. The choice not to see you at night was mine."

She pointed to a park bench. "Shall we sit? For a few minutes?"

"Ruby—"

"It's broad daylight. I can see your coaster is running, and your men seem to have things well in hand." Ruby leaned a bit closer. "And *she's* nowhere in sight."

Nick sighed. He might as well get this over with. He motioned to the bench, and she gave him a triumphant smile.

Once she'd settled and arranged her skirt, she folded her hands in her lap. "So, where do we start? What would you like to know about me?"

"Not much." He couldn't believe he'd said the words out loud.

She playfully slapped his arm. "Nick Perrin, I'm going to forget you said that. Well, I've had several prominent roles. Did you hear of *The Chorus Lady* by James Forbes?"

"I don't go to the theater much."

"It was a modern vaudeville show. You know, more of a play with music and dance worked in it than a variety of acts. I had a major role as a chorus girl." She flicked her auburn hair off her shoulder. "I only took this particular job at the last minute. Mr. Crowell contacted me and offered me a considerable sum if I'd come here for the month with his troupe." She smiled. "He was lucky I happened to be available."

"Fascinating." The word fell flat as it came out of Nick's mouth.

"Oh, it was. Now, you must tell me how you came to have this prestigious position. When we parted, you were merely a laborer on one of Ingersoll's crews."

"There's not much to tell. I watched Mr. Ingersoll and learned all about the construction of the coasters. And I asked so many questions he probably wanted to send me packing. After a while, Mr. Ingersoll promoted me to being a building supervisor. This is the first coaster where I've been both designer and builder."

"That is simply wonderful! I'm so proud of you."

Nick glanced at her, and for a minute, he saw the young woman he'd once fallen in love with. They'd both been so full of dreams, and she seemed genuinely happy he'd achieved some of his. Perhaps he'd been too hard on her. They could possibly be friends. After all, he was the only one she knew at the lake.

He shook his head. No. No. No. This was Ruby—the actress. She could sell a glass of water to a drowning man. If there was anyone he shouldn't trust, it was her.

"Mr. Nick!"

Nick turned and spotted Levi break free from Mark Westing and race toward the bench where Nick sat with Ruby. He stood, caught Levi in his hands, and swung him in a wide circle several times. When Nick set him down, Levi wobbled until he plopped onto the ground in a fit of giggles.

After he stood, Nick squatted in front of him. "Morning, Chipmunk. Where's Chipmunk Mama?"

Levi frowned. "Workin'. She said she was too busy making beans to come see you, so Mr. Mark said he'd bring me."

"Beans are more important than seeing me?"

"Yep. I told her it wasn't true. Beans are beans, and you're . . ."

"I'm what?"

Levi scrunched his brow in thought. "You're better-er than beans."

Nick chuckled. He stood and shook Mark's hand. "Thanks for escorting Levi. I know he gets under Lilly's feet sometimes."

"I don't get under Mama's feet, but sometimes I accidentally step on top of them."

Both men laughed, and Ruby came to stand beside Nick. She laid a hand on his arm, and he stiffened. Truth be told, he'd almost forgotten her. "Miss Ruby Rawlins, may I introduce Mr. Mark Westing. Miss Rawlins is an actress and is performing here at the vaudeville theater."

Mark tipped his hat. "A pleasure, miss." He glanced at Nick. "I do hope I wasn't interrupting anything by bringing Levi by now."

"No, Miss Rawlins and I were simply catching up on old times." He glanced at Mark, who seemed to be studying the coaster. "Did you want to take a ride this morning?"

"Me too!" Levi bounced.

Nick placed a hand on his shoulder. "Not yet, Levi. Your mama doesn't want you to do that. She's afraid you'll get hurt."

Mark faced Ruby. "Miss Rawlins, would you care to join me?"

She glanced at Nick as if she hoped he'd say something on her behalf, but he looked away. She was no longer his responsibility.

"I'm not much of a roller coaster enthusiast." She pressed her hand against her chest as if the mere thought of riding on the coaster gave her the vapors.

285

"In all the time I've known her, I've never gotten her to ride a single time."

"Ah, so you two never took the plunge together." Mark chuckled.

Nick held his fist to his mouth and coughed.

Mark shrugged. "Since I have no one to ride with, I'll pass for now, but thanks for offering." He glanced around. "Where's Levi? I promised to bring him back safe and sound."

Nick scanned the area. Where had Levi gotten off to? The last he'd seen him, he was headed to the loading station.

The coaster! His heart slammed against his ribs, and he took off running. Blood pumping, he raced up the stairs to the loading station. "Levi!"

"Here I am." Levi peeked out from one of the extra cars in the loading shed. "If I can't ride, I can pretend. Right, Mr. Nick?"

Nick took a deep breath. "Sure you can, but next time would you please tell us where you're going?"

Levi scrambled out of the roller coaster car. "Okay."

Mark jogged up the steps. "I see you found him."

"He was in one of the extra cars." Nick ruffled the boy's soft hair. "Will you give your mama a message for me? Tell her to put away the beans and make sure she has tomorrow afternoon free."

"Me too?" Levi asked.

"Yes, sirree. We're going to have fun."

"So you have special plans tomorrow?" Ruby walked across the platform, the heels of her shoes clicking on the station's wood floor.

When he nodded, hurt flickered in her moss-green eyes. He took a deep breath. He hadn't meant to hurt her, but if she held any ideas of them rekindling a romance, she might as well know nothing of the sort was going to happen.

Mark cleared his throat. "Well, Levi, we'd better be getting back."

They all turned when the engine started and the chain lift began to move. Percy pushed the first car around to the foot of the lift hill and hopped inside. Usually Nick took the first ride of the day, but he guessed Sean told Percy to do it for him. The boy had worked hard enough to earn the privilege, and so far the roller coaster had performed flawlessly.

He turned back to Mark. "I forgot to ask you what you're doing at the lake. Lilly said you got a job working for her former father-in-law."

"And I appreciate you not holding that against me."

"My beef is with him, not you."

"I'm here because I had some papers to deliver, and of course, I couldn't miss out on Lilly's pie."

"Lilly's pie or Eugenia's?" Nick sucked his cheeks in to keep from laughing.

"Does Lilly tell you everything?" Mark chuckled. "Eugenia's a sweet girl, but she seems a little nervous around men. I thought maybe I could put her at ease." He turned to Ruby. "Miss Rawlins, may Levi and I escort you back to the theater?"

"Yes, I'd appreciate that." She flashed one more flirty smile toward Nick and tapped his chest with her gloved finger. "And I'll be seeing you again soon."

Nick watched the three of them go and sighed. Apparently Ruby was not taking no for an answer.

⚘

Mark glanced at the few shopkeepers and hawkers opening their places along the Midway. They rolled back their canvas curtains, polished their windows, and swept the area in front of their stalls. By late morning, the sleepy place would come alive with patrons. Right now, it almost looked like any block on Main Street.

After telling Levi he could walk ahead of them, Mark whirled toward Ruby. "Didn't Victor Crowell make the reason we wanted you to come here clear? What's taking you so long?"

"Yes, but it takes time to set these things up." Ruby popped her parasol open. "Nick Perrin is a smart man, and he isn't going to welcome me back with open arms right away. Besides, I never promised I could get him to rekindle our romance."

"I doubt you can." Mark glanced at Levi, who was looking at something beneath a bush. "You're being paid to make Lilly think he wants you back."

"Don't worry, Mr. Westing. She'll have no doubts when I get through here."

Mark studied the woman beside him. There was no doubt she was beautiful, and he was certain she meant what she said. She'd make sure Lilly doubted every word Nick told her.

An unfamiliar feeling nudged him. Guilt? Even if Lilly had been nothing more than their family's maid, he'd always admired her dry wit and kindness, and Nick Perrin seemed genuinely taken with her. Still, he understood Claude Hart's position. If Lilly continued her relationship with Nick, it would most likely end in marriage, which would mean the happy couple would take Levi away with them. If he were in Mr. Hart's place, he might be doing the same thing.

Levi started back toward him. He was a cute kid, and Mark liked kids. With Claude Hart's influence and financial assistance, a lot of doors could open for the boy. And he was lucky to have a mother who let him be himself, something Mark had never enjoyed.

"Look what I found." From behind his back, Levi displayed a dotted salamander on his outstretched palm.

Ruby shrieked. "Get that wretched thing away from me!"

"Miss Ruby, don't be scared. This is Spot, and he's nice."

Mark laughed. "Levi, I think you've discovered a tiger salamander. I was quite a creature collector myself when I was your age. Your Spot is only a youngster. See how pale his color is? When he gets older, he'll be a lot brighter and could get this long." He held his hands a foot apart.

Levi's eyes rounded. "You think Mama will let me keep him till he gets bigger and bigger and bigger?"

Mark shrugged. "My mother wouldn't have, but I don't know about yours."

"Miss Ruby, you want to hold him now?" Levi held the salamander to his cheek.

"No, and you should put that nasty thing back where you found him, and don't you dare touch me with those filthy hands. Go on, now. Toss that creature away."

"Then how would I show Spot to Mr. Nick?"

"He has no interest in your lizard, you silly boy."

"He does too."

"No he doesn't. I've been friends with Nick for a long time."

"But he's my friend now." Levi stomped his foot and stuck out his tongue.

The actress glared at him. "You incorrigible boy! I ought to take a switch to you!"

"Miss Rawlins." Mark dropped his voice low. "Remember, Nick Perrin is quite fond of the boy. You don't want to upset *him*." Mark turned to Levi, who still had a pout scrunching his chubby cheeks. "It's never good to be impolite to a lady, Levi, no matter how rude she is."

"Never?"

Mark sighed and took Levi's hand. "Not even when she deserves it."

33

Excitement electrified the air around Lake Manawa. From her seat in the rowboat, Lilly studied the crowds. Thousands had gathered. But why?

"All right, I'm officially dying of curiosity." The oar splashed when Nick lowered it in the water, and she wiped a bead of water from her cheek. Levi giggled from his seat beside her. "What is going on out here?"

Barely out of breath despite his rowing effort, Nick grinned. "Why, Lilly, I would have thought you had this all figured out by now. Haven't you been reading the newspapers?"

"And when would I do that?" She twisted in her seat when she heard a shout. "Is there a parade? I thought I heard someone at the café mention something big was coming today."

"You might say that." Nick stopped rowing as they neared the other boats bobbing in the water.

"I see them!" a man shouted from another rowboat. "Look! Here they come."

The crowd on the shore divided as if Moses himself were doing the parting. Single file, eleven enormous beasts entered the water under the direction of their shirtless Indian guides.

"Elephants?" Lilly rubbed her eyes. She had to be seeing things.

"Well, they aren't camels." Nick twisted his waist to get a better look. "The Hagenbeck Circus came to town today. They've been advertising this all week."

"Look, here they come!" Levi stood and pointed.

Lilly pulled him back down. "You can't stand in a boat, sweetheart."

The guides directed five full-grown adult elephants farther into the lake. Behind them, six smaller elephants followed. Two of the younger elephants were so small Lilly wondered if they'd been born this year.

Once the elephants lumbered into the lake, Nick rowed until they were within yards of the beasts.

"Do we dare get this near? What if they're dangerous?" Lilly draped her arm around Levi.

"The mahouts will tell us if we get too close."

"Mahouts?" Lilly asked.

"The elephants' keepers are called *mahouts*." Nick pointed to the elephant that one of the mahouts had started scrubbing with soap and a brush.

The two babies played near the shore, firing cannons of water toward one another. Then one of the larger ones filled his trunk with water and shot it over his back. The crowd cheered.

"Nick, there's one coming this way." Lilly grabbed the side of the boat. "He's huge."

"Can I pet him?" Levi waved to the elephant.

"Not this time." Lilly placed a restraining hand on Levi's leg.

"Mama, you're squeezing my leg plumb off."

"Sorry." She pulled her hand away and shared a smile with Nick. "That one doesn't seem to even know we're here."

"Hi there, Mr. Elephant!" Levi cupped his hands to his mouth and shouted. "Come over and see us."

Lilly clamped her hand over her son's mouth. "Levi!"

The pachyderm dipped his trunk into the lake, then raised it in the air. He pointed it at their boat and sent a shower of water in their direction.

Lilly laughed and sputtered. "He doused us!"

"More! More!" Levi applauded.

Nick took off his dripping straw hat and shook it. "Let's not encourage him, Chipmunk."

Mopping her face with a handkerchief, Lilly couldn't stop grinning. What would the proper Harts think if they saw her now?

Nick glanced at Lilly. "Do you know how elephants are trained? When they're still young, they are chained to a stake. No matter how much they strain and struggle, they can't break free. When they're older, you can chain them with only a rope because they still believe they can't break free even though they could pull the whole circus tent down if they wanted."

"So it's all in their heads?"

He nodded. "They create their own prison."

"That's hard to believe." Lilly watched one of the elephants turn when the mahout gave it an order. "They're beautiful."

Nick gave her a crooked grin. "And so are you."

She giggled. "Mr. Perrin, are you comparing me to an elephant?"

"That probably wouldn't be in my best interest, would it?"

She laughed. "My, but you are a smart fellow."

Dried off and wearing a fresh black suit, Nick arrived to pick up Lilly. To his delight, earlier that day Emily had offered to keep Levi while he and Lilly went to dinner, then to the ball. He and Emily, however, had kept the ball a secret from Lilly.

The timing couldn't be more perfect since he needed to tell Lilly he'd be leaving sooner than he planned. His stomach wadded in a tangle every time he thought about broaching the subject, but as tempted as he was to keep the news a secret, it wasn't fair to her.

"Emily and Lilly should be out in a minute." Carter patted a fussy baby Katie on his shoulder.

"Why can't I go with you?" Levi looked up from the drawing he was making with his Crayola crayons.

"Hey, buddy," Carter said, "you can't leave me here all alone, surrounded by girls. Besides, as soon as I put Katie in her crib, I was hoping we could play ball."

Nick squeezed the boy's shoulder. "You'll have more fun here with Uncle Carter than you will at some fancy restaurant and dance."

Emily came out of the cottage first, but soon Lilly followed. Nick sucked in a breath as she glided down the stairs dressed in an ivory, lace-covered dinner gown. A matching satin sash accentuated her tiny waist, and her chestnut waves hung loosely about her shoulders, looking so soft he ached to touch them. The neckline plunged slightly, revealing her creamy skin.

"You're absolutely stunning."

Her cheeks filled with color, and she smiled. "Thank you."

"You're a lucky man, Nick." Carter stood and glanced at Emily. "And so am I, of course."

She playfully slapped his arm. "Lilly, don't worry about your son. Carter's needed a playmate for a couple of days now."

Nick held out his arm. "Shall we?"

Slipping her hand into the crook of his elbow, Lilly glanced at Levi. "You be good for Aunt Emily."

"I will, Mama."

Emily waved. "Have fun. We'll be fine here."

∽⧼⧽∼

The steak, so tender she could cut it with a butter knife, melted on Lilly's tongue. Creamed potatoes and sprigs of asparagus rounded out the dinner at the Fish and Game Club's restaurant.

"I don't think a soul at the lake missed seeing us riding this evening." Lilly took a drink from her water goblet, the cut-glass crystal pressing against her fingers. She turned the goblet a bit to the right and watched how it caught the light from the gas chandeliers. All around her, silverware clinked against plates, creating its own symphony.

"I hope word gets back to your former in-laws we were out parading about. I want Claude Hart to know we aren't scared of him." Nick speared another piece of steak.

"Speak for yourself."

Nick locked his gaze with hers. "Lilly, I won't let him bother you."

"It's not me I worry about. Besides, what about when you're gone?" She bit her lip. "I'm sorry. We promised not to talk about that tonight."

Nick blotted his lips with his napkin. "We will discuss it later. I promise. But right now, we've got a ball to get to."

"We're going to the ball at the Kursaal? But . . ."

He took a drink from his water glass. "You do know how to dance, don't you?"

"Of course I do. Who do you think had to practice with Marguerite all those years? It's just that—" She dropped her gaze and pushed a sprig of asparagus around her plate.

"What?"

"People who work at the lake don't associate with those who are here for entertainment. It's an unwritten rule."

"But it was Mr. Nash, the park manager, who suggested I go, and I work here."

She dabbed her mouth with her napkin and folded it beside her plate. "Nick, you're practically famous around here. Don't you know people all over town are talking about you and your roller coaster?"

He took out his wallet and placed several bills on the table. Then he stood and held out his hand to Lilly. "Well, this famous fellow wants to take his girl to the dance at the Kursaal."

One look into his determined eyes told her arguing would be useless.

Within a few minutes, they'd walked the short distance to the brightly lit pavilion. Upstairs in the Kursaal, Nick swept her into his arms and onto the dance floor. Dance after dance, they whirled and laughed. So much time with one partner was scandalous, and a Midway cook dancing at one of the Kursaal's balls would be the talk of the lake tomorrow. But for once in her life, Lilly didn't care.

Tomorrow she would.

But not tonight.

❧

Bearing two lemon ices, Nick zigzagged through the crowd, searching for Lilly. Perhaps she wasn't back from freshening up yet.

"Nick?"

He turned to find Ruby, resplendent in a beaded gold gown. "Good evening, Ruby."

"Where is your dance partner?" She licked her lips.

He nodded toward the second lemon ice. "She said she wanted to freshen up while I got these."

"Hmmm. I don't see her anywhere. Maybe you could put those down and dance with me. Once? For old times' sake?"

Her forwardness caught him off guard. "I—I don't think so. I think I see Lilly. If you'll excuse me." After bowing slightly, he made a hasty departure.

Lilly accepted the lemon ice. "Was that Ruby you were speaking to?"

"Yes. She wanted to dance." He frowned.

"It would've been fine." Lilly dipped her spoon into the cold mixture.

"It might have been fine with you, but it wasn't with me," he snapped. "I'm sorry. Ruby unnerves me. All this bringing up the 'old days.' I don't want to remember the old days. It took me years to forget them."

"I think she's lonely."

"Then she can find some other man to ease her loneliness, or get a puppy." He took her empty glass and set it along with his own on one of the waiters' trays. "And now I'd like to dance one more time with the most beautiful woman at the ball."

"Marguerite already left."

He gave her a teasing grin. "Too bad. I guess I have to settle for you then." He leaned close and pressed his lips to her ear. "And by the way, Marguerite is nothing compared to you."

The skin on her neck prickled beneath his warm breath. "Don't let her hear that."

⚛

"No peeking." Lilly glanced at Nick through the bush a quarter mile from the Kursaal. The darkness made maneuvering difficult.

"I wouldn't dare." Nick chuckled.

She rolled one silk stocking over her calf and tugged on

296

the stocking's toe. How had he convinced her to do this? She should be heading home to her son. "I can't believe you talked me into wading with you."

"It was as hot as soup in there." Nick rolled up his pant legs. "Besides, it's a beautiful night. Look at those stars."

She glanced skyward. Stars winked against an ebony curtain. A full moon cast a silvery glow on the lake while a soft breeze blew the tendrils of hair framing her face. She brushed them away and took a deep breath. Everything smelled fresh and alive. Hiking up the hem of her dress, she eased from her spot behind the bush and stepped onto the sand. The surface was still warm from the day's sun, but as she stepped, the cooler sand oozed between her toes. She dipped one foot into the water and winced. "It's really chilly."

"It'll feel good." Nick joined her and took her elbow. "On three. One, two—"

Before he got to three, he nudged her into the water. She sucked in a breath. "You can't count, and this is cold."

"I thought you were a hardy Iowa girl."

"I am—in the summer, but this is late spring, and the water's not had a chance to get warm yet." She shivered. If she stood still any longer, she'd have frostbite.

"Can't you handle it?"

She heard the dare in his voice. He flicked water from his fingers toward her.

"What do you think?" She cupped a handful of water and splashed it in Nick's face. "Did that cool you off?"

He bent and scooped her into his arms. When he spoke, his voice was husky. "Nothing you do cools me off."

"Nick—"

"But for splashing me, I should dunk you."

"No!" she squealed and held him tighter. "I can't go back to Emily's soaking wet again."

"You could tell her a rogue elephant got you." He laughed and feigned tossing her in.

She giggled. "That only works once in a lifetime. You should put me down. Nicely. Like the gentleman I know you are."

"Ah, but remember, I'm a pirate."

She couldn't see his face clearly, but she could imagine his pirate grin.

"Aargh, and what if I don't want to?"

"We all have to do things we don't want to."

With a sigh, he lowered her feet onto the sand but kept his hands on her waist. He tugged her toward him. She placed her hands on his chest, so warm, so inviting. The cold lake water lapped at her feet. The bottom of her dress would be wet now, but it didn't matter.

Nick cupped her cheek. "I don't want to tell you this."

"Tell me what?"

"I have to leave sooner than I planned. Mr. Ingersoll needs me in Kansas City after the Fourth of July."

The breath whooshed from her lungs, and hot tears filled her eyes. "That only gives us a little less than a month."

He pressed his forehead to hers. "I know."

"A month." Beneath her hand, his heartbeat quickened. The tears trailed down her cheeks in the darkness. "Maybe it would be easier to say goodbye now."

"No." He thumbed away one of the tears. "No. This is not the end. I know you're not ready to promise me a future. I understand that. But I've got a month to change your mind, and I plan to use every second. Starting now."

Before she could say another word, he covered her lips with his own in a kiss full of promise. The kiss deepened, and her heart and soul answered.

Oh, Lord, how am I going to let him go?

34

Cradling her sleeping boy after he'd been awakened by a nightmare, Lilly brushed the hair from his forehead. She held his chubby hand, still soft with baby fat, and pressed a kiss to his fingertips.

She held her whole world.

Her heart snagged. *Not anymore.*

Somehow Nick Perrin had broken down her walls and taken up residence. And every time she was with him, her whole life seemed to be on one of his roller coasters. He made her feel twists and turns and dips and rushes that no one ever had.

Including Ben.

She looked down at her sandy-haired son, so like his father. Her love for Ben had been a sweet, steady love. Her love for Nick was a thrill-a-minute love. Yet could she really count on him in the long haul? They hadn't known each other but such a short time. How could she not believe that at the end of this month, he would go and she'd never hear from him again?

Easing Levi back into his bed, she sighed. What if she'd made a mistake letting Nick into their lives?

She drew the cover to Levi's shoulders and kissed his cheek. *Lord, keep my baby safe. Don't let him suffer because of my choices. He's all I have left.*

❧

"Mr. Nick said he has a present for me."

With Levi's hand clasped in her own, Lilly could almost feel his excitement like an electrical current.

"Sweetheart, please don't ask to ride the roller coaster again today."

"But, Mama—"

"Levi." Her voice, stern, ended the discussion. All week she'd taken him to see Nick's roller coaster in the afternoon, and without fail he asked to ride it every time. She had no doubt he pestered Nick some more when she wasn't around.

This morning Nick had asked her to bring her son over again, as he had made him something that might help with his roller coaster obsession.

"Hurry, Mama." Levi nearly dragged her down the paved walk to the coaster. When they reached the turnstile, Forest motioned them through, and Nick met them at the loading station.

"And why are you here, Chipmunk?" Nick winked at Lilly.

"My present!"

"Oh, yes. I do recall something about a present." He rubbed his square jaw. "Hmmm. Where do you think I put that?"

Lilly giggled. "It looks like Nick has forgotten where it is. Maybe we should come back later."

"No!" Levi hopped up and down. "Please, Mr. Nick. Please 'member."

Nick lifted Levi and balanced him on his arm. "I think it may be in the engine shed. Let's go see."

"Mama too?"

"Posilutely."

Lilly rolled her eyes at her two boys, her heart warming. In the days since the ball, her doubts had eased some, but they'd never truly abated. She guessed it was simply her nature. Trusting didn't come easy.

As they approached, Percy came out of the engine shed. Nick's brows drew together. "Is there a problem somewhere?"

"No, sir. Sean asked me to check something for him."

Nick nodded. "Thanks." After the young man departed, Nick tickled Levi's belly. "Ready for your surprise?"

"Yes, sir!"

Nick held the door for Lilly. She entered, greeted by a strong odor. She pressed a handkerchief to her nose. "What's that smell?"

"Mostly motor oil and the hot engine. Some of it may be Sean's scent lingering here after a hard day."

She laughed, and her gaze fell on something covered by a small tarp.

Levi spotted it too. "Is that my present?"

"Sure is, Chipmunk." He set Levi down. "Now, you close your eyes while I take the tarp off."

With a whoosh, he yanked the covering away. Lilly gasped, then pressed her fist to her mouth and bit her knuckle.

"Can I look?"

"You sure can."

Levi squealed when he saw the replica of Lake Manawa's Velvet Roller Coaster. "It's my own roller coaster?"

"It sure is, and you can give your bugs a ride anytime you want." Nick slipped his arm around Lilly's waist.

"It's amazing, Nick." Lilly leaned in closer to get a better view. The tiny trestles, all mounted on one larger board, matched that of the large coaster perfectly, and even the cars had been painted with the same red paint with yellow curlicue designs. "You must have been working on this for weeks."

He grinned. "Some of the boys helped. Especially Sean."

"Can I take it back to the diner?" Levi let the first car go at the top of the lift hill and watched it follow the track, up and down, to the end.

"You better. I can't keep it here or Sean might sneak in and start playing with it—again."

Levi grabbed Nick's legs, squeezing so hard Nick held on to Lilly's shoulder to keep from toppling. "Easy there, Levi."

"This is the bestest present ever."

Lilly caught Nick's gaze and smiled, hoping he could see the smile in her heart as well. Being people who believed toys were unnecessary, the Harts had refused to indulge their grandson's fancies except for a few items like the wooden blocks. How many times had she watched her son eye the toys in the department store and wished she could purchase him one?

She laid her hand on Nick's arm. "*Thank you* hardly seems adequate."

He winked at her. "Then you can thank me personally—later."

Hauling the wooden roller coaster toy back to the diner took Nick less time than he expected. It wasn't so heavy that Levi couldn't move it around or Lilly couldn't carry it inside, but it was a bit too much for her to carry the distance of the Midway.

He set it down in the shade where Levi usually played and watched the boy immerse himself in a roller coaster play world. Although he'd hoped the toy would appease Levi's desire to ride the real coaster, looking at the boy now, he guessed his plan had probably backfired.

"He loves it." Lilly sat down on the bench not far from the front door. "I bet he'll be playing with it until dark."

"Nick!" a man's voice shouted.

Nick turned and spotted Mark running toward him.

"I've been searching all over for you. Ruby fell off the vaudeville stage and got hurt. She's asking for you."

"Hurt? How bad?" A strange mixture of concern and doubt tumbled inside him.

"I don't know." Out of breath, Mark paused before he continued. "The doctor is on his way. I happened to be there dropping off some contracts."

Nick glanced at Lilly. What would she think if he went racing off to his former fiancée?

Lilly tipped her head in the direction of the theater. "Go. She needs you. She doesn't have anyone else here."

"Thank you for understanding."

She flashed him a cheeky grin. "You can thank me personally—later."

He squeezed her hand and took off with Mark. When they arrived at the theater, they were directed to Ruby's dressing room. Mark knocked on the door, and the woman who'd had the trained poodles in the show opened the door. "Are you Nick?"

He nodded. "And this is Mark Westing."

The woman opened the door. "I'll let you two be alone with her."

Nick frowned and glanced at Mark, who merely shrugged.

Stepping into the dressing room, he eyed Ruby lying on a fainting couch and did his own visual examination. Her right foot lay propped on two pillows, and a wet cloth had been draped across her forehead.

Mark cleared his throat. "Remember those contracts? I need to take care of them. I'll be back in a few minutes."

"Wait, Mark—" Nick hadn't wanted to be alone with Ruby, but his words came out too late. At least Mark had left the door open.

Ruby's eyes filled with tears. "Thank you for coming."

Compassion nudged him forward. "How badly are you hurt?"

"I sprained my ankle, and I have an awful headache."

Pain etched her face, but he imagined she could act that part without even trying. "The doctor will have you fixed up in no time."

"I can't walk. How will I get back to my hotel room?"

"I'm sure something can be arranged." *But I'm not volunteering.*

She patted an empty spot on the fainting couch. "Why don't you sit down? I don't want to be alone."

He glanced around for another seat and decided his options were to sit next to her on the fainting couch or to sit on the pink ruffled stool at her dressing table. Then again, he didn't need to sit at all. "Ruby, I'm glad it's not more serious. I'd better be going."

"No, you can't go yet. I'm scared. I don't know if it's—" She moaned and pressed a hand to her head.

Nick sighed and chose the ruffled chair. If he were lucky, maybe the flimsy stool would break and he'd get a concussion.

The doctor arrived, and Nick stepped out of the room. Where had Mark gone? Smart fellow probably saw his opportunity and took off. Nick could leave now too, but it seemed a little cowardly. Leaning against the doorjamb, he waited, counting the chipped paint spots on the pea-green walls.

When he reached forty-three, the door opened. "You can come in now."

Nick stepped inside as the doctor began to put his stethoscope back into his bag. "She'll be fine. Two days of bed rest for the ankle should take care of the headache too." He placed his hand on Nick's shoulder. "A little time and attention will do wonders."

Time and attention? From him? That was not going to happen.

"Do you have a carriage?"

Nick nodded. "But, Doctor—"

"Good. I don't think she should be riding on the streetcar." The doctor glanced at Ruby. "My, your color is improving already. This young man appears to be just the medicine you needed."

Ruby smiled. "I think so too, Doctor."

He'd taken her to a hotel room?

Lilly's heart hammered at Mark's news. He'd said Nick seemed quite concerned over the whole matter. Not only had he fetched his rented carriage, but he'd also carried Ruby to it, and then he'd whisked her off to her hotel room in the city to convalesce.

"You'd be proud of him, Lilly. He was quite attentive. He's probably there now, making sure she's all tucked in for the day." Mark took a swig of coffee. "Like you said, she doesn't have anyone else around here. I'd have stayed and helped him get her settled, but he seemed to have it all in hand."

305

She gave him a halfhearted smile. "Nick's very thoughtful."

"And who wouldn't be to someone who looks like Ruby Rawlins?" He stopped. "Sorry, Lilly, that didn't come out right."

"I understand. She is a beautiful lady." She pushed the jealousy down. Nick had no choice but to take care of Ruby. "Speaking of ladies, I believe there's a special lady in the kitchen who just pulled another batch of cinnamon rolls from the oven. They're so popular, Eugenia can't make enough of them. Would you like one? That is why you're here, right?"

"Why I'm here?"

"To see Eugenia."

"Oh, yes." Mark grinned. "Sure, I'd love a roll. Can she join me for a few minutes?"

"I think that can be arranged." With coffeepot in hand, Lilly slipped into the kitchen. "Eugenia, guess who's here?"

To her credit, Eugenia didn't shriek or faint. In the last two weeks since Eugenia had dumped the pie on Mark, she'd made an amazing turnaround. Nora had helped her fashion her hair in a much more attractive manner, and Lilly had helped her go shopping for a couple of suitable work outfits in appropriate colors. "Does he want a cinnamon roll?"

"Two, actually. One for you and one for him."

A smile bloomed on Eugenia's face. "It will be my pleasure."

Lilly smiled. "I'm sure it will."

❧

"Nick, will you please bring me a copy of *The Delineator* this evening?"

A deep sigh slipped through Nick's lips. A day of running back and forth seeing to Ruby's needs had taken its toll on him. Lilly seemed to understand he had no choice but to assist his former fiancée, but he didn't know how long Lilly's generous nature would hold out.

His own was certainly fading fast.

"I told you I wouldn't be back today. I've arranged for one of the hotel's maids to deliver your supper and check on you before bed to see if you need anything. She'll also tend to you tomorrow."

Ruby's lip jutted out. "I'd rather have you come check on me."

"And I'd rather spend the evening with Lilly and Levi." He placed his hand on the crystal doorknob of the hotel room. "And on Sunday, I attend church services with them."

"But I'll be so lonesome."

"Perhaps I can stop by briefly."

"The doctor said I could be up and around on Monday. Will you come take me to the lake?"

"Ruby—"

"Please, Nick. I don't know anyone else, and I can't imagine walking all the way to a streetcar stop."

He opened the door. "I have a roller coaster to run in the morning."

"That will work perfectly, because I don't have to go into the theater until the afternoon." She pressed her hand to her head as if the conversation had exhausted her. "I don't know what I would have done without you."

Nick's stomach soured. Maybe he should have let her find out.

❦

Flopping into the chair in Mrs. Whitson's boardinghouse parlor, Nick released a heavy sigh.

"Problems, boyo?" Sean looked up from the ship model

of the USS *Constitution* he'd been working on since they'd finished the toy roller coaster.

"Ruby."

"Ah, the old girlfriend's takin' up all yer time, eh?" He pointed to a board and handed Nick some sandpaper. "Make yerself useful."

"When did I agree to work on your ship?"

"My frigate." Sean chuckled and pointed to the book with the photo he'd used for inspiration. "Commissioned by President George Washington himself. And if yer wanting a listenin' ear, then ya can help me out. I've sure helped ya plenty on yer project for the lass."

Taking one of the three would-be masts in hand, Nick rubbed sandpaper over it until it was smooth. "Ruby is milking this sprained ankle and the bump on her head for all they're worth. I have to go pick her up tomorrow and bring her to the lake."

"And what does yer Lilly say?" Sean glued a tiny cannon onto its wheeled mounts.

"She says she understands." Nick set the mast down, took the next long dowel mast Sean indicated, and sanded it.

Sean held his pieces in place while the glue set. "Is that so?"

Nick glanced up. "You don't think she does?"

Sean grunted and shrugged.

"Lilly isn't like most women."

"Boyo." Sean released the pieces he'd been holding and smiled when they stayed. "There's not a woman on earth who'd be happy about the man she's sparkin' with spendin' time with the woman he'd promised to marry. And could you blame her? How would ya feel if the tables be turned?"

The muscles in Nick's neck knotted tighter. How did he explain to Sean that he shared Lilly every day? A part of her

308

heart would always belong to Ben. But Ben was gone and Ruby was here.

Nick tipped his head to one side then the other, attempting to stretch the kinks out of his neck.

"So, laddie, where do ya feel God's leadin' ya in all this?"

"I don't know. I guess I haven't asked Him."

Sean ran his hand along the hull of the ship. "Do ya know why the USS *Constitution* was so strong? Southern live oak made up her hull, and it was a wee bit denser than all the other woods. The hull was built twenty-five inches thick at the waterline. She took an acre of sailcloth and miles of riggin'. Can you imagine?"

Nick glanced at the picture in the book.

"Her nickname was Old Ironsides. But do ya know, as tough as she always was, if God's hand hadn't been on her, she'd have gone down."

35

He'd failed.

Maybe not failed completely, but from the deep scowl on Claude Hart's face, Mark had no doubts he hadn't made the powerful man happy.

"We didn't count on Ruby getting injured, but I must say she's used the situation to her advantage." Mark tugged on his waistcoat. "I can tell Lilly is having doubts about Nick seeing to our actress's whims."

The muscle beneath Mr. Hart's right eye twitched. "But they are still a couple. You said they were at the ball together."

"Yes, sir, but I think with a little more time—"

"Do I seem like the kind of man who likes to wait?"

Mark met the man's gaze. "No, sir."

Mr. Hart stood and walked to his bookshelf. He removed a heavy volume. "I believe you need another plan. To discredit Nick Perrin once and for all."

"Wouldn't that be a last resort, sir?" Claude Hart seemed

to be pushing things. There wasn't any hurry. It wasn't like Lilly was ready to rush to the altar on the arm of Nick Perrin.

Mr. Hart dropped the book on his desk, making a thunderous noise. Mark jumped and the attorney laughed. "In view of your present success, I'd say it's time for plan B."

❧

The knock at the back door startled Lilly. She dropped the tin measuring cup into the heavy pottery mixing bowl with a clatter, then wiped her hands on her apron. She turned as the door opened.

"Good morning." Nick grinned, his blue eyes twinkling. "I couldn't wait another minute to see you."

"Don't you need to go check on Ruby?" She winced at the sarcastic tone that layered her voice. She picked up her rolling pin and rolled out the biscuit dough with a vengeance, exasperated she'd revealed her jealousy. "I'm sorry. I know she needs your help."

"I'm the one who's sorry," he said, removing the rolling pin from her hand and turning her toward him. "I haven't been around much. I've let Ruby call the shots, and I haven't been praying about what to do with her."

"You're doing what you have to."

He laid his hand on her arm. "But not what I want to do. As long as you understand that. Surely you know you can trust me."

She blinked away the tear threatening to escape. "With her, yes."

"What do I have to do to prove myself to you?"

She leaned her cheek against his chest, hearing the solid, steady heartbeat beneath her ear. She could ask him to not see Ruby again, but would that really make her trust him completely? The problem wasn't him. It was her.

311

Fear or faith. The preacher had said every storm required one of those responses. She was so tired of being afraid. Afraid of losing Levi. Afraid of being alone. Afraid of her world crashing in on her again. How could she explain to Nick the tempest raging inside her?

Nick kissed the top of her head. "Why don't I take Levi with me after lunch today? I haven't seen much of him either."

Lilly pulled back and looked into Nick's lethal blue eyes. "He'd like that, and it will be good for him. He hasn't moved more than a foot from that toy roller coaster since you gave it to him."

He traced her lower lip with his finger. "I love you."

"And I love you, but what if that isn't enough?"

"My beautiful, pragmatic, sensible Lilly, we can make this work." He cupped her chin, nudging it upward so he could claim her lips.

Her heart skipped a beat, and she leaned into the kiss. Oh, how she wanted to believe. Thankfully, Nick could be quite convincing.

⬡

After giving Lilly one last kiss, Nick slipped out the back door. Eugenia and Nora would arrive soon, and he didn't want to embarrass Lilly by being caught there alone with her.

Nick plucked a blade of grass from the ground, the color reminding him of the dress Lilly wore on the day they first went out for breakfast together. Over the last couple of days, he'd had a lot of time to think about their relationship. He wished Lilly understood that seeing Ruby again only reminded him of how lucky he was to have Lilly in his life. While Ruby was concerned about herself and her career, Lilly was concerned about helping others any way she could. While Ruby made him feel like he was never quite good enough, Lilly made him believe he could do anything. While Ruby seemed like a dozen other women he'd met at one time or another, Lilly was one in a million.

He rounded the corner and stopped short. Who was the broad-shouldered man kneeling beside Levi?

Nick sauntered over. When Levi spotted him, he jumped up and ran to him.

"Hi there, Chipmunk. Who's your friend?"

"This is Mr. Whiskers."

The full-bearded man stood and turned.

With a chuckle, Nick held out his hand. "Hi, I'm Nick Perrin, and I'm assuming your name is not Mr. Whiskers."

"No." The man grinned. "My name is Clifford Black. I was admiring your son's roller coaster. Did you make it?"

Nick didn't correct the man's assumption about Levi. "Yes. He likes the real one so much I thought he'd enjoy having one of his own."

"Oh, you're the roller coaster designer, right? I heard about you."

"And if I don't get over there, I may be the unemployed roller coaster designer."

"I want to go with you." Levi looked at Nick with pleading eyes.

Nick took off his hat and ran his hand through his hair. "I already talked to your mama. You're coming with me after lunch."

"To ride the roller coaster?"

"To *see* the roller coaster."

"But I'm bigger today." Levi wobbled as he stood on his tiptoes.

"Not big enough." Nick tapped his nose. He glanced at Mr.

Black, surprised the man had not excused himself and gone inside to eat. A strange sensation tightened inside him. He was becoming as paranoid as Lilly. Perhaps the man simply didn't want to be rude by slipping away during a conversation. Still, it wouldn't hurt to make sure Levi was with his mother before he left.

He squeezed Levi's shoulder. "Why don't you head on in? I think your mama has your breakfast ready."

"Yes, sir!" Levi galloped up the steps and let the diner's screen door bang shut behind him.

Nick tipped his head toward Mr. Black. "Nice meeting you, Mr. Black."

"You too." He nodded. "If building big roller coasters doesn't work out, you could always consider making toys."

Nick smiled. "Thanks. I may do that."

⤜∙⤚

"Hello, sister dear."

Marguerite smiled at the sound of her brother's voice as he joined her on the Midway. She paid the salesman and sniffed her bag of freshly roasted peanuts. "Morning, Mark."

"Cravings already?"

"Who told you?"

"Trip." He snagged a handful of nuts from her bag.

She swatted his hand. "But I wanted to tell you."

"Sorry. He said it seemed like everyone knew except him, so he thought I did too. Congratulations." He cracked the shell of a peanut and dropped the insides into his mouth. "What brings you to this side of the lake?"

She started down the sidewalk toward the diner. "I wanted to speak with Lilly."

"Why?"

"And here I thought you graduated with honors," Marguerite teased.

"I did."

"Then you should already know why I want to talk to her. She's my best friend. I tell her everything. By the way, shouldn't you be working?"

"I am." He hooked his fingers in the pockets of his vest. "I had to deliver some important papers."

"You do an awful lot of that. Are you sure there isn't another reason you keep coming to the diner—a special someone, perhaps?"

"Apparently Lilly tells you everything too." He chuckled. "Don't make more of something than it is. I like to be nice to Eugenia. I thought it would be good for her."

"Then you're not really interested."

"Not in a permanent sort of way."

Marguerite slipped her hand into Mark's elbow. "You have to be careful with a girl's affections—especially with someone like Eugenia."

"Perhaps you should be saving your lectures about being careful with someone's affections for Nick Perrin."

She stopped. "What do you mean?"

"Only that he's been spending a lot of time with his former fiancée, the vaudeville actress Ruby Rawlins."

Marguerite sighed. When she'd stopped by yesterday, Lilly had told her about Ruby's injury and Nick rendering the woman assistance. Was there more? Did her brother know something she didn't?

"Mark, do you think Nick is sweet on Ruby again?"

"He carries her to his buggy, he takes her to her hotel room, and he sees to her needs. What does that tell you?"

"How do you know all this? Furthermore, why do you even care?"

He shrugged. "Lake gossip. It gets to the best of us."

She frowned and poked his chest. "Keep this lake gossip to yourself, understand? We don't know what is going on between Nick and Ruby."

"But you'll speak to Lilly? She should know."

Tipping her head to the side, she eyed him. "Did you grow up when I wasn't looking?"

◈

Everything was perfect.

With Levi's chubby fingers safely tucked in his hand, Nick skirted the crowds and headed toward the roller coaster. How had he been so lucky to have Mark offer to retrieve Ruby this afternoon? Actually, it didn't take a genius to realize it was Marguerite who'd arranged the situation. He'd have to thank her later.

The offer had allowed him to spend a few extra minutes with Lilly, and now he could spend some time with his favorite small person. He didn't even have to worry about Ruby. With any luck, Mark would have her nearly back to the theater by now.

At least that nightmare was over.

"You want some ice cream, Levi?" Nick nodded toward a vendor's cart.

"Yes, please!"

After securing two vanilla ice cream cones, Nick and Levi took their time walking the rest of the way to the roller coaster.

"We're a pretty good team." Levi looked up at Nick, then licked his cone. "Aren't we?"

"I'd say so."

"Forever and ever."

"I'm working on that." Nick ruffled Levi's hair as they passed through the turnstile.

Glancing at the loading station, Nick halted. Ruby stood at the top of the stairs waiting with Mark. Why had he brought Ruby here and not to the theater?

Nick directed Levi around the side of the building. The last thing he needed was for the boy to go back and tell his mama that Ruby had come there after all.

"Percy." Nick called the young man over. "I need you to do me a favor."

"What now?"

Nick scowled at the youth's tone but decided to let it go this time. "I need you to keep an eye on Levi here while I handle another matter."

"I'm no nanny."

"I didn't say you were. You're doing me a favor." Nick nudged Levi forward. "Have you met Percy?"

"Yes, sir."

"You're going to spend some time with him, okay?"

Levi nodded.

"Nick, what do I do with him?"

"You were a boy once. Do what you would have wanted to do. But keep an eye on him." He ruffled Levi's hair. "You do what Percy tells you to, Chipmunk. I'll be back in a few minutes."

❦

Ruby's wide-brimmed hat had so many feathers Nick wondered if a good gust would send it flying. And should someone's hat be wider than any other part of their body? He was no expert on women's clothing, but it didn't seem right.

For the first time all week, only a dozen or so customers

were present. Maybe Tuesdays were going to be slower days. That'd be okay with him, but the investors might not like it.

At least the small crowd would allow him to talk to Ruby. He'd deal with her now rather than later. His father always said putting off a task didn't make it any less unpleasant, but it made the suffering longer.

"Ruby." He tipped his hat. "You're looking refreshed."

"I told Mark he had to bring me here so I could properly thank you for all you've done."

"You're welcome, and I was happy to help."

She laid her hand on his arm. "Do you mean that?"

"Well—yes."

"I'm so glad to hear you say so." She linked her arm in his and drew him off to the car shed on the side. "We're fortunate things aren't busy right now. I need to talk to you about a private matter."

An uneasy feeling took root inside Nick, but he remained. "What do you want to discuss with me?"

"Us."

Nick stepped back. "There isn't an 'us,' Ruby. I thought you understood."

"I know that's what you said, but are you certain there's no hope for reconciliation?"

"I love Lilly."

"The cook?"

"Yes, and she's a fine woman."

"And she has a son. Are you ready to be a father? What do you know about children?"

"I had a lot of brothers and sisters, you know that, and yes, I love Levi like he's my own."

She laughed. "Then maybe you should look to see where your future son is right now."

He followed the direction of her gaze, and his heart thudded to a complete stop. Halfway up the lift hill, Levi sat beside Percy in the front car of the roller coaster.

If Nick didn't die of a heart attack, Lilly was sure to kill him.

Slowly. Painfully. Inch by inch, with her paring knife.

His stomach churned. Maybe they wouldn't have to tell her.

He heard a gasp. He stepped from the car shed. With Ruby right behind him, he turned and saw Lilly. Her eyes, filled with tears, bore into him.

Betrayal.

Nick's heart plunged.

Lord, what have I done?

36

Every nerve pulled taut as Lilly watched the car carrying her son whiz around the roller coaster rails. Agonizing seconds flew by. Up and down. Around and around. Her head swam with dizziness, and she grabbed for the railing.

Her son.

Her baby.

On that *thing*.

Nick laid his hand on her shoulder. She jerked away. How could he have let Levi ride the roller coaster when he knew how she felt about it?

"Lilly, he'll be okay."

"You don't know that," she spat. "There are no guarantees."

The car rolled into the station, and Sean applied the brake. Levi jumped out and ran to her. She knelt and crushed him against her chest, holding him, drinking in his sweaty little boy scent and pressing kisses to his downy hair. She held him as long as he'd allow.

At last he wriggled free. "Did you see me? I was flying." Levi made a hilly motion with his hand. "It was sooooo much fun! Mama, you gotta try it."

She patted his head. "Levi, go sit on the bench down by the steps and wait for me."

"But, Mama, I want to go again. See, I'm big enough."

"Now, Levi." Her tone left no room for argument.

With his shoulders slumped, Levi trudged away.

Lilly whirled toward Nick. Anger boiled inside her like a pot left on a hot stove. He'd put her son in danger. That was unforgivable. She glared at him. "I have one question. Why? Why did you let him do it?"

Nick took her arm and propelled her to a more secluded spot. He crossed his arms over his chest. "I didn't let him. I left him with Percy, and the boy must have taken him on the ride. Don't blow this out of proportion. He's fine."

"Why did you leave him with Percy? I thought you wanted to spend time with him."

"I had something I needed to take care of." Nick glanced toward Ruby, who stood several yards away beside Mark.

Lilly followed his line of sight, not missing the triumphant smile on the actress's face. She wiggled her fingers in Lilly's direction.

"Her? You weren't watching Levi because you were talk-ing to Ruby?"

"It's not like that." Nick held out his arms. "Maybe now isn't the time to talk about this. Maybe we should discuss it later after you've calmed down."

"There won't be a later." Tears, hot and angry, filled Lilly's eyes. "I can't do this. I can't trust you with my son. Levi could have been hurt."

"But he wasn't." Nick ran his hand down her arm.

She pulled away. She stared into his blue eyes flashing with hurt and anger. "I can't."

He shook his head and ran his hand through his hair. "This isn't about letting Levi ride on a roller coaster. This isn't even about us. This is about you. You don't want to be hurt. But I'll tell you something, Lilly. Life hurts sometimes."

"I know all about how much life hurts." Tears fought their way down her cheeks, and she swiped them away.

"This is the excuse you've been looking for so you can go back to your safe world—the one you control—without feeling guilty. But the truth is you're afraid."

"Afraid of what? You?"

"Everything." His voice dropped low. "But most of all, you're afraid we'll all see you're a coward."

"You insufferable, arrogant—" She stopped and clamped her lips together. She would not say another word.

Getting involved with Nick Perrin had been a mistake—a mistake she wished she could erase as easily as chalk on a board.

⌘

Drawing his fist back, Nick prepared to let the punch fly.

He slammed his knuckles into his open palm. The collision stung. The pain almost felt good. It was certainly better than the frustration building inside him.

Behind Percy, the roller coaster's engine putted along as if nothing had happened. Wide-eyed, Percy looked as if he expected Nick's next punch to land in his face. Still, Nick couldn't muster any sympathy for him. Irresponsible boy. Why had Percy let Levi ride the roller coaster? Did he even realize the grief he'd caused Nick?

Nick glared at him. "What in the blazes were you thinking?"

Percy looked at the floor and shrugged. "You said to let the boy do what I would have wanted to do."

"I said to watch him. I trusted you to keep an eye on him."

Percy looked up, defiant. "And I never took my eyes off him. What harm was there in letting him ride the roller coaster? Other kids do it all the time."

"But Levi isn't any other kid. He's—" Nick swallowed the lump in his throat. "He's Lilly's son, and I know you heard me talking about how she wouldn't let him ride."

"Okay, I'm sorry. I didn't think it was a major concern."

"Well, you were wrong." The pulse in Nick's temple drummed an annoying beat, accusing him of being the truly guilty party. If only he'd ignored Ruby and tended to Levi himself. "Get out of here." Nick turned his back on Percy and waved his hand in the air.

"Are you firing me?"

"No, but I don't want to see your face right now."

Percy slammed the door to the motor shed so hard the building shook. Nick's chest heaved. He ought to throttle that boy.

He kicked a bucket and it clattered against the wall. The anger seething inside wasn't all directed at the boy.

Lilly. Her implications. Her doubts about him. Her lack of faith in him. Each thing seemed like another shot to his bruised heart.

Or was it his bruised pride?

He rubbed his throbbing temple. He didn't need this. His life had been fine before Lilly Hart, and it would be fine without her too.

"Jury, what say you?"

Mark sat down at the back of the gallery, watching the

conclusion of one of Claude Hart's trials. His client, Ralph Veenstra, had been accused of assault with a deadly weapon, and after watching Mr. Hart deliver the closing argument, he'd not been surprised the jury returned twenty minutes later with a verdict.

The jury foreman stood. "We find the defendant not guilty."

Ralph pumped Mr. Hart's hand, thanking him over and over. Mark waited patiently for his employer to finish and met him in the hallway outside the courtroom.

"Congratulations, sir." Mark fell in step beside Mr. Hart, the heels of their shoes pounding out a beat on the courthouse's polished hardwood floor.

"Thank you." He glanced at Mark. "Do you have news?"

"Yes, sir, but perhaps we can discuss it someplace . . . less public."

"Good idea."

Mark followed Mr. Hart out of the courthouse and down the block to his law office. The older lawyer pressed his hand against the frosted glass panel on his office door and turned to Mark. "I hope you have good news."

"Excellent, in fact."

The two men entered, and Mark ran his hand along one of the walnut bookcases. "Our efforts have been successful. Nick and Lilly are no longer courting."

"Are you certain?" Mr. Hart sat down at his massive rolltop desk.

"Yes. I witnessed their parting exchange myself." Mark walked to the decanter set and poured himself a whiskey. "You no longer have any concerns."

"As long as Lilly still has my grandson, then I have concerns." Mr. Hart stroked his snowy beard.

"But you said you believed Lilly's financial situation would eventually make her turn to you for assistance and acquiesce to your will for Levi. Did your son really not leave a will to provide for her?"

Mr. Hart's eyes darkened. "That's something I won't discuss with you."

Mark's stomach instantly knotted. Clearly he'd hit a raw nerve. Something was wrong here. Lilly might be a former maid, but she deserved what her husband wanted her to have, and so did Levi. Did Claude Hart need control so badly he'd make them all suffer until he got his way?

Still, Mark couldn't risk offending the powerful man. His whole career was on the line. "Sir, I apologize. I didn't mean to infer you were being dishonest. I merely found it odd a lawyer—"

Mr. Hart shot Mark a warning look. After several seconds, the older man pinched the bridge of his nose. "Well, your news is good, but it's too late to stop my other plans."

"Other plans?"

Mr. Hart gave a halfhearted laugh. "You didn't believe I entrusted something as important as this solely to you." He stood and went to his safe. With a twist of his hand, he opened it and removed an envelope. "I want you to go to the lake and find a man named Mr. Black."

"Where will I find him?"

"Near the roller coaster."

"And do what?"

"Give him this. It's payment for a job I expect him to finish."

Mark stared at the envelope in Mr. Hart's extended hand. Everything in him said not to take it, but what choice did he have? Finally, he accepted it.

"You're a smart young man. You already understand some things cannot be left to chance." He laid a hand on Mark's shoulder. "Keep this up and you'll be a trial lawyer here in no time."

Mark swallowed the lump in his throat. What had he gotten himself into?

⁂

Lilly punched the dough.

A coward? He'd called her a coward?

She turned the dough ball out onto the floured countertop and pressed it flat with the heels of her hands. Punishing the dough, she folded it and pushed down hard again and again.

Why would he say that? She was no coward. She'd stood up to her in-laws. She'd gotten her son out of that house. She'd started a new life for herself.

The dough seemed sticky, so she sprinkled in a little more flour and began to knead some more. Her mother had once said kneading dough had saved many a marriage. Lilly pressed hard into the spongy mixture. There wasn't any marriage to save, but it sure felt good to take her anger out on something.

"Lilly?" Marguerite slipped into the kitchen of the diner carrying a rubberized bag. "Are you ready to go?"

"Go where?"

"Swimming. Remember?" She pulled the stool to the counter and sat down. "Lilly, what's wrong? It looks like you've been crying. Is Nick okay?"

"Nick's fine. Unless I decide to break the sixth commandment, in which case I can assure you he'd no longer be fine."

"I see." Marguerite poured herself a glass of water and handed Lilly a dish towel. "You're going to make your dough salty with those tears. Talk to me."

Lilly blotted her face and went back to kneading. "Maybe later."

"We'll talk while we're swimming."

"Marguerite, I'm not really in the mood." After dividing the dough, Lilly plopped it into two glass pans and set it on the back of the stove to rise.

"You, my friend, need a break. And you know you're going to have to tell Emily and me what's wrong sooner or later, so you might as well tell us both at the same time. Think about this outing as saving you time."

Lilly sighed and shook her head. Only Marguerite would think of that. Knowing her friend, she might as well give in and go. Marguerite always seemed to get what she wanted eventually.

After making sure Eugenia and Nora had things covered, Lilly and Marguerite, along with their children, went to Emily's cottage. Lilly quickly gathered their bathing costumes and hurried back outside to join her friends.

"I'll be back in an hour or so." Emily kissed baby Katie then Carter goodbye.

"Have a good time. Katie and I will be fine. We have packing to do."

Lilly's heart lurched. "Packing?"

"I was going to tell you later, but Carter and I have decided to return to traveling with the team. My aunt Ethel is improving, and Carter says we'll be fine as long as we're together."

"Both of you? And the baby?" Lilly asked as they started toward the lake.

"Well, we weren't planning on leaving her behind." Emily's lips curled. "But, Lilly, I want you to know I already spoke to my grandmother, and she told me to make it clear you're free to stay here even after Carter and I leave."

"I'm not so sure I could do that." She eyed Tate, Faith, and Levi up ahead. What would she and Levi do now?

Emily waved her hand in the air. "Of course you can. Grandma insists."

"I'll have to think about it." They reached Lake Manawa's shore, and after Marguerite admonished Tate to help Levi change in the men's bathhouse, they hurried into the ladies' bathhouse to put on their bathing costumes.

It didn't take Lilly long to slip out of her skirt and shirt-waist and into her dark blue bathing costume. Since she was already wearing her black wool stockings, she didn't need to put those on. The square neck, tucked bodice, and flared skirt of her bathing costume showed more current trends than a lot of those donned by other women. Last season it had been one of her frivolous purchases from the meager allowance the Harts provided. She traced the yellow piping with her finger. Nick would have liked it.

Standing in front of the mirror, she tied a large, sunny-yellow kerchief around her hair, securing the bow in the front. Marguerite emerged from the stall along with Faith. She smiled at Lilly. "I know I told you this before, but that is the cutest bathing costume I've ever seen."

"Thank you."

"What did Nick—" Marguerite stopped. "Sorry."

Lilly's heart pinched, and tears pricked her eyes. Nick hadn't seen her in the bathing costume. Until the last few days, the water hadn't been warm enough to consider a swim.

"What's wrong?" Emily came out of her stall, adjusting her flowered swimming cap. "Did I miss something?"

"Nick and Lilly are on the outs."

"Nick and I"—Lilly placed her hand on the door's latch—"are over."

37

Drenched and tired from frolicking, Marguerite sat on the warm beach. She dug her fingers into the deep, wet layers of sand. Worry wrapped its tendrils around her heart. Lilly refused to speak about what had happened with Nick, so how could she help if she didn't know what was wrong?

Emily sat down beside her. "Did you come up with a plan yet?"

Out in the lake, Lilly held a prone Faith on her arm, trying to teach her to float. Marguerite smiled, remembering when Lilly had taught her to swim. "You know our Lilly. You can't make her do anything."

"Or say anything." Emily sighed. "I guess we'll have to trust her to talk when she's ready."

Lilly left the water and walked up the beach. Her steps stilled for a moment when she glanced in the direction of the Midway, and then she hurried to join them. She sank into the sand beside them.

Emily placed a hand on her friend's damp arm. "Tell us what happened."

"He let Levi ride the roller coaster." Lilly thrust her fists into the sand.

"Is that all?" Marguerite asked. "Men do a lot of things with their children a mother might not think is safe. Trip even took Tate out in the sailboat during a storm. He said he needed to learn what to do if one came up."

"Tate's a lot older than Levi, and Tate is Trip's child. Levi is mine."

"I see." Marguerite crossed her arms.

"It sounds like there's more to the story." Emily's voice was gentle and filled with concern.

Lilly pressed her lips together.

Marguerite huffed. "Oh, good grief. Just tell us. We aren't going to leave you alone until you do."

❧

The advertisement in the newspaper was a godsend.

Lilly clutched the paper in her hand and glanced at Marguerite walking beside her. Levi trailed behind them, looking for cicada skins. He'd already found a couple and delighted in showing them to his aunt Marguerite.

The ad said the four-room house for sale was only a half mile from the lake. It would take every penny Lilly had saved, but she believed she could afford it. They might have to do with sleeping on the floor for a month until she could buy beds, but they'd manage.

She'd been glad Marguerite readily agreed to go with her to see it. The last couple of days had taken their toll on Lilly, and she hadn't wanted to do any convincing. Every movement right now made her feel like she was walking through a wet field of cockleburs. Her sandpapery eyes drooped, still thick from last night's crying, and her heart was as heavy as Eugenia's oatmeal.

Her friends had been supportive of her decision to stop seeing Nick, but she sensed Marguerite had an earful of opinion ready to deliver this morning.

"Lilly, are you sure this is what you want?" Marguerite snagged a bushy green foxtail from the weeds along the road and stripped it with her fingers.

"I don't know. I haven't seen the house yet."

"That's not what I mean." Marguerite glanced at her. "Are you certain you and Nick can't try again? Buying a house closes that door quite soundly."

"I didn't tell you the worst of what he said."

"Oh?"

"He called me a coward."

Marguerite's eyebrows peaked. "I hope he ducked when he said it."

Lilly almost smiled.

"Now, do you promise not to hit me?" Marguerite pushed a branch out of the way.

"Yes."

"Is he right?"

Lilly stopped. "You think I'm a coward too?"

"I think you're afraid, and I don't blame you, but I worry you're letting your fear control your choices. Building all these walls isn't going to keep you from getting hurt. It's only going to keep you from being loved."

They started walking again. "Can I hit you now?"

Marguerite shrugged. "If you have to."

"I'll forfeit." Lilly looked at her dearest friend. That hadn't been easy for Marguerite to say. But was she right? Was fear controlling Lilly?

Marguerite shielded her eyes from the sun. "If that's the house, then you may be living at Emily's a while longer."

Lilly saw a crude "For Sale" sign nailed to a tree in the front yard. Shoving an overgrown bush out of the way, she walked to the front porch, making sure to skip over the second step, which was rotted through. "Levi, you stay out here with Aunt Marguerite until I see what the inside looks like."

"Are you sure it's safe?" Marguerite asked. "I can have Trip come check it out."

"Now who's the coward?" She laughed and nudged the front door open. Nothing scurried out. That was a good sign.

Clearly the house had lain empty for quite some time. Cobwebs filled the corners, and only broken pieces of furniture remained. The threadbare rug on the floor spoke of some rodent visitors. She shuddered. Wouldn't Levi be happy to know the house came with pets?

"Lilly?" Marguerite stuck her head inside the doorway. "Are you okay?"

"Yes, come on in. It's dirty, but it's not in horrible shape. There's a nice fireplace." Lilly blew on the mantel and dust filled the air. She coughed. "It will need a little elbow grease."

Marguerite surveyed the room while Levi began opening every door and cupboard. "This place would need an army of elbows. Why can't you stay at Emily's cottage?"

"I know you can't understand this." Tears sprang to Lilly's eyes. "But it's time for Levi to have a home. I have to at least give him that."

⤐⤏

"I still can't believe the lassie bought a house. Has she gone ape on ya?"

Nick chuckled at Sean's surprise, which mirrored his own a few hours ago. He snapped the reins, and the horse picked up speed on the dirt road. The wagon bounced in the ruts.

If Lilly's new house was only a half mile from the lake on this road, they should have no trouble finding it—especially given the description Marguerite had provided.

When Marguerite had come to the roller coaster this afternoon and told him Lilly had purchased a house, he'd been shocked. If he were to admit it, the news hurt too. Was it so easy for her to move on without him? Still, he couldn't bear the thought of her living in a house Marguerite claimed was better fit for Levi's critters than for mankind.

"Marguerite says it's not in the best shape, and I want to see for myself."

"See it? Then why did ya borrow this wagon and fill it with supplies for fixin' things up?"

"I don't want Levi living somewhere with rotten steps. He could get hurt. That's all."

"Is that a fact?"

Nick spotted what must be the house and drew the wagon to a halt. It was worse than he thought. Had she even looked at the roof?

Sean whistled. "This place is in need of a wee bit of repairs, eh?"

"I'll say." Nick hopped down. "How much do you think we can get done before Lilly returns?"

Eyeing the heavy rain clouds in the sky, Sean shrugged. "If we're lucky, we can patch those holes on the roof before nary a raindrop falls."

Nick clapped Sean's shoulder. "Sounds like a plan."

They worked side by side for two hours. Even though this wasn't a roller coaster, Nick enjoyed working with Sean. He found that the years of building they'd done together meant few words needed to pass between them.

Nick took a swig from the canteen and handed it to Sean.

"I'm glad they won't get wet. Thanks for helping me, Sean. I only wish I could do more."

Sean eyed him. "Boyo, ya can't be fixin' everything."

"I wouldn't fix it all, but I'd repair those porch steps, maybe make a couple of beds, and see to the cracked plaster in the parlor."

"And the hole in Lilly's heart?"

Nick quirked his eyebrows in question. "I can't fix that."

"Ah, but ya have to admit ya sure have been tryin'."

Crossing his arms over his knees, Nick sighed. "All right. You've got something on your mind. Out with it."

"It's a wee thought that's been nigglin' around in me head." Sean tapped his temple. "Yer a man who likes to fix things, right?"

"Yes."

"And maybe ya been trying to fix Lilly's life." Nick started to protest, but Sean held up his hand. "I don't mean it in a bad way, laddie."

"She's afraid, but she's too stubborn to admit it. When Ben died, I think she realized bad things do happen to God's children." Nick sighed again. "Doesn't the Bible say perfect love casts out fear? I love her. She can trust me. Why didn't it work?"

"That's an easy one. Yer not perfect."

The words stung. Another reminder of his pride. Did he believe he was the answer to all of Lilly's problems? Sometimes the Lord's lessons seemed to come one on top of the other.

Nick rose to his feet, careful to keep his balance on the roof. "So you're saying I'm trying to fix all the hurts in her life, but I can't do it. Only He can."

Sean chuckled. "And here I thought I'd have to use a hammer to get that through yer thick head."

⬥

Lilly's arms ached from scrubbing. She'd sent Emily and Marguerite home hours ago. Emily had taken Levi with her too. And now, with the solitary lamp casting shadows on the walls of the house, Lilly wished she'd gone with them.

Instead, her stubbornness had taken over and she'd insisted on staying the night here in her own home.

She ran her hand along the now dust-free mantel. It was hers. All hers. But this place didn't seem like a home yet. It had four walls, windows, and doors, but it wasn't filled with love. Tonight it felt eerie and empty.

At least the freshly mopped floors were dry and the place aired out. She spread a quilt out on her would-be parlor floor and piled another heavy blanket on top of it. Too tired to worry about undressing, she tossed the pillow on the pallet, then plopped down beside it. Her skirts flew up. She laughed, glad no one was there to see it. After removing her shoes and stockings, she fell onto the downy pillow.

Her head struck something. *Ow!* With a sigh, she reached inside the embroidered pillowcase and felt for the offending object. Her fingers wrapped around the leather of a book. She pulled the volume free and held it toward the lamp.

Her Bible. The one that once belonged to her mother. She'd given it to Lilly on the day she married Ben. Emily must have packed it.

She set it aside and drew the last blanket over herself. The lamp flickered, but she didn't extinguish it. Tonight she'd leave it burning.

Above her, thunder rumbled and the clouds released their burden in a downpour. She glanced at the ceiling. She was dry. Thanks to Nick.

She'd been shocked—and a little angry—that he'd fixed the roof. But now the gesture overwhelmed her with a bitter-sweetness that wouldn't wash away with the rain. Tears filled her eyes, casting a watery globe around the solitary lamp. She blinked and the tears escaped.

Rolling onto her side, she bunched the pillow beneath her head. *No, I will not cry tonight. Not again. I have a new home. I'm starting over. I'll be fine.*

Her heart didn't listen, and soon the corner of the pillow lay soaked. Lightning flashed outside, and she rolled onto her stomach. The heavy stomping of thunder only made the little house seem more empty, and the solitude engulfed her.

But she was safe.

Dry.

Thanks to Nick.

After wiping her eyes, she propped herself on her elbows before pulling the Bible closer. She didn't want to open it. God had let too many storms occur in her life, and He hadn't exactly been stilling them.

Trust Me.

She felt the words press again on her heart. But why should she? She flipped the Bible open to the book of Luke and the story of Jesus stilling the storm. What had Brother Hamilton said? That Jesus doesn't still every storm, but He's in the boat with you?

But where were You in my storm? Were You sleeping? Didn't You care?

She wanted to pull the words back. Who was she to question the Lord? Her eyes dropped to the Bible splayed in front of her. She read the story again. The apostles questioned Jesus, but He questioned their faith. They missed the greatness of the One in the boat with them.

But it was the words written in the margin in her mother's hand that caught her eye. *Faith entrusts oneself and one's children to God in the midst of danger.*

Her mother had told her she was leaning on her own wisdom and not the power of God. Had her own mother struggled with the same things when Lilly's father died?

Lilly's heart throbbed. *Lord, I see what I've been doing. When the storms came, I had the same choice the apostles had, the same choice my mother had. I could've responded with fear or faith. And I chose fear. I stopped trusting You and started trusting only myself. Please, Lord, please forgive me.*

Though the thunder continued to rumble, a quiet surrounded her heart. She chose to believe in the greatness of the One who calmed the storms.

She traced her fingers over her mother's words again, saying them aloud. "Faith entrusts oneself and one's children to God in the midst of danger."

Mama, I hope I never have to find out if I have your kind of faith.

38

If rain healed, then the whole lake had undergone a miracle. Nick inhaled the refreshing scent of everything washed clean. Last night's churning lake now lay placid, and the whole Midway—signs, awnings, buildings—sported vibrant colors, free of dust and still damp from the rain.

Despite the renewed morning, heaviness pressed against Nick's chest. He needed to let Lilly go. It had been a week now, and she'd bought a house. She was moving on fine without him.

As he approached the lunch counter, Nick squinted against the too-bright sun. He spotted Sean and Forest entering. He knew those two had left the boardinghouse before him, but where was Percy? Probably still sulking. The boy remained sore with Nick even after he'd apologized yesterday for yelling at him. He didn't blame Percy, but how long would the young man hold a grudge?

Levi galloped toward him. "Morning, Mr. Nick. Come see who's riding on my roller coaster." His chubby fingers

338

wrapped around Nick's calloused hand and pulled him forward.

"Whoa, Chipmunk. I haven't even had any coffee yet."

"Mama's fruster-ated. Coffee burned."

"Did Eugenia do it?"

Levi stopped in front of his toy, looked up, and shook his head. "Nope. Mama did. Then she told me to go outside and play." He pointed to the roller coaster. "See?"

Nick squatted down to get a good look at Levi's passengers. "Night crawlers?"

Levi nodded. "And they like it!"

"How can you tell?"

"They get all wiggly and excited like I do."

A chuckle erupted from Nick's chest as he stood. "You be sure to give them a good ride, and then put them back so they can go home."

Percy finally arrived and slipped in the diner's front door, but Nick didn't feel like addressing the surly young man right now.

"I have a home." Levi dug his toe in the ground. "But Mama says it's for us. Not for you."

Nick cleared his throat, but the lump lodged there refused to budge. "I'm glad you and your mama have your own place. I want you both to be happy."

"The house doesn't make her happy. It makes her sad."

"Why do you say that, Levi?"

"All she does is cry. Clean and cry. Clean and cry. I didn't even get to stay there with her last night. I had to go back with baby Katie." Levi scrunched his forehead and crossed his arms over his chest. "And all she does is cry too."

A bitter smile twisted Nick's mouth. "I'm sure things will get better."

"It's all my fault Mama's crying."

"What do you mean?"

"I rode the roller coaster, and she got mad at you for letting me. That's why she bought a house for just me and her and not you."

"No, Levi, it isn't your fault." His heart ached for Levi. How could he make the little boy see? "Sometimes grown-up problems are hard to understand and explain, but all you need to know is your mama and I love you."

"So you'll be here forever?"

Nick sat down on the lunch counter's stoop and drew Levi close. "Listen, buddy. I need you to understand something, and I need you to be brave, okay?"

"I'm brave."

"I know you are." Nick kissed the top of Levi's head. "I will have to go to another place soon to build a new roller coaster. But if your mama says it's okay, I'll come back to visit you."

Levi's lower lip trembled. "You're leaving?"

"Not for a while yet." Moisture gathered in Nick's eyes, and he blinked. "I'm sorry, Levi. I wish I could stay with you forever, but I can't. I've got a job to do. Someday I'm going to own Perrin's Park Amusements, and maybe you can come work for me. Would you like that? To build roller coasters?"

Levi shrugged, and tears trickled down his round cheeks. "Only if I can build stuff with you." He threw his arms around Nick's neck and squeezed hard. "I love you, Mr. Nick."

"I love you too, Levi, and I always will."

❧

Why did things always go wrong on Tuesdays?

Lilly dumped the blackened bread pudding into the trash

and set the pan in the sink to soak. Not only would she have to make another dessert, but cleaning that pan would take at least half an hour.

Breakfast had been a disaster. She'd burned the coffee, and her oatmeal looked like Eugenia's early attempts. And seeing Nick stirred her already churning stomach into a frothing mess.

If guests hadn't already been in the diner, she'd have let Eugenia do all the serving by herself.

Lilly wiped her hands on a dish towel and went outside to check on Levi. He'd been unusually quiet all morning. When she'd questioned him, he said he was sad about Mr. Nick.

She sighed. It was better this way. Saying goodbye to Nick now was best for both of them. She only wished it didn't hurt so much.

Pushing open the screen door, Lilly glanced outside at Levi's play area. Worms crawled out of one of the roller coaster cars, but Levi didn't seem to be around to push them back in. His cast-iron fire wagon with its two white horses lay overturned in the mud. Where had he gone now?

With her hands cupping her mouth, Lilly called for him and waited for an answer.

None.

Her eyes fell again to the toy coaster, and Levi's tearstained cheeks filled her mind.

Levi had been so upset. Would he have gone to find Nick again?

❧

"Mark, what a pleasant surprise." Marguerite opened the door and motioned her brother inside the boat shop. "What brings you here so early in the morning?"

"I doubt if you'll think this is a pleasant surprise by the time I leave. Could we go somewhere alone to talk?"

"I guess." She untied her apron strings. "Let me tell Trip to keep an eye on the children."

A few minutes later, Marguerite found herself sitting on one of the boardwalk's park benches outside the massive brick Rowing Association. She glanced at the tranquil lake, so different from the trouble she saw brewing in Mark's eyes. "What's wrong?"

"You sure know how to get to the point." Mark leaned forward, placing his elbows on his knees and clasping his hands in front of him. "I think Lilly's in trouble."

"Why? What's going on?"

"I think I've made a big mistake, Marguerite." He turned to look at her. "I've been helping Claude Hart."

"Of course you have. You do law work for him."

"No, I've been helping him in his efforts to get Lilly to send Levi to boarding school."

Marguerite gasped. "How could you? Lilly is family."

Mark stood. "No, she's not. She was your personal maid, and I truly believed the Harts could provide more for Levi in both education and opportunities."

"But Levi belongs with his mother. He's all she has left. I don't understand how you could help that man."

Mark held up his hand. "I know you don't, and you can box my ears later, but right now I need your help with something else."

Marguerite sucked in a lungful of rain-freshened air and rubbed the bridge of her nose. "All right, what is going on? What kind of trouble are you talking about?"

"Promise me you'll listen."

"Okay." She dropped her hand to her lap.

"My job was to make sure Nick and Lilly's courting didn't get serious. I'm the one who told Mr. Hart how close they were getting, and I'm the one who arranged for Ruby to come to work here this season."

Marguerite glared at him but remembered her promise to be quiet. Besides, if there was more, she needed to hear it.

Mark sat down again. "After I learned they'd called off their courting, I figured Mr. Hart would be done with them because he'd told me he simply didn't want Lilly marrying Nick and taking his grandson halfway across the country."

"I can see his concerns, but I'm guessing he wasn't satisfied."

"He wasn't. He does care about Levi, but I think he's also worried about Levi being his only heir. He's afraid Levi won't know how to live like a Hart. But the more I've been around Levi, the more I've seen how happy he is, and this job kept getting harder to do."

"So what's the trouble now?"

"Mr. Hart hired another man named Mr. Black. I don't know what Mr. Black is supposed to do, but I have a bad feeling about it, and I'm afraid whatever it is will happen today."

Marguerite shook her head. "Like what?"

"Something involving the roller coaster, maybe? I don't know."

"We need to tell Lilly."

"You're not mad?"

She harrumphed. "Mark, I'm furious, but I'm even more disappointed. I also know we don't have time to address this right now." She started walking, and he fell in step beside her. "Let's go tell Lilly what's going on, and then we'll have to talk to Nick."

"Nick?"

"Well, yes, if you think they may do something to his roller coaster."

"He'll probably deck me."

She raised an eyebrow. "He might, but I'll do my best to protect you—little brother."

❦

The steady chug of the engine seemed like the only thing in Nick's life he could count on. With the roller coaster set to open in less than fifteen minutes, it was time for his customary safety ride. Although he knew every twist, turn, dip, and plunge of the Velvet Roller Coaster, he found he still got a little thrill from the ride each morning. It was his creation—squeaks, clacks, and all.

"Percy, wheel that car on around."

With a shove, the youth pushed the car to the loading position. "Do you want me to take the ride today? You look tired."

Nick smiled. Maybe Percy would forgive him after all. Nick climbed into the backseat. "No, but thanks for the offer."

"If you're sure."

Nick studied the chain as it turned while he waited for Percy to push the car to the bottom of the lift hill. One of the links seemed to have a bit of a kink in it. He'd have Sean check it out after his ride and before the patrons got on. It couldn't be anything serious. Sean said he'd checked it all before breakfast, and little got past that man's inspection.

The car jolted as the chain dog connected. Nick glanced at the Midway below as the car began to climb. He spotted the bandstand in the distance and heard the faint strains of Nordin's concert band practicing a fast-paced tune. Clack, clack, clack—he counted the green anti-rollback boards as he passed each of them. Twenty of the twenty-three clicks.

344

Only three left. He'd be at the top in seconds. Best view in the park.

A high-pitched *ching* made Nick grab for the safety bar. The car suddenly jerked backward, giving him whiplash. Air whooshed from his lungs. The car hit the first anti-rollback board hard, splintering it.

The car continued to plunge backward down the steep incline. Each time the car hit a green board, the decent slowed, but the boards snapped in the process. Nick's chest constricted. He was traveling too fast. Would he run out of boards before the car slowed enough to come to a stop?

He whirled around. Only a handful of green boards remained. If the car didn't stop, it would keep flying backward until it hit the waiting set of cars in the loading station. He'd heard of those collisions. They weren't pretty.

Lord, please!

Snap! Another green board gave way to the weight of the car. The car dropped, but the next board stopped it.

Deathly still, Nick waited. Would this one hold?

39

Below him, Nick heard Sean bark orders and then heard the footfalls of someone approaching, climbing on the rails.

Whatever you do, don't shake it.

When he dared to look behind him, he saw Sean balanced precariously on the track, jamming a piece of wood behind the back of the car. What was he doing? If the car slipped now, Sean could be killed.

The car jerked, but the crunch of wood told him the brace held.

"Boyo, ya ready to climb out, or do ya need a minute to stop shakin'?" Sean asked.

Nick drew in a shaky breath. "I think I'll take the minute and thank God."

"Sounds like a good idea, but I dunna think God would mind if ya thanked Him on the ground either."

Nick took the hand Sean offered, climbed over the back of the car, and lowered his feet onto the two narrow maple boards making up the track. They crouched low and backed the rest of the way down the incline.

Sean reached the bottom first and climbed onto the loading platform. He took Nick's arm. "Easy now, boyo. Ya hurt?"

Nick rubbed his neck. "No, but I bet I'll be sore tomorrow. Let's go have a look at that lift chain."

"You could sit down and rest a wee bit first if ya like."

"No, I need to see what happened." He turned to Percy and Forest, who had joined them. After answering some of their questions, he said, "You two go make sure the gates remain closed. Don't let anyone in, and keep the reason why quiet. Tell them we have some repairs to do."

When they'd gone, Sean and Nick headed beneath the lift hill. The chain hung from the trestle like a dangling kite string, with the end reaching the ground. Sean located the severed link and picked it up.

Nick joined him. "What do you think? Did we miss something?"

"You mean, did I miss something?"

"Sean, I'm not blaming you."

"No need to. I'm doin' enough of that all by me lonesome." He turned the broken chain dog over in his hand and frowned. "What does this look like to you?"

"How could the metal give way like that?" Nick examined the link. His blood ran cold in his veins. "This didn't break off. Someone cut this with a torch."

"But why would anyone do that? Passengers could have been killed."

"Go fetch the sheriff. We need to report this." Nick nodded toward the gate. "Send Forest up. We'll see what it's going to take to fix this chain."

"Ya realize, Nick my boy, we need to find the bugger who

did this. Whoever it was had to have access, and only a hand-ful of folks have a key to the padlock on the gate."

"No, I think they had to do it while we ate breakfast. You did your inspection before we ate, and you wouldn't have missed the kink it put in the chain." Nick swept the area with his gaze. "I'll look around while you're gone and see if I can find anything that points to someone in particular. I'm afraid this could be Claude Hart's doing, and we may never know who he had working for him."

❧

"I have to see Nick!"

Lilly tried to push past Forest. Instead of letting her through, Forest grabbed the wooden turnstile and held it fast. "Mrs. Hart, there's been a mechanical problem with the roller coaster, and we were told to keep everyone out."

"*Everyone* doesn't include me, I'm sure." Lilly glared at the man. A few seconds later, she softened. "Please, Levi is missing, and he had to have come here to see Nick."

"Forest, is there a problem?" Sean laid a hand on the crew member's shoulder. "Did ya say something about the laddie, Mrs. Hart?"

"Yes, I believe Levi's come here to see Nick. You have to let me in to look for him."

"We haven't seen the boy, but I'm sure Nick will want to know he's missing." He motioned Forest to let her pass. "Go on. If you don't see Nick, he's in the engine shed."

Not even taking the time to thank Sean properly, Lilly pushed the wooden bar on the turnstile. She hurried up the paved walkway to the roller coaster, scanning the area for any sight of her son. The uneasy feeling inside her chest grew. If Levi wasn't here, where could he be? She and Eugenia had checked the Midway, and no one had seen him.

Mr. Thorton's words came back to her. *You never know when a boy is going to get a hankering for an adventure.* Had Levi wandered off? What if he'd gone down to the lake?

No. She couldn't think that. She had to keep focused. Pushing the threatening panic back down, she climbed the steps to the loading station. Not seeing Nick, she hiked her skirt and raced across the station platform. She cast a fleeting glance at the roller coaster car wedged on the lift hill. The mechanical problem? Had Nick been inside that car? And he'd said the roller coaster was safe enough for her son.

Slamming the engine shed door open, she peered inside. "Nick?"

He spun around. "Lilly!" His gaze swept her face. "What's wrong?"

"Have you seen Levi?"

Concern creased his brow. "No, why? Is he missing?"

"I can't find him anywhere. Nick, what if he went to the lake?" Lilly's eyes misted.

Nick crossed the distance between them in two broad steps and pulled her into his arms. "Shhh, don't say that. He knows better. He wouldn't go there. We'll find him."

She pulled back. She couldn't let Nick comfort her—even now. "I need to look for him."

Nick pressed his lips into a thin line and held the door for her. "I said *we'll* find him. Come on."

"Where do we start?" Lilly scanned the area.

Nick pointed to the car shed where the extra roller coaster cars were housed. "Look in all of them. He likes to play there. I'll look around the coaster." He placed his hand on her shoulder. "And, Lilly, we'll find him. I promise."

A sob stuck in her throat, making her unable to respond. After his hand slipped away, she hurried up the back steps to the car shed. The red cars with their yellow curlicues seemed like adult-sized toys. She craned her neck to look inside each empty car.

"Levi!"

Nick hopped onto the platform. "He's not around the coaster." He nodded toward the suspended car on the lift hill. "Where else might he go? Back to Emily's? To your new place?"

Footfalls on the front steps made them both turn. Sean and the sheriff came into view, and Lilly's heart thudded to a stop. What had the lawman discovered? Her knees threatened to give way, and she grabbed for the wall.

Nick caught her elbow. "Lilly, I sent for the sheriff. He's not here because of Levi."

"You? Why?"

He led her to a bench and urged her to sit. "Rest here a minute."

"I can't rest. I have to find my son."

Squatting before her, he took her hands in his and bowed his head. "Lord, we're so scared right now, but we know You have Levi in the palm of Your hand. Give us the wisdom to know where to look for him and the faith to trust You to guide us to him. And please, Lord, bless and comfort this mother. No one has ever loved a son more than Lilly does."

Sean called for him just as Nick said, "Amen," and he stood. "I'll be right back. Keep thinking about where to look next. We'll get the sheriff and the men to help."

◈

"Sheriff, we've got two problems." Nick wasted no time with a greeting. "First, I think someone sabotaged the roller coaster. One of the links had been cut, and I found the wand for the cutting torch lying on the ground in the engine shed."

"Any idea who would want to do that?"

"Only one, but he'd never do it himself." Nick sighed. "Claude Hart hasn't been happy with me seeing his former daughter-in-law."

"I recall he wanted me to take her son from her."

"Which brings me to the second, much more important problem. Lilly's son, Levi, is missing. We need to get men out looking for him. She's looked in all the normal spots, but we haven't found him. She's not sure where he may have wandered off to."

Sean looked from Nick to Lilly, who was sitting on a bench with her hands clasped in her lap. "But the lad is only six years old? How far would he go?"

"I don't think he'd go far, but he does like adventure and this is a big place."

The sheriff pulled off his hat and ran his hand through his peppered hair. "I know you don't want to consider this, but I have to ask. Would he go to the lake?"

Nick's throat clogged, and he cleared it. "I don't think so."

"I'll get some men and bring them back here to start looking."

"No, bring them to Thorton's Lunch Counter. That's where Lilly works and where she last saw him." He nodded toward Sean. "I'll have my men search here again and then join us there."

"Boyo, here she comes."

Nick glanced behind him and confirmed Sean's words.

"You'll need to keep the lady calm." The sheriff tugged his hat back on his head. "I don't want to have to deal with hysterics on top of finding a lost boy."

"I won't be hysterical, sir." Lilly stepped into the circle. "You can wipe that shocked look off your face. Half the

351

patrons at the park probably heard you." She started down the steps.

Nick caught her arm. "Where are you going?"

"To find my son."

"I can't just sit here!"

"Lilly, the sheriff wants you to stay here in case he comes back." Nick stilled Lilly's pacing with a touch of his hand. The sheriff had arrived with a handful of men, and they'd divided to the locations Lilly had given as possible places Levi might go—the zoo, the cottage, their fishing hole. "I promise I'll come back and find you as soon as I've checked out the ice cream parlor, the carousel, and the miniature train."

"Let me go with you. Please, the waiting is killing me."

The bell over the door jingled, and Lilly turned to it, hope in her eyes. The hope disappeared at the sight of Marguerite and Mark.

Marguerite looked at Lilly. "What's wrong?"

"Levi's missing." Lilly hugged herself.

"Do you think—" Marguerite shot a fearful look at Mark. "We need to talk to both of you."

Nick pushed the chair in after he stood, making it screech on the floorboards. "Can't it wait? I'm heading out to look for him."

Marguerite held out her arm. "We need to talk—now."

"Why? Do you know something?" Nick demanded.

"Let's sit down." Marguerite wrapped an arm around Lilly.

"No!" Lilly jerked away. "I can't."

"Please." Marguerite pulled out a chair. "Mark has some things he needs to tell you both."

The four of them took seats around the table, and with muscles stretched so tight they could snap, Nick listened to Mark relay the information about his role in helping Claude Hart, including trying to keep Lilly and Nick apart. Nick clenched his fists, fighting the urge to deliver a star-spangled blow to Mark's jaw. That wouldn't help right now.

Sean and Percy entered and took a seat.

"But what does this have to do with Levi?" Lilly dug her nails into Mark's arm.

The young man winced. "I believe your father-in-law had another plan in the works involving a man named Clifford Black. He had me deliver some money to him and tell him he wanted him to finish the job they'd planned."

Nick felt the blood drain from his face. Clifford Black. The man who'd unnerved him while speaking with Levi the other day. "Like sabotage my roller coaster?"

Mark shrugged. "I don't know."

"What do you know about this Black?"

"Not much. Honestly. I was willing to help him keep you and Lilly apart. That's all. Maybe this Clifford Black is helping him with some other plans. I don't know." Mark locked eyes with Nick. "I knew what I was doing was wrong, but it wasn't illegal."

Nick hit the table with his fist. "Didn't you realize someone could have been hurt or killed?"

"Like I said, I had no idea Mr. Hart would go that far, and you have no proof that he did. I find it hard to believe Mr. Hart would risk that."

"So why are you telling us this now?" Lilly clutched her coffee cup, her knuckles whitening. "And what does it have to do with my son?"

Nick draped his arm around her chair and pulled her close.

"He thinks this Mr. Black and your former father-in-law were planning something else."

"Like taking Levi?" Lilly whispered.

"It's something he'd consider," Mark said with a sigh.

Nick's heart hammered in his chest. "Lilly, you know them better than anyone. Where would Claude take Levi?"

"Claude and Evangeline would never hurt Levi—not physically anyway." She bit her lip to quell its trembling. "They'd keep him with them at the estate until they made arrangements to send him away to that school."

"Would they have that Black fellow take him straight there?" Marguerite started to lift her coffee cup to her lips but set it back down when it shook in her hands.

Lilly met her gaze. "He'd work fast, but I don't think he'd let a stranger take him. Claude's a stern man, but he's never been cruel. Besides, I think he'd want to present his grandson to the school's headmaster himself."

Memories of those first days in the orphanage, when he'd been ripped from his family, fired through Nick's thoughts. Even surrounded by reasonably kind people, the fear and loneliness had swallowed him. Levi was not going to go through that. Someone would come for him.

Nick stood. "Then he's most likely at the estate."

"What are you doing?" Lilly grabbed his sleeve. "You can't march in there and expect them to turn him over to you."

"Lilly, I'm getting him back."

"Should I trust you?" She stood and tipped her face toward his, her eyes bleak.

The bitterness in her voice made him cringe. He cupped her jaw, tracing her tearstained cheek with his thumb. "No, Lilly. Trust God."

40

Why had she let Nick Perrin walk out of the diner without her?

She pressed her hand to the glass on the window, watching him jog away. Maybe she let him go because he countered every argument she'd given him. Or perhaps she knew the more she delayed him, the longer it would take to get Levi home. Even the discussion about Levi not being at the Harts' but being at the lake had merit.

Still, deep inside, the tiny bud of truth bloomed.

She let him go because she trusted him.

"I wish he would have taken me with him." Mark downed the last of his coffee.

"Nick was right. If you get caught breaking into Claude Hart's home, your law career will be over." Marguerite carried the empty cups to the counter. "At least he stayed long enough for Lilly to describe the layout of the home. He's not going in totally blind."

Mark stood and walked to the door. "But I need to do something. I'm going to Mr. Hart's office to see if I can find any train tickets. At least then we'll know the time frame of his plans."

"Are you sure that's a good idea?" Marguerite asked. "Lilly, what do you think?"

She turned toward him. "Take me with you."

Mark lowered his hand from the knob. "But Nick said you're supposed to stay here."

"Mark, you owe me."

With a sigh, he nodded. "You're right. I do."

⁂

Coal dust filled Nick's nostrils. The chunks of coal shifted beneath his body with every step. Thank goodness the Harts had a large coal-shoot door. As it was, he barely cleared the shaft. He made it to the door and cracked it open.

The basement, used mostly for cold storage, remained devoid of any staff. He stepped from the room and dusted off his clothes. Tracking through the house would hardly keep his efforts hidden.

Nick found the staircase and began his ascent. On the first floor, he heard the banging of pots. It made sense for this to be the servants' staircase. A swinging door barred anyone from inside the stairwell. He continued climbing. Lilly had said the nursery was on the second floor in the west wing. Levi couldn't be far now.

At the top of the second set of stairs, he paused to listen. Lilly said the household staff usually took care of the bedrooms first thing in the morning and then moved to the main floor. If they hadn't finished here, he'd have to find somewhere to hide.

Hearing nothing, he slipped into the narrow servants' hallway. He followed it until it opened to the much brighter and wider regular hall. In front of him, he could see the expanse of stairs leading down to the main floor with a formal dining room and a parlor flanking it.

Giggling on the main floor below halted him. He pressed his body against the wall, his heart beating like the wings of a bat. The sound of the maids' chatter died off. Keeping one hand on the ivy-patterned wallpaper, he again started for the nursery. The thick Oriental rug muffled his steps.

A board creaked. He stopped. Listened. Moved on.

Lilly said the nursery was the fourth room on the right. With another prayer on his lips, Nick counted the oak-paneled doors as he passed them. He laid his hand on the ornate brass door handle of the fourth door and pressed his ear to the solid surface.

Crying. His heart grabbed, and everything in him told him to burst into the room and scoop Levi into his arms. But what if Levi wasn't alone?

The room adjacent to the nursery on the left had been Lilly's. She said a pocket door joined the two rooms. Since no one was likely to be in her old room, Nick abandoned the nursery door and eased the next door open.

He glanced around the enormous bedchamber. Dusty blue wallpaper loaded with white chrysanthemums seemed to fit Lilly. A four-poster mahogany bed stood sentry in the center. A massive wardrobe lined one wall with a door to a water closet beyond. He pictured Lilly sitting in the rocking chair holding a sleeping baby Levi. The table by the window, he imagined, had been a sanctuary for the young couple to enjoy occasional meals together.

He felt like a voyeur peeking into Lilly's private world. He shook his head. To go from all this to a tent, and none of it ever hers. No wonder she wanted a home.

357

His gaze fell on the pocket door she'd told him about. Easing it open ever so slightly, Nick surveyed the nursery. For a playroom, few toys lined the shelves. He'd expected hobby horses and trains and instead saw a single basket of blocks, a few cast-iron horses and carts, and a top. Where were the balls and bats? Where were the books?

But what he did see excited him.

Levi sat drawing at a child-sized table—alone.

After pushing the pocket door into the wall far enough for him to slip through, Nick stepped into the room. Levi spun around. He started to squeal, but Nick held a finger to his lips. Levi ran across the room and launched himself into Nick's waiting arms.

The boy squeezed Nick's neck so hard he could barely breathe. When Levi finished hugging, he delivered a plethora of slobbery kisses to Nick's cheeks.

"Are you okay, Chipmunk?" Nick whispered, brushing the hair from Levi's forehead. Levi pulled back, and Nick grinned at the coal-dust-speckled boy. What a sight the two of them made.

Tears glistened in Levi's eyes. "I want my mama."

"I know, and I'll take you to her as soon as I can."

"That mean man made me come here. I told Grandfather I need to go home, but he said we're going on a big trip to-morrow." Levi scowled. "I don't want to go on a trip. I want to go home."

"Home? To your new house? The diner?"

Levi shook his head. "Wherever you and Mama are."

When he heard voices in the hallway, Nick held up his hand to signal Levi to be quiet. Setting Levi down behind him, Nick strained to hear if those outside were entering or merely passing.

A voice he recognized echoed in the corridor. Nick's pulse drummed.

They'd been betrayed.

⟨⟨⟩⟩

Telling Lilly no was the hardest thing Mark had done in a long time.

He did owe her, but letting her get in trouble or get hurt wasn't any way to pay her back. Besides, the last thing Mark needed was to give Nick Perrin another reason for punching him. Already he'd seen Nick's struggle to keep from dealing with him in a very concrete manner.

Lilly finally backed down from her demands after Marguerite reminded her that Levi could still be at the park and not at the Hart estate, and Mark left, promising he'd telephone the lake with word as soon as he heard anything.

"Miss Fallwell, good morning." Mark tipped his hat in greeting to Mr. Hart's stenographer.

"I'm sorry, but Mr. Hart's not been in today."

"That's okay. I'm supposed to collect some papers from his desk to deliver. Mind if I go on in?"

Miss Fallwell worried her lower lip between her teeth. "He doesn't usually let anyone in, but given as you work here, I guess it would be okay."

"'Course it's okay, beautiful." He flashed his best college grin, and the full-faced, bespectacled, middle-aged woman turned as crimson as the draperies.

Inside Claude Hart's office, Mark went directly to the roll-top desk and slid the louvered door up. He scanned the many drawers and the desktop for train tickets. Seeing none on the surface, he began to go through the tiny drawers, starting in the right corner.

Miss Fallwell rapped on the doorjamb. "Mr. Westing, did you find what you were looking for? I could come in and help you search for them."

"No, no. Don't trouble yourself on my account."

"It wouldn't be any trouble." Her singsong voice made her wishes clear.

"I've found the papers, Miss Fallwell, and I'm merely reading through them to make sure they're in order."

"Oh, all right," she said, the disappointment in her voice clear.

Mark rifled through the central pigeonholes on the desk. Nothing. He stopped. Something was off. He went back to the three stacked center drawers and pulled them all out. They were shorter than the other drawers.

He studied the wood panel behind them. One board seemed a bit different. He leaned close and examined it. With the three drawers extended, it allowed for him to slide the one panel over. Would it move?

Pressing his fingers to it, he found it slid easily, revealing a hiding space. He reached inside and removed a set of folded papers.

Mark opened the documents and gave a low whistle. Wait till he showed these to Lilly and Nick.

❦

Hiding would serve no purpose now.

Nick crouched in front of Levi and took his hands. "Any second, I think your grandfather and some other men may be coming in here. It may look like I'm in some trouble for coming to get you, but no matter what happens, I don't want you to be afraid. I'll come back and get you as soon as I get things straightened out. And, Levi, I promise you'll be back with your mama by tonight."

360

Levi put his arms around Nick's neck. "Please don't go. Please."

The door opened, but Nick didn't release Levi. Instead, he held him tighter and whispered, "Remember, I love you, and I will be back."

Nick let go of Levi and turned toward the doorway, where Claude Hart stood like a judge ready to deliver a death sentence. Behind him stood three other men.

"Percy, why?"

"Mr. Black forced me to tell him where you'd gone. He said he'd tell the sheriff what I'd done."

"Which was?"

Percy dropped his gaze to the floor.

"It was you? You cut the chain on the coaster? Why would you do that?"

"I—"

Claude Hart cut him off. "Enough idle talk. Officer Morris, please arrest this man. I will be pressing charges."

Nick met Claude's gaze. "You know this boy belongs with his mother."

The officer looked from Claude to Nick to Levi. "Sir, what's he talking about?"

"Nothing of consequence."

"I'm taking Levi home." Nick scooped the boy into his arms.

"I don't think you're in any position to make demands, Mr. Perrin. Breaking and entering is a serious crime."

"So is kidnapping."

"Give me the child." Claude held out his arms.

"No!" Levi cried. "Please don't let them take me, Mr. Nick."

Rivers of tears rolled down Levi's cheeks, and Nick's heart splintered.

"Officer, as you can see from the child's address, this man is not a relative," Claude said. "I'm his grandfather, and the boy is under my protection. Do your duty. Arrest this man and get him out of my house." He pointed to Percy. "And take him as well. He confessed to sabotaging the roller coaster at Lake Manawa. I'm sure the sheriff there will be happy to deal with him."

"Please, Grandfather, don't make Mr. Nick go away." Levi clung to Nick's neck, his breath hot against Nick's skin.

Nick smoothed Levi's hair, trying to soothe the boy's sobs shaking his six-year-old frame. "Hey, Chipmunk, remember what I said earlier. Now you have to be brave for a little while longer for your mama—and for me."

"Sir." The officer's tone said the time had come.

Pressing a final kiss to Levi's sandy hair, Nick pried Levi's arms away from his neck and handed him to Claude Hart. Hot tears burned the back of his eyes.

The officer rattled a set of handcuffs.

Nick swallowed hard. "Please, not in front of the boy."

"Sorry. That's the way it has to be."

Slowly Nick placed his arms behind his back and felt the cold metal rings clink around each wrist. But it was the dejected look on Levi's face that tore his heart to pieces. How was he going to get out of this and get Levi back to Lilly?

41

From the outside, Council Bluff's three-story Squirrel Cage Jail looked more like a gothic brick church than a prison. Lilly adjusted her hat pin, then allowed Mark to lift her from the carriage to the ground.

"Have you been in there?"

Mark took her elbow. "Not as a prisoner, but yes. There are three floors of revolving pie-shaped cells inside a large cage. The jailer can rotate the cells so only one cell on each floor has access to a door at any time. A regular marvel of ingenuity."

"But it sounds like something for an animal."

"It's not so bad. There are some windows for sunlight, and they feed them pretty well." Mark raised his eyebrows. "But it is nearly impossible to escape."

"Will they let me see Nick?"

"I'm going in as his lawyer, and you're with me, so it should be fine."

"But you aren't an attorney yet."

"That's okay. I don't think there will be a trial." Mark patted his coat pocket. "I think Mr. Hart will be willing to negotiate a release."

Lilly climbed the stairs and preceded Mark inside. Mark told her to wait while he spoke to the jailer. She surveyed the entry and wished she could see more of the jail, but from her vantage point, she could only see the kitchen on the left and the offices on the right.

A few minutes later, the jailer joined them. He gave her a critical once-over. "I'm not sure this is a fit place for a lady. I won't be responsible for how the men act toward you."

"I'll be fine."

"So be it. He's here on the first floor. Follow me."

They followed the jailer down a hall. Lilly glanced upward at the "cage" holding the cells. The brick, the sparse windows, and the cold metal bars made her shiver. The unmistakable stench of unwashed bodies caused her stomach to turn. How was Nick handling this horrid place?

The jailer went to the wall and connected a crank to a large gear. As he turned the crank, the cells turned on their axes with a groan. Metal grated against metal with an eerie screech. Lilly could see each of the prisoners housed in the small, pie-shaped cells as they passed by. Several made ungentlemanly comments to her in the process. Finally Nick's cell appeared. She started toward it, but Mark grabbed her arm.

"Can you let him out so we can talk?" Mark asked the jailer, nodding toward Lilly. "She shouldn't be subjected to seeing him here."

"Sorry. That's against the rules."

Mark released her. "Go ahead. I'll give you some time alone first."

Lilly's heels clinked against the metal floor, and she wrapped her fingers around the thick metal slats.

Clothes blackened and face smudged, Nick met her, covering her hands with his own. "He has Levi. I found him, but I got caught before we could get out."

"Is he okay?"

"He's upset, but he's fine. I told him to be brave."

"Why is Percy here?" She glanced at the boy sitting behind Nick.

"It's a long story." Nick cleared his throat. "I'm sorry. I failed you."

"How can you say that? You said you'd do anything for Levi and me, but I never dreamed it could come to this." Her eyes filled with tears.

"Hey, none of that." He laughed, but it sounded hollow and sad. "I'll get out of this, and I'll make sure you get Levi back. Then I think you and I need to have a nice long talk."

"Nick, I still don't know how we can make it work. Levi needs a home. He needs security now more than ever. Think about what this has done to him, and you have a job that takes you all over the country." She dropped her gaze to the chipped paint on the metal floor.

He tipped her chin up until her eyes met his. "I have a job. It's not my life. There are other things I could do."

"But—"

He pressed his fingers to her lips. "Not here. Not now." He glanced over her shoulder. "Mark."

The younger man strode over. "How are you holding up?"

"I'm fine. Levi has to be your priority, not me. How can we get him out of that house?"

"Lilly, has anyone been a witness to the problems you've been having with Claude Hart?" Mark asked.

"He spoke to Mr. Thorton and threatened his diner if I didn't let him see Levi, and Marguerite and Emily were there when Claude and Evangeline dragged the sheriff in to accuse me of being an unfit mother."

"The sheriff? I take it he didn't find any of their allegations true."

"Heavens no! He wasn't a bit happy with them and told them to leave me alone."

"Perfect."

"And I can testify." Percy joined them at the cell door. "Mr. Black paid me to sabotage the roller coaster. He was careful not to use Mr. Hart's name, but I think he'd turn on Mr. Hart before he'd take the blame himself."

"Good." Mark cupped Lilly's elbow.

"Mark, what do you plan to do?" Nick asked.

The soon-to-be attorney turned to Lilly. "You and I, Lilly, are going to make a little deal with the devil."

❦

An hour later, Lilly and Mark found the sheriff at Lake Manawa's jail. Thankfully he'd gotten the message that Levi had been found, but he was furious to learn why the morning's search had been unnecessary. He readily agreed to come to the city to help them straighten out the whole affair.

Once they reached the police department, they followed the sheriff inside.

"Sheriff Walter Boone, what can I do for you?" The police captain set down his papers and leaned forward at his desk.

Sheriff Boone held a chair for Lilly, then took a seat himself. "Andrew, I'm here about a missing little boy."

"My men will be glad to help you find him."

"Actually, he's been found. He's at the home of Claude Hart."

The captain picked up the sheet of paper on top of his pile and passed it to the sheriff. "We arrested a man for breaking and entering there today. Any connection?"

"The man you arrested was trying to get the boy back. Hart had arranged for the boy, his grandson, to be taken from his mother."

The police captain turned toward Lilly. "Is that you?"

She pressed her hand to her wildly beating heart. "Yes, sir."

"And who are you?" He studied Mark.

"Mark Westing. I'm a friend of the family, and I work for Claude Hart."

"You another lawyer?" The captain's eyebrows rose.

"Not yet, sir." Mark shifted. "Sir, we'd like to ask you to release Nick Perrin."

"Based on what? He still broke the law."

The sheriff nodded. "You're right, he did, but so did Mr. Hart. I'm thinking I might be able to look the other way concerning the kidnapping if you can get Mr. Hart to agree not to press charges against Nick Perrin."

"You can't charge Claude Hart with kidnapping. He's a powerful man. No judge in this city would find him guilty if the child was his own grandson. Besides, you said he arranged to have the child taken. Who did the actual kidnapping?"

"Clifford Black. But he's either at the Hart residence or long gone." The sheriff rubbed his peppery beard. "You're right, though, about Hart and the judges of this town, but the kidnapping happened at Lake Manawa, my jurisdiction. I have no problem arresting the arrogant man and keeping him in my jail as long as I possibly can."

The police captain turned to Lilly. "Are you agreeable to not pressing charges?"

"I only want my son returned and Nick released."

"Then maybe this will work. We'll go talk to Mr. Hart first thing in the morning."

"No!" The word burst from Lilly's lips. "We'll talk to him now."

"We?" The police captain looked from Lilly to the sheriff.

The sheriff smiled. "Andrew, the lady's been through enough today. First she couldn't find her son, and we all feared he was lost or drowned. Then she found out he'd been kidnapped, and now the man she loves is in jail. I don't know about you, but I think we shouldn't put her through any more. What do you say? Shall we reunite a child and his mother?"

"What if Hart won't go along with the exchange?"

Mark patted his coat pocket again. "I can guarantee you, he will."

The captain turned toward the officer sitting nearby. "In that case, Officer Rainer, fetch Mr. Perrin from the jail and bring him to the Hart residence. I'm sure he'd like to be there when we get the boy."

"But I need to go with you." Lilly met the captain's gaze. "Please."

The captain sighed, then stood. "I hope I don't regret this."

When Nick got back to the boardinghouse, he planned to take the longest bath in history. He might even take two.

Thankfully the officer who'd come didn't insist on handcuffing him, but he'd been tight-lipped about where Nick was being taken. At least the time in the cell had allowed him to speak with Percy about why he'd sabotaged the coaster. How he'd missed Percy's growing resentment, he'd never know. Percy admitted he first got angry when Nick sent him to work in the kitchen and he got sprayed by the skunk. It only grew worse when Nick yelled at him for letting Levi ride on the coaster.

When Clifford Black had approached Percy and offered him money to do a little roller coaster damage, he'd agreed—partly because of the money, but mostly because he was angry with Nick. He figured the lift chain would break before it ever hauled a car up the hill. When Nick got in the car, Percy was too afraid to say anything. In the cell, Percy's guilt over Nick's almost being hurt seemed to be tearing the boy apart.

After the officer came to get Nick, Percy looked like a lost little boy, and it had been hard to leave the young man. Not that the officer gave Nick another option. Nick assured Percy they'd get him out somehow. He prayed he'd be able to keep that promise.

The officer pulled his horse and police wagon to a stop in front of the Hart estate. The late afternoon sun hung low in the sky, casting an orange haze on Lilly, who stood on the Harts' veranda. But where was Levi? Why hadn't her son been returned to her?

The officer tilted his head in her direction. "The captain said you can stay with her."

Not waiting a second, Nick hopped down and ran up the walk. Lilly looked tired and worn, but she wasn't distraught. Did he see a peace about her?

"Nick, thank God you're here."

He crossed the veranda and pulled her into his arms. She melted into his embrace, and he stroked her hair. "Are you okay?"

She pulled back and forced a tremulous smile. "I've had better days, but I trust God to make this work."

"You do?"

"Don't act so surprised. I've had a lot of time to think

today." She brushed a tendril of hair from her face. "Do you know what I prayed yesterday? In my mother's Bible, I read some words she'd written in the margin. 'Faith entrusts oneself and one's children to God in the midst of danger.' I prayed I'd never have to do that. But God had other plans."

"And?"

"I put the two people I love most in the world in God's hands."

He smiled. "So you've mastered the storms?"

"No." She shook her head. "I only know who's in the boat with me. But one thing I've learned in all this is that faith means putting your trust in God over and over and over, every day." She sighed and filled him in on all that had transpired while he'd been in the jail.

Nick brushed a kiss on her forehead. "Let's go inside and get Levi."

"But—"

"Hey." He grinned, pulling her behind him. "Trust me."

❦

No one stopped them from entering. With her hand nestled inside Nick's, Lilly led him toward the formal parlor, where she heard voices. They paused at the door.

"And I believe," Mark said, "since you hid this from Lilly for several years, not pressing charges against Nick should be the least you could do for her."

Lilly gave Nick a puzzled look. What was Mark talking about? She peeked around the corner, but Levi wasn't in the room.

"But I want to see my mama now!"

Lilly grabbed Nick's sleeve and breathed, "That's Levi." She wanted to bolt to him, but Nick kept her firmly by his side. A woman responded to her son, and Nick motioned in the direction of their voices.

"I think he's in the kitchen," Lilly whispered. Still, she found it odd how quiet her son had suddenly become. Had the woman with Levi threatened him to keep his voice down?

They crept down the hallway, and Lilly stopped in the doorway. A round-faced cook stood by the stove stirring a pot, and at the kitchen table sat Levi with a pile of cookies and a huge glass of milk in front of him. He looked up with a cookie protruding halfway from his lips and smiled. So much for being threatened.

He spit the cookie on the table, hopped down from the chair, and raced across the room. "Mama!"

Lilly caught her son in her arms, raining kisses on his face. After several minutes, she loosened her grip, and Levi wriggled free.

He tipped his face toward Nick. "I knew you'd come 'cause you promised."

42

Until Lilly saw Mark sitting in the dining room of the lunch counter, she'd almost forgotten about the comments she'd overheard in the Harts' parlor a few days ago. What had her former in-laws hidden from her? She made a mental note to ask him later.

Trip and Marguerite sat across from Mark at the large table. Emily and Carter joined them, and a few minutes later, Nick entered, spoke to Mr. Thorton, and then sat at the same table. She noticed he pulled up an additional chair. If they thought she could join them, they were sadly mistaken. Customers at four other tables waited to be served.

Mr. Thorton laid a hand on her shoulder. "Go on. They need to talk to you."

"Are you sure?"

"This may surprise you, but I can pour coffee too." He winked at her. "And, Lilly, I'm sorry if you thought I was on Claude Hart's side with Levi. I should have stood up to him when he started pressuring me. I hope you know I was truly concerned for you and Levi."

"I do, Mr. Thorton." She smiled as he picked up the coffeepot and headed toward a table in the corner.

Eugenia nudged Lilly's arm, a plate of cinnamon rolls in her hand. "Didn't I hear Uncle Clyde say your friends need to speak with you? Why are you still standing here? I can handle the customers. You've trained me well."

Lilly smiled at the girl and untied her apron. "Don't you want to say hello to Mark?"

Eugenia giggled. "We'll be saying hello tonight when he picks me up. We're going to the vaudeville show."

Lilly draped her arm around the girl's shoulders for a quick hug, then walked over to the table where Nick stood waiting. He pulled out her chair, and she slowly sat down. Why were all her friends grinning like children who'd gotten a pony on Christmas morning?

"Okay, you all had better fess up." She scanned their faces. "What's going on?"

Mark lifted a set of papers from his inside coat pocket and passed them to her. She opened them and read the words at the top. *Last Will and Testament of Benjamin Davis Hurt.*

Her heart skipped. "Where did you get this? Claude told me Ben never made a will."

"I found it hidden in Claude Hart's desk." Mark beamed at her. "I owed you."

"Is it real?"

"As real as the money Ben left you." He pointed to the last paragraph on the page. "The reason I didn't tell you right away was I wanted to check everything out. Lilly, you have enough money to fix your house, furnish it, and still not work another day ever again if you don't want to. And if you choose to press charges, your father-in-law could be disbarred."

With her mouth so dry it tasted like flour, Lilly couldn't

speak. A strange mixture of anger and joy churned inside her. Ben had provided for her and Levi. Not only had he not forgotten about them, but he'd also made his wishes known about Levi's education. But how dare Claude Hart lie to her? She hadn't even needed to scrape every penny since she'd left their house!

She took a deep breath and swallowed. He and Evangeline were Ben's parents. She'd have to come to terms with their place in her life for Levi's sake. Allowing Claude to be disbarred would only be seeking revenge and not honoring Ben's memory.

"Lilly?" Emily touched her arm. "What do you think?"

She blinked. "I'm speechless."

Marguerite chuckled. "Now, there's a first."

⸙

At Mr. Thorton's insistence, Lilly took the rest of the day off. Marguerite offered to keep Levi, and Nick announced he had plans for her. However, he said, they first needed to stop at the roller coaster.

She slipped her hand into the crook of his arm. "Did you get everything settled with Percy?"

"The sheriff agreed to let him go in my custody, and I arranged for him to work off the cost of the repairs. He's a good worker, but he needs a lot more encouragement than I realized."

Her chest warmed. Nick was such a natural father.

"Ruby dropped by today." He hesitated and gave her a grin that made her heart whirl. "She told me to tell you that you are one lucky lady, but I told her that I was the lucky one."

"Nick, we still have so much to talk about."

"I know, but nothing is going to make me stop loving you."

374

They strolled down the sidewalk toward the roller coaster. "Nick, I've been wretched this week. How could you still like me, let alone love me? I didn't even like myself. Are you out of your mind?"

"I must be," he rasped, his voice barely audible.

Tears burned her eyes.

They stopped at the base of the stairs. Holding her face in both of his hands, he thumbed away the tears. "I love all of you—the good, the bad, the funny, the angry, the slightly insane. I even love it when you're jealous of someone who couldn't hold a candle to you. That's not going to change."

"How can you be sure?"

"If you couldn't scare me away this week, do you really think I'm going anywhere? There's no other shoe that's going to drop. I didn't plan on asking you to marry me today, so I won't, but I'm putting you on official notice. I *am* going to ask."

She swallowed hard and waited until he'd lowered his hands before she spoke again. "Nick, there was a time when I thought I'd never love again, but you turned that upside down, and I want to be with you. Truly, I do. But I have to do what's best for Levi, and he needs a home. This is his home. My mother is here. His grandparents are here. He has people who love him here. He can't move around every couple of months the rest of his life."

"I agree." He led her up the steps of the loading station. "That's why I already wrote a letter of resignation to Mr. Ingersoll. I'll mail it tomorrow if you say the word. I'll quit this business so we can give him a normal life."

"I couldn't let you do that. Roller coasters are too important to you."

"No, Lilly, you and Levi are important, and I'd do anything

for you. But will you do me one favor? Ride my coaster with me."

She couldn't refuse him. Minutes later, Nick helped her into a waiting car and sat down beside her. Butterflies did somersaults in her stomach.

Percy wheeled their car around to the bottom of the lift hill. She glanced at the incline and at Nick's face. He draped his arm around her, and she pressed into him, finding a solidness she yearned to lean on forever. He was willing to give all this up for her. What was she willing to give up for him?

Her mother? She could join them whenever she wanted to. The Harts? They wouldn't be hard to say goodbye to, but she'd have to make arrangements for them to see Levi. Her friends?

Her throat clogged as the car began its ascent. She'd find a way to keep in touch with her friends.

Her home? They could keep the house. She could hire someone to tend to it, but if she married Nick, there'd be no permanent, year-round place to call home. Her head demanded she take the safe path, but her heart told her to risk it all.

"Look around, Lilly. Isn't the view beautiful?"

"It is. You can see all of Lake Manawa." The car rounded the curve at the top. Her heart skittering, she turned to him. It was now or never. For once in her life, her heart won over practicality. "Nick, I want a life with you. I want this life. Complete with all the thrills and dips. Will you, well, you know . . ."

"Are you asking me to marry you?"

She didn't get to answer. Instead, the first dip sucked the air from her lungs. She screamed. He pulled her tighter.

The ride, a mix of hills, valleys, and sudden turns, sent

her stomach lurching, and she loved every second. Why had she waited so long to enjoy it?

As the car slowed, she glanced at him.

"Lilly, is that what you were asking?"

Love shone in the cobalt-blue depths of his eyes. She nodded. "I was asking if you're ready for the ride of your life."

He grinned. "I don't think you can ever be ready for something like that. You just have to take the plunge. Like this." Cradling the back of her head in his hand, he lowered his lips to hers, making her believe every word he'd ever said—a roller coaster of emotions, dizzily spinning her fears into oblivion.

Finally, in his arms, she was home.

Author's Note

Trolley parks like Lake Manawa began to grow in popularity more and more in the early part of the century. Funded by streetcar companies, these trolley parks were the first amusement parks. Streetcar companies made a wise investment in them. Visitors would pay to get to the park, spend money once they arrived, and pay again to go home—a winning situation all the way around. Between 1899 and 1905, amusement park popularity exploded, with an average of seventy-five new parks being built each year. It is estimated that the United States saw the appearance of two thousand parks before the Great Depression.

Fred Ingersoll, inventor, designer, and builder, was the first to create an amusement park chain known collectively as Luna Parks. Records indicate that his company built over 277 roller coasters and forty-four complete Luna Parks, although more lost "Lunas" are being discovered all the time throughout the world. A number of park workers made their start building Luna Parks, including Joseph McKee, who went on to build over three hundred roller coasters.

The name of Lake Manawa's roller coaster designer and builder does not appear to have survived the test of time, but given the details we know of the coaster, it seems possible that the Velvet Coaster could have been one of the roller coasters built by the Ingersoll Company or someone who once worked there.

The world's oldest operating coaster, Leap-the-Dips, is still providing fun at Lakemont Park in Altoona, Pennsylvania. It was built in 1902 by the Edward Joy Morris Company. It is North America's last surviving side-friction roller coaster and reaches an average speed of 10 miles per hour. In contrast, today's fastest coasters top speeds of 120 miles per hour.

Lake Manawa's Velvet Coaster burned to the ground in 1922. Without its star attraction, the once opulent park came to a close only five years later—a victim of the automobile, tornadoes and fires, and changing times. The buildings that remained were sold off or torn down. My grandfather purchased one of the bath houses, moved it to a lot on what was once part of the Midway, and made it into a home. My father lived there as a boy.

Today, Lake Manawa State Park is a popular boating, fishing, and camping area, but sadly, nothing remains of its time as a resort. Stop by the state park and the Squirrel Cage Jail Museum when you visit Council Bluffs, Iowa.

Acknowledgments

Saying goodbye to Marguerite, Emily, Lilly, and Lake Manawa has been harder than I expected, but I am excited about the new characters already filling up pages on my computer. Thank you, dear reader, for sharing in these women's stories and joining me on this journey. Your letters and notes have brought me so much encouragement. Please know that I'm praying for you all.

I am grateful to all those at Revell who work so hard to create the best product possible. My wonderful editors, Andrea Doering and Jessica English, make the words sing. Cheryl and her art department design the most beautiful covers. Deonne, Donna, Twila, Michele, and each of their teams deserve a round of applause for publicity, marketing, and sales work.

A big thanks goes to my agent, Wendy Lawton, of Books & Such Literary Agency for her business savvy and ongoing support.

Research is one of the parts of writing historical novels that I enjoy most. I want to thank B. Derek Shaw, board member for the National Roller Coaster Museum and Archives, for his help, as well as the Council Bluffs Public Library. Any errors are mine alone.

A special thank you to Judy Miller, who answers all my questions, holds my "writer" hand, reads my chapters, and reminds me of what is really important. You are one of greatest blessings in my life.

I want to send a big hug to my wonderful crit partners, Brenda Anderson and Shannon Vannatter, who make sure all my characters are dressed and that Lake Manawa comes alive.

Laura Frantz, Dawn Ford, Marlene Garand, and all the Inkspirational Messagers—you mean the world to me.

To my husband, David, my constant support and the love of my life—words cannot express my gratitude. And to my children, Parker, Caroline, and Emma—thank you for handling my deadlines with grace, for reading pages, and for being proud to tell your friends that your mom is an author.

Most of all, I thank God for the privilege of writing stories, and I pray that my words bring glory and honor to Him. May you always know His unfailing love (Rom. 8:38–39).

A history buff, antique collector, and freelance graphic designer, **Lorna Seilstad** is the author of *Making Waves* and *A Great Catch* and draws her setting from her home state of Iowa. A former high school English and journalism teacher, she has won several online writing awards and is a member of American Christian Fiction Writers. Contact her and find out more at www.lornaseilstad.com.

LORNA SEILSTAD IS SURE TO MAKE WAVES!

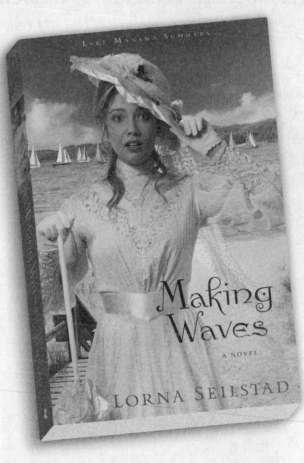

"You'll set sail on a wonderful adventure in Lorna Seilstad's new series set at Lake Manawa, Iowa. Her quick wit and captivating characters are mixed into a little-known slice of history that will keep you turning the pages and wishing for more when the story ends. Fortunately, there's another book to follow. I can't wait!"

—Judith Miller, author of *Somewhere to Belong*

Revell
a division of Baker Publishing Group
www.RevellBooks.com

"*A Great Catch* weaves humor, history, romance, and spiritual truths into a delicious story that will delight readers' hearts. What a fun, relaxing read! I'd like to remain at Lake Manawa forever."

—LAURA FRANTZ, author of *The Colonel's Lady*

The perfect summer novel, *A Great Catch* will enchant you with its breezy setting and endearing characters.